NEBULA AWARDS

SHOWCASE 2000

NEBULA AWARDS

SHOWCASE 2000

*The Year's Best SF and Fantasy
Chosen by the Science Fiction
and Fantasy Writers of America*

EDITED BY

Gregory Benford

HARCOURT, INC.
New York San Diego London

The Library of Congress has cataloged this serial as follows:
The Nebula awards. — No. 19 — New York [N.Y.]: Arbor House, c1983–v.; 22cm.
Annual.
Published: San Diego, Calif.: Harcourt, Inc., 1984–
Published for: Science Fiction and Fantasy Writers of America, 1983–
Continues: Nebula award stories (New York, N.Y.: 1982)
ISSN 0741-5567 = The Nebula awards
1. Science fiction. American — Periodicals.
1. Science Fiction and Fantasy Writers of America.
PS648.S3N38   83-647399
813'.0876'08–dc19
AACR 2 MARC-S
Library of Congress [8709r84]rev

ISBN 0-15-100479-x
ISBN 0-15-600705-3 (pbk)

Text set in Electra
Designed by Kaelin Chappell

Printed in the United States of America
First edition
E D C B A

Permissions acknowledgments appear on pages 287–288, which constitute a continuation
of the copyright page.

IN MEMORIAM

Robert A. W. ("Doc") Lowndes
Paul Lehr
Naomi Mitchison
Rachel Cosgrove Payes
T. A. Waters
Jo Clayton
Jean-Claude Forest
Allen Drury
Lawrence Sanders
Alain Doremieux
Shin'ichi Hoshi
Sean A. Moore
Ernst Jünger
Peter Nilson
Wayland Drew
Ted Hughes
Frank D. McSherry Jr.
John L. Millard
Aubery Vincent Clarke
John V. Baltadonis
T. Bruce Yerke
Richard Wright
Ardis Waters

CONTENTS

Introduction
THE SCIENCE FICTIONAL CENTURY

GREGORY BENFORD

This volume celebrates some of the best science fiction published during a particularly engaging period, the years just a bit before the century turns over and delivers unto us a millennium. A suitable moment to cast a backward glance.

Several pieces in this anthology reflect on science fiction's place in literature overall. (See, in particular, the piece by Jonathan Lethem and the responses to it.) Others revel in the genre's history. Both views are particularly germane to a field that has come to dominate the visual media, while remaining largely neglected by the conventional literary world.

Nebula volumes are not collections of the best of the year; for those, see the annual productions of Messrs. Hartwell and Dozois. Instead, Nebula nominees and winners are the favorites of a club, the Science Fiction Writers of America, which is as riddled with highly opinionated folk as any small town. Winners can represent a compromise, the resultant of divergent forces. Factions and even bloc voting can carry the day, and have. Since a large number of fantasy writers migrated into the SFWA, making it the SFFWA, we see more fantasy among those honored by nomination. So any Nebula volume is more like a momentary reading of the pulse than a pinnacle of effort. That given, I have tried to frame the fiction here with commentary by others on how the genre looks in the waning moments of a millennium. Only in this introduction shall I hold forth from my own, rather unusual, perspective.

Here I mingle my own opinions with some incidents I found clarifying, from the genre's other source: science. As a professor of physics (at the University of California at Irvine) and an SF writer, I feel myself at the intersection of both these illuminating spotlights.

Consider these quotations from across the century:

> *"It is the business of the future to be dangerous; and it is among the merits of science that it equips the future for its duties."*   —Alfred North Whitehead, 1911

> *"Denied the magic of mythology, we must have it in science — hence science fiction."*   —Edward Harrison, 1980

> *"Science is my territory, but science fiction is the landscape of my dreams."*   —Freeman Dyson, 1997

To me, this bespeaks a culture thinking aloud. Whitehead was a philosopher, Harrison is an astronomer, and Dyson is a physicist, futurist, and an excellent writer. They all felt the quick pulse of science's heartbeat beneath society's skin.

In 1997 David Hartwell presented a mammoth tome titled *The Science Fiction Century,* making the broad claim that in this last remarkable hundred years, "Science fiction did not aspire to take over literature, but reality."

Furthermore, in his view, "the overwhelming evidence is that American science fiction and the American market drive the SF world." SF has "now outlasted all the other counterculture or outsider literary movements of the century" and "is read with ease and comprehension by the teenage children of educated adults who can derive little or no pleasure from it." Hartwell sees the genre as "attempts to get at the truth of the human condition in this century, so contoured and conditioned by science and technology."

Alas, I wish more people believed this were so.

Much of our culture still does not see science fiction this way — principally, I think, because we all have a built-in reflex: to accept the present as a given, ordinary, unremarkable.

Yet today would have been a wonder to anyone living in 1899, simply because of changes wrought by science. Unthinkingly anchoring ourselves in our moving Now, we do not realize how it came from Then. We cannot see our lives as taking place in our great-grandparents' awesome future.

Fundamentally, Hartwell was right—SF speaks for science more than any other fiction (and often more tellingly than nonfiction). Its goal is to take over the real world, because slowly scientists became quite aware that, like it or not, their culture was doing just that.

Of course, it was easy to make mistakes, but more often through timidity than bravado ("... computers in the future may have only 1,000 vacuum tubes and weigh only ½ a ton."—*Popular Mechanics*, March 1949).

As change accelerated over the last two centuries, literature expressed anxieties and anticipations about it. In Mary Shelley's seminal novel, Frankenstein was the scientist's name, yet revealingly, most remember it as the monster's.

A telling hit. Often SF makes scientists into heroes, while conventional fiction (and much of Hollywood) fears them. Yet a century ago scientists were more likely to be depicted heroically. Why?

Another way of getting at what we in this genre have all been about is to inquire into how scientists make their own culture through SF. I have had a long, winding involvement with modern science and fiction, the inevitable clash of the noble and imaginary elements in both science and fiction on one clean hand, with the gritty and practical way the world uses it on the other soiled hand.

I estimate that half the scientists I know have been heavy-duty SF fans, even if they now read little fiction at all. Many notable figures I knew—Edward Teller, Freeman Dyson, Leo Szilard, Stephen Hawking, Marvin Minsky, Martin Rees—read SF, and some even wrote it. Though some deride SF, science feels the genre at its back, breathing on its neck in the race into the future.

This has been principally a century driven by physics. The nineteenth century was dominated by the metaphors and technological implication of two more applied sciences: chemistry and mechanics.

Starting around 1899, electromagnetic theory and experiment gave us the telephone, radio, TV, and computers, and made the internal combustion engine practical—thus, the car and airplane, leading inevitably to the rocket and outer space. That fateful wedding of the rocket with the other monumental product of physics, the nuclear bomb, led to the end of large-scale strategic warfare—as profound a change as any in modern times.

Personally, I have never settled emotionally the tensions between the huge impact of physics and its abstract graces. They represent two quite different modes of thinking. I grew up amid the shattered ruins of Germany and Japan, with a father who had fought through World War II and then spent long years occupying the fallen enemy lands.

I took as a given that physics had stopped strategic warfare, not by uplifting mankind to higher consciousness but by scaring it silly. Nothing in the half century since has changed my mind.

At the time, I did not realize how much that resolution came from ideas developed in SF. For the central lesson of SF as a medium is that the highway between it and science runs both ways.

In the Wellsian era, 1890–1910, physics was exploring electromagnetic wonders and inventing both relativity and early quantum mechanics. Meanwhile, SF was concerned mostly with voyages in an ever-expanding landscape. It lagged science considerably, though its flights made without much scientific backing—time travel, other dimensions—were certainly imaginative.

Yet SF did take on ideas long before the general culture would face them. Throughout this century, conventional literature persistently avoided the gathering prospect of a conceptually altered tomorrow, retreating into a realist posture of fiction of ever-smaller compass.

Even as a boy, when I started reading Heinlein, Clarke, and the other modern masters, it took a while before I realized that most people thought that a "science fictional" concept meant it was somehow unreal, even absurd.

In orthodox literature this is the common, unspoken assumption; the present world, so soon to be the stuff of nostalgia, enjoys an automatic, unearned privilege. In this the humanist tradition resists the culture of science—for SF is, fundamentally, best seen that way.

In America the genre came about through scruffy pulp magazines, beneath the contempt of modernist savants. This bias remains today, isolating the genre as no other is from the springs of mainstream attention. High-church mysteries receive respectful notice (P. D. James,

John le Carré); our best receive a paragraph of notice in the back of the literary bus.

All this began back at the Wells–James fracture. Foregrounding personal relations, the novel of character came — in a classic pre–World War I debate between Henry James and H. G. Wells — to claim the pinnacle of orthodox fiction. James won that argument, banishing Wells from the citadel of high literature and conceding to him a popularity James did not enjoy in his time. But in so doing, James surrendered more than sales; he left the future to the genre that would later increasingly set the terms of social debate.

Of course, the genre is not a simple predictive machine. The science fictional shotgun blast into tomorrow is bound to hit some targets. H. G. Wells, the Shakespeare of the genre, fired off more speculative rounds than anyone, and indeed helped bring about the tank in his 1903 "The Land Ironclads." Churchill remembered this tale during World War I and began the research that led to its battlefield use.

When Hugo Gernsback founded *Amazing Stories* in 1926, full-bodied quantum mechanics was being invented, mostly in Germany. Pulp SF dealt mostly with the wonders issuing from the physics of the Wellsian era — electromagnetism, wider explorations of the planets.

In World War II we saw John Campbell's Golden Age at *Astounding*, and simultaneously, the great explosion of physics into the perceptual world of the public.

By this time SF was breathing on the neck of physics, running just slightly behind the implications of discoveries. Since then, the two have been closely linked, yet this is seldom known in the larger culture.

That speculation leads to serious study I learned more and more in my career. The usual version of the scientific method speaks of how anomalies in data lead theorists to explore new models, which are then checked by dutiful experimenters, and so on. Reality is wilder than that. More fun, too.

No one has impressed me more with the power of speculation in science than Freeman Dyson. Without knowing who he was, I found him a like-minded soul at the daily physics department coffee breaks, when I was still a graduate student at the University of California at San Diego, in the mid-1960s.

I was especially impressed that he had the audacity to give actual department colloquia on his odd ideas: notions about space exploration by using nuclear weapons as explosive pushers, and speculations on odd variants of life in the universe. He had just published a short note on what came to be called Dyson spheres — vast civilizations that swarm around their star, soaking up all available sunlight and emitting infrared. We might well study infrared emitters to detect civilizations, then.

Dyson at age eight wrote an SF novel, *Sir Phillip Roberts's Erolunar Collision*, about scientists directing the orbits of asteroids. He was unafraid to publish conjectural, even rather outrageous ideas in the solemn pages of physics journals. When I remarked on this, he answered with a smile, "You'll find I'm not the first."

Indeed, he descended from a line of futurist British thinkers, from J. D. Bernal of *The World, the Flesh and the Devil* to Olaf Stapledon to Arthur C. Clarke. In *Infinite in All Directions* Dyson remarked that "Science fiction is, after all, nothing more than the exploration of the future using the tools of science."

This was a fairly common view in those burgeoning times. In 1963, my first year of graduate school, I met Leo Szilard at department colloquia, avidly holding forth on his myriad ideas. Szilard had persuaded Einstein to write the famous letter to Roosevelt explaining that an A-bomb was possible, and advocating the Manhattan Project. He had a genius for seizing the moment. Szilard had seen the potential in nuclear physics early, even urging his fellow physicists in the mid-1930s to keep their research secret. And he read SF. He even wrote it.

I had read Szilard's satirical SF novel *The Voice of the Dolphins* in 1961, and his SF short stories, and from him heard the story, famous in the genre, of how in the spring of 1944 Cleve Cartmill published a clear description of how an atomic bomb worked in *Astounding Science Fiction*, titled "Deadline." Szilard mentioned to me that Cartmill's bomb would not have worked, but the story did stress that the key problem was separating nonfissionable isotopes from the crucial uranium 235.

This story became legend, proudly touted by fans after the war as proof of SF's predictive powers. It was a tale of an evil alliance called the Axis — oops, no, the Sixa — who are prevented from dropping the A-bomb, while their opponents, the Allies — no, oops, that's the Seilla — refrain from using the weapon, fearing its implications.

As Campbell never tired of telling, in March 1944 a captain in the Intelligence and Security Division of the Manhattan Project called for an investigation of Cartmill. He suspected a breach in security, and wanted to trace it backward. U.S. security descended on Campbell's office, but Campbell truthfully told them that Cartmill had researched his story using only materials in public libraries.

Indeed, a special agent nosed around Cartmill himself, going so far as to enlist his postman to casually quiz him about how the story came to be written. The postman remembered that Campbell had sent Cartmill a letter several days before the special agent clamped a mail cover on Cartmill's correspondence. This fit the day when agents had already visited Campbell's office. Campbell was alerting his writer, posthaste. Soon enough, security came calling.

SF writers are often asked where they get their ideas. This was one time when the answer mattered.

Cartmill had worked for a radium products company in the 1920s, he told the agent, which had in turn interested him in uranium research. He also fished forth two letters from Campbell, one written ten days short of two years before the Hiroshima bombing, in which Campbell urged him to explore these ideas: "U 235 has—I'm stating fact, not theory—been separated in quantity easily sufficient for preliminary atomic power research, and the like. They got it out of regular uranium ores by new atomic isotope separation methods; they have quantities measured in pounds..." Since a minimum critical mass is less than a hundred pounds, this was sniffing close to Top Secret data.

"Now it might be that you found the story worked better in allegory," Campbell had advised, neatly leading Cartmill to distance the yet-unwritten tale from current events.

Plainly Campbell was trying to skirt close to secrets he must have guessed. The literary historian Albert Berger obtained the formerly secret files on the Cartmill case, and as he points out in *Analog* (September 1984), Campbell never told Cartmill that wartime censorship directives forbade *any* mention of atomic energy. Campbell was urging his writer out into risky territory.

Cartmill was edgy, responding that he didn't want to be so close to home as to be "ridiculous. And there is the possible danger of actually suggesting a means of action which might be employed." Still, he had used the leaden device of simply inverting the Axis and Allies names, thin cover indeed. Campbell did not ask him to change this, suggesting that both men were tantalized by the lure of reality behind their dreams.

The Office of Censorship came into play. Some suggested withholding *Astounding*'s mailing privileges, which would have ended the magazine. In the end, not attracting attention to the Cartmill story and the magazine seemed a smarter strategy. Security feared that "... such articles coming to the attention of personnel connected with the Project are apt to lead to an undue amount of speculation."

Only those sitting atop the Manhattan Project knew what was going on. "Deadline" might make workers in the far-flung separation plants and machining shops figure out what all this uranium was for, and talk about it. The Project was afraid of imagination, particularly disciplined dreaming with numbers and facts well marshaled. They feared science fiction itself.

This set the mold. For in the 1940s Henry Luce's *Time Magazine* announced that this was the American Century.

H. Bruce Franklin's *War Stars: The Superweapon and the American Imagination* has made the case that SF, particularly in the pulp magazines, strongly influenced U.S. foreign policy. In the 1930s Harry Truman had read lurid pulp magazine SF yarns of superweapons settling the hash of evil powers. Often they were held in readiness after, insuring the country against an uncertain future.

Truman wasn't alone. Popular culture's roots run deep. Time and again at Livermore I heard physicists quote SF works as arguments for or against the utility of hypothetical inventions, especially weapons.

One day while we were working on a different sort of problem, Edward Teller took a break and pointed out to me an interesting paragraph in an old paperback:

> *We were searching ... for a way to use U235 in a controlled explosion. We had a vision of a one-ton bomb that would be a whole air raid in itself, a single explosion that would flatten out an entire industrial center.... If we could devise a really practical rocket fuel at the same time, one capable of driving a*

*war rocket at a thousand miles an hour, or more, then we
would be in a position to make most anybody say "uncle" to
Uncle Sam.*

*We fiddled around with it all the rest of 1943 and well into
1944. The war in Europe and the troubles in Asia dragged on.
After Italy folded up . . .*

The story was by Robert A. Heinlein, writing as "Anson MacDonald," titled "Solution Unsatisfactory" (May 1941, *Astounding*).

Teller noted that the story even gets the principal events in the war in the right order. "I found that remarkable," Teller said, describing how Manhattan Project physicists would sometimes talk at lunch about SF stories they had read.

Someone had thought that Heinlein's ideas were uncannily accurate. Not in the details, of course, because he described not a bomb, but rather using radioactive dust as an ultimate weapon. Spread over a country, it could be decisive.

In a way Heinlein had been proved right. The fallout from nuclear bursts can kill many more than the blast. Luckily, Hiroshima and Nagasaki were air bursts, which scooped up little topsoil and so yielded very low fallout. For hydrogen bombs, fallout is usually much more deadly.

In Heinlein's description of the strategic situation, Teller said, the physicists found a sobering warning. Ultimate weapons lead to a strategic standoff with no way back—a solution unsatisfactory. How to avoid this, and the whole general problem of nuclear weapons in the hands of brutal states, preoccupied the physicists laboring to make them. Nowhere in literature had anyone else confronted such a Faustian dilemma as directly, concretely.

Coming three years later in the same magazine, Cleve Cartmill's "Deadline" provoked astonishment in the lunch-table discussions at Los Alamos, Teller said. It really did describe isotope separation and the bomb itself in detail, and raised as its principal plot pivot the issue the physicists were then debating among themselves: Should the Allies use it?

To the physicists from many countries clustered in the high mountain strangeness of New Mexico, cut off from their familiar sources of humanist learning, it must have seemed particularly striking that Cartmill described an allied effort, a joint responsibility laid upon many nations.

Discussion of Cartmill's "Deadline" was significant. The story's detail was remarkable, its sentiments even more so. Did this rather obscure story hint at what the American public really thought about such a superweapon, or would think if they only knew?

Talk attracts attention. Teller recalled a security officer who took a decided interest, making notes, saying little. In retrospect, it was easy to see what a wartime intelligence monitor would make of the physicists' conversations. Who was this guy Cartmill, anyway? Where did he get these details? Who tipped him to the isotope separation problem? "And that is why Mr. Campbell received his visitors," said Teller.

I blinked. So the great, resonant legend of early hard SF was, in fact, triggered by the quiet, distant "fan" community among the scientists themselves.

For me, closing the connection in this fundamental fable of the field completed my own quizzical thinking about the link between the science I practice and the fiction I deploy in order to think about the larger implications of my work, and of others. Events tinged with fable have an odd quality, looping back on themselves to bring us messages more tangled and subtle than we sometimes guess.

That era was not the zenith of SF's influence, though.

To the larger culture, after the 1950s, visual SF was at least as important as anything in print.

Today, in visual media SF rules. It delivers regular megahits. Fantasy, SF's market ally, enjoys exactly the reverse.

Huge fantasy trilogies dominate the best-seller lists, while little SF gets there in the 1990s. Yet fantasy has never led to large grosses for Hollywood, despite its apparent compatibility with the rise of special effects.

This suggests that SF penetrates a very different part of the culture, and that its most effective tools may be its visions, as in Stanley Kubrick's 2001, rather than its idea-heavy fictions. Fantasy may best appeal to deep emotional needs, and not depend as much on special effects (seen one elf, seen 'em all) or wonders.

Space travel was the signature imagery of the genre — and it photographs well, too. (Biotech is not going to have it so easy.)

As far back as 1869 Edward Everett Hale's "The Brick Moon" envisioned manned artificial satellites. SF had played out this idea in great detail by the time Arthur C. Clarke anticipated the huge impact of global communications satellites in 1945 (without patenting the idea, alas).

Space was an intuitive choice, mingling technology with vast horizons — and an easy one. Most SF advocates have hailed each predictive bull's-eye as though the authors were using rifles, when in fact the genre sprays forth a shotgun blast of *what ifs*. Heinlein anticipated the water bed and remote-control waldoes. Wells and others foresaw nuclear weaponry, mass bombing, and space travel.

Indeed, ever since Jules Verne's cannon-propelled expedition to the moon, SF used space as a metaphor for the opening of the human prospect. Verne correctly set his cannon very near Cape Canaveral, arguing that the U.S. would probably lead the world in technological innovation, and southern Florida was energetically useful for launching, since one gained there the most centrifugal boost from the Earth's rotation. His choice of cannon over rockets seems to have come from a novelistic desire to link space with military means, another prescient shot.

Contrary to a common observation, half a dozen authors foresaw first moon landings watched by the whole world on television. Though visionaries like Heinlein incorrectly depicted the first moon rockets as built by private capital, in fact such companies did build the Apollo-era hardware; the money was first laundered through the government, though.

Some authors even saw that a U.S.-U.S.S.R. rivalry would be necessary to launch the Space Age. Large ideas needed big causes to drive them, a lesson we should not forget. Nothing grand is done offhandedly.

SF has a love of the large, a reaction to Jamesian sitting-room drama. Changes in everyday life, which most concern real people, SF uses as background verisimilitude, not the focus.

While early optimistic SF thought automation would yield an easy cornucopia, by the 1950s Kurt Vonnegut's *Player Piano* saw how marginalized some people would become, a persistent problem. Few authors have seen any solution to this predicament, other than republics of leisure that inevitably run into the trap of bread-and-circuses distractions — an uncomfortable resemblance to many aspects of our present, with our exaggerated sports and entertainment, which increasingly infiltrates politics and even science.

Rudyard Kipling predicted transatlantic air express in "With the Night Mail." Even the pulp-era death rays found their vindication in the laser beam, but in our lives lasers read CDs and serve as tiny, smart servants bearing information, not death.

Still, the genre did a conspicuous pratfall over computers. Well into the 1960s, writers clung to the image of a monolithic single machine worshiped by attentive mathematicians, missing the personal computer revolution.

Worse, starting in the 1930s they assumed that robots would confront us with the most profound puzzles of human identity. SF robots were humanoid with advanced intelligence. Few imagined robots as routine monomaniac factory laborers, bolted in place.

This meant that the issues of artificial intelligence were acted out by metal men we now know to be implausible, missing many of the deep conceptual problems the field confronts today. Artificial intelligences shouldn't look like us, because they won't really be like us.

How technology looks has become, thanks to TV and movies, more important than ever. Movie imagery matters; when President Reagan advocated missile defense (advised in part by SF writers like Jerry Pournelle) the media dubbed it "Star Wars"—though Reagan never said the defense would be space-based. If politics is at basis a discussion of where we are going, what then is its natural literary medium?

We have come a long way from unblinking wonder at technology and from the top-down social engineering doctrines that accompanied the brooding optimism of a century ago. SF now more often employs the self-organizing principles popular in biology, economics, artificial intelligence, and even physics.

Virginia Postrel in 1998's *The Future and Its Enemies* argues that the essential political differences today are between stasists and dynamists. In a sense, these terms reflect two sciences: biology vs. mechanics. SF now usually sides with futures run not by Wellsian savant technocrats but by the masses, innovating from below and running their own lives, thank you very much.

This gathering belief in dynamic change driven by freedom and information flow contrasts with the oddly static tone of much earlier thinking. Mundane literature has carried an unspoken agenda, assuming that the present's preoccupations stand for eternal themes.

Even early SF presumed that elites should rule and that information should flow downward, enlightening the shadowed many. Wells was welcomed to speak by the Petrograd Soviet, the Reichstag, Stalin, and both Roosevelt presidents—a company that never doubted their managerial agenda.

Today, such mechanistic, pseudo-scientific self-confidence seems quaintly smug. Control dominated much SF thinking, perhaps more strikingly in Asimov's psychohistory. I recently wrote a novel set in his Empire, and tried to update how psychohistory could work—but it's a tough job. Clockwork theories are not in vogue.

Now, the genre looks to more vibrant metaphors, while cocking a wary eye at our many looming problems.

SF writers are now much less interested in predicting and thus determining the future, precisely because they do not believe that linear, programmatic determinism is the right angle of attack. They see themselves more as conceptual gardeners, planting for fruitful growth, rather than engineers designing eternal, gray social machines.

What does this portend for the next century? Grand physical measures still beckon.

We could build a sea-level canal across Central America, explore Mars in person, use asteroidal resources to uplift the bulk of humanity. Siberia could be a fresh frontier, better run by American metaphors than the failed, top-down Russian ones.

Biological analogies will probably shape much political thinking to come. We will gain control of our own reproduction, cloning and altering our children. Genetic modification is surely a dynamist agenda, for the many mingled effects of changed genes defy detailed prediction.

Though the converging powers of computers and biology will give us much mastery, how such forces play out in an intensely cyber-quick world will be unknowable, arising from emergent properties, not stasist plans.

Unlike physics, biology is going to be hard to direct in a top-down manner. Parents will make major decisions, seeking biotech to better the prospects of their children.

Despite our rather dark impulses to control the shadowy future landscape, to know the morrow, it will be even harder in the science fictional worlds to come.

Scientists used to pay more attention to SF than anybody. (I mean the thinking genre, not the knockoff Hollywood product.) I doubt that is so today, though surely it is still the genre that best expresses the unique power of their worldview. I am sure that the writers of SF's founding era, and perhaps of this one as well, would be pleased to hear that they have been so influential. From the vantage of a few decades hence, as history comes into focus, the mainstream culture may fathom that we have passed through The Science Fictional American Century.

Somebody really was listening out there. Our writers are bards of science, as Poul Anderson has remarked.

Perhaps they are as well the unacknowledged legislators of tomorrow.

In the nineteenth century, missing the mark by a mile, Shelley (Mary's husband) thought that job fell to the poets.

The 1998 Nebula Awards Final Ballot

FOR NOVEL

The Last Hawk, Catherine Asaro (Tor Books)
*Forever Peace, Joe Haldeman (Ace)
Moonfall, Jack McDevitt (HarperPrism)
How Few Remain, Harry Turtledove (Del Rey)
Death of the Necromancer, Martha Wells
To Say Nothing of the Dog, Connie Willis (Bantam Spectra)

FOR NOVELLA

"Aurora in Four Voices," Catherine Asaro (*Analog Science Fiction and Fact*)
"The Boss in the Wall," Avram Davidson & Grania Davis (Tachyon Publications)
*"Reading the Bones," Sheila Finch (*The Magazine of Fantasy & Science Fiction*)
"Izzy and the Father of Terror," Eliot Fintushel (*Asimov's Science Fiction*)
"Jumping Off the Planet," David Gerrold (*SF Age*)
"Ecopoiesis," Geoffrey A. Landis (*SF Age*)

*Indicates winner.

FOR NOVELETTE

"The Truest Chill," Gregory Feeley (*SF Age*)

"Time Gypsy," Ellen Klages (*Bending the Landscape: SF*, Overlook Press)

"The Mercy Gate," Mark J. McGarry (*The Magazine of Fantasy &
Science Fiction*)

"Echea," Kristine Kathryn Rusch (*Asimov's Science Fiction*)

"Lethe," Walter Jon Williams (*Asimov's Science Fiction*)

*"Lost Girls," Jane Yolen (*Realms of Fantasy*)

FOR SHORT STORY

"When the Bough Breaks," Steven Brust (*The Essential Bordertown*,
Tor)

"Standing Room Only," Karen Joy Fowler (*Asimov's Science Fiction*)

"Fortune and Misfortune," Lisa Goldstein (*Asimov's Science Fiction*)

"Winter Fire," Geoffrey A. Landis (*Asimov's Science Fiction*)

*"Thirteen Ways to Water," Bruce Holland Rogers (*Black Cats and
Broken Mirrors*, Martin Greenberg and John Helfers, Ed., DAW)

"Tall One," K. D. Wentworth (*The Magazine of Fantasy & Science
Fiction*)

NEBULA AWARDS

AWARDS

SHOWCASE 2000

Reading the Bones

SHEILA FINCH

Sheila Finch was born and reared in London, attended Bishop Otter College, then taught a year in the docklands before they became trendy. She came to the United States and did graduate work in medieval literature and linguistics with Harold Whitehall at Indiana University. She has lived in California since 1962 and has published six novels, including her latest, *David Brin's Out of Time: Tiger in the Sky,* a young-adult novel. With thirty short stories and several nonfiction pieces about SF published, she has long been interested in the more intellectual component of the field. She also has published poetry and other non-SF writing. She has taught at El Camino College since 1980 and has conducted summer workshops in Idyllwild, California. Her "lingster" series, to which *Reading the Bones* belongs, is the foremost study of linguistic problems with aliens, bringing a thorough understanding of modern theory, plus imagination. This striking novella won the Nebula and is part of an in-progress "lingster" novel.

I

Someone was trying to tell him something.

Ries Danyo wallowed round on the bench, peering through the

tavern's thick haze, eyes unfocused by too much *zyth*. The sitar he didn't remember setting on the bench beside him crashed to the floor. The gourd cracked as it hit stone.

A male Freh sat beside him, the alien's almost lipless mouth moving urgently. The Freh had a peculiar swirling design tattooed from his forehead down the nose, and one of his hands was wrapped in a filthy rag. Ries stared at dark blood seeping through the folds. The alien spoke again, the pitch of his voice writhing like smoke.

Ries didn't catch a word.

Sometimes he wondered if the native vocalizations on this planet should even be called anything as advanced as language—especially the impoverished version the Freh males used. Not that his human employers were interested in actually having a conversation with these aliens. Just as well. He wasn't the lingster he'd been just five years ago.

The native liquor had given him a pounding headache and he needed to sleep it off.

The Freh's unbandaged, bird-claw hand shook his arm, urging him to pay attention. Dizziness took him. For a moment, he drifted untethered in a matrix of protolanguage, unable to grasp either the alien's Frehti or his own native Inglis to form a reply, a sensation closely resembling what he remembered of the condition lingsters called interface, but without the resolution.

A harsh burst of noise battered his eardrums, booming and echoing around the low-roofed tavern. He squinted, trying to clear his clouded vision. Two male Freh capered across the floor, arms windmilling. He started to rise—

And was knocked down off his chair and dragged behind the overturned table.

Thuds. Screams. The crowded tavern erupted into shrill pandemonium. Freh voices ululating at the upper end of the scale. Something else—a deeper footnote that brought the hairs up on his neck.

He tried to stand. The room cartwheeled dizzily around him. A pungent odor filled his nostrils—a stench like rotten flesh, decaying fungus. He had a sudden image of nightmare beasts rutting. The meal he'd just eaten rushed back up into his throat.

Something slammed into his back, toppling him again. He struggled out from underneath the weight. A pudgy juvenile Freh, shapeless in layers of thick, stinking rags, stared down at him for a moment, then scrambled away hastily. Ries sat on the floor in the wreckage, his head throbbing, his mind blank.

Tongues of flame flickered across the low ceiling; acrid smoke filled his lungs and made him cough. The coughing caused him to retch again. He doubled over.

"Talker." The alien with a bloody hand shook his arm. "Talker. Danger."

The sound of Frehti was like birdsong. Trying to make sense of such warbling, twittering, and chirruping—problematic at the best of times—was impossible in his present state. He got maybe one Frehti word in every two.

He closed his eyes against the stinging smoke, the piercing screeches. *Maybe I really am dying*, he thought.

No exaggeration. Maybe not tonight, or tomorrow or even a month from now. But he sensed his body succumbing to death little by little, felt the slow tightening of *zyth's* grip around his heart. He had a sudden vision—a splinter view of green foothills and sapphire lake—that closed down as rapidly as it opened. If he didn't give it up, he wouldn't live long enough to see Earth again.

Then he was aware of the bump and scrape of being hauled over benches, broken crockery, other bodies in the way.

He was too tired to resist.

One of the aliens had tried to give him a message last night.

The memory pricked him as he dropped a step behind the Deputy Commissioner's wife and her companions moving through the cloth merchants' bazaar. He shielded the flask of *zyth* he was opening from their sight and took a medicinal gulp. The demon that lived in that flask raced through his blood like liquid flame, and he felt his heartbeat quicken.

In his experience, stone sober or drunk like last night, the Freh had the most stunted language of any sentient beings in the Orion Arm. Even very early linguists from pre-Guild days had taught there was no such thing as a primitive language, and what was true on Earth had proved true through the Orion Arm: All languages the Guild of Xeno-linguists had ever found were as sophisticated as their speakers needed.

On the other hand, the Guild could be wrong; Frehti, the language spoken here on Krishna, could turn out to be an exception.

His head pounded as if he'd slammed it repeatedly into a stone wall, his skin was clammy, and his throat seemed to have been scrubbed with sand. He had no recollection of how he got back to his quarters in New Bombay.

It was not yet noon, but the heat was already fierce. Dust rose as he walked, making his eyes water. He sneezed, startling a small cloud of insects hovering about his face. Already he could smell the rich, chocolate odor of the river moving sluggishly past the edge of the native town. The monsoon would be here any day, bringing its own set of problems. There were no pleasant seasons on Krishna.

The native name for the planet was Not-Here. *"How can anybody say their own world isn't here?"* the Deputy Commissioner's wife had demanded when he'd translated this for her. *"No wonder they're all so useless!"* Krishna was too benign a deity to give name to this planet, he thought. Kali would've been more appropriate.

The DepCom's wife and fifteen-year-old daughter moved slowly down the line of stalls in the silk merchants' section, followed by the wife of some minor official in the human colony. The women dabbed sweat from their cheeks with one hand, fended off flying insects with the other. They took their time, the DepCom's spoiled daughter plucking with obvious irritation at her mother's sleeve. The girl's red hair which she'd piled on her head in a style much too old for her had come loose, and he could see damp strands of it stuck to the back of her slender neck.

The bazaar was crowded with small, plump aliens whose skin had a color and texture that reminded him of scrubbed potatoes. The males' faces were decorated with tattoos, crude as a child's scribbled designs, done in dark purple ink; the females went unadorned. Like many races he'd seen in the Orion Arm, the Freh were humanoid—as if once having found a good recipe, Mother Nature was loathe to throw it away—and no taller than ten-year-old human children. Their mouths had almost no lip, and their eyes were round and lacked lids. Like a bird or a reptile, they had a nictitating membrane that could veil their gaze, and their hands were four-fingered. The oddest thing about them was that such lumpish beings had mellifluous, birdlike voices.

Almost all of them here in the bazaar were male. They squatted along the edges of the narrow path between the stalls, leaned on poles supporting tattered silk awnings, or crowded around the stalls of food-sellers. Two-thirds of the male population never seemed to have any-thing to do; their sole purpose in life seemed to be standing about half-naked, staring at each other and at the humans.

No more details surfaced from the events in the tavern. When he'd been younger, he'd bounced back vibrantly from nights like last night. Now they left him feeling a hundred years old, his body demanding more of what was killing it to function at all. He took another sip—the alcohol flamed in his throat—put the flask back in his pocket, and caught up with the women.

He despised these shopping trips. The women argued and dispar-aged and forced the prices down to a level he was ashamed to translate. And then they'd take their shimmering purchases back up to the Resi-dence and have something fussy made out of them. The DepCom's women liked the delicate textiles on Krishna, but they preferred the elab-orate fashions they remembered from Earth, however inappropriate they might be in this climate. But even that wasn't the heart of his discontent. This was no job for a lingster, even one who'd fallen as far as he had.

Ragged awnings over each stall hung limp in the still air. The ever-present smells of the bazaar, rotting vegetables, flyblown meat, sewage running in open ditches behind the stalls, and the merchants' sweat-soaked rags filled his nose. A hand dimpled like a child's plucked at his sleeve, and he turned to see half-raw meat on a stick offered to him. The seller of the meat gazed at him.

He recognized a juvenile, still carrying the rolls of fat about its neck that marked immaturity. Behind the juvenile, rows of small, feath-erless, flying creatures the natives trapped were set to roast over a bed of coals alongside succulent red-brown tubers. He shook his head and regretted it when the hangover pounded again in his temples. The ju-venile grinned. There was a youthfulness in all their faces, a bland childlike expression that never seemed to mature. The only difference between them as they grew was that while they stayed pudgy they tended to lose the exaggerated neck fat.

He'd never seen an old Freh, male or female, or even an obviously middle-aged one. He didn't know if this meant they died young, if they simply kept their old out of sight, or even if they put them all to death above a certain age. It was a mark of how little importance humans placed on the natives of this world, their customs or their language, that no xenoanthropologists had spent time here, and the xenolinguists initially sent by the Guild had spent precious little.

Across the alluvial plain on which the Freh town was built, Krishna's sun climbed the Maker's Bones till the eroded mountains glowed fiercely white like the skeleton of some extinct mammoth. He wiped a trickle of sweat from his neck, willing the women to hurry up. Sometimes they could go on like this for a couple of hours, examining bolts of iridescent material, picking and complaining.

The squatting merchants held their wares up silently, gazing incuriously at the human women, occasionally scratching simple marks on small squares of damp clay to keep track of their sales. They had no written language, and their arithmetic, on a base of eight, seemed not to be very flexible either. He glanced at an alien infant lying in a makeshift cradle underneath a stall; its parent paid no attention or perhaps was too lazy to swat the insects swarming over its face. The DepCom's wife had organized a wives' committee to teach Krishna's natives elementary hygiene; it didn't seem to be having much success.

"Danyo." Mem Patel crooked a finger at him. "See that bolt? Find out what this shifty-eyed thief wants for it."

For this elementary task the DepCom's wife required the expensive services of a Guild lingster. Mem Patel, like the rest of the human colony, hadn't bothered to learn anything of this language beyond "Kitchen Frehti," an impoverished pidgin of a very few alien words and her own native Inglis, which she used with the female Freh who worked in the Residence.

"Danyo! The brocade this boy's holding!"

Beside the male alien, a female stood up, ready to bargain. She wore a shapeless brown garment and a necklace of plaited vines with a few gray clay beads that was no match for the garish blue designs on her mate's face. On Krishna it seemed to be the female's job to communicate; he wondered if perhaps males found it beneath their dignity to talk too much.

Before he could begin, the comlink the DepCom insisted he wear on these outings buzzed at his wrist. He held the tiny receiver to his ear. *"Ries. I need you up here. Right away."* Deputy Commissioner

Chandra Patel's voice echoed inside his skull, disturbing the brooding hangover again as if it were a flock of bats.

Ries stared at his shaking hand. "Sir?"

"*Intelligence just in,*" the DepCom's voice said. "*Mules massing across Separation River.*"

In the little more than two years Ries had been here, he'd seen the pattern repeat every year. A handful of the second race on Krishna, nick-named "Mules" by the humans for their long, horsey faces, came into the native town and ran wild for a few days just before the monsoon struck. Nothing serious, as far as anyone could tell. A few fights with their Freh neighbors, an occasional native shack burned to the ground. One of the DepCom's hobbies had been gathering information, anecdotal for the most part, about the Mules.

"It's monsoon weather, the silly season," he said, watching the women plucking fretfully at rainbow silks. "Mules don't pay attention to New Bombay."

"*Maybe. But I found a record of an attack when the colony was founded fifteen years ago. Almost wiped them out.*"

The DepCom's daughter turned and, catching Ries's gaze on her, stuck her tongue out at him. He frowned at the girl and saw her laugh.

"*The early commissioners kept very poor records,*" Patel said. "*Maybe we can't trust them. But I don't want to take chances.*"

"Nothing the *Star of Calcutta* can't take care of, surely?"

"*Bring the women back to the Residence, Ries. Immediately.*"

The DepCom's women hadn't been pleased. Ries had let their indignation wash over him, ignoring their shrill protests.

Back in his own quarters in the Residence, he poured a shot of *zyth* in a small glass. They'd been wrong at the Mother House to think he couldn't handle it. There was a lot of pressure in lingstering; some of the Guild's best people broke under the strain.

He leaned down to the computer on his desk and touched a key; the screen became a mirror. The action reminded him how long since he'd used the AI for the purpose it was intended; hours spent browsing through its copious files on the flora and fauna of Krishna didn't count. It was as superfluous here as he felt himself to be. A highly trained lingster and a superior AI with nothing to do, what a waste.

He frowned at his swollen face under tangled curls of dark brown hair—no gray showing yet—the line of his cheekbones blurred under the flushed skin, the blue eyes bloodshot like the tracks of a wounded bird over snow. He stepped away and noticed an extra couple of kilos around the waist.

He changed into fresh tropical whites, tugged a comb through his hair, erased the mirror, and went out of his room. At the top of the stairs, he changed his mind, ducked back inside, and grabbed the flask, which he tucked into a thigh pocket.

On the ground floor, a Freh houseboy with no understanding of how a central air system worked had left the doors of the Residence's great entrance hall wide open. A faint breath of humid air moved sluggishly inside, already laced with aerosols from the distant ocean's seasonal diatom bloom. Soon the monsoon would turn the streets of human enclave and native town alike into rivers of mud and the air into a smothering blanket laden with infection. He closed the doors.

Turning back, he found one of the houseboys silently moving across the hall. This one was draped in gaudy layers of red and orange silk. But today something fierce moved through the houseboy's small eyes before it was replaced by the servile, grinning expression the Freh adopted in human presence.

An arched alcove revealed a closed door. Ries knocked.

"Come in."

Chandra Patel glanced up from a large desk dominated by an oversize screen. The only sign of luxury here was the antique scarlet and gold carpet with a design of thatched huts and water buffalo that lay on the polished wood floor. Purchased from an impoverished museum in India and imported at great cost, it soothed Patel's occasional bouts of homesickness.

On the desk today Ries saw an uncharacteristically disorderly heap of papers, infocubes, and disks, as if the DepCom had lost patience and banged a fist down in their midst, jumbling them. The usually immaculate diplomat hadn't taken time to shave this morning, and the burgundy silk lounging robe he wore looked as if he'd slept in it.

"What haven't you told me?" Ries asked.

Across the room, Patel's tea kettle on a hot-stone and two cups of delicate porcelain waited on a small table. Ries took a pinch of aromatic black tea leaves from a canister, put some into each cup, then filled the cups with boiling water. Back turned to the DepCom, he poured a few drops of *zyth* from the flask into his own tea. He handed the other cup to the DepCom.

Patel said heavily, "The *Calcutta's* on training maneuvers. Out of the sector. It'll take too long for her to get back."

Tea forgotten for a moment, Ries stared at the DepCom. When humans had first arrived on this planet, the Freh who lived mainly in the lowlands along Separation River had been easily impressed by the display of superior technology into letting them settle peacefully. The Dep-Com was fond of pointing out that most Freh were living better now than they'd been before the advent of human colonists. Not to mention the stuff they managed to steal from the humans they worked for, his wife would add; colony wives had developed the necessary ritual of inventorying household property at least once a month.

The Mules seemed to be a different species than the Freh. Almost nothing was known about their history or their culture; their only observed behavior was this once-a-year mayhem visited on their neighbors. Ries himself had never even seen one close up. But the purpose of the small starship, *The Star of Calcutta*, was mainly to guard the planet against attack by the Venatixi, an alien race who bore no love for humans and whose violence intermittently scarred this sector of the Arm. Yet it seemed somebody had blundered, having the ship gone right now.

"But that isn't why I called you down here, Ries. Look at this." The DepCom indicated the screen with a brown hand. "I know you're interested in the Freh language. I think I've found something more bizarre."

Curious, Ries moved over to the desk to look. The one thing that had made his employment here bearable was Patel's friendship. It was the DepCom who suggested Ries make use of the sitar that had been his. The sitar, Ries remembered now, that had been damaged and then forgotten in a native tavern.

Before Patel could elaborate on what he'd found, the door opened and his wife hurried in. Nayana Patel—a short woman who might've been voluptuous in her youth—had changed into an elaborate red gown with voluminous skirts heavily embroidered in silver. He could see hints of the gown's Indian ancestry, but overornamented and fussy; the embroidery must've added at least a kilo to its weight.

"Chan!" she said sharply to her husband. "You must say something to the servants. Amah ruined my breakfast this morning. You'd think after all this while she'd have learned how to prepare naan. Now I find that she's run away."

Nayana Patel called all the female house servants "Amah," refusing to learn their names in retaliation for what she saw as their refusal to prepare the vegetarian diet the Patels followed, and claiming she couldn't tell one from another in any case.

"Find yourself another servant, Naya."

Half a dozen silver bracelets on her wrist chimed musically as she moved in front of his desk. "That's what I'm trying to tell you, Chan. They've all gone."

Patel stared at her for a second, then abruptly turned back to his desk and pressed a button on a small pad. They waited in silence. He banged his hand on the pad again. Nothing happened.

"You see?" Mem Patel said. "We're alone in this great awful house. Left to fend for ourselves."

Remembering the odd, veiled look the houseboy had given him, Ries felt a tremor of apprehension slide up his spine.

"Ries," Patel said. "Get my family to the *Calcutta*'s base. Take my skipcar."

Mem Patel said petulantly, "I'm not going anywhere without you, Chandra."

"Stop arguing for once, Naya, and go with Ries. I'll follow as soon as I can."

She stared at him. "But I need to pack—"

"Get the children." Patel took her arm and steered her out the door. When she'd gone, he gazed at Ries. "I can trust you with my family, can't I?"

"Sir?"

"You're a good man when you're not drinking," Patel said bluntly. Anger burned in his stomach. "You can rely on me."

"The bottom line, Ries," Magister Kai had said, "is that we can't rely on you anymore."

The Head of the Mother House of the Guild of Xenolinguists had turned his gaze out the arched window of his study as if autumnal rain-clouds slowly obliterating Alpine peaks absorbed his full attention. Ries had been summoned back to the Mother House for retraining, something all lingsters were encouraged to do at regular intervals. Other lingsters caught up on new technology and techniques, but he was subjected to lectures from a new Head, a man less inclined to be indulgent than the one he'd known as a student twenty years ago.

"I see from the record that the Guild has given you a number of chances over the last three years." Magister Kai turned to face him again. "You were a very talented lingster in the beginning. But your addiction to native alcohols is a serious problem."

"It's under control now, Magister." What choice did he have but stay sober on Earth? They would've found and confiscated his supply at the port if he'd tried to bring any home with him.

"Is it, Ries? I'd like to think so. I'd like to think that all the years the Guild spent preparing you for service haven't been wasted after all. I'd like to believe that we could send you out into the field without worrying whether or not you'd be sober enough to do your job. But I find that belief hard to sustain."

His last assignment had been a disaster. He knew the Guild would've much preferred to send someone other than himself, but the client alien had expressed urgency, and he'd been the only experienced lingster close enough to take the assignment at the time.

"I was sick. Picked up some kind of native virus — "

"And dosed it with native alcohol," Magister Kai said. "Dangerously compromising the interface because you were out of control. Another time you, and the Guild, may not be so lucky. You do realize the risk you take?"

Lingstering was more of an art than a science for all the Guild proclaimed otherwise, and as an artist he'd found that some native liquors set his considerable talent free. That last time he'd managed to scare himself because it had taken him days to shake the demons that stalked through his skull.

There were hazards to mixing alcohol or any pharmaceutical, alien or otherwise, with the already volatile drugs of interface. The Guild had long ago learned to weed out candidates with sensitivity to Terran intoxicants, narcotics, stimulants, and hallucinogens, not even bothering to send them for treatment. Yet it was impossible to know in advance all the alien substances a human could become addicted to and develop appropriate immunogens.

He'd begun the slide three years earlier when his young wife died. He'd promised her he'd be the rock under her feet; instead he'd let her die. The Guild told him there was nothing he could have done for Yv, even if he'd been there. There was nothing anybody could've done, they said. He didn't believe them; the Guild didn't approve of lingsters marrying. He'd been out of it on some native potion that morning, incapable of helping her when she needed him. Later, he drank to forget the damage the drinking had caused. And then he'd found he couldn't stop. The Guild had moved him from planet to planet, and on each he'd found something to ease his pain, something they couldn't immunize him against in advance. He didn't need some sanctimonious representative of the Guild telling him he should quit; he knew it. But he knew he wasn't ready just yet.

He said tersely, "I'm sober now."

"Perhaps you mean it this time," Magister Kai gazed at him for a moment. "And because of that, I'm giving you one last chance. The colony on Krishna was founded a dozen years ago. The aboriginal population is placid with the rudiments of a simple language. The lingsters who forged the interface set up the AI to handle it."

"Then why does anybody still need a lingster?"

"The Deputy Commissioner on Krishna, Chandra Patel, is an old friend of mine," Magister Kai said. "He wants a personal translator for his family."

Shopping facilitator was more like it, he thought, as he left the DepCom's study. There wasn't even enough work here for a grade one translator. But he'd kept his word to Magister Kai. He hadn't missed a day of this boring and demeaning duty.

He crossed the hall. Through the high windows he saw the first wisps of cloud gathering over the jagged ribcage of the Maker's Bones. If Patel was right and the Mules intended to attack the human compound this time while the ship was offworld, there'd be real trouble.

He entered his own room and gazed at the mess he lived in. While the DepCom's wife packed, he'd better pull together a few things of his own. The only object of real importance he possessed was the fieldpack of interface drugs that all lingsters carried when they were on assignment. Not that he'd had any opportunity to use either the alpha or beta sequences in the whole two years he'd spent on Krishna, but no lingster ever walked off and left his fieldpack behind.

He thought of apocryphal stories of lingsters who'd come through disasters, triumphantly hefting their packs as if they'd faced nothing more than a routine interface. The stories were more propaganda than actual history, but the habit lingered. He strapped it on the hip opposite the flash.

To himself at least, he had to admit that he'd loved the Guild once, when he was young. He still thought with fondness of his student days. It had seemed an almost holy endeavor to immerse himself in the mystery of language, and the Guild, monastic in its foundation in any case, did little to discourage this religious fervor in its lingsters. Yet there was something about the Guild that ate up a lingster's productive years, then spat him out, exhausted, cynical, and bereft.

Somewhere in the silent house he heard a muffled thud. Mem Patel, probably, bumping a trunk full of expensive clothes and baubles, and he'd be the one stuck with carrying it up to the roof. In a sour mood, he started up the stairs that led to the family's private apartments.

Another thump, behind him this time. Then a sharp crash of furniture overturned. And a scream.

He turned back too fast, triggering a giddy spell. For a second the stairs tilted crazily under his feet and he lost his footing, slipping down two steps. He grabbed at the stair rail for balance, then moved with great care across the hall till the dizziness subsided. The noise was coming from Patel's study.

Nausea rose in his stomach. He hesitated outside the door.

Another scream.

He flung the door open on a nightmare scene and came instantly, sharply sober.

The DepCom lay on the antique carpet by his desk, the spreading pool of his blood obliterating its pastoral designs. One of Patel's hands clutched the shattered keypad of his terminal. Standing over him, a small, naked alien, with a face so covered in tattoos that the natural color of the skin hardly showed, held a blade like an elongated thin pyramid in one bloodstained hand.

It took Ries several seconds to comprehend the incredible scene. Not Mule. The assassin was Freh. His heart lurched.

The plump little alien glanced at Ries. Two others, wearing only the Freh version of a loincloth, were ransacking the room, overturning chairs and emptying bookshelves.

He screamed at them in Kitchen Frehti: "Scum, obey your master." Lingster or not, it was all he could remember of the language in his shock.

The Freh holding the three-edged knife crimson with Patel's blood jabbered nervously. The other assassins reverted to familiar native behavior, shoving each other in their haste to scramble out the open window through which they'd entered.

Sick with horror, he let his eyes come back to the DepCom's lifeless body, glazed with its own blood. Then he dropped to his knees. Patel's fingers had flickered briefly.

Something clattered to the floor as he knelt. Ignoring it, he cradled the DepCom's bloody head in his lap. Close up, he caught the faint iron smell of the spreading blood.

"Ries," Patel whispered hoarsely. "I must tell you—Mules—Something I just learned—"

"Save your strength, Chan. I'll get help."

Weak fingers scrabbled at his sleeve. "Important. You *must* know this. The Freh—"

Patel's voice stopped. His head lolled back, his eyes stared unseeing into the lingster's own. Then his colorless lips moved soundlessly, and Ries read his last words: "Save my family."

He stared down at the dead man in his arms for a moment longer. Then he laid the head gently back down on the Indian carpet and stood up.

The assassin still stood, knife in hand, gaping stupidly at the result of his treachery. Ries took a step forward, and the alien bolted, scrambling out the window in his turn.

He glanced back one more time at the body, feeding a growing rage. The broken flask lay beside Patel, *zyth* running like a fiery oil slick over his bloody body.

The family's private apartment was at the end of a long hallway on the third floor. Ries skidded on wooden tile polished slick every morning by grinning Freh houseboys, the same ones—or their friends and neighbors—who now had the blood of Chandra Patel on their hands. Never in the fifteen years the human colony had been on Krishna had the Freh given any indication they could turn into killers.

The fogginess of the hangover he'd experienced earlier came back, clouding his thoughts as the shocking clarity of Patel's murder faded. He could use a drink—but he knew he had to stay sober now.

The DepCom's bedroom door stood ajar, and he heard the *skreek* of trunks being dragged across the wooden floor, the thud and thump of the family's frantic packing. He knocked once to announce his presence, then went inside without waiting for a reply.

Three-year-old Jilan, the Patels's late-in-life child, sat in a heap of vivid scarlet and turquoise pillows on the huge bed, silently clutching a stuffed toy. He'd always thought there was something fey about this child who'd been born on Krishna. The older daughter was adding her weight to her mother's as they tried to close an overstuffed traveling chest. Lita's eyes were deep brown flecked with gold, and when she'd finished growing out of her awkward years he imagined she'd be as exotic as a tiger. For now, she was a moody teenager, unpredictable as a cat.

"Danyo." Nayana Patel looked up and spotted him. "I can't find a boy to help us. Give me a hand with this."

"Respect, Mem, but we have to get out now. Leave it."

She stared at him, fussing absently at the long, elaborately pleated gown. "I can't go without—"

He grabbed the woman's elbow and turned her toward the door.

The younger daughter wailed. But the older daughter snatched at his sleeve, and he saw scarlet, long-nailed fingers.

"Don't touch my mother!" the girl ordered.

He removed her hands from his sleeve. "We don't have time to waste."

Mem Patel's eyes widened as she caught sight of the blood on his hands where her husband's head had rested. "Chandra?" she whispered. Color drained out of her dark face leaving it gray.

He was afraid she'd break down helplessly if he gave her the truth. But she obviously guessed the news was bad. She clapped a heavily ringed hand over her mouth, stifling her exclamation. Then she turned back to the bed, bracelets tinkling, and swept her younger child up. The toddler whimpered as the stuffed toy fell out of her arms. The big case she'd been packing forgotten now, the woman moved to the door.

Lita scowled, pushing a loose strand of copper hair back up on her head. He watched her grab up a smaller case that had been on the floor by the bed, feeling the heat of her dislike. "*What are you, Danyo?*" she'd once asked. "*Monk or fairy? Do you ever even look at women?*" How close she'd come to the truth; since his wife's death, he hadn't been with a woman.

Lita followed her mother to the door.

"Wait." He stepped in front of Mem Patel and looked cautiously around the open door.

The upstairs hallway was deserted, the great house silent, giving no hint of the carnage he'd witnessed downstairs. A sense of wrongness suffused the place. The stairwell leading up to the rooftop was at the opposite end of the hallway from the main staircase. No rooms opened off the hall at this point, no balconies or even windows that opened, and if they were challenged here they'd be cornered.

As the fugitives moved down the hall, a row of holo-portraits of former Deputy Commissioners watched grim-faced, white-robed men and women in ceremonial saris, whose most serious threat during their tenure on Krishna had been the upholding of Hindu customs in the face of Freh indifference and incompetence. To make eye contact with any one of them was enough to activate circuits that would deliver snippets of wisdom in the subject's voice. Some had chosen favorite axioms of diplomacy, others repeated cherished lines from the *Bhagavad Gita*. He didn't look at them. There was no advice modern or archaic they could give him; not one of them had faced a nightmare like this.

"You might not want to tell Mama the truth, Danyo," Lita's low voice said just behind him. "But you'd better soon tell *me* or I'm not going anywhere with you."

He glanced back at the girl's sullen face. "You don't have much of a choice."

"Pah! Your breath stinks of liquor," she said.

Jilan wailed and Mem Patel smothered her child's face against her own breast, muffling the sound. The woman's eyes glittered with tears, but she held her grief in silence. He shepherded the family along until they reached a door that led to the roof stairs. Opening it cautiously, he listened for sounds.

They were directly above a small, walled garden the Patels used for meditation, with a holo-statue of Krishna in a niche surrounded by flowers. It struck him then how the Patels clung to the things of home, how little they'd adjusted to this new life. Yet in this they were no different from the rest of New Bombay colony.

A damp wind was picking up, soughing through the trees on the other side of the wall. Tall and skinny, they reached as high as the flat roof of the Residence. The Freh called the trees "Spirit-Trap," the name serving to suggest again how little he really understood of the Freh or their language. The air was heavy with the clotted green smell of the coming monsoon. His sinuses tingled.

He stepped cautiously outside. Beyond the trees, he saw the other wall, the one that shut New Bombay off from the native town squatting at its feet like a scruffy beggar, and south of the town, Separation River. To the north and east was a great chain of mountains dropping down to foothills in the northwest where it was possible to cross to the rolling sweep of grasslands where the starship was based. Their only hope of safety lay in the *Star of Calcutta*'s base.

The DepCom's silver skipcar crouched on a bull's-eye pad in the center of the roof, an oversized mosquito about to launch itself into the sky. It was small enough that Mem Patel's luggage, if he'd let her bring it, would've made it unbearably crowded. He didn't need to know much about flying; the onboard AI would take care of most of it. The sooner they got on board the better. He beckoned to the women.

His way was suddenly blocked by a Freh in a voluminous ankle-length, orange-brown garment. A white silk scarf, like all the natives wore during the season of blowing spores, covered his face.

"Talker. Wait," the alien said in Frehti. "No harm."

Mem Patel gasped, but if the mother was scared, the wildcat daughter certainly wasn't.

"Go from our way," Lita said in a high-pitched Frehti that Ries hadn't known she could speak.

The Freh stepped back a pace and allowed the white scarf to slide down, revealing sallow features and one lone tattoo squiggle that began on his forehead and ran down over one cheek. Ries recognized the male alien who'd been in the tavern last night; his name was Born-Bent. The Freh's spine seemed twisted out of alignment, raising one shoulder higher than the other and throwing the head off balance. One eye was dull amber, the other gray. *"What they'd call back home a sport,"* the

DepCom had once commented, coming upon the malformed alien in the marketplace.

"What are you doing here?" Ries demanded in Frehti.

Born-Bent had done small services for him from time to time, but he'd never trusted the Freh.

Behind him, he heard the child's voice start up again in a rising whine of protest, and the mother's urgent hushing.

The Freh made a half servile, half nervous gesture with his head. "Danger here."

He became aware of the tremor in his hands and shut his fists to still it. "What do you want with me?"

The lipless mouth pulled up in an ugly caricature of a grin. "I do service. Then Talker do service."

He wondered suddenly if the name the aliens called him indicated respect or contempt. Probably the latter, since males didn't seem to hold conversations.

"What service?"

At that point, the little girl screeched loudly.

"What is it, precious one?" Mem Patel asked anxiously.

Born-Bent reached into his tentlike robe with his bandaged hand and pulled something out. "Take."

His hand rose instinctively to ward off attack before he saw what it was the alien held out: the sitar he'd left in the tavern. The cracked gourd that had formed the instrument's resonator at its base had been replaced with the shell of a large, native nut.

"This also."

Ries looked down at a second object the alien laid on his palm. It seemed to be a small bone from an animal with some kind of marks scratched on its surface; at first glance, they resembled the scrawl of the primitive counting system used by the merchants in the bazaar. Yet as he gazed at the bone, something stirred in him, some sense of mystery.

"What is it?"

"Soul bone. Give to the mothers."

He had to raise his own voice over the sound of the child's wailing. "What mothers? Where?"

"Beneath the bones. Go. Great danger."

The last thing he had time to do was carry a native relic to an alien graveyard. Ries shoved the bone into a pocket and looped the carry-cord of the sitar over his shoulder.

He turned back to Lita. "Get in the 'car."

"I don't take orders from servants."

"Lita!" Mem Patel scolded.

"Well—he is."

"Your papa wishes us to go with Danyo, and so we will."

The girl scowled but turned toward the vehicle. He took the still shrieking, red-faced child from her mother. Jilan pummeled his arms with her fists.

Mem Patel suddenly seemed to understand the cause of her child's distress. "Where is it, sweetheart? Tell Mama."

Jilan pointed back toward the open door at the top of the narrow stairwell.

His skin prickled. For a moment he thought he'd heard the rumble of voices rising up the stairwell, the echo of tramping feet. He listened. Nothing.

"We have to leave, Mem. Now!"

The older girl was already in the skipcar; she leaned back out the door, holding her arms out to take her sister. He lifted the child up to Lita's waiting arms, then turned to help the DepCom's widow.

Nayana Patel was running back toward the stairwell door to fetch the child's toy, one hand clutching the ridiculously ornate skirt above her knees. Lita screamed. He lunged after Mem Patel, but Born-Bent grabbed him, pinning his arms. The Freh was surprisingly strong for his small size.

"Talker!" The alien said urgently. "You understand how words make."

As Nayana Patel reached the door, another alien appeared, his body naked but his face scarved in white. Ries caught the prismatic glint of a three-sided knife. Mem Patel screamed, the sound dwindling away into a gurgle as bright red arterial blood spurted high, hitting the lintel as she fell.

"Mama!" Lita wailed.

Two more Freh spilled out onto the roof, stepping carelessly over the downed woman.

He threw his weight against the sport. His head spun dizzily, but he caught Born-Bent off-balance and almost broke free.

Born-Bent punched him full in the stomach.

His knees buckled under him and air rushed out of his lungs. The alien dragged him across the roof and shoved him like a sack of vegetables through the door of the skipcar. Inside, the child's deafening noise echoed round the confined metal space. His belly scraped painfully over the ridged floor. Lita's long-nailed fingers scrabbled at his arm, pulling him in; her red hair had come loose from the clip, and long curls spilled over her face.

He glanced out the door again, just in time to see Born-Bent go down under the flash of a blade.

II

The skipcar was flying low over leafy Spirit-Trap treetops glowing olive by storm light. High crests whipped past only centimeters away. Lita Patel sat in the pilot's seat, frowning out the forward port at the horizon, where the gray-green of the jungle met the iron gray of the clouded sky. She'd had the presence of mind to get the skipcar airborne after Born-Bent shoved him aboard.

"Flying too low," he observed. His eyes were raw and his stomach felt bruised.

"Glad you're feeling better."

"Onboard AI—"

"Overrode it. I'm keeping us under the storm clouds."

He squinted at the jungle flowing like a dark river beneath them. "Didn't know you knew anything about flying."

"More than you, apparently." She turned to look at him. "You drink too much."

In the watery light he saw smudges under her eyes which were bloodshot as if she'd been crying. Her red hair had come completely loose now, tumbling over her shoulders.

And suddenly he knew that one of the things about her that irritated him so much was that her hair was the same rich color as his young wife's had been. Looking at this half-grown vixen triggered painful memories of his lost, sweet Yv. The sooner they reached the base and he could hand these two over to somebody else the better.

His head felt as if it had been hollowed out; the sound of his own voice when he spoke boomed and echoed inside his skull. He leaned forward and punched up the 'car's automap and studied it. The terrain between New Bombay and the base was hilly and wild; their route passed over a ridge thick with unbroken jungle, a tapestry in vermilion and umber.

"Danyo, I expect you to explain—"

"Not now."

"Then advise me. I've been trying to raise *Calcutta's* base, but I get no response."

Even with the starship gone, there should be a skeleton maintenance crew left behind. He deactivated the map. "Try again."

She leaned forward and keyed a command into the pad. Nothing happened. "Why don't they answer? Is something wrong?"

He considered possibilities but decided not to share them. Ahead, a jagged spike of lightning streaked out of the black clouds and raced to the ground.

After a moment, she said in a whisper that couldn't hide the shakiness of her voice, "Tell me the truth now, Danyo. My father's dead too, isn't he?"

If they were going to have any chance of getting through this, she would have to grow up. There was no way he could make it painless. "The Freh killed him."

She closed her eyes, and he saw her small white teeth biting her lower lip. She had her mother's ability to absorb terrible news and not cry out. He couldn't remember the death of his own parents—he'd already been on assignment for the Guild—but he knew it wasn't under terrible circumstances like these. He felt there was something he ought to say to her but couldn't think of anything appropriate.

They skimmed over the wind-churned treetops in silence again for a few seconds. Rain spattered in a crazy staccato on the forward port. They'd be lucky to make it to the base before the storm caught them.

Finally, he said lamely, "I'm sorry."

She stared resolutely ahead. "We have to get to the *Calcutta* now."

He hadn't been able to weep after Yv's death. Like Lita, he'd found no time for grief. Instead, he'd taken the way past the pain of living through a bottle of whatever a planet offered. But that had been just another kind of lie.

"The ship isn't at the base right now."

"Not there? Then — "

She didn't get to finish her thought. The little skipcar shuddered as if hit by a giant fist, rolled tail over nose, and headed straight down for the forest floor.

When he opened his eyes again, he was dangling upside down from the seat webbing, the floor of the skipcar above his head. Branches poked their way in through broken ports. A long jagged spike of what was supposed to be shatterproof plastiglass was poised above his neck. It took him a moment to figure out that the 'car must have been caught in a tree that had broken their fall.

What the hell're we going to do now?

The silence made him nervous. Supporting his weight with one hand on a strut, he wriggled cautiously round until the glass no longer threatened to impale him. Now he could see the pilot's seat.

Empty.

He craved a shot of *zyth* to steady his nerves, but he knew he was going to have to do this alone from now on. The thought scared him. Then he abandoned caution and twisted in the web until he could see the back. Also empty. If they'd been ejected —

"You're conscious," Lita said, leaning in the window, careless of the splintered glass.

He stared upside down at her. "I thought you might've been killed."

"You don't have that much luck, Danyo." Her expression, wan beneath the coffee-brown skin, gave the lie to the bravado of her words.

"We must've been struck by lightning." He wondered if the onboard AI had been badly damaged, and if it contained a self-repair program.

"I got Jilan out first in case the 'car burned."

She indicated where her sister sat, finger in her mouth, at the foot of a tangle of slender jungle trees. Long emerald fronds dripped rainwater on her.

He noticed that Lita had removed the ornate overskirt she'd been wearing at home — the thought brought back an unwelcome image of Mem Patel's skirt spattered in blood — revealing sturdy brown legs in serviceable shorts. She carried the skirt slung over one shoulder like a cloak. The little strap sandals on her feet were not so practical.

His seat web was jammed and it took time to free himself. Lita helped, supporting him to take tension off the web's fastening.

"Devi! You weigh too much," she grumbled.

He turned, allowing his legs to slide slowly down to the ceiling that was now the floor, and felt the sitar bump against his head. For a moment he considered leaving it behind. But it had been Patel's, and Born-Bent had gone out of his way to mend it and bring it back. It really didn't weigh that much, he thought. The sitar's carry cord had caught in the seat web and had to be untangled. A lightweight jacket he'd thrown into his pack had snagged on the cord too, and came with it.

He rolled himself cautiously out of the wrecked 'car and stood beside the girl in the wet forest. Immediately, his sensitive sinuses tingled painfully.

"Jilan's hungry," Lita said. "She hasn't eaten since — "

He felt heat on the back of his neck and turned to see the skipcar burning. He stared at it for a moment. The forest was too damp for the fire to become a threat, but he hadn't had time to get their belongings out.

"You see?" she said. "Now what?"

Krishna wasn't a world that invited tourism. He knew few things about the foothills other than they were wild and dotted with small Freh villages where some of the bazaar's vendors lived. He'd trusted the skipcar's AI to get them to the base without knowing exactly where it was. Now he was certain of only one thing: They dared not stay here in the jungle, so close to the chaos in New Bombay.

"Now we go on foot," he said.

Lita scuffed a toe in the grass that formed a thick, waist-high carpet under the trees, and drops of water flew off the stalks. "Not much of a path. And what about Jilan? This is over her head."

He glanced in the direction she indicated and saw the little girl pushing her way through grass that reached her shoulders. As he watched, she stumbled and fell, disappearing under a green wave that closed over her. If she went off on her own, they could easily lose track of her.

"I'll carry Jilan."

"Do you know what direction we should take?"

He didn't, but he wasn't going to admit that. Spirit-Trap trees hid the mountains from sight, and the sky was too overcast for him to get his bearings from the sun. If he climbed one of the trees, he'd get a better sense of which way to go, but these trees were too thin to take his weight. He had no idea how many hours had passed since they'd fled New Bombay. He had to do it soon, or what little daylight was left would be fading.

He picked up the toddler and settled her on his shoulders where she twined her fingers in his hair, leaning her head drowsily against his. She was heavy, but at least she'd given up that awful screaming. He wasn't used to children, and he'd never had much contact with this one in New Bombay; she'd stayed most of the time in the nursery with the family's personal servants.

"Be careful with my sister," Lita warned. "She's very upset."

He glanced at the older girl. It wasn't the first time he'd noticed her interpreting for her silent sibling. "Doesn't she speak for herself?"

"Why should she? My mother spoiled her. And the amahs did everything for her. Everybody around her did the talking."

Three was late for a child to begin talking, he thought. All healthy human babies were born with impressive linguistic skills. Jilan should be conveying her thoughts with some fluency by now, not relying on others to do it for her.

Somewhere a stream rushed by, hidden in the dense undergrowth, chattering urgently to itself. The sharp, clear scent of water lay like a descant over the darker notes of wet soil and thick plant-life. Enormous magenta and scarlet blossoms hung from vines that climbed the tree trunks; smaller, acid yellow flowers lit up the shadows beneath them. Clouds of eyeless insects whirred by; guided only by the smell of the flowers, they blundered constantly into the humans' faces. He pushed his way through the high grass and Lita followed.

"These sandals are rubbing my feet," she complained at one point.

He wouldn't have believed the brutal carnage they'd left behind in the Residence was the work of Freh if he hadn't seen them himself. Something had caused the normally placid aliens to rise up against the humans. If they'd been harboring deep resentment against the colonists all these years, they'd done a good job of hiding it. He tried to remember if he'd ever sensed anger or even reluctance in the native behavior, but all the images he conjured up were of bland, incurious, passive faces.

"You understand how words make." Born-Bent had been wrong; he didn't understand at all. There were obviously huge gaps in his knowledge of how Frehti operated. He wished he could take the problem back to the Guild, let his old teachers play with it. He imagined them as he'd known them in his youth. Magistra Eiluned, old already when he'd first come to the Mother House, and Dom Houston, who'd believed that every language served only to disguise. Was Frehti disguising something he should know? In memory he saw them gathered round the seminar table while the warm green smell of summer flowed through tall windows and cuckoos spoke from sunlit apple orchards.

A stifled exclamation at his side brought him back. Lita had caught one of her flimsy sandals in a wiry grass strand. He put out a hand and steadied her.

When the sandal was settled back on her foot, she glanced up at him. "Do you have any idea what caused that . . . that . . . what happened back there?"

Her voice wavered, but he could tell she was determined not to let him see her terror. Hair in disarray, clothing streaked and torn, she was, after all, hardly out of childhood herself.

"Time to talk about it later," he said.

Something had happened in the native tavern. Born-Bent had tried to give him a message and perhaps been killed for it. Then the DepCom had tried to share something he'd learned. Again, something important enough for a man to waste his dying breath trying to communicate. Ries had a sense of huge pieces of information lacking, questions without answers. Until he understood the deadly puzzle, he and the DepCom's children were in mortal danger.

When they'd gone a few hundred meters through the dense undergrowth, he found what he was looking for. An old Spirit-Trap with a thick, gnarled trunk shoved its head up through the canopy formed by its younger neighbors. He let the child and the sitar slide gently down to the wet grass. Jilan clung to his leg for a moment, staring up at him wideeyed, but she made no sound. He was beginning to find the child's silence unnerving.

"Wait here a minute," he said. "Okay?"

Jilan didn't answer.

"What're you doing now? Lita asked as he began to climb. She seemed to have pulled herself together again. "You'll never make that, Danyo. You're out of shape."

The smooth trunk was slick from the rain but free of the clinging vines. Near the top, the main trunk split into three, and he could go no further as each thin limb bent under his weight. He sat in the security of this three-pronged Y, blood pounding in his temples, leaning out precariously to gaze over the surrounding forest.

The rain had stopped and the sun had already set, leaving a diffuse glow in the banked clouds on the horizon. To his left, the storm had cleared, and he saw the first faint spark of the constellation the Freh called "The Thief." Below it, a white smear, a tail end of the home galaxy that the Freh knew as "Sorrow-Crossing," gleamed faintly. Somewhere down that soft wash of light, a small blue planet orbited a sun too insignificant to be visible this far away.

He looked away. Fugitives couldn't afford the luxury of being homesick.

They were on the slope of one of the foothills, a gentle rise that he hadn't noticed as they'd trudged through the thick jungle. He gazed across canyons choked with dark vegetation and saw Separation River, glowing like a pewter ribbon in the twilight, winding across the alluvial plain. He thought of his first impressions of Krishna as the shuttle ferrying him down from the starship came in through the atmosphere: a lush green planet laced with shining waterways, signs of squalid habitation appearing only after the shuttle landed.

In the foreground, downslope, he noticed a number of trees seemed to be leaning crazily, and he realized he was staring at the skipcar's crash site. Then his attention was pulled back to the distant human settlement on the banks of the river. It seemed as if it were illuminated. As he stared, it erupted in a fountain of flame that turned the bluffs crimson. New Bombay was on fire.

"How much longer are you going to stay up there?"

It was completely dark on the forest floor when he slid back down the tree again, but his eyes retained the afterimage of flame. The Dep-Com had thought danger would come from the wild Mules, yet it was the placid Freh who'd rebelled, and that was more frightening.

"Well, did you find which way we have to go?"

"I think so."

No sense passing on to her what he'd learned from the AI of car-
nivores on Krishna. As if to underline his concern, the leathery black
shape of a huge nightbird slipped between the trees and swept past his
shoulder. He heard the slap and creak of its featherless wings.

And he heard something else. Something more menacing than a
wild animal.

"What? Danyo, why're you pushing me?"

"Up there." He jerked his chin at the tree he'd just climbed down.
"We'll wait up there till it's light."

"But I don't climb trees. And what about Jilan?"

He shoved the hesitating girl toward the tree. "Get your foot up on
that bole there. Then the other. Keep going!" He slung the sitar over his
shoulder, grabbed the child up and held her close to his chest with one
hand, reaching into the tree's darkness for a handhold with the other.
The fieldpack dug into his hip as the child clasped her legs around him.

Lita seemed to pick up his urgency and she climbed quickly. He
followed, burdened by the child and the sitar, which he couldn't leave
behind in the damp grass. It banged into his shoulder blades with each
movement. Scared by the ascent, the little girl made it worse by clinging
tightly to his hair. Lita's foot slipped twice on the damp trunk and struck
his fingers, almost knocking him off. The child struggled, and he had a
hard time hanging on to the slippery bark.

"Stay calm!" he commanded.

She whimpered but stopped struggling. Lita had now reached the
Y where he'd stopped earlier; he pushed the child up into her down-
stretched hands. Relieved of Jilan's weight, he scrambled up after her.

He heard the harsh intake of Lita's breath as she turned toward the
plain of Separation River. The entire sky to the south and east was lit by
the lurid glow of the fire, and under it the wet leaves of the forest canopy
glittered redly as if they'd been drenched in blood.

Below them, the forest suddenly filled with screams — the crash of
bodies running blindly through undergrowth — a high-pitched keening
that brought the hairs up on his neck and arms. A sudden smell like pu-
trefying flesh rose up to his nostrils.

"Merciful Lord Krishna!" Lita exclaimed, her hands clasped over
her nose. "What is it?"

At the foot of the tree that sheltered them, a naked, spindly legged creature, its corpse-white skin hanging in folds like a too-big overcoat hastily thrown over spikes of underlying bone, wrestled a plump Freh female to the ground. The Freh shrieked and thrashed about as the other alien covered her. Ries could see her fists pummeling the larger alien's shoulders—a male, he could see its elongated penis and scrotal sack—and he heard the stream of scolding she gave vent to in her birdlike voice. The male made no sound in reply.

This was the first Mule he'd ever seen close up, and he was stunned by the height and emaciation of the alien. The powerful reek of their violent mating rose up in a thick cloud till he thought he would vomit.

Then it was over. The Mule stood up, his long, horselike head turning slowly, the overlarge ears pricked as if they were listening to sounds out of human range. Then he vanished wraithlike into the trees. A moment later, the Freh female picked herself up from the ground, brushed leaves and dirt off, then strolled away as if nothing had happened.

It made no sense. The Freh and the Mules were separate species; that was obvious at a glance. Had he misunderstood what was happening?

Lita was crying now. The mask of arrogance and precociousness that marked the teenager in the bazaar this morning had dropped away. The younger daughter stared up at him, her eyes wide with fright, her hands gripping the front of his jumpsuit.

"She looked like one of Jilan's amahs," Lita said in a wobbly voice. "What're we going to do, Danyo?"

"We'll stay up here for the night. In the morning, we'll make plans."

He put one arm around each of them, drew them close to share a little warmth, and thought about what she'd just said. The girl obviously didn't share her mother's boast that she couldn't tell one Freh from another.

The lurid glow in the sky over New Bombay gradually faded. The storm had blown over for the time being, leaving a sky bright with alien constellations and the white trail of Sorrow-Crossing. The planet had no companion in its orbit round its sun; Krishna's night sky was perpetually moonless. He looked down. Now the wet leaves mirrored the fierce glitter of stars.

When it was light again in the morning, he'd try to remember information browsed in the computer's library about edible plants and roots. One protein-rich, red-brown tuber the natives roasted over hot coals, he'd tasted in the bazaar. The Freh used the husks to make the dye they favored for their own robes. If he could find some tomorrow it would solve the food problem.

Something dug into his ribs where the child clung to him. He took Born-Bent's soul bone out and examined it curiously. It was about the size and width of his own index finger, and in the starlight its surface gleamed almost as though it were translucent. He ran his finger over the symbol scratched on it, but it yielded no secrets to him. The mothers — whoever and wherever they were — would know what to do with it, the Freh had said. If he survived long enough to find them.

After a while, the girls slept, but he remained awake and watchful for a long time, listening to the sounds of flight and evasion and bestial rutting that came from all directions, punctuated with an ominous animal roaring that brought to mind the chilling sights and sounds of jungle life he'd found in the AI's library.

He slept fitfully. Shortly before dawn, he dreamed Yv was drowning in Separation River. She was wearing the sky-blue dress she'd worn on their wedding day, and her outstretched hands implored him to help while he stood on the other bank, unable to reach her.

When he woke, his head had the sticky, cobweb-filled feeling he knew well, a clogged dullness that *zyth* caused and only *zyth* could remove.

His muscles jumped and trembled this morning. Fire raced down the nerve paths, and sweat broke out on his brow in spite of the cool morning. He felt weak, drained, ready to give up, desperate for the courage *zyth* could give him, even if it didn't last.

The forest had dissolved in a pearl-white mist that dripped off the leaves. He looked down at Jilan, still nestled in the crook of his arm. She was awake, gazing up at him, thumb in mouth, her face puffy and tear-streaked. *This wasn't part of my Guild oath!* But for the child's sake, he had to pull himself together.

Lita was kneeling in the tall grass in the gray light, emptying something out of her skirt, which she'd used as a basket. Wisps of fog drifted slowly over the ground.

She glanced up at him. "I found breakfast while you were still snoring."

He wouldn't give her the satisfaction of seeing her barbs strike home. He let the sitar slide down until it was low enough to drop safely into her outstretched hands. Then he grasped Jilan with one shaky hand and with the other lowered himself down to stand beside Lita. The little girl wriggled free and clutched her sister's arm. Lita pulled her sister down to sit on the ground close beside her, then indicated a mound of thumbnail-sized, dark purple berries.

"The houseboys sometimes brought us berries," she said. "They looked a bit like these."

He picked one out of the mound and raised it cautiously to his nose, then broke the berry open with a fingernail and gazed at the honeycomb of tiny segments surrounding a small oval seed. "This one's okay."

He handed it to her and picked up another.

"You mean you're going to do that with each one?" she asked, her disbelief obvious. "But they all came from the same bush. If one's okay—"

"Three kinds of berries all grow on one bush. They all look alike on the outside. The one I gave you is female, safe to eat. Another kind contains the male chromosomes, a kind of red dust that will make you sneeze and your stomach cramp, but it won't kill you. The third is sexually neuter. It's designed to kill the plant's enemies that mistake it for one of the other two."

She clapped her hands over her mouth. "But I was so hungry, and they looked— Danyo, I already ate one!"

"Does your stomach hurt?"

She shook her head.

"You were lucky. Next time, wait for me."

"I was only trying to help," she said in a small voice.

He sat cross-legged on the wet ground and sniffed, split, and sorted the berries, discarding most of them, stopping to sneeze frequently. Both sisters watched him work. Finally he took a berry from the smallest pile and—to reassure Lita—put it with great show into his own mouth. Then he turned that pile over to her.

"Those you can eat safely."

"You're only going to eat one berry?"

"I'm not hungry."

He didn't tell her that *zyth* was distilled from the poisonous form of these berries, made safe only after a long period of fermentation, and perhaps not even then. Hunger for *zyth* rose up from his bowels like a starved beast, all claws and teeth, overwhelming his body's need for food. For a moment he considered saving the dangerous berries. If he put one under his tongue, sucked it, didn't chew —

He stood up abruptly and walked away from temptation.

While the children ate their meager breakfast, the sun rose and the mist gradually melted off the grass. A fallen tree trunk provided a place to sit. He unslung the sitar from his shoulder, settled it in his lap, and began to explore the strings with a hand that wouldn't stop trembling. The native nut that had replaced the cracked gourd changed the resonance, and he compensated for it as much as he could. He really needed a wire plectrum to pluck the strings, but that hadn't been in his pocket when Born-Bent returned the lost instrument to him.

His fingernails were still caked in the DepCom's blood. He wiped his hand clean in the wet grass.

Lita came over to sit beside him as he finished. Her red hair tangled over her shoulders, and pink juice from the berries stained her mouth. Jilan was drawing on a patch of bare ground, using a piece of dry grass she'd pulled from the forest floor. Absorbed by her work, the child paid no attention to them. The two looked nothing alike, he thought. Lita would be as voluptuous as her mother but taller when she matured; the child was elfin-faced and seemed destined to be small and delicate.

"That was my father's sitar," Lita said.

"Yes."

"Play something."

He picked out an old song he'd learned as a student, a lament for time past and homeland lost, like a thousand similar dirges sung in different languages over the millennia by humans who'd been explorers and wanderers since they emerged from the primal ocean.

"Sad. It reminds me of Earth."

He set the instrument down on the ground beside him.

"I never learned to play. I think it would've pleased my father if I had." She ran one fingertip down the length of a string. "I've been away so long, it's hard to remember Earth, let alone India. Have you ever been to India?"

He shook his head and stood up, working on tension in his neck and shoulders.

"One thing I remember is a white house in the mountains, near the headwaters of the Ganges. We lived there in the summertime. We had peacocks and monkeys in the gardens—"

She broke off. He watched her staring into the distance, the rising sun illuminating half her face, highlighting the dark cheekbones so that she seemed a bas-relief carving of a young goddess on a temple wall.

In the silence, he bent down and retrieved the sitar, sliding an arm through its carry-cord. "Time to move on."

After a while she said, "You must've met lots of aliens."

"A number. They're not all pleased to meet Homo sapiens."

She scrambled to her feet and took her sister's hand. They stepped out through tough, wiry grass that grew up to the height of the child's head. He took Jilan from Lita and swung her up onto his shoulders. The child grasped the neck of the sitar as she rode, which didn't prevent it from banging his back but tightened the carry-cord as it passed across his throat.

Lita walked beside him. "How did you know about the berries?"

"There was a wealth of information in the AI's library. Your father seemed to be the only person in New Bombay who was interested in it."

She was silent for a moment, then she said, "You don't like me very much, do you?"

"Not important. I have to get you to safety."

"Well, maybe it's mutual." She halted, staring at the stark peaks, bones shrouded in funereal gray mist. "I hate this planet. Especially those ugly mountains."

He glanced up without slowing his pace. "The Maker's Bones?"

She caught up with him again. "And why do they have that name? Do the Freh believe in a god called the Maker? Is he supposed to be buried up there or what?"

"I haven't seen any evidence the Freh have a god."

"How can that be? All primitive races have gods or goddesses."

Before he could answer, something crashed through the undergrowth ahead of them. He seized Lita's arm and pulled them all down behind a tall clump of the bushes. Jilan whimpered and pressed her face against his chest.

The noise grew closer, and now they could hear snuffling — growling — keening —

"What is it?" Lita whispered, her breath warm at his ear.

Three figures emerged from the trees, a tall Mule male with deep-set eyes and two male Freh, one a juvenile, wrapped in rags and still showing the distinctive rolls of adolescent neck fat. The Mule tackled the naked adult Freh and wrestled him to the ground. They rolled over and over in the grass, the Mule grunting, the Freh screeching, and both pounding each other, at one point coming so dangerously close to the humans' hiding place that Ries smelled the Freh's sour sweat and the rancid odor of the Mule.

The Mule appeared to be trying to sink long fangs into the Freh's arms while the juvenile stood by, shrilling and gesturing with his four-fingered hands. Ries would never have guessed from the starved look of the Mule that he would be so strong, but he was obviously getting the better of the sturdier-looking Freh.

As abruptly as the sexual encounter had ended last night, this fight ended. Now the combatants separated, not looking at each other, sat up, and brushed dirt off themselves. A long moment passed. When he finally stood, the Mule's thin arms were as long as his legs; Ries saw the bones clearly through the skin as if the alien were a walking anatomy demonstration.

The Freh turned unblinking eyes in the direction of the hidden humans, but far from signaling defeat, there was something that seemed glutted and satisfied in that expression. There was some unexplained connection here, some clue he was missing that would explain the bizarre interaction between these two species that he'd witnessed last night and today, but he had no idea what it could be.

Through all this, the juvenile continued to wail. Suddenly, the Mule seemed to become aware of the noise for the first time. With a roar that was almost too deep to come from such a sunken chest, he now turned on the younger Freh. At first Ries thought he meant to kill the juvenile, but he saw that the Mule's intention was to drive him away. The juvenile took a step back, his eyes large with fear, arms flapping ineffectually in front of his face. The Mule lunged forward.

Then, to Ries's astonishment, the adult Freh joined the chase. At this, the juvenile turned and ran. The Mule and the adult Freh both ran after him. The sounds of the chase gradually died away behind them and the silence of the forest returned. Ries blew breath out, releasing tension.

"I want to go home!" Lita clutched her little sister.

He sighed. "New Bombay burned last night. You saw the fire."

"Not New Bombay. Earth."

He didn't think any of them had much chance of ever seeing Earth again.

Warm rain pelted them without ceasing, and sodden blind bugs crashed against their faces and hands. He'd given his light jacket to Lita, who was carrying her sister on her back; both of them huddled under it. Their hair hung limp and wet over faces streaked with mud. Lita's flimsy sandals had disintegrated in the rain, and now she wore his boots, lashed around her ankles with vines to prevent them from falling off. His own feet were protected only by socks with strips of tree bark to fortify the soles, also secured with vines; leaves jiggled festively as they walked. The tropical white jumpsuit he'd put on yesterday morning was now filthy and ripped.

Lita seemed in better spirits this morning. He heard her murmuring to her sister, telling her how close they were to the *Calcutta's* base, how soon they'd be there. Maybe he'd had the same optimistic resiliency when he was her age; he certainly didn't now. He trudged, head down, water pouring down his back. His empty stomach protested constantly and his tired muscles ached. His nerves shivered with need, and it was hard to stop thinking about *zyth*. One shot of it would be like grabbing power lines in his bare hands, electricity racing across the connection, burning, energizing.

It would be so much easier to give up, lie down, surrender —

I am a channel. . . . Through me flows the meaning of the Universe. . . .

The words of the lingster's mantra rose unbidden in his mind, dragging him back from the abyss. *First was the Word and I am its carrier.*

He had to go on. There was no choice; the Guild had seen to that. The Guild had branded him, and there was no removing the mark from his soul. Alien alcohol was his attempt to break the bond and it had failed, just as it had failed to take away the pain of Yv's death.

He swatted insects and moved on. He was glad for the small relief of being rid of the younger child for a while, and not just because of the

burden of carrying her extra weight on his back. Jilan's continuing silence was unnerving. She didn't respond to anything he said to her. He
had no idea what to do about her.

If Yv had lived, he wondered, would she have wanted children?
One of them would've had to leave the Guild since the Guild discour-
aged child-raising by its lingsters. Would she have done so gladly? Could
he have accepted her decision, whatever it might've been? A memory
surfaced: She lay under him in a grove of giant, singing ferns on an exotic world, the first time they'd made love; the wild red hair spilled over
her small, firm breasts, her eyes in shadow the color of moss, a sprinkling
of rosy freckles over her nose. He ached to realize there were things
about his young wife he hadn't had time to learn.

Underneath his thoughts, like an evil mantra, the need for *zyth*
pulsed. He should've gathered the berries. He could go back — just a
small detour — it took all his fading strength to prevent his feet from leaving the path and turning back.

First was the Word . . .

The depth of his need for *zyth* terrified him. He had to escape this
nightmare addiction before it was too late, and abstinence was the only
way to free himself.

The jungle gave way slowly to the sparser vegetation of the hill
country; trees were not so towering here, their leaves sprouting higher
up the trunk. And the grass no longer grew so tall. With a sigh of relief,
Lita put her sister down on the ground.

They heard it first: an insistent murmur like faraway traffic, growing to an animal roar. Then the ground sloped under their feet and they
came out suddenly from the forest to stand on a bank where trees
tumbled down a ravine to the west. Through the bare branches they
glimpsed water, an emerald cascade flashing over the rock face in the
subdued light and racing away through the undergrowth. One of the
many tributaries of Separation River with its headwaters in the mountain range they were skirting, it lay directly in their path, too wide and
flowing much too fast for them to cross.

His mind woozy with fatigue, he stared at it, trying to remember
the automap he'd consulted before the skipcar crashed. There shouldn't
have been a river that size anywhere near. How had he gone wrong?

"What do we do now?" Lita asked, her voice husky.

It was a fair question. New Bombay was gone. The *Calcutta's* base was probably deserted but better than nothing if he could've been certain he could find his way across this country. Which apparently he couldn't.

Then he thought of something. "You speak Frehti."

A spot of color came and went on her high cheekbones. "Well, I've learned a little."

More than a little, I'll wager, he thought. "Do you remember what the Freh sport said to us as we left the Residence?"

She frowned. "Something about his mother?"

"Not his mother. 'The Mothers.' I think it's a title."

"Well, where do we find them?"

"*Under the bones,*" the misshapen alien had said, and he'd imagined a graveyard of some sort. But now he realized it meant the Maker's Bones, the sharp-toothed mountains to the north. They'd been heading northwest when the skipcar went down, crossing the foothills to get to the base. They needed to change course.

"Northeast and uphill, I think."

"Up *there?*" she asked, her voice full of skepticism.

"Could be our only hope for help."

"Who's to say these 'Mothers' will be friendly? The rest of the natives aren't."

"We don't have a lot of options."

She heaved a deep sigh for his benefit. "How far?"

"Far enough."

He gazed up at the distant peaks. Perhaps a two-day journey on foot, maybe longer because of the child. The rain was bad enough here where the thinning trees still provided some shelter. Up on the ridge, they would be exposed to the full force of monsoon winds and torrential rain, and the cold of high altitude at night. It would take all his strength to get them through this, but he had no strength anymore. They needed — deserved — a far better guide.

Lita was right; whether the Mothers would shelter them was doubtful, but he couldn't think of an alternative. And there was nobody else around to help them.

He selected a peak shaped like the broken tooth of a jungle beast as a reference point, then lifted Jilan off her sister's back.

"Let's get moving," he said.

III

For the next two days they made slow progress over rugged ground, keeping the distinctively shaped peak in sight at all times. The land sloped steeply up through the boulders and rocky outcropping; the tall, tropical growth of the jungle floor gave way swiftly to low, wind-battered trees with sharp needles instead of leaves. Cold rain sleeted down all day. The ground beneath their feet turned to mud, slowing their progress further.

"We'll take a break here." He indicated an isolated clump of stunted Spirit-Traps that seemed as lost and out of place as the human fugitives on these high slopes and in almost as much danger of not surviving.

They huddled together in the meager shelter, watching the rain. Lita leaned back against a knobby trunk and closed her eyes; after a while, her regular breathing told him she slept. He needed sleep too, but the constant itch of his craving for *zyth* prevented him from finding it.

Jilan seemed unable to sleep. He studied her. There was nothing dull or retarded about the eyes that gazed back at him, and he knew she wasn't deaf. Then why didn't she talk like a normal three-year-old? He seemed to remember hearing her exploring pre-speech sounds like all human children, trying out the full range available before settling on the ones selected by the language that would become their native tongue and forgetting how to make the others. But she hadn't progressed to the next stage.

"Baby," he said softly, so as not to wake Lita. "Talk to me. Say: 'Ries. Hello, Ries.'"

He sounded ridiculous to himself. It gave him a sudden respect for mothers everywhere who provided models for their children to learn language from. The little girl stared at her hands in her lap.

"Try 'Hello, Lita.'"

Nothing. He pondered for a moment, made another decision.

"*Taq'na*," he said. Food, in Frehti.

Her dark eyes flicked briefly over him. Not much, but more reaction than he'd got for Inglis. Encouraged, he tried again.

"*Yati.* How about that one? *Yati.* Mama."

She blinked at him and he feared for a moment she was going to cry. Idiot! he thought. Why bring up bad memories? But she'd obviously grown bored already; she began to trace patterns in the mud with her fingers. Not surprising that she reacted to Frehti, he decided. She'd probably had more interaction with her alien amahs than she'd had with her parents.

His musings were interrupted by a bout of sneezing. His nose was constantly on fire with invading spores. The DepCom's daughters didn't seem to be as bothered by the phenomenon; Lita sneezed occasionally and rubbed her eyes, Jilan's nose was runny, but neither one was seriously affected. His immune system was challenged more than theirs. The AI had warned about *zyth* addiction's side effects, but he hadn't paid attention, at first arrogantly certain none of it was ever going to happen to him. And later, not caring.

After a while, Lita woke up, and they continued their journey. Along the way, he kept his gaze on the ground, searching for signs of the nutritious tuber that would solve one of their problems, not daring to venture far off the path he'd set for fear of getting them further lost. He didn't find any.

Their second night out, he had better luck and found a sheltered place between a jumble of huge boulders where he could light a small fire to dry their clothes. That night he also found the last of the edible berries for their supper, but not enough for all three. Even with his share added to hers, the child whimpered from hunger, her face wan and pinched with distress.

It wasn't hunger that sent the spasm through his body, and it took all his willpower not to put one of the poison berries under his tongue. *Just one—How could one hurt?—You'd feel so much better—*the seductive voice inside his head pleaded and cajoled. *You could handle one.*

His hands shook so badly as he handed Lita her share of the berries that she noticed.

"It's *zyth*, isn't it? You need some."

He sat down on the other side of the fire from her. "Who told you that?"

"Mama said you were an incurable drunkard. She said it was a scandal the Guild sent you to us."

"A lot of things your mother never understood."

"She said it was good we didn't have to pay the Guild too much for your services because you were squandering all your share in the native taverns."

"None of her business what I did with my money."

"My father always defended you when they argued, did you know that?"

He felt too sick to be angry. "I don't want to hear any more. Get some rest."

"Well, don't go and die on us during the night, will you?"

She lay down and covered herself and her sister with his jacket and was soon sleeping soundly. He stared at the little fire till the flames flickered out. It took him a long time before anger and need both subsided, allowing him to fall asleep for a little while too.

The third night, they were not so lucky. After a long, exhausting day when at times he despaired of finding a way around the huge boulders in their path while the child cried constantly from hunger, they camped out on stony ground on a windswept ridge where even the thorny bushes couldn't take hold. The rain held off when the sun went down, but it was bitterly cold and he found nothing to burn.

For a long time after Jilan had closed her eyes, he heard the soft muffled sound of Lita weeping. After the girl finally fell asleep, he sat stiffly beside them, every muscle in his body aching from physical exertion, his nerves vibrating with a desperate craving for *zyth* that wouldn't let him sleep.

It was time he faced the truth. He didn't know these mountains. He had no clear idea where he was going. He was incapable of looking after himself; how could he hope to take care of these two children? Only a fool would take seriously native superstitions about "souls" and "Mothers" who might or might not exist. How could they help him even if they did? He'd made a bad decision. They should've tried to get across the river to the base. There was no way they would survive this ordeal, and just as he felt he'd been indirectly responsible for Yv's death, he would now be to blame for the death of the DepCom's children.

He pulled Born-Bent's bone out of his pocket and peered at the symbol carved on it. Disgusted, he flipped the bone into the darkness. He heard it glance off a rock.

Then he lay down, and immediately distinguished the uncomfortable lump of the fieldpack from the sharp stones digging into his ribs. Even now, he couldn't violate his training and throw the thing away. He hadn't thought so much about the Guild in years, and now he could hardly get it out of his mind. It rode on his heartbeat and slid through his veins; he was as addicted to the Guild as he was to *zyth*. He couldn't lift his hands without its laws springing up in his path. He had never hated the Guild so fiercely nor needed it so much.

He shifted the pack so it wasn't directly beneath him, and closed his eyes. At once, all the useless, stupid, shameful scenes out of his past sprang vividly to his mind. The opportunities the Guild had given him that he'd wasted, his constant failure to live up to the lingster code, the way he'd ultimately betrayed Yv, he relived them all. Dark thoughts skittered through his brain, tormenting him late into the night.

He came suddenly awake just before sunup, conscious of someone bending over him. His skin crawled as he forced himself to bear the silent scrutiny without flinching. Whoever it was could've killed him as he slept but hadn't. Beside him, he could feel Jilan's small body, wedged between him and her sister for warmth. Both girls were still sleeping.

He heard a sudden intake of breath above him. Cautiously, he slitted his eyes and looked up.

A pudgy, adult male Freh knelt over him, layered in the familiar ankle-length, orange-brown cloth. The Freh's head was turned, tilted as if he were listening to some sound coming from the direction of the jagged peaks that loomed white as snow this morning in cold predawn light, looking more like the fangs of a beast than bones.

Then the alien became aware the human was awake, and his head swiveled back in alarm. Ries stared at him. One half of the Freh's face was covered with an ugly red blotch that spread from just below the hairline to well below the chin. The nose was twisted and warped off-center, a defect that pulled one eye down with it and trapped the nictitating membrane halfway over the eyeball.

The Freh scrambled to his feet, keening anxiously. Something slipped out of his fingers. Ries sat up. Now he could see that behind the male there was a female gesturing to him.

"What do you want?" he said in Frehti.

At the sound of his voice, Lita woke up. She took one look at the Freh and shrieked. The Freh stumbled away in obvious panic. The female clutched his arm and hobbled beside him, half pulling her companion, half being dragged along by him.

"Devi!" Lita said. "I've never seen such an ugly one."

The native was another sport, only the second he'd seen.

The child was awake and whimpering now. Lita stooped and picked her sister up. "Are we just going to let them get away?"

The two Freh were scrambling up a rocky incline toward the nearest peak. He watched their awkward progress; they seemed to know where they were going. And if they could do it, so could humans.

"No. We're going to follow them."

"Jilan can't go much farther without food."

As he bent down to retrieve the sitar, something caught his eye. The bone lay out in the open where the alien had dropped it. He picked it up; a crack obliterated part of the markings. He dropped it back in his pocket.

Lita took two shuffling steps forward with her sister perched on one hip. The girl's exhaustion was apparent in the slump of her shoulders, her pinched expression. He caught up with her and took Jilan from her.

"I'll carry my father's sitar," Lita said.

They stumbled forward silently for a while, no energy left over for talk, while the land rose inexorably beneath their feet.

The rising sun brought no warmth, and the dazzle it struck from the bare peaks hurt his eyes. At least it had stopped raining, and his nose seemed a little less sore. Lita had shut her eyes against the fierce light and walked blindly, clinging to his arm. He squinted through lowered eyelids, his vision narrowed down to the point where he felt as if he were sleepwalking. With his free hand, he adjusted the way the fieldpack rode at his waist. One good thing had come from so much exercise and so little food: his belt fit looser now than it had a few days ago.

Yet in spite of his exhaustion and the pressing need for food, he felt better in spirit than he had in a long time. Miraculously, his mind was clear and pure as spring water this morning. The self-hatred of the night before seemed to have burned away; possibilities spun in the bright air like butterflies in the apple orchards at the Mother House. He looked deep into his being and found it miraculously free of the demon that had bound him for so long. He took a deep breath. He might not have a coherent plan for their survival, but for the first time since Chandra Patel's murder he knew hope.

It was such a ludicrous emotion under the circumstances that he laughed aloud. In the thin air of this high altitude, the laughter soon turned to gasping for breath.

"Come not nearer."

The Frehti words cut short his amusement. Shielding his eyes against the sun with one hand, he peered at the small, bent figure of an old Freh female standing directly in his path.

His heart jumped with the realization: an *old* female.

She wore a long, shapeless brown garment of some coarse, woven material, the hood thrown back from her lined face revealing thin, graying fur on her head. She was holding a three-edged Freh knife ready to strike, reminding him powerfully of Patel's assassins. Belatedly, he set Jilan down, pushing her and Lita behind him.

"Name yourself," the old female said. "Tell what you seek here."

"I am Ries Danyo. I seek the Mothers."

"You have found. I am called First-Among-Mothers."

The word she used was *Na-freh'm-ya*, and he heard a common root in it, but she didn't give him time to think about it. She gestured with one clawlike hand, and they were suddenly surrounded by three more hooded figures who had come up on his blind side where they'd been hidden in sun dazzle. All three carried the vicious-looking triple-edged knives.

Before he could react, the little girl was taken from his grasp. Seeing one of the hooded figures lifting her sister, Lita yelled and kicked at her own captors. Ries's arms were seized and rapidly bound to his sides; his nose filled with the powdery scent he associated with old age, and something danker, an underground smell that clung to their robes.

Every one of their captors, he saw, was bent, wrinkled, gray-furred, skinny-necked, and female. It would've been funny, he thought, a gang of old alien females struggling uphill with a furious human teenager and a wailing human child, if he could've been sure they wouldn't resort to using those knives.

First-Among-Mothers held up one hand, cutting off Lita's noisy protest. "Little one safer here than Danyo."

"Why is Danyo not safe with the Mothers?" he asked.

She stopped abruptly in his path and he almost fell. One of the other females yanked his bonds, pulling him upright. First-Among-

Mothers's face was an arm's length away from his. In spite of the situation, he was fascinated by this close view.

There was nothing here of the blandness that had marked every Freh's features he'd seen until now, yet she was no sport. The round, amber eyes, curdled with age till they resembled milky opals, held a depth of intelligence that was unmistakable. He read anger in them, but also a touch of humor in the lines at their edges as if she laughed at herself for a role she was playing. Something in her expression seemed to say this was all an elaborate joke. The effect was so human that he felt convinced he could read her basic goodwill. It was almost impossible not to anthropomorphize and think of her as an old woman.

He knew instantly to distrust his naive reaction. He'd forgotten a lot of the Guild's teachings over the years, and disobeyed more, but this stayed in his mind: The closer to human an alien appeared, the more difficult it was for a human to read its intentions.

"Danyo male," First-Among-Mothers said.

"But Danyo not Freh," he countered.

She considered this for a moment. "No trust here."

At that, they all resumed their uphill journey. The old Freh females urged the humans to hurry with kicks and slaps and the occasional warning prick from the tip of a knife, though he noticed that they were easier on Lita than they were on him.

He felt like Gulliver captured by the Lilliputians.

It was past noon when the party halted in the shadow of the broken peak he'd used as a bearing.

"In," First-Among-Mothers said.

The females escorting Lita and Jilan went ahead through a narrow opening in the rock. He did as he was told, and found himself at the top of a flight of steps carved into rock walls. Torchlight made shadows leap on the walls.

"Down."

He went down.

The steps opened up into a cavern, broad and high-ceilinged, with rough-hewn pillars supporting balconies that overhung shadowy side aisles. The stone floor was covered with a layer of rushes, and plainly woven hangings gave privacy to different areas. While it was still cool down here, it was several degrees warmer than the air outside, for which he was grateful. But he was mostly struck by its resemblance to the monastic design of the refectory, the oldest building of the Guild's Mother House. The cavern lacked only modern means of lighting and windows to look out on high mountains rather than be buried beneath them as here. A long wooden table down the center completed the resemblance.

Old females sat together on stone benches in groups of two or three, all wearing the same kind of homespun robes. The scene was almost reassuring in its domesticity, until he noticed the glitter of a knife tucked in one old crone's belt.

They were stared at with a good deal of open-mouthed curiosity, but unlike just about every Freh he'd ever come in contact with, these old females didn't grin in the presence of humans. It was always an odd sensation to be stared at as a human on an alien world, one he'd had many times but never managed to get used to. Suddenly, when he least expected it, the tables would be turned and he'd perceive himself as the alien in the crowd, the man far from home.

From somewhere in the vast cave came the aroma of food being prepared. The smell made his knees buckle with hunger. Now he was pushed back against one of the columns. He resisted and a female slapped him across the mouth, making him taste blood. His thighs encountered a hard edge, and he slumped awkwardly onto a narrow stone bench while one of the aliens secured his arms to the column.

He was suddenly aware of how filthy and repulsive he must seem, more like a wild man than the neatly dressed colonists of New Bombay with their emphasis on hygiene. He could smell his own sweat, sour from days of not bathing.

Across the way, he saw Lita and Jilan seated at a long wooden table where First-Among-Mothers sat with them. There seemed to be no menace in the alien's actions toward the girls. He tested the bonds; they were flimsy enough that he could burst free if he had to, but he saw only one exit from the cave that would lead up to the ground, the one they'd come down.

Soon other females appeared carrying large pots made from gourds like the one Born-Bent had used to mend the DepCom's sitar; they began ladling the contents out into clay bowls to serve the girls. He, apparently, was not going to be given food.

As if she sensed his thought, Lita turned and glanced at him. "Danyo hungers too," she said in very clear Frehti.

First-Among-Mothers leaned forward and gazed at Lita. "No male eats here but the kipiq."

She used a word Ries had never heard before. In spite of his stomach's protests and the presence of danger, he was excited. He felt an adrenaline rush at the unfolding revelation of mystery. While the form of Frehti First-Among-Mothers used ranged from the simpler, chirping utterances of males in the marketplace to more complex constructions, he knew that no lingster encountering it would question the high sentience quotient of the speaker. He had difficulty following it at times, accustomed as he was to the male form of the language.

And he understood now why those first lingsters had been so mistaken in their judgment: They'd forged interface with the wrong sex.

"Danyo is a..." Lita struggled but didn't find a word for it in Frehti. "...a *lingster*."

Lightheaded from hunger, he almost laughed, remembering an old student joke: *What comes in two sexes but has no sex life? A lingster.*

First-Among-Mothers glanced at him. "The tale arrives before the male. A vragim comes from Sorrow-Crossing and speaks our words."

"I am vragim too," Lita said, jutting her chin stubbornly.

It surprised him to find the girl arguing in his defense. There were a lot of things about her that he still didn't understand. Her handling of Frehti was one; the DepCom's daughter used the new word as confidently as if she'd always known what it meant.

First-Among-Mothers got up and came over to him.

"Vragim. *Lingster*," she said. If she'd been human he would've read contempt in her tone, but he must resist making connections that might not be there at all. "And do you know how words make, as the tale is told to me?"

He blinked, hearing Born-Bent's voice in memory, "*You understand how words make.*" He jumped suddenly between the known and the hidden, the leap of faith every lingster performed at some point, the lucky guess that was also one of humankind's most basic tools for learning language.

"I bring the kipiq's soul home for the Mothers to make words with," he said.

The effect in the stone cavern was electrifying. Every Mother set down her work or her food and stared. Others crowded in from rooms off the main hall till there were at least forty old Freh females gaping at him, round-eyed as owls. A long silence followed, broken only by the clatter of the child's bowl; Jilan seemed the only one in the cavern not affected by his words.

He closed his eyes for a second against his body's weakness, seeking strength to prevail in the battle of wills he sensed had been set in motion.

First-Among-Mothers held out her hand, palm up, and he was startled by her look of almost desperate desire.

"Give."

"No."

She thought about that for a moment, then turned and snapped her fingers. A bent figure hobbled quickly forward and undid the bonds holding his arms. Another followed with a bowl full of the thick stew.

So she thought she was going to bribe him with food?

His stomach insisted it was a fine idea.

First-Among-Mothers waited while he wolfed the contents down without tasting. A second bowl appeared, and he devoured that too, barely noticing how rich and spicy it was this time. When the third bowlful arrived, he was able to eat with a semblance of manners that would've been acceptable in the Guild's refectory.

First-Among-Mothers gestured to the gathered females and they moved silently away. He saw one old alien carrying Jilan, and Lita following them. The main cavern emptied slowly out.

"Now," First-Among-Mothers said. "We make the words together."

He followed her through a low arch at the far end of the big cavern, and came to a smaller cave. The light was dimmer here, and it took a moment for his eyes to adjust. When they did, he saw the Mothers waiting silently in a circle. His breath caught in his chest.

The old aliens had stripped off and discarded their shapeless robes. The flickering light of wax tapers glowed on naked flanks and fleshless rumps, touching with silver the gray fur on their heads, sliding past bony shoulders and spilling over flat, shriveled breasts. One emaciated female turned her back to him, and he saw clearly knobs of vertebrae and sharp blades of bone outlined under the skin that he identified as ribs, though they didn't appear to be assembled in the human plan. Although Freh females' faces were never tattooed, decoration covered their trunks and all four limbs in scrolls, swirls, leaves, and vines. Primitive, by the standards of high civilizations in the Arm, but full of energy and power, the tattoos were dark purple, the color of *zyth* berries.

He'd never seen a roomful of nude women, let alone old women — it was next to impossible not to think of them as women; they seemed more human unclothed, as if spirit was more important than species — but he felt no awkwardness. They wore their years with dignity and a kind of patient beauty like a ring of wise elder goddesses.

Now First-Among-Mothers also dropped her garments on the floor, kicking them impatiently against the cave wall. Nakedness seemed to make her grow taller than the others, her body straighter than theirs though no less slack and wrinkled, her gray head fur still partly dark. Like the others, her body was covered in intricate purple designs. The circle opened to let her through.

She walked slowly clockwise inside the ring, which began to move counterclockwise around her. There was something on the ground inside the ring, a center that First-Among-Mothers was circling, an irregularly shaped mosaic formed by small bones, all about the same width and length of the one Born-Bent had entrusted to him. To one side, there were several haphazard, smaller piles. There must've been well over two hundred bones in the pattern, but it looked unfinished, with many spaces and gaps interrupting whatever design was in the process of being formed.

Some kind of religious ceremony, he guessed, watching her circling slowly, her bare feet marking an intricate rhythm on the stone floor. Then she stopped, caught up a bone from the pattern, raised her arms, and began to gesture. Her hands caught the tapers' light, sweeping in a broad arc above her head. She seemed to be inscribing some kind of ephemeral calligraphy on the air. As she did so, she opened her mouth and sang one note. Now all the Mothers followed her lead, performing the looping arm movements, the singing tone in unison.

First-Among-Mothers repeated this with each of the bones in turn, marking each with a different sound. Then, after a long while, the group fell silent, the outer circle opened again, and the malformed male Freh who'd stood over Ries on the mountain appeared. The kipiq, who was naked too, entered the circle humbly, shuffling forward over the stone floor on bare knees and holding one hand high above his head. In it, Ries saw another small bone like the one in his pocket.

Now a low, animal hum broke the silence, rising quickly in pitch and volume. The sound became almost deafening in the confined space, then stopped abruptly as the kipiq reached the center of the ring. He took his time choosing a place to set the bone he carried. In the silence, First-Among-Mothers squatted to see it. The kipiq remained on his knees, head bowed.

She examined the bone, holding it close, turning it, shifting its position, exchanging it with others. At times she seemed to change her mind and returned a bone to its original position, removing another that had now apparently become less desirable and tossing it on the outer piles. Whatever these decisions meant, Ries sensed they were of the utmost importance to the assembled Freh. At last she put a hand on the kipiq's shoulder and the ring of Mothers gave a long drawn-out sigh.

First-Among-Mothers turned, and Ries could see her owl eyes glowing in the light from the nearest taper. She held up the kipiq's bone. Now he saw it had marks scratched on it, like the one in his pocket. Then accompanied by another elaborate hand movement above her head, she sang out a clear, distinct syllable. As she did so, the Mothers followed her arm movements and repeated the sound after her like children performing rote learning. It reminded him suddenly of how, hundreds of years ago on Earth, Chinese children had learned by tracing the characters of their language on the air.

The revelation of what she was doing stunned him. First-Among-Mothers was reading the bones.

But these couldn't be complete words, he realized in a great rush of comprehension, not even morphemes, the smallest units of meaning. The Freh had no written language. She was taking the first step, inventing a system of codifying the phonemes, the individual units of sound. From the gathered bones at her feet, she was choosing the best symbols to begin writing her language.

It was obvious from what he'd observed that not just any shape on a bone would do. Creating a written language was a sacred job, not one to be completed hastily. *Through me flows the meaning of the universe.*

He thought First-Among-Mothers would understand the Guild's philosophy very well.

Runes, hieroglyphs, logograms, ideograms, pictograms, alphabets, humans had tried them all through long millennia of experimentation. The Guild taught lingsters in a few years what had taken centuries to unlock, the secrets of these scripts. All but the main one: how they had come into being in the first place. He'd always wondered what accidents of chance and intelligence had caused early humans to take the first step, associating sounds with symbols, then developing them into script. And from that to go on to write laws and poems, shopping lists and equations that guided starships across the darkness of space to a world that still stood on the threshold.

The Guild itself with all its research hadn't been able to answer that question, not even for one Terran language. A great wave of exhilaration washed over him. He was witnessing an alien race set out on that mysterious journey. Yet he could also see First-Among-Mothers had a long way to go before the symbols she was collecting were usable.

After a while, she fell silent. The kipiq shuffled back out of the circle into the shadows at the edge of the cave. Ries was aware of her gaze on him now.

It was his turn. The bone containing the symbol Born-Bent found so vital he called it his "soul" must be added to the collection growing at the feet of First-Among-Mothers. The ring of old females gazed at him, waiting patiently. But even in his excited state, a sense of human pride restrained him. He was not going to remove his clothes, nor would he enter the circle on his knees. If the Mothers wanted Born-Bent's soul, they would have to take it his way or not at all.

Conscious of the weight of a shared destiny, human and Freh, he walked solemnly forward in the silence and leaned down, placing the bone in a vacant space.

First-Among-Mothers squatted, peering at the bone as she had done before. Now she reached for it, squinting in the glimmering light. For a long time she studied the symbol scratched there. Then her hand dropped slowly to her side. She stood and faced Ries, her expression bleak.

"Broken," First-Among-Mothers said. "The soul is gone."

Around the ring, old Mothers began to wail.

IV

"Think about the waste," Lita said to him. "The tragedy, as the Mothers see it."

The girl had been his only visitor since a group of females had dragged him off to a small niche in a corridor off the main cavern and barred the entrance with a strong lattice of wooden branches lashed with vines. The alcove had probably been a vegetable storage area, he guessed from the lingering smells.

Lita passed a cup of water through the lattice gate and he took a sip. In her other hand she held a slim taper that made deep shadows jump in his cell. He felt exhausted; all emotion and energy had been sucked out of him.

It was hard to estimate the passage of time in this darkness, but he guessed a day had passed since First-Among-Mothers's ceremonial reading of the symbols on the bones. While he'd been stuck here, contemplating the consequences of one moment of bad temper, Lita had apparently been deep in conversation with First-Among-Mothers.

Her ability shouldn't have been surprising. She'd been about eight or nine when the family came to Krishna, an age when children still learned languages with some ease, and she must've been exposed to the more complex forms used by the house servants who were largely female. She'd just never let him see evidence of it.

"Freh males don't contribute to the work. Except the kipiq, of course, and not too many of them make it to adulthood."

"I imagine not," he agreed, thinking of the day he and the Dep-Com had encountered Born-Bent in the bazaar. In his experience of cultures of the Arm including early human, such deformities had usually signaled a short life for the child born with them.

"Do you understand how serious this is, Danyo?" Her face in half-shadow, she looked as if she were thinking about leaving him alone again. "The race doesn't use language like humans. Freh males have a very simple version. Sort of like Kitchen Frehti. Without the Inglis words, of course."

He had the absurd fantasy he was back at the Mother House taking an exam about pidgins and creoles. "It's uncommon to find such a wide division in ability between the sexes."

"The females are *much* better at it! But the big thing is, up here, year after year for a long time, the Mothers've been working on finding a way to get the language written down."

"You've learned an impressive amount in such a short time."

"Well," she said, softening her tone a little, "I might've missed a few things. I'm not really perfect in Frehti yet. Anyway, every Mother who manages to come up here contributes something. And the one who is 'First-Among-Mothers' puts it all together."

"Why are symbols from the sports so important?"

"The *kipiq*," she corrected, "are male. First-Among-Mothers says the language must balance between male and female or the race will eventually destroy itself. But regular males don't use language well, and kipiqs usually don't survive to be adults, so they don't get very many male symbols. So when the one you brought was broken, they were upset."

It was as if he could hear First-Among-Mothers's words echoing through Lita's, and he had the sense that the Freh meant something he couldn't fathom yet.

"The Mothers believe if they can write the language down, they'll have a chance to prevent something bad from happening. Do you understand, Danyo? Can you follow this?"

"Does she say why there are no old males up here, only old females?"

"She said it was the—the—oh, a word I don't understand. *Sem yaj*—something."

"Sem yaji nuq," First-Among-Mothers said. She had come to stand in the shadows behind Lita.

"Tell me in other words, words I can understand," he said, switching to Frehti.

"Sem yaji nuq. No other words." She turned to Lita and said kindly, "The little one calls you."

Lita went away, taking the taper with her. In the darkness, he was aware of First-Among-Mothers's soft breathing.

"No male comes here except the kipiq who brings his soul bone," she said. "Now I must kill you."

He was suddenly exasperated with her mysteries and evasions. "Explain the death of these children's father, and maybe I can help you speed up the work."

"You bargain with me?"

"Yes, I bargain with you."

She hesitated, thinking it over. Then she said, "He learned about sem yaji nuq."

"I do not understand those words! Use others."

"I have not your skill."

"You accepted my bargain."

Her voice rose in anger. "He knew about Those-Who-Have-Gone-Over. You call them *Mules*, but that is your word, not ours."

He peered through darkness, wishing he could see her expression. Lingsters learned to use visual clues as well as aural ones to decipher meanings. "*Something I just learned...*" Patel had said. "What is this connection, so important a man must die for knowing it?"

"You have the answer you sought. Keep your word."

If so, he thought, it was an answer he didn't understand, but he was apparently not going to get any further explanation at the moment.

"I have seen many worlds, First-Among-Mothers, spoken many languages. You are not the first people to wrestle with this problem."

She was silent for so long he began to think she'd gone away. Then she said, "In the market they call you Talker. But you cannot help with this."

"You have nothing to lose by letting me try."

He had the feeling she was reading his face, as if her milky old eyes could see in the dark. Then he heard her sigh.

"We have a saying, 'Bone defeats bone, but stone outlives.' I think perhaps you are stone."

"Let me look at the bones, First-Among-Mothers."

In the darkness, he heard her slice the vines holding the lattice with her knife.

He squatted on the stone floor, examining the bone pattern, while First-Among-Mothers held a taper so he could see. The air was thick and fragrant with the incense smell of tapers, making his eyes heavy. He frowned, concentrating. Somewhere in the main cavern, he heard the sounds of the sitar: Lita picking out tunes to soothe her sister.

He stared at the symbols on the bones. The fine etching had been colored with a dark, rusty ink that might very well have been blood. He was aware of an almost religious quality to the moment. Spread out before him on the rough stone floor of the cave was the birth of a writing system, a script that could capture a language and its speakers' vision of their world. No modern human had ever witnessed such a moment.

Then he remembered Born-Bent's hand in its bloody bandage and he examined the bones more carefully. They were all a similar length and shape, and all of them had once been fingers, he was sure of it. The symbolism of the Mothers's task began with the medium on which it appeared. He was awed that these aliens — judged simple aborigines by the human colonists — cared so much about a project that many of them couldn't possibly even comprehend. He glanced up at First-Among-Mothers.

"Each Mother gives one," she said. "Except the First. She gives all before her death. One by one."

She held up her hands for his inspection. Freh were four-fingered, three forward and a flexible fourth below the palm. He counted three fingers gone out of eight, two from the left hand and one from the right. An alphabet forged in blood, a ritual as demanding as interface and as dangerous, he thought, given the primitive state of medicine on this world. He wondered if he could've found the courage if it had been his ritual.

"The work has taken many, many years," she told him. "The shapes must be just right to hold the sounds that make up our language. Not every one that is given is accepted. It is the work of the First to choose."

She gestured with the taper, indicating he should continue. After a while, she squatted beside him and gazed at the bones as if she too was seeing them for the first time. Forgotten, the taper dripped wax on the floor.

Some of the symbols he examined were carefully and lovingly inscribed; others resembled the first scratchings of a child. Champollion seeing an Egyptian cartouche for the first time might have felt light-headed like this, he thought, and Niebuhr copying cuneiform inscriptions may have caught his breath in just the same manner as connections became clear. Ries Danyo, drunkard and failed Guild lingster, was becoming part of the galaxy's history.

Many of the finger bones carried obvious pictograms, tiny exquisite glyphs that were suggestive even at first glance of objects from the world of the writers, though he knew better than to suppose the picture necessarily gave the meaning of the sign any more than it had in Egyptian hieroglyphs. Others bore what were apparently semantic symbols, abstract representations of the sounds of Frehti, and these delicately carved logograms had an austere beauty of their own.

Mixed systems were not unprecedented; Earth had seen several, most notably the Egyptian and Mayan scripts. He wasn't particularly surprised to find one evolving here. But eventually all the languages of Earth had found it more convenient to adopt alphabets. The first problem was not the mix of symbols for sounds and glyphs for whole words, but that there were still far too many choices here at present. Some would need to be eliminated.

First-Among-Mothers touched his shoulder. "I will tell the sound of each one."

Then she began essentially to repeat the ceremony he'd witnessed earlier. One by one she picked up the bones and pronounced the sound that went with it, but where earlier she had sung these phonemes as part of a venerable ceremony with the assembled Mothers, now she was content just to vocalize.

Almost immediately he realized the impossibility of working this way. It was like trying to catch one drop out of a stream of water. He didn't have the stamina to sustain this concentration for very long. He needed to impose some kind of order.

Not for the first time since he'd fled New Bombay he thought with regret of the AI left behind. Sorting and identifying so many alien signs without help was a daunting task. But there'd been translators and interpreters long before there'd been lingsters, before computers too; those early pioneers had worked under primitive conditions.

"I need wet clay. And something to mark with, like a cloth merchant keeping tally."

First-Among-Mothers made no reply to the request, and he wondered if the idea of reducing her exalted goal to humble clay seemed like sacrilege to her. If so, she'd have to get used to it; humanity's profoundest laws had first been scratched in clay. She set the taper on the floor and clapped her hands. A moment later, a figure appeared in the cave's low archway. First-Among-Mothers said something in rapid Frehti and the Mother withdrew. They waited in silence.

After a while, the Mother came back with a lump of clay the size of his fist, clammy from the storage bin. He took it and flattened it out, stretching it into a tablet he could use to make a syllabic grid to plot the signs of written Frehti.

The work progressed slowly over a number of hours; he lost track how many. Twice, First-Among-Mothers sent for more tapers and refreshment. He drank water gratefully, and splashed some on his face to ward off drowsiness, but in spite of his recent hunger he couldn't eat. Gradually, he familiarized himself with the symbols so that similarities and repetitions began to appear, and together they weeded the redundancies out. Over and over again, she patiently repeated the sounds that accompanied glyphs and logograms. It was tedious work.

"It goes too slowly," First-Among-Mothers commented.

She was right. It was an enormous task and would take days at this rate, possibly weeks. The early scholars on Earth had spent years unraveling the secrets of cuneiform or Linear B; if he didn't want to spend that much time here in this cave he needed to find some way to speed things up.

In this fieldpack there was a way.

He touched it now, still safe on his belt; since he'd arrived on Krishna, there'd been no occasion to use it. In it, there were two sequences of drugs that lingsters used in interface. The alpha sequence consisted basically of sophisticated neurotransmitters that increased alertness and enhanced the lingster's ability to work at high speed, especially at such routine tasks as analyzing, cataloging, and memorizing. He'd used them many times on other worlds, always when working with an AI that also monitored the dosage; he knew how effective the alpha sequence could be.

That had all been a long time ago, before he'd begun poisoning himself with *zyth*. No way of telling if there'd be a drug interaction, or how severe. He hadn't had any of the Krishnan liquor for several days; perhaps that would lessen the danger. And if not? *"Another time,"* Magister Kai's voice said in his memory, *"you may not be so lucky."* In all his career, he'd done very little to make the Guild proud of him, and much he was ashamed of. This was a risk he had to take.

"I can make it go faster," he said.

He took out the rack of small plastivials and thought about the pills they contained. First-Among-Mothers gazed steadily at him, her round eyes luminous as a nocturnal animal's in the taper light. She'd asked no questions since he'd begun studying the bones, even when he disturbed the careful way she'd laid them out, accepting that whatever he did it would advance her work. He hoped he could reward her faith.

He shook two small brown ovals onto the palm of his hand, then swallowed them. Within seconds, he felt the sudden jolt of the alpha drugs streaming through his veins. Thoughts sped through his brain too fast for words to catch them; his vision sharpened till microscopic details sprang into vivid display, and he could see individual hairs on First-Among-Mothers's head even in this dim light, the wrinkles on her face like the paths of long-dry rivers.

Something else, too, something different this time, something flickering at the back of his mind, disappearing when he turned his attention to it. Then it vanished in a great rush of endorphins that lifted and tossed him like a cork.

The work went faster. Connections seemed suddenly illuminated for his recognition, correspondences jumped out at him, were considered, and First-Among-Mothers indicated her choices, which he then recorded. A workable Frehti alphabet began to emerge on the clay tablet.

"One sound is missing."

His nerves jumped at the sound of her voice. Absorbed by the work, he'd lost awareness of his surroundings and again he was confused by the passage of time. Disoriented, he gazed at the last of the tapers burning low, flickering in the draft she caused as she stood up from the work. He squinted through the wavering light at the neat chart he'd inscribed on the clay tablet, sixty-seven symbols that best represented the consonants, vowels, and diphthongs of First-Among-Mothers's language, chosen from the drawings on the assembled bones.

"A small sound," she continued dreamily. "Not often used. But the very highest of all. I have waited a long time to find its symbol."

"What sound is that, First-Among-Mothers?"

In answer, she formed a small 0 with her mouth and allowed breath to come sighing through; he could see her curled tongue almost touching her lips, shaping the sound. What emerged was a diphthong with an initial labial, a singing tone as if it came from a flute. She repeated it for him twice more.

A small scuffling noise behind them drew First-Among-Mothers's attention and she fell silent.

"I — I am sorry, First-Among-Mothers," Lita said nervously in Frehti from the shadows in the archway. "My sister wandered off — and I just found her. I will take her away."

"Do so."

For the first time, he wondered what First-Among-Mothers's life was like before she came up here to live beneath the Maker's Bones. Had she worked in the bazaar for a cloth-merchant mate, or had she cleaned and cooked in a human residence? Had she borne children, and were any of them male, and if so, did she ever think of what had become of them?

First-Among-Mothers waited until the sounds of the children faded. Then she inclined her head toward the small pile of bones remaining on the stone floor, urging him back to work.

He glanced at them, seeing only duplications of symbols that had already been assigned or obvious clumsily drawn discards. There was no sign left over that could correspond to the new sound she'd just made.

She raised a hand and he was aware of the missing fingers. "A holy sound. Not one Talker hears in the market. It is Wiu, The White Bird. You will not find its sign there among the ordinary ones. It is a male sound, and a kipiq should give it shape. Now, Talker-from-Sorrow-Crossing must replace the kipiq's soul that he lost."

The high mood of the alpha sequence deserted him as fast as it had come on. Cataloging the symbols on the bones with her help was one thing; that was no different from the regular duties lingsters often performed for their employers. Deliberately adding a human element to an emerging alien alphabet was another.

It was such a temptingly simple thing she asked of him: one sign, just one, from all the possibilities he'd encountered in human history, or from any of the worlds along the Arm for that matter. But even that little gift would be interference from one culture in another's development, and even minor interference was strictly forbidden. Nothing good ever came from violating this rule, however much the people of the less-advanced culture wanted it. Like all lingsters, he'd sworn an oath to respect that prime prohibition.

"I cannot do it," he said. "I am sorry."

"Why can you not?"

"I cannot give you a sign that has its roots on the other side of Sorrow-Crossing. Nothing good would come from such a gift."

"I wish the work completed before my death, Talker," she said, her voice as calm as if she discussed the price of a bolt of silk. "And I do not have much time. You will do it or you will die. I will give you one day's turning to decide."

Two Mothers had appeared as if they'd been waiting for her command, and taken him back to his alcove prison.

Alone in the darkness once again, exhausted, his thoughts drifted. First-Among-Mothers had posed a dilemma for him. To give her what she wanted he must violate his oath. Never in his life had he knowingly done anything big or small that would alter the natural destiny of any of the alien races he'd come in contact with. But to die for the sake of that oath now meant he must violate the promise he'd made Chandra Patel to protect his family. If he died, the girls had no hope of ever reaching the *Calcutta*'s base.

Which was more important, interference in a developing culture—such a tiny touch at that, just the one symbol—or the suffering and perhaps death of the DepCom's children? How would the Guild decide?

"Danyo."

He jumped at the sound of her voice. Without knowing the boundary, he'd drifted from thought to sleep. This time Lita hadn't brought water or a taper.

"Danyo, something's wrong with Jilan. She seems very hot and—"

"As you may have noticed, I'm a prisoner here."

"Devi! Why don't you just open the door and walk out?"

He heard the sound of the lattice gate opening.

"How stupid you are sometimes, Danyo. I could tell as soon as I touched it they hadn't lashed the lattice together again."

If First-Among-Mothers had allowed the opportunity for him to escape, then it was because she knew there was nowhere he could escape to, with or without Lita and her sister. The thought frustrated him; he didn't like being defeated by an old Freh female, even one so obviously intelligent.

"Now will you come and see Jilan?"

He felt Lita's impatient hand on his arm, tugging him through the open gate; he let her guide him through the darkness until light seeped into the corridor from the central cavern.

"I don't know what good I can do. I'm not a medic."

"Keep to the wall just to be safe. No sense letting them see you out here."

"Maybe the food didn't agree with her."

"She's been eating Freh food all her life. That's all the amahs ever made for her after they stopped wet-nursing her. She never touched what Mama and I ate. Do hurry up!"

Jilan was sitting cross-legged on a wide stone bench cushioned in bright silk. Tapers burned in a sconce fixed to the cave wall above her head. In their yellow light, he saw colored clay beads strung on a thong, a crude doll made of wood and covered in fur, toys he'd seen Freh children play with under the stalls in the bazaar. Jilan was making marks with a cut reed on a small lump of clay the size of a cloth merchant's tally. By the uneven flamelight, he could see her pixie face looked flushed. He laid a hand on her cheek and felt how warm it was. Lita bent quickly to wipe saliva from the corner of her sister's mouth.

"I've been giving her water."

"Good."

"What else should we do?"

The child didn't look too sick to him.

Then he became aware Jilan was saying something, very softly, almost under her breath, over and over again. No, not saying, *singing—* But not that exactly either. He felt chilled. Possibility shivered up his spine, moved like the touch of a feather across his nerves. He knelt quickly on the pad beside the child, who immediately stopped vocalizing.

"Baby, say it again for me," he said. "Please?"

"What is it?" Lita asked.

Jilan stuck a thumb in the corner of her mouth and stared wide-eyed at him.

"Where's the sitar? Get it for me."

Lita scrambled away and was back a moment later with the instrument. He ran his fingers over the five melody strings, searching for the right notes that described the pitch values of Frehti: G sharp, A, B flat, B.

Jilan seemed to be listening intently. Encouraged, he let his fingers wander among these four tones, the drone strings humming under the impromptu melody.

"What're you doing, Danyo?"

Jilan opened her mouth and sang a note.

Not B, he realized, somewhere in between B and C, a flattened C. The native nut altered the tones he produced, fitting the sounds of the language better than the original gourd. He quickly adjusted the tuning pegs to reflect the subtly different harmonics of the semitone. Now she gave shape to the sound. His hands shook as he realized what he was hearing, the diphthong First-Among-Mothers had pronounced for him: *Wiu.*

"Danyo?"

"Get First-Among-Mothers and meet me in the cave with the bones."

He hooked the sitar over his shoulder, grabbed up the clay block and the writing utensil in one hand, and tucked the child under the other arm. He felt her cheek burning against his as he ran back to the cave.

New tapers flickered in the small cave, eerily lighting the disturbed pattern he and First-Among-Mothers had left behind. He set Jilan down on the stone floor. Silent again, she gazed up at him, her breathing heavy and quick.

"This won't take long, baby."

"*Children invent language,*" the Guild taught. Why not the alphabet too, or at least a small part of it? The child was as close to a pure source as he was likely to find. Her parents might've come from Earth, but she was born on Not-Here—the planet's alien name was suddenly more appropriate than the one the colonists had given it—and she'd never spoken a word of Inglis. It was a near-perfect compromise. As long as First-Among-Mothers accepted it.

"Have you changed your mind, Talker?"

The clouded eyes gleamed like mother-of-pearl in the taper light when he turned to face her. She stood very erect, almost as tall as Lita.

He chose his words with care. "I offer a compromise, First-Among-Mothers."

"No more bargaining. Only one solution. Make the sign to hold that last, holiest of sounds."

"I cannot give you the sign you desire. It is not my gift to give and would only bring you evil. Instead I offer a child from Sorrow-Crossing but born on Not-Here. A vragim from her mother's womb, but nourished with a Freh mother's milk. Let this child make the sign."

First-Among-Mothers gazed skeptically at him in silence.

"The symbol you want from me," he said gently, "would be male, but it would be alien to your world. What I offer now is better. Trust here."

He waited for several long moments more. She said nothing, but she didn't specifically forbid the attempt either. He took the sitar and plucked the flattened C with the nail of his right forefinger. The child gazed up at him, thumb in mouth. She was drooling again.

"Come on, baby," he coaxed. "Sing for me."

He plucked the note again. She removed the thumb from her mouth and copied the semitone the sitar sang.

He heard the smothered gasp of surprise from First-Among-Mothers, and as the note died away he sounded it again. The child gave voice to the diphthong a second time, and this time her small pure voice was joined by the old woman's larger, mellower one.

He laid his palm flat across the strings, cutting off the vibration. The child gazed up at him. He set the sitar down and held out the clay tablet to her.

"Draw the sound, Jilan," he said. "Draw *Wiu* here, in the clay."

She took the tablet and the stylus from him and stared at them for a moment, then began to draw. Apart from the child's labored breathing there was no sound at all in the cave. From time to time she smoothed over what she'd done and began again. Finally, she held the tablet up and tilted her head, examining it. Then she held it out, not to him, but to First-Among-Mothers.

Over the child's head, her sister shot him a startled look.

First-Among-Mothers squatted down and took the tablet reverently as if it were holy, peering at it in the dim light. She took her time.

Then, in a soft voice, she said, "I accept the last sign."

He let the breath he'd been holding come sighing out in a whoosh of relief. Leaning forward, he peered at the symbol the child had drawn. The clay tablet held the crude, stick figure of a bird. He discovered that where a moment before he'd been chilled, now he was sweating heavily.

First-Among-Mothers laid the tablet down and took the child's hand in both her own, closing her fingers over it. "But it must be written on bone."

Lita got the significance first. "You can't cut a finger off my sister's hand. I won't let you!"

She threw herself at First-Among-Mothers, almost knocking the Freh and the child over.

First-Among-Mothers didn't appear upset by the outburst; instead, she smiled at Ries over the angry girl's head, a terrifying rictus grin from that almost lipless mouth. Taking the child's hand had been an act of provocation, showing him who held the power here.

"A child's sign, a male's bone together complete the work." She released the child and stood swiftly. Her hand came up with the three-edged knife glittering in it.

His vision seemed clouded, splitting the light from the knife into a rainbow of fire that stung his eyeballs. The universe was full of wonder and beauty, the Guild taught, but it also held much that was painful and cruel. The first lesson Earth's earliest astronauts had learned hundreds of years ago was that space offered suffering as well as glory. *The faint of heart among you,* the Guild warned its young students, *should stay at home.*

It was a small sacrifice she asked of him, and far better him than the child. Humans had been given an extra finger, as if long ago Nature had foreseen this moment and the need for one of her children to help another. He would think of it as payment for the privilege of witnessing the birth of a written language; no other lingster could say that. His head ached with the burden of such knowledge.

"And in return, will you give us safe passage over the mountains to the starship's base?"

"We will guide you to your people, Talker."

"Take Jilan away now," he said to Lita.

"No, Danyo! We're staying right here with you."

First-Among-Mothers nodded as if their presence too was an acceptable part of the ritual. She held out her hand to him, and hesitantly he put his left hand in it. For the first time in days he thought how good a shot of *zyth* would be to steady his nerves.

She drew him down until both of them were on their knees on the floor in a circle of golden light. With one hand, she positioned his on the stone. The other raised the knife.

At the last moment, he found a center of calm within. He didn't flinch as the knife descended.

The weather was cold and clear as they crossed over the stony summit of the Maker's Bones. It was still two hours before dawn, and alien constellations blazed above them in a forever moonless sky. He stopped to gaze at the brilliant river of light that was the home galaxy, Sorrow-Crossing. Somehow the name seemed to fit better here, in the farthest reach of the Arm, than "Milky Way." Dark sky and high altitude combined to make a magnifying lens of the thin air; he squinted at the enormous treasure of stars spilled across black space, half convinced he could distinguish the one dim pinpoint of light from all the rest that was Earth's Sol.

Lita touched his arm and he started walking again. First-Among-Mothers had given them food for the journey, and she'd sent along two females who knew the mountain paths as guides. The group moved purposefully, not wasting breath on conversation. From time to time a creature chirruped sleepily from an unseen nest, fooled by their passage into thinking it was morning.

Gradually, the pageantry overhead faded, and a breeze came up followed by the first rays of Not-Here's star. Within the hour, the sun shone fiercely down on them; there was little heat in it yet, but he started to sweat again. The air had the clean, clear smell of sun-warmed stone, and it was mercifully free of spores, but he had difficulty breathing and stumbled often on the uneven ground.

Below them on one side of the ridge, the land swept down a hundred kilometers to the valley of Separation River and the alluvial plain where the human colony had been. The other side fell less steeply to the golden sweep of grassland and the starship base. From up here, the planet appeared suddenly new, as if he'd never seen it before, more exotic than his memory of its strangeness the first day he'd landed. Knowing some of its secrets made it more alien, not less.

He felt light-headed, an aftereffect of the wound to his left hand that still throbbed, and the fact that he'd had no desire to eat much in the days that followed the reading of the bones. Lita scolded him for his lack of interest in food, but he was relieved to be free of both the promptings of hunger and the need for *zyth.*

First-Among-Mothers had bandaged the wound herself, stopping the blood by packing a native moss into the space left by his severed finger, then wrapping it securely in layers of silk. While he still lay on the bed where Jilan had played, he'd seen the Mothers reverently preparing a small cauldron of boiling water into which they'd added herbs to boil his flesh off the bone so the child's symbol could be inscribed properly on it; his head still rang with the sound of their chanting.

For a moment his mind teetered between past and present, then First-Among-Mothers's face rose up before him as she'd stood by his bed. *"I am well pleased with the work,"* she'd said. And he'd argued, *"But mysteries remain. Tell me why language belongs to Freh females but not Freh males." "Have you forgotten what Freh means?"* She held up one of her remaining fingers. He'd never really thought about the literal meaning of a word he'd used so casually for two years. He guessed, *"One? First?"* Then he knew: Those-Who-Come-First.

The memory faded and he staggered against one of the Mothers. She grabbed his arm, steadying him, her old eyes peering into his as if assessing his ability to continue the journey. The two Freh females had caught their long skirts up over bony knees and wore animal-skin boots laced above their ankles. The level of their energy surprised him; old as they seemed to be, they'd been taking turns carrying Jilan on their backs over the uneven ground.

But at that moment the child skipped beside them, gathering pebbles and flowers along the way, and chattering in Frehti like any three-year-old who'd been born on this world. Since that first sound uttered over the bones, she hadn't stopped babbling in First-Among-Mothers's language. As if a wall had been breached, he thought, allowing the child to express everything she'd saved up for just this moment. Yet it was just another irony of the human experience on this world that the child had found her native tongue at the very moment when she must leave the company of those who spoke it.

"Are you all right, Danyo?" Lita asked, coming alongside him. "We could rest for a few minutes."

He couldn't rest until he'd fulfilled his promise and brought the DepCom's daughters to the safety of the starship's base.

Lita's cool hand touched his forehead. "You're very hot."

He attempted a joke. "Teething. Like Jilan."

He remembered Lita visiting him soon after his *donation*—a word he could deal with without self-pity. She'd tried to distract him from the pain in his hand with gossip: The Mothers were busy practicing writing out the alphabet under First-Among-Mothers's direction; the girl had laughed, describing their first clumsy attempts. She also told him Jilan had cut a late molar and her fever had gone away.

"Let me look at your hand again. Maybe it's infected."

"Antibiotics at the base."

"Danyo," the girl said, "stop trying to be such a hero all the time."

He stared at her, uncomprehending. She stalked off ahead down the rough path. The ferocious sun dazzled his eyes, and his head throbbed again.

"*What has this to do with Those-Who-Have-Gone-Over?*" he'd asked First-Among-Mothers. "*We are one and the same,*" she'd said, "*only you do not see it yet.*"

He thought about her words now as he stood on the path, one hand pressed to his chest, catching his breath. Metamorphosis was not uncommon among species in the Orion Arm; humans had encountered it more frequently than they'd found sentience on the worlds they'd visited. Even on Earth, caterpillars turned into butterflies and tadpoles became frogs without anyone being too surprised. Why shouldn't a pudgy Freh transform into a gaunt Mule? And if it only happened to one sex, it would still be no stranger than a hundred other quirks and tricks of Mother Nature he'd seen elsewhere. Yet butterflies weren't prone to do violence on caterpillars.

"*There is more to it than that,*" he'd argued, thinking of First-Among-Mothers's urgent need to write the language out. "*Some secrets remain hidden until their time comes,*" the old Freh had replied. "*And will you tell me then, First-Among-Mothers?*" "*If we both live, Talker.*"

An hour later—two hours? Three? He seemed to have lost the ability to keep track of time—the party stopped. They'd reached an overlook, the land falling perhaps two hundred meters straight down a cliff. Spirals of dust rose in the heat, and the view before him shimmered hazily as if it were underwater. A vast plain spread out before them, an enormous valley stretching like a lake of grass to a range of mountains on the misty horizon. Huge flocks of bright-skinned, featherless birds rose and fell over gold-green fields, and the sweet smell of the grasslands drifted up on the warm air.

Sweat started out on his forehead and neck, instantly evaporating, and he sneezed once. He squinted through watering eyes into brightness at the goal they'd struggled to reach for so long, the end of their journey.

"There," one of the Mothers said, pointing.

"The *Star of Calcutta*'s base. I see it!" Lita said.

"We go no further," the second Mother said.

"We can make it from here, can't we, Danyo?"

He nodded and wished he hadn't as the sparkling world spun around him. Drunk without *zyth*, he thought.

One Mother handed Lita the sitar she'd been carrying, the other gave her package of food to the girl.

"You are stone," one of them said to him, touching his head gently.

Stone was a much more humble position to aspire to than rock, he thought.

Then both of them started back up the path. He knew they were anxious to rejoin the frenzy of work going on in the cave, writing out the history of their race in order to preserve its memory. And perhaps put an end to violence in some manner he didn't understand. What excitement there'd be in the Mother House when this story got back to the Guild. He could almost see the Head—whoever it would be now—summoning the teachers and the senior students—

"You really are feverish," Lita said.

"I'll get you there. Don't worry."

She stared at him. "*You'll* get *us* there?"

For the next few minutes she was distracted by the antics of her little sister who scampered back and forth across the path, chasing small flying creatures into the thickets. He was able to direct all of his strength into putting one foot in front of the other instead of having to spend it making conversation. For some reason, going downhill was more difficult and took concentration.

The gleaming white domes and communication towers of the star-base grew steadily bigger as they followed the zigzagging path, but the heat increased, slowing their progress so that the nearer they came to the valley floor the longer it seemed to be taking. It didn't seem to bother the two girls, but he found it harder and harder to lift his feet.

"No use," he said, after a while. "I can't go any farther."

"We're almost there." Lita adjusted the sitar over her shoulder. "Look. Only about another hundred meters to the perimeter. I can see the gate and the guard house."

He slumped down by the side of the path. Jilan came skipping back and gazed at him, a spray of crimson wildflowers in her fist. The small blooms were the color of the blood that spurted from his hand when First-Among-Mothers's knife descended. He put his bandaged hand up to support his head, which seemed to weigh more than he remembered.

The child opened her mouth and sang, "*Wiu*," a note as pure as a bird's.

"Please, get up," Lita said urgently. "I can't carry you."

"You go. I'll wait here."

"They'll be able to help you down there. You just need some good human pharmaceuticals..."

As she stared down at him, the hot breeze rising from below teased the coppery hair and brought its faint scent like woodsmoke to his nose, so that for a moment he had the illusion he was looking at Yv.

So long ago. He'd fallen in love with the way Yv's long hair lifted in the warm wind, the hair with its smoky perfume that bewitched him. He could see her clearly in memory, sitting in the shade of a tree when he'd first seen her, her arm around one of that world's younglings who was teaching her to name the flowers that surrounded them. Though he'd always been sharply aware of his alienness on each world he'd visited, Yv had always seemed at home.

Then he knew one question was answered: Yv would've wanted children. And he would've come to love them, too. If felt good just to sit here and think about his wife.

"There. I can see a guard." Lita stood on tiptoe and waved her arms excitedly. "Oh, he doesn't see us. But I'll go get him, and then somebody'll come back for you."

Jilan put her bouquet of wildflowers in his lap and their perfume was so rich it made his head spin. She danced away from him into the light, her slight figure shattering in a myriad diamond points that hurt his eyes to watch. She seemed more an elemental spirit of this world than a human child, and he recognized in that one scintillating moment that there were mysteries that were not given to him to understand.

"You'll be all right?" Lita asked. "It won't take very long."

"Yes. Go."

She hesitated for a moment longer, then leaned down and kissed him quickly on the cheek. "When we get back to Earth, Ries," she said, "I'm going to become a lingster, like you."

He put his hand up to touch his cheek and found it wet with his own tears.

The DepCom's daughters ran down the path to the base, the Dep-Com's sitar bouncing on the older daughter's back. The running figures became smaller and smaller. Then a tall figure emerged from the gate-house and hurried toward them. Ries watched till the radiance forced his eyes closed.

When he opened them again, his wife was standing in the wild-flowers at the edge of the path, hair spilling like flame over her shoulders. She was wearing the sky-blue wedding dress.

Yv held out her arms to him, welcoming him home.

Lost Girls

JANE YOLEN

Called alternatively the "Hans Christian Andersen of America" (*Newsweek*) and "the Aesop of the twentieth century" (*New York Times*), Jane Yolen is a storyteller, novelist, children's book author, poet, playwright, and author of more than 200 books for children, young adults, and adults.

Ms. Yolen's books, poems, and stories have won so many awards, they cannot all be listed, but include: the Caldecott Medal, Nebula Award, the Rhysling, an *Asimov's Magazine* Readers' Poll award, World Fantasy Award, a National Book Award nomination, three Mythopoeic Awards, the Golden Kite Award, the Skylark Award, Jewish Book Award, the Christopher Medal, the Association of Jewish Libraries Award, the Charlotte Award, etc. She has six body-of-work awards from such diverse groups as the Catholic Library Association, the universities of Minnesota and Keene State, the Oklahoma Libraries, and the New England Science Fiction Association.

Her writings have been made into television shows, audio books, theatrical presentations, and one full-length movie— *The Devil's Arithmetic,* starring Kirsten Dunst.

Her story here earned her a second Nebula.

"It isn't fair!" Darla complained to her mom for the third time during their bedtime reading. She meant it wasn't fair that Wendy only did the housework in Neverland and that Peter Pan and the boys got to fight Captain Hook.

"Well, I can't change it," Mom said in her even, lawyer voice. "That's just the way it is in the book. Your argument is with Mr. Barrie, the author, and he's long dead. Should I go on?"

"Yes. No. I don't know," Darla said, coming down on both sides of the question, as she often did.

Mom shrugged and closed the book, and *that* was the end of the night's reading.

Darla watched impassively as her mom got up and left the room, snapping off the bedside lamp as she went. When she closed the door there was just a rim of light from the hall showing around three sides of the door, making it look like something out of a science fiction movie. Darla pulled the covers up over her nose. Her breath made the space feel like a little oven.

"Not fair at all," Darla said to the dark, and she didn't just mean the book. She wasn't the least bit sleepy.

But the house made its comfortable night-settling noises around her: the breathy whispers of the hot air through the vents, the ticking of the grandfather clock in the hall, the sound of the maple branch *scritch-scratch*ing against the clapboard siding. They were a familiar lullaby, comforting and soothing. Darla didn't mean to go to sleep, but she did.

Either that or she stepped out of her bed and walked through the closed door into Neverland.

Take your pick.

It didn't feel at all like a dream to Darla. The details were too exact. And she could *smell* things. She'd never smelled anything in a dream before. So Darla had no reason to believe that what happened to her next was anything but real.

One minute she had gotten up out of bed, heading for the bathroom, and the very next she was sliding down the trunk of a very large, smooth tree. The trunk was unlike any of the maples in her yard, being a kind of yellowish color. It felt almost slippery under her hands and smelled like bananas gone slightly bad. Her nightgown made a sound like *whooosh* as she slid along.

When she landed on the ground, she tripped over a large root and stubbed her toe.

"Ow!" she said.

"Shhh!" cautioned someone near her.

She looked up and saw two boys in matching ragged cutoffs and T-shirts staring at her. "Shhh! yourselves," she said, wondering at the same time who they were.

But it hadn't been those boys who spoke. A third boy, behind her, tapped her on the shoulder and whispered, "If you aren't quiet, *He* will find us."

She turned, ready to ask who *He* was. But the boy, dressed in green tights and a green shirt and a rather silly green hat, and smelling like fresh lavender, held a finger up to his lips. They were perfect lips. Like a movie star's. Darla knew him at once.

"Peter," she whispered. "Peter Pan."

He swept the hat off and gave her a deep bow. "Wendy," he countered.

"Well, Darla, actually," she said.

"Wendy Darla," he said. "Give us a thimble."

She and her mom had read that part in the book already, where Peter got kiss and thimble mixed up, and she guessed what it was he really meant, but she wasn't about to kiss him. She was much too young to be kissing boys. Especially boys she'd just met. And he had to be more a man than a boy, anyway, no matter how young he looked. The copy of *Peter Pan* she and her mother had been reading had belonged to her grandmother originally. Besides, Darla wasn't sure she liked Peter. Of course, she wasn't sure she *didn't* like him. It was a bit confusing. Darla hated things being confusing, like her parents' divorce and her dad's new young wife and their twins who were—and who weren't exactly—her brothers.

"I don't have a thimble," she said, pretending not to understand.

"I have," he said, smiling with persuasive boyish charm. "Can I give it to you?"

But she looked down at her feet in order not to answer, which was how she mostly responded to her dad these days, and that was that. At least for the moment. She didn't want to think any further ahead, and neither, it seemed, did Peter.

He shrugged and took her hand, dragging her down a path that smelled of moldy old leaves. Darla was too surprised to protest. And besides, Peter was lots stronger than she was. The two boys followed. When they got to a large dark brown tree whose odor reminded Darla of her grandmother's wardrobe, musty and ancient, Peter stopped. He let go of her hand and jumped up on one of the twisted roots that were looped over and around one another like woody snakes. Darla was suddenly reminded of her school principal when he towered above the students at assembly. He was a tall man but the dais he stood on made him seem even taller. When you sat in the front row, you could look up his nose. She could look up Peter's nose now. Like her principal, he didn't look so grand that way. Or so threatening.

"Here's where we live," Peter said, his hand in a large sweeping motion. Throwing his head back, he crowed like a rooster; he no longer seemed afraid of making noise. Then he said, "You'll like it."

"Maybe I will. Maybe I won't," Darla answered, talking to her feet again.

Peter's perfect mouth made a small pout as if that weren't the response he'd been expecting. Then he jumped down into a dark space between the roots. The other boys followed him. Not to be left behind, in case that rooster crow really had called something awful to them, Darla went after the boys into the dark place. She found what they had actually gone through was a door that was still slightly ajar.

The door opened on to a long, even darker passage that wound into the very center of the tree; the passage smelled damp, like bathing suits left still wet in a closet. Peter and the boys seemed to know the way without any need of light. But Darla was constantly afraid of stumbling and she was glad when someone reached out and held her hand.

Then one last turn and there was suddenly plenty of light from hundreds of little candles set in holders that were screwed right into the living heart of the wood. By the candlelight she saw it was Peter who had hold of her hand.

"Welcome to Neverland," Peter said, as if this were supposed to be a big surprise.

Darla took her hand away from his. "It's smaller than I thought it would be," she said. This time she looked right at him.

Peter's perfect mouth turned down again. "It's big enough for us," he said. Then as if a sudden thought had struck him, he smiled. "But too small for *Him*." He put his back to Darla and shouted, "Let's have a party. We've got us a new Wendy."

Suddenly, from all corners of the room, boys came tumbling and stumbling and dancing, and pushing one another to get a look at her. They were shockingly noisy and all smelled like unwashed socks. One of them made fart noises with his mouth. She wondered if any of them had taken a bath recently. They were worse — Darla thought — than her Stemple cousins, who were so awful their parents never took them anywhere anymore, not out to a restaurant or the movies or anyplace at all.

"Stop it!" she said.

The boys stopped at once.

"I told you," Peter said. "She's a regular Wendy, all right. She's even given me a thimble."

Darla's jaw dropped at the lie. *How could he?*

She started to say "I did not!" but the boys were already cheering so loudly her protestations went unheard.

"Tink," Peter called, and one of the candles detached itself from the heartwood to flutter around his head, "tell the Wendys we want a Welcome Feast."

The Wendys? Darla bit her lip. *What did Peter mean by that?*

The little light flickered on and off. *A kind of code*, Darla thought. She assumed it was the fairy Tinker Bell, but she couldn't really make out what this Tink looked like except for that flickering, fluttering presence. But as if understanding Peter's request, the flicker took off toward a black corner and, shedding but a little light, flew right into the dark.

"Good old Tink," Peter said, and he smiled at Darla with such practice, dimples appeared simultaneously on both sides of his mouth.

"What kind of food . . ." Darla began.

"Everything parents won't let you have," Peter answered. "Sticky buns and tipsy cake and Butterfingers and brownies and . . ."

The boys gathered around them, chanting the names as if they were the lyrics to some kind of song, adding, ". . . apple tarts and gingerbread and chocolate mousse and trifle and . . ."

"And stomachaches and sugar highs," Darla said stubbornly. "My dad's a nutritionist. I'm only allowed healthy food."

Peter turned his practiced dimpled smile on her again. "Forget your father. You're in Neverland now, and no one need ever go back home from here."

At that Darla burst into tears, half in frustration and half in fear. She actually liked her dad, as well as loved him, despite the fact that he'd left her for his new wife, and despite the fact of the twins, who were actually adorable as long as she didn't have to live with them. The thought that she'd been caught in Neverland with no way to return was so awful, she couldn't help crying.

Peter shrugged and turned to the boys. "*Girls!*" he said with real disgust.

"All Wendys!" they shouted back at him.

Darla wiped her eyes, and spoke right to Peter. "My name is *not* Wendy," she said clearly. "It's Darla."

Peter looked at her, and there was nothing nice or laughing or young about his eyes. They were dark and cold and very very old.

Darla shivered.

"*Here* you're a Wendy," he said.

And with that, the dark place where Tink had disappeared grew increasingly light, as a door opened and fifteen girls carrying trays piled high with cakes, cookies, biscuits, buns, and other kinds of goodies marched single file into the hall. They were led by a tall, slender, pretty girl with brown hair that fell straight to her shoulders.

The room suddenly smelled overpoweringly of that sickly sweetness of children's birthday parties at school, when their mothers brought in sloppy cupcakes greasy with icing. Darla shuddered.

"Welcome Feast!" shouted the boy who was closest to the door. He made a deep bow.

"Welcome Feast!" they all shouted, laughing and gathering around a great center table.

Only Darla seemed to notice that not one of the Wendys was smiling.

The Feast went on for ages, because each of the boys had to stand up and give a little speech. Of course, most of them only said, "Welcome, Wendy!" and "Glad to meet you!" before sitting down again. A few elaborated a little bit more. But Peter more than made up for it with a long, rambling talk about duty and dessert and how no one loved them out in the World Above as much as he did here in Neverland, and how the cakes proved that.

The boys cheered and clapped at each of Peter's pronouncements, and threw buns and scones across the table at one another as a kind of punctuation. Tink circled Peter's head continuously like a crown of stars, though she never really settled.

But the girls, standing behind the boys like banquet waitresses, did not applaud. Rather they shifted from foot to foot, looking alternately apprehensive and bored. One, no more than four years old, kept yawning behind a chubby hand.

After a polite bite of an apple tart, which she couldn't swallow but spit into her napkin, Darla didn't even try to pretend. The little pie had been much too sweet, not tart at all. And even though Peter kept urging her between the welcomes to eat something, she just couldn't. That small rebellion seemed to annoy him enormously and he stood up once again, this time on the tabletop, to rant on about how some people lacked gratitude, and how difficult it was to provide for so many, especially with *Him* about.

Peter never actually looked at Darla as he spoke, but she knew — and everyone else knew — that he meant *she* was the ungrateful one. That bothered her some, but not as much as it might have. She even found herself enjoying the fact that he was annoyed, and that realization almost made her smile.

When Peter ended with "No more Feasts for them with Bad Attitudes!" the boys leaped from their benches and overturned the big table, mashing the remaining food into the floor. Then they all disappeared, diving down a variety of bolt-holes, with Tink after them, leaving the girls alone in the big candlelit room.

"Now see what you've done," said the oldest girl, the pretty one with the straight brown hair. Obviously the leader of the Wendys, she wore a simple dark dress — *like a uniform,* Darla thought, *a school uniform that's badly stained.* "It's going to take forever to get that stuff off the floor. Ages and ages. Mops and buckets. And nothing left for us to eat."

The other girls agreed loudly.

"*They* made the mess," Darla said sensibly. "Let *them* clean it up! That's how it's done at my house."

There was a horrified silence. For a moment none of the girls said a word, but their mouths opened and shut like fish on beaches. Finally the littlest one spoke.

"Peter won't 'ike it."

"Well, I don't '*ike* Peter!" Darla answered quickly. "He's nothing but a long-winded bully."

"But," said the little Wendy, "you gave him a thimble." She actually said "simble."

"No," Darla said. "Peter lied. I didn't."

The girls all seemed dumbstruck by that revelation. Without a word more, they began to clean the room, first righting the table and then laboriously picking up what they could with their fingers before resorting, at last, to the dreaded buckets and mops. Soon the place smelled like any institution after a cleaning, like a school bathroom or a hospital corridor, Lysol-fresh with an overcast of pine.

Shaking her head, Darla just watched them until the littlest Wendy handed her a mop.

Darla flung the mop to the floor. "I won't do it," she said. "It's not fair."

The oldest Wendy came over to her and put her hand on Darla's shoulder. "Who ever told you that life is fair?" she asked. "Certainly not a navvy, nor an upstairs maid, nor a poor man trying to feed his family."

"Nor my da," put in one of the girls. She was pale skinned, sharp nosed, gap toothed, homely to a fault. "He allas said life was a crapshoot and all usn's got was snake-eyes."

"And not my father," said another, a whey-faced, doughy-looking eight-year-old. "He used to always say that the world didn't treat him right."

"What I mean is that it's not fair that *they* get to have the adventures and you get to clean the house," Darla explained carefully.

"Who will clean it if we don't?" Wendy asked. She picked up the mop and handed it back to Darla. "Not *them*. Not ever. So if we want it done, we do it. Fair is not the matter here." She went back to her place in the line of girls mopping the floor.

With a sigh that was less a capitulation and more a show of solidarity with the Wendys, Darla picked up her own mop and followed.

When the room was set to rights again, the Wendys—with Darla following close behind—tromped into the kitchen, a cheerless, windowless room they had obviously tried to make homey. There were little stick dollies stuck in every possible niche and hand-painted birch bark signs on the wall.

SMILE, one sign said, YOU ARE ON CANDIED CAMERA. And another: WENDYS ARE WONDERFUL. A third, in very childish script, read: WENDYS ARE WINERS. Darla wondered idly if that was meant to be WINNERS or WHINERS, but she decided not to ask.

Depressing as the kitchen was, it was redolent with bakery smells that seemed to dissipate the effect of a prison. Darla sighed, remembering her own kitchen at home, with the windows overlooking her mother's herb garden and the rockery where four kinds of heather flowered till the first snows of winter.

The girls all sat down—on the floor, on the table, in little bumpy, woody niches. There were only two chairs in the kitchen, a tatty overstuffed chair whose gold brocaded covering had seen much better days, and a rocker. The rocker was taken by the oldest Wendy; the other chair remained empty.

At last, seeing that no one else was going to claim the stuffed chair, Darla sat down on it, and a collective gasp went up from the girls.

"'At's Peter's chair," the littlest one finally volunteered.

"Well, Peter's not here to sit on it," Darla said. But she did not relax back against the cushion, just in case he should suddenly appear.

"I'm hungry, Wendy," said one of the girls, who had two gold braids down to her waist. "Isn't there *anything* left to eat?" She addressed the girl in the rocker.

"You are always hungry, Madja," Wendy said. But she smiled, and it was a smile of such sweetness, Darla was immediately reminded of her mom, in the days before the divorce and her dad's new wife.

"So you *do* have names, and not just Wendy," Darla said.

They looked at her as if she were stupid.

"Of course we have names," said the girl in the rocker. "I'm the only one *truly* named Wendy. But I've been here from the first. So that's what Peter calls us all. That's Madja," she said, pointing to the girl with the braids. "And that's Lizzy." The youngest girl. "And that's Martha, Pansy, Nina, Nancy, Heidi, Betsy, Maddy, JoAnne, Shula, Annie, Corrie, Barbara . . ." She went around the circle of girls.

Darla interrupted. "Then why doesn't Peter—"

"Because he can't be bothered remembering," said Wendy. "And we can't be bothered reminding him."

"And it's all right," said Madja. "Really. He has so much else to worry about. Like—"

"*Him!*" They all breathed the word together quietly, as if saying it aloud would summon the horror to them.

"Him? You mean Hook, don't you?" asked Darla. "Captain Hook."

The look they gave her was compounded of anger and alarm. Little Lizzy put her hands over her mouth as if she had said the name herself.

"Well, isn't it?"

"You are an extremely stupid girl," said Wendy. "As well as a dangerous one." Then she smiled again—that luminous smile—at all the other girls, excluding Darla, as if Wendy had not just said something that was both rude and horrible. "Now, darlings, how many of you are as hungry as Madja?"

One by one, the hands went up, Lizzy's first. Only Darla kept her hand down and her eyes down as well.

"Not hungry in the slightest?" Wendy asked, and everyone went silent.

Darla felt forced to look up and saw that Wendy's eyes were staring at her, glittering strangely in the candlelight.

It was too much. Darla shivered and then, all of a sudden, she wanted to get back at Wendy, who seemed as much of a bully as Peter, only in a softer, sneakier way. *But how to do it?* And then she recalled how her mom said that telling a story in a very quiet voice always made a jury lean forward to concentrate that much more. *Maybe,* Darla thought, *I could try that.*

"I remember..." Darla began quietly. "...I remember a story my mom read to me about a Greek girl who was stolen away by the king of the underworld. He tricked her into eating six seeds and so she had to remain in the underworld six months of every year because of them."

The girls had all gone quiet and were clearly listening. *It works!* Darla thought.

"Don't be daft," Wendy said, her voice loud with authority.

"But Wendy, I remember that story, too," said the whey-faced girl, Nancy, in a kind of whisper, as if by speaking quietly she could later deny having said anything at all.

"And I," put in Madja, in a similarly whispery voice.

"And the fairies," said Lizzy. She was much too young to worry about loud or soft, so she spoke in her normal tone of voice. "If you eat anything in their hall, my mum allas said... you never get to go home again. Not ever. I miss my mum." Quite suddenly she began to cry.

"Now see what you've gone," said Wendy, standing and stamping her foot. Darla was shocked. She'd never seen anyone over four years old do such a thing. "They'll all be blubbing now, remembering their folks, even the ones who'd been badly beaten at home or worse. And not a sticky bun left to comfort them with. You — girl — ought to be ashamed!"

"Well, it isn't *my* fault!" said Darla, loudly, but she stood, too. The thought of Wendy towering over her just now made her feel edgy and even a bit afraid. "And my name isn't *girl*. It's Darla!"

They glared at one another.

Just then there was a brilliant whistle. A flash of light circled the kitchen like a demented firefly.

"It's Tink!" Lizzy cried, clapping her hands together. "Oh! Oh! It's the signal. 'Larm! 'Larm!"

"Come on, you lot," Wendy cried. "Places, all." She turned her back to Darla, grabbed up a soup ladle, and ran out of the room.

Each of the girls picked up one of the kitchen implements and followed. Not to be left behind, Darla pounced on the only thing left, a pair of silver sugar tongs, and pounded out after them.

They didn't go far, just to the main room again. There they stood silent guard over the bolt-holes. After a while — not quite fifteen minutes, Darla guessed — Tink fluttered in with a more melodic *all clear* and the boys slowly slid back down into the room.

Peter was the last to arrive.

"Oh, Peter, we were so worried," Wendy said.

The other girls crowded around. "We were scared silly," Madja added.

"Weepers!" cried Nancy.

"Knees all knocking," added JoAnne.

"Oh, this is really *too* stupid for words!" Darla said. "All we did was stand around with kitchen tools. Was I supposed to brain a pirate with these?" She held out the sugar tongs as she spoke.

The hush that followed her outcry was enormous. Without another word, Peter disappeared back into the dark. One by one, the Lost Boys followed him. Tink was the last to go, flickering out like a candle in the wind.

"Now," said Madja with a pout, "we won't even get to hear about the fight. And it's the very best part of being a Wendy."

Darla stared at the girls for a long moment. "What you all need," she said grimly, "is a backbone transplant." And when no one responded, she added, "It's clear the Wendys need to go out on strike." Being the daughter of a labor lawyer had its advantages. She knew all about strikes.

"What the Wendys *need*," Wendy responded sternly, "is to give the cupboards a good shaking-out." She patted her hair down and looked daggers at Darla. "But first, cups of tea all 'round." Turning on her heel, she started back toward the kitchen. Only four girls remained behind.

Little Lizzy crept over to Darla's side. "What's a strike?" she asked.

"Work stoppage," Darla said. "Signs and lines."

Nancy, Martha, and JoAnne, who had also stayed to listen, looked equally puzzled.

"Signs?" Nancy said.

"Lines?" JoAnne said.

"*Hello*..." Darla couldn't help the exasperation in her voice. "What year do you all live in? I mean, haven't you ever heard of strikes? Watched CNN? Endured social studies?"

"Nineteen fourteen," said Martha.

"Nineteen thirty-three," said Nancy.

"Nineteen seventy-two," said JoAnne.

"Do you mean to say that none of you are..." Darla couldn't think of what to call it, so added lamely, "new?"

Lizzy slipped her hand into Darla's. "You are the onliest new Wendy we've had in years."

"Oh," Darla said. "I guess that explains it." But she wasn't sure.

"Explains what?" they asked. Before Darla could answer, Wendy called from the kitchen doorway, "Are you lot coming? Tea's on." She did not sound as if she were including Darla in the invitation.

Martha scurried to Wendy's side, but Nancy and JoAnne hesitated a moment before joining her. That left only Lizzy with Darla.

"Can I help?" Lizzy asked. "For the signs. And the 'ines? I be a good worker. Even Wendy says so."

"You're my only..." Darla said, smiling down at her and giving her little hand a squeeze. "My *onliest* worker. Still, as my mom always says, Start with one, you're halfway done."

Lizzy repeated the rhyme. "Start with one, you're halfway done. Start with one..."

"Just remember it. No need to say it aloud," Darla said.

Lizzy looked up at her, eyes like sky-blue marbles. "But I 'ike the way that poem sounds."

"Then 'ike it quietly. We have a long way to go yet before we're ready for any chants." Darla went into the kitchen hand-in-hand with Lizzy, who skipped beside her, mouthing the words silently.

Fourteen Wendys stared at them. Not a one was smiling. Each had a teacup—unmatched, chipped, or cracked—in her hand.

"A long way to go where?" Wendy asked in a chilly voice.

"A long way before you can be free of this yoke of oppression," said Darla. *Yoke of oppression* was a favorite expression of her mother's.

"We are not yoked," Wendy said slowly. "And we are not oppressed."

"What's o-ppressed?" asked Lizzy.

"Made to do what you don't want to do," explained Darla, but she never took her eyes off of Wendy. "Treated harshly. Ruled unjustly. Governed with cruelty." Those were the three definitions she'd had to memorize for her last social studies exam. She never thought she'd ever actually get to use them in the real world. *If*, she thought suddenly, *this world is real.*

"No one treats us harshly or rules us unjustly. And the only cruel ones in Neverland are the pirates," Wendy explained carefully, as if talking to someone feebleminded or slow.

None of the other Wendys said a word. Most of them stared into their cups, *a little*—Darla thought—*like the way I always stare down at my shoes when Mom or Dad wants to talk about something that hurts.*

Lizzy pulled her hand from Darla's. "I think it harsh that we always have to clean up after the boys." Her voice was tiny but still it carried.

"And unjust," someone put in.

"Who said that?" Wendy demanded, staring around the table. "Who *dares* to say that Peter is unjust?"

Darla pursed her lips, wondering how her mom would answer such a question. She was about to lean forward to say something when JoAnne stood in a rush.

"I said it. And it *is* unjust. I came to Neverland to get away from that sort of thing. Well... and to get away from my stepfather, too," she said. "I mean, I don't mind cleaning up my own mess. And even someone else's, occasionally. But..." She sat down as quickly as she had stood, looking accusingly into her cup, as if the cup had spoken and not she.

"*Well!*" Wendy said, sounding so much like Darla's home ec teacher that Darla had to laugh out loud.

As if the laugh freed them, the girls suddenly stood up one after another, voicing complaints. And as each one rose, little Lizzy clapped her hands and skipped around the table, chanting, "Start with one, you're halfway done! Start with one, you're halfway done!"

Darla didn't say a word more. She didn't have to. She just listened as the first trickle of angry voices became a stream and the stream turned into a flood. The girls spoke of the boys' mess and being underappreciated and wanting a larger share of the food. They spoke about needing to go outside every once in a while. They spoke of longing for new stockings and a bathing room all to themselves, not one shared with the boys, who left rings around the tub and dirty underwear everywhere. They spoke of the long hours and the lack of fresh air, and Barbara said they really could use every other Saturday off, at least. It seemed once they started complaining they couldn't stop.

Darla's mom would have understood what had just happened, but Darla was clearly as stunned as Wendy by the rush of demands. They stared at one another, almost like comrades.

The other girls kept on for long minutes, each one stumbling over the next to be heard, until the room positively rocked with complaints. And then, as suddenly as they had begun, they stopped. Red faced, they all sat down again, except for Lizzy, who still capered around the room, but now did it wordlessly.

Into the sudden silence, Wendy rose. "How *could* you...," she began. She leaned over the table, clutching the top, her entire body trembling. "After all Peter has done for you, taking you in when no one else wanted you, when you had been tossed aside by the world, when you'd been crushed and corrupted and canceled. How *could* you?"

Lizzy stopped skipping in front of Darla. "Is it time for signs and 'ines now?" she asked, her marble-blue eyes wide.

Darla couldn't help it. She laughed again. Then she held out her arms to Lizzy, who cuddled right in. "Time indeed," Darla said. She looked up at Wendy. "Like it or not, Miss Management, the Lost Girls are going out on strike."

————

Wendy sat in her rocker, arms folded, a scowl on her face. She looked like a four-year-old having a temper tantrum. But of course it was something worse than that.

The girls ignored her. They threw themselves into making signs with a kind of manic energy and in about an hour they had a whole range of them, using the backs of their old signs, pages torn from cookbooks, and flattened flour bags.

WENDYS WON'T WORK, one read. EQUAL PLAY FOR EQUAL WORK, went another. MY NAME'S NOT WENDY! said a third, and FRESH AIR IS ONLY FAIR a fourth. Lizzy's sign was decorated with stick figures carrying what Darla took to be swords, or maybe wands. Lizzy had spelled out—or rather misspelled out—what became the girls' marching words: WE AIN'T LOST, WE'RE JUST MIZ-PLAYST.

It turned out that JoAnne was musical. She made up lyrics to the tune of "Yankee Doodle Dandy" and taught them to the others:

We ain't lost, we're just misplaced,
The outside foe we've never faced.
Give us a chance to fight and win
And we'll be sure to keep Neverland neat as a pin.

The girls argued for a while over that last line, which Betsy said had too many syllables and the wrong sentiment, until Madja suggested, rather timidly, that if they actually wanted a chance to fight the pirates, maybe the boys should take a turn at cleaning the house. "Fair's fair," she added.

That got a cheer. "Fair's fair," they told one another, and Patsy scrawled that sentiment on yet another sign.

The cheer caused Wendy to get up grumpily from her chair and leave the kitchen in a snit. She must have called for the boys then, because no sooner had the girls decided on an amended line (which still had too many syllables but felt right otherwise)—

And you can keep Neverland neat as a pin!

—than the boys could be heard coming back noisily into the dining room. They shouted and whistled and banged their fists on the table, calling out for the girls and for food. Tink's high-pitched cry overrode the noise, piercing the air. The girls managed to ignore it all until Peter suddenly appeared in the kitchen doorway.

"What's this I hear?" he said, smiling slightly to show he was more amused than angry. Somehow that only made his face seem both sinister and untrustworthy.

But his appearance in the doorway was electrifying. For a moment not one of the girls could speak. It was as if they had all taken a collective breath and were waiting to see which of them had the courage to breathe out first.

Then Lizzy held up her sign. "We're going on strike," she said brightly.

"And what, little Wendy, is that?" Peter asked, leaning forward and speaking in the kind of voice grown-ups use with children. He pointed at her sign. "Is it . . ." he said slyly, "like a thimble?"

"Silly Peter," said Lizzy, "it's signs and 'ines."

"I see the signs, all right," said Peter. "But what do they mean? WENDYS WON'T WORK. Why, Neverland counts on Wendys working. And I count on it, too. You Wendys are the most important part of what we have made here."

"Oh," said Lizzy, turning to Darla, her face shining with pleasure. "*We're* the mostest important . . ."

Darla sighed heavily. "If you are so important, Lizzy, why can't he remember your name? If you're so important, why do you have all the work and none of the fun?"

"Right!" cried JoAnne suddenly, and immediately burst into her song. It was picked up at once by the other girls. Lizzy, caught up in the music, began to march in time all around the table with her sign. The others, still singing, fell in line behind her. They marched once around the kitchen and then right out into the dining room. Darla was at the rear.

At first the Lost Boys were stunned at the sight of the girls and their signs. Then they, too, got caught up in the song and began to pound their hands on the table in rhythm.

Tink flew around and around Wendy's head, flickering on and off and on angrily, looking for all the world like an electric hair-cutting machine. Peter glared at them all until he suddenly seemed to come to some conclusion. Then he leaped onto the dining room table, threw back his head, and crowed loudly.

At that everyone went dead silent. Even Tink.

Peter let the silence prolong itself until it was almost painful. At last he turned and addressed Darla and, through her, all the girls. "What is it you want?" he asked. "What is it you truly want? Because you'd better be careful what you ask for. In Neverland wishes are granted in very strange ways."

"It's not," Darla said carefully, "what *I* want. It's what *they* want."

In a tight voice, Wendy cried out, "They never wanted for anything until *she* came, Peter. They never needed or asked . . ."

"What we want . . ." JoAnne interrupted, "is to be equals."

Peter wheeled about on the table and stared down at JoAnne and she, poor thing, turned gray under his gaze. "No one is asking you," he said pointedly.

"We want to be equals!" Lizzy shouted. "To the boys. To Peter!"

The dam burst again, and the girls began shouting and singing and crying and laughing all together. "Equal . . . equal . . . equal . . ."

Even the boys took it up.

Tink flickered frantically, then took off up one of the bolt-holes, emerging almost immediately down another, her piercing alarm signal so loud that everyone stopped chanting, except for Lizzy, whose little voice only trailed off after a bit.

"So," said Peter, "you want equal share in the fighting? Then here's your chance."

Tink's light was sputtering with excitement and she whistled non-stop.

"Tink says Hook's entire crew is out there, waiting. And, boy! are they angry. You want to fight them? Then go ahead." He crossed his arms over his chest and turned his face away from the girls. "I won't stop you."

No longer gray but now pink with excitement, JoAnne grabbed up a knife from the nearest Lost Boy. "I'm not afraid!" she said. She headed up one of the bolt-holes.

Weaponless, Barbara, Pansy, and Betsy followed right after.

"But that's not what I meant them to do," Darla said. "I mean, weren't we supposed to work out some sort of compromise?"

Peter turned back slowly and looked at Darla, his face stern and unforgiving. "I'm Peter Pan. I don't have to compromise in Neverland." Wendy reached up to help him off the tabletop.

The other girls had already scattered up the holes, and only Lizzy was left. And Darla.

"Are you coming to the fight?" Lizzy asked Darla, holding out her hand.

Darla gulped and nodded. They walked to the bolt-hole hand-in-hand. Darla wasn't sure what to expect, but they began rising up as if in some sort of air elevator. Behind them one of the boys was whining to Peter, "But what are we going to do without them?"

The last thing Darla heard Peter say was "Don't worry. There are always more Wendys where they came from."

The air outside was crisp and autumny and smelled of apples. There was a full moon, orange and huge. *Harvest moon,* Darla thought, which was odd since it had been spring in her bedroom.

Ahead she saw the other girls. *And* the pirates. Or at least she saw their silhouettes. It obviously hadn't been much of a fight. The smallest of the girls—Martha, Nina, and Heidi—were already captured and riding atop their captors' shoulders. The others, with the exception of JoAnne, were being carried off fireman-style. JoAnne still had her knife and she was standing off one of the largest of the men; she got in one good swipe before being disarmed, and lifted up.

Darla was just digesting this when Lizzy was pulled from her.

"Up you go, little darlin'," came a deep voice.

Lizzy screamed. "Wendy! Wendy!"

Darla had no time to answer her before she, too, was gathered up in enormous arms and carted off.

In less time than it takes to tell of it, they were through the woods and over a shingle, dumped into boats, and rowed out to the pirate ship. There they were hauled up by ropes and—except for Betsy, who struggled so hard she landed in the water and had to be fished out, wrung out, and then hauled up again—it was a silent and well-practiced operation.

The girls stood in a huddle on the well-lit deck and awaited their fate. Darla was glad no one said anything. She felt awful. She hadn't meant them to come to this. Peter had been right. Wishes in Neverland were dangerous.

"Here come the captains," said one of the pirates. It was the first thing anyone had said since the capture.

He must mean captain, singular, thought Darla. But when she heard footsteps nearing them and dared to look up, there were, indeed, two figures coming forward. One was an old man about her grandfather's age, his white hair in two braids, a three-cornered hat on his head. She looked for the infamous hook but he had two regular hands, though the right one was clutching a pen.

The other captain was ... a woman.

"Welcome to Hook's ship," the woman said. "I'm Mrs. Hook. Also known as Mother Jane. Also known as Pirate Lil. Also called The Pirate Queen. We've been hoping we could get you away from Peter for a very long time." She shook hands with each of the girls and gave Lizzy a hug.

"I need to get to the doctor, ma'am," said one of the pirates. "That little girl ..." he pointed to JoAnne "... gave me quite a slice."

JoAnne blanched and shrank back into herself.

But Captain Hook only laughed. It was a hearty laugh, full of good humor. "Good for her. You're getting careless in your old age, Smee," he said. "Stitches will remind you to stay alert. Peter would have got your throat, and even here on the boat that could take a long while to heal."

"Now," said Mrs. Hook, "it's time for a good meal. Pizza, I think. With plenty of veggies on top. Peppers, mushrooms, carrots, onions. But no anchovies. I have never understood why anyone wants a hairy fish on top of pizza."

"What's pizza?" asked Lizzy.

"Ah ... something you will love, my dear," answered Mrs. Hook. "Things never do change in Peter's Neverland, but up here on Hook's ship we move with the times."

"Who will do the dishes after?" asked Betsy cautiously.

The crew rustled behind them.

"I'm on dishes this week," said one, a burly, ugly man with a black eyepatch.

"And I," said another. She was as big as the ugly man, but attractive in a rough sort of way.

"There's a duty roster on the wall by the galley," explained Mrs. Hook. "That's ship talk for the kitchen. You'll get used to it. We all take turns. A pirate ship is a very democratic place."

"What's demo-rat-ic?" asked Lizzy.

They all laughed. "You will have a long time to learn," said Mrs. Hook. "Time moves more swiftly here than in the stuffy confines of a Neverland tree. But not so swiftly as out in the world. Now let's have that pizza, a hot bath, and a bedtime story, and then tomorrow we'll try and answer your questions."

The girls cheered, JoAnne loudest of them all.

"I *am* hungry," Lizzy added, as if that were all the answer Mrs. Hook needed.

"But I'm not," Darla said. "And I don't want to stay here. Not in Neverland or on Hook's ship. I want to go home."

Captain Hook came over and put his good hand under her chin. Gently he lifted her face into the light. "Father beat you?" he asked.

"Never," Darla said.

"Mother desert you?" he asked.

"Fat chance," said Darla.

"Starving? Miserable? Alone?"

"No. And no. And *no*."

Hook turned to his wife and shrugged. She shrugged back, then asked, "Ever think that the world was unfair, child?"

"Who hasn't?" asked Darla, and Mrs. Hook smiled.

"Thinking it and meaning it are two very different things," Mrs. Hook said at last. "I expect you must have been awfully convincing to have landed at Peter's door. Never mind, have pizza with us, and then you can go. I want to hear the latest from outside, anyway. You never know what we might find useful. Pizza was the last really useful thing we learned from one of the girls we snagged before Peter found her. And that—I can tell you—has been a major success."

"Can't I go home with Darla?" Lizzy asked.

Mrs. Hook knelt down till she and Lizzy were face-to-face. "I am afraid that would make for an awful lot of awkward questions," she said.

Lizzy's blue eyes filled up with tears.

"My mom is a lawyer," Darla put in quickly. "Awkward questions are her specialty."

The pizza was great, with a crust that was thin and delicious. And when Darla awoke to the ticking of the grandfather clock on the hall and the sound of the maple branch *scritch-scratch*ing against the clapboard siding, the taste of the pizza was still in her mouth. She felt a lump at her feet, raised up, and saw Lizzy fast asleep under the covers at the foot of the bed.

"I sure hope Mom is as good as I think she is," Darla whispered. Because there was no going back on this one—fair, unfair, or anywhere in between.

Thirteen Ways to Water

BRUCE HOLLAND ROGERS

Bruce Holland Rogers has published both popular and literary fiction, including science fiction, fantasy and horror stories, mystery, and romance fiction. In all he has sold more than seventy short stories. Rogers has published two poetry chapbooks: *Breathing in the World* (Phase & Cycle Press) and *Tales and Declarations* (Trout Creek Press/Dog River Review).

Rogers won the Nebula for Best Novelette of 1996 for "Lifeboat on a Burning Sea" and a second Nebula for this tale. He was a 1994 nominee for the Edgar Allan Poe Award for his mystery story, "Enduring as Dust." In 1989 he won first prize in the Writers of the Future Contest for his dark fantasy story, "A Branch in the Wind."

Rogers holds an M.A. in English literature from the University of Colorado. After he finished his degree, he stayed on for four years to teach classes in American literature, creative writing, science fiction, and college composition. He and his wife, Holly Arrow, now live in Eugene, Oregon, where she is a psychology professor at the University of Oregon and he devotes his energies full time to writing. He sometimes teaches seminars in creativity and conducts private fiction-writing workshops.

1. With Blood

When Jack Salter was seventeen, two other guys held his arms while Bull Wilson punched his face. Three times. Hard.

"You stay away from Diane," Bull said. "Don't even *talk* to her."

Later, on the riverbank, Jack washed the blood from his face and thought, *I'll never forget this. I will never forgive.*

2. Because She Asks Him To

When Diane Wilson comes to Jack this time, it isn't out of the mists of fantasy. She comes in a BMW, and she's her real self, a woman almost fifty.

He's sitting under the overhang of his tin roof when she drives up. The blue Beemer looks strange on the gravel road that generally sees VW bugs or beat-up Hondas or more often no traffic at all. Diane wears a suit and jacket. She goes from crisp to wilted the minute she gets out of the car's air-conditioning. He puts his book down but doesn't stand.

"Jack," she says.

He nods but can think of nothing to say that won't seem like a formula. Not, *This is a surprise.* Not, *How've you been?*

The silence grows between them. He thinks it is strange at his age to feel this sort of awkwardness. At last she tells him, "I need your help, Jack."

"My help," he says.

"Actually," she says, "Bull needs your help."

He could laugh then. He could shake his head. He could say, *The son of a bitch you married needs* my *help?* But instead he folds his hands and says, "Tell me."

"He's down by the river," she says. "He's been there for days. I looked and looked, and when I found him, he told me it was for the water. So he could drown."

"I don't understand," Jack says.

"I don't either." She begins to cry.

He doesn't stand up, go to her, embrace her. He lets her stand there, wet-faced, hugging herself, shaking, until she is finished. She opens her purse and takes out a tissue.

"Why don't you call the police?"

"I guess you won't do it," she says.

"I didn't say that."

"If I call the police, they'll hospitalize him. We've been through that once. The doctors can't do anything for him. The headaches come right back, and he hates me for doing that, for handing him over like that as if he'd done something."

"What headaches?"

She tells him, then, about the cluster headaches, a dozen attacks some days that make Bull Wilson stalk the floor, wail, beat his fists against his head or his head against the wall. Like fire in his head, like a blade in his skull boring in, digging and scraping.

Like guilt.

No, not guilt. Bull Wilson would never feel guilty.

Jack says, "Why me?"

"He talks about the war. Not to me. But to men—his friends or even strangers who find him there by the river. He tells his war stories. And you were there."

"A lot of men in town were there."

"But you ... I just have this feeling about you. About the kind of person you are. Bull's friends can't help him. They don't know what to do."

"And I will?"

She looks at him long and hard. "Maybe."

Jack nods then. He wonders if she knows what he did in the war, if she knows that she is asking him to do it again, thirty years later. Although this won't be the same. This will be altogether different, if he can do it at all.

He says, "I'll try."

3. Under the Cottonwoods

He finds Bull Wilson just where Diane says he'll be, crouched among the blackberry brambles along the riverbank, in the shade of black cottonwoods.

Bull still wears his tie, hasn't even loosened it, but three nights of sleeping beside the Willamette have left mud stains on his suit. His hair is a mess. Bull's eyes are red. Veins show on his blistered nose.

Even so, when Jack makes his way through the poison oak, Bull meets him with a blue gaze so steady that Jack thinks for a moment that this will be easy, that he'll just say, as if they were old friends, *Come on, Bull. Let's go home,* and reclaim him.

But the gaze is more than steady. Bull stares. He stares *beyond* Jack. If he knows who Jack is, he gives no sign.

A thin chain is wrapped around Bull's hand like a rosary. A fifty-caliber shell dangles from the end.

"Hey, Bull," Jack says.

"Ghosts," Bull whispers. Then he says, "They won't leave me." He pounds his forehead with his fist and shouts, "They won't fucking stop!" He grimaces, keeps hitting himself.

Jack sits down, not too close, and watches the green churn of the Willamette, waits for Bull's headache to pass. He waits for Bull to say the next thing he will say.

4. Downhill

When Jack Salter was a boy, his father showed him the mountains. They hiked the rain-soaked Siskiyous, the big timber of the Cascades, the scrubby Sheepshead Mountains. And his father taught him that if he was lost, he should go the way that water goes. He should follow a slope to a stream, follow the stream to a river, follow the river to safety.

5. Lethe

They were far north of the DMZ, two Jolly Green Giants hovering above the treetops. They'd had to wait for their Skyraider escort to fly up from Da Nang. That gave the NVA time to locate the pilot, set a trap.

As the Skyraiders circled, Jack rode the cable down, found his man in the underbrush, loaded him onto the litter. When the two of them reached the helicopter doorway, the enemy opened up. A rocket seemed to pass harmlessly through the rotors, but heavy rounds clapped the armor, or pierced it. The Jolly Green started to pitch and rock. As she climbed away, she was burning. Jack strapped a parachute on his injured man, donned one himself.

When the helicopter exploded, the blast threw Jack out the open door. His parachute opened just above the trees.

Jack's ears were ringing so badly that when the PJ for the other Jolly Green came down to get him, he couldn't hear what the man was saying, could barely hear the thundering of the engines when the second bird hoisted him up, carried him away.

His crewmates were gone, along with the man they'd come for. Quick as that.

When his head cleared, he thought, *I can forgive anything. I can forget anything.*

6. Under the Full Moon

The Willamette has rolled on for a few minutes, and Bull hasn't spoken again. But now he says, "The first action I saw was on the night of a full moon." He lets that sentence rest. "We went out on an ambush. The dikes of the rice paddy were slippery. We were careful, trying not to fall down. Quiet."

Bull watches the river, but Jack thinks he must be seeing something else.

"We walked through the village. Eyes on us. I felt them. Now and then, the moon appeared in the rice paddies. The sergeant with the starlight scope said, real soft, 'There!' And he spread us out. These guys were walking right toward us, toward the village, and when the sergeant popped off the first rounds, the rest of us joined in."

Bull falls silent. Jack waits. And goes on waiting until Bull says, "We went forward. Two bodies, and a third guy, shot up, who begged for his life. The sergeant said no dice. He said, 'You.'"

Bull taps his chest. "I did a fucking good job. Had to wrap him like meat to take back. We always had to take them back unless we had the lieutenant. Only officers could confirm. Carrying him back, I felt him watching."

Bull shakes the chain, the dangling cartridge.

"In here. There was mud on my boots from the paddies. I cleaned it off, put it in here. Mud from the place where it happened would keep him from following me, would keep him out of my dreams. And it worked. It worked like a charm. After every ambush, every firefight, I would scrape a little mud, and they couldn't come after me."

7. Names

Jack's father taught him to fish. By the time he was fourteen, Jack had taken trout out of the Rogue River and steelhead from the Umpqua; he'd stood hip-deep in the Deschutes, fished the John Day in the shadow of the Umatilla Mountains. Every kid in his class knew where the Columbia was, knew the Willamette flowed through their town, but Jack knew Bully Creek, the Sprague, Crooked River, and the Applegate. He could draw them from memory, and he knew how it was to stand in their waters.

Naming the rivers was the first thing. Second was naming the rocks they flowed over: granite, schist, basalt. Then he learned the names of the birds that shared the river with him: osprey, green heron, great blue. He learned the differences between pine and fir, hemlock and spruce, could tell the Scouler willow apart from the Mackenzie willow.

Names were powerful, like incantations. He'd tried using them to weave a spell around Diane Dailey, teaching her, in walks along the river, the names of things she'd grown up never really seeing because she didn't have the names.

Names were so important that when the C-130 flying him to Quang Tri came under fire, the dull dread of his training found its focus: He hadn't been in the country for two days, and people were trying to kill him. He was lost. He knew the names of nothing.

On his first mission, standing in the helicopter doorway, he watched rivers pass below. But which rivers? He looked out at the jungle, and the only name he had was *green*.

He knew that he'd never find his way home if he didn't know where he was. He studied the map in the briefing room, learned the shapes and names of the Cam Lo River, the Ia Drang, the Mekong, and the Ma. As for the jungle, no one on base could tell him the names of anything but bamboo. He bought books by mail order, felt exposed until they came, and at last began to learn: *Mangrove. Rubber tree. Banyan. Strangler fig.* He learned the difference between bamboo and Tonkin cane.

Knowing the names was protection. When the cable lowered him into the jungle to find an injured pilot, he'd look on the way down for something he knew the name of: Blackleaf. Scarlet banana. And sometimes he'd see, coiled in the branches and staring at him as if it knew *his* name, a reticulated python.

He would get home.

8. Thunder for Rainfall

Every man who came home different was different in his own way.

Jack traded the thunder of the helicopter's twin engines for the sound of rain rattling a tin roof. It was not so different from where he might have ended up without the war, except that the spruce and pine, the fir and hemlock of home meant more to him now, were more precious. He couldn't live in town or work in town, but needed his solitude. He spent most of his time reading or looking across the vale at a stand of Douglas fir and the crows that glided over. When he needed work, he did odd jobs.

Bull came home hungry, traded the jungle rains for the roar of chain saws. It was not so different from where he might have ended up without the war, except that he was harder now, more aggressive. One summer, he supervised the crews that clear-cut that stand of Douglas fir.

9. In a Boat

"It was the monsoon," Bull says. "No way to get anywhere but boat or helicopter, so they sent us up this river in flatbed boats, one squad to a boat. All Charlie needed was patience. The ambush that got us was from both banks of the river. And they had snipers in the trees.

"I tried to get my rifle up, start returning fire like we were supposed to do in an ambush. But I noticed that two guys in my squad were dead, and the thing I kept thinking was, 'Shit. How am I going to get dirt out of a fucking river?' Because it wasn't just the enemy dead. Your own dead would follow you if they could."

Jack waits, then asks, "What did you do?"

"As soon as we were clear, I took off my helmet and dipped it in the river. The corporal in our boat says, 'What the fuck?' But I had it. Muddy water. I didn't need a lot. When the lining dried, I scraped it for a few flakes."

He shakes the cartridge again.

"I kept them here, and they left me alone. For years. For years! But now it's wearing off. I get these headaches. They want me dead. And dead is better than the headaches."

"How do you know it's the ghosts?"

"They tell me. I hear them."

So Jack listens, but hears only the river.

10. Shall We Gather at the River?

Jack met the protesters down by the river because he didn't want to make his speech at the access gate. They'd be too keyed up. He wouldn't have their attention.

"Remember that the loggers aren't our enemies," he said. "Notice what you're carrying in your hearts."

His beard was gray. He was, by now, an elder of the movement and could say these things without seeming naive.

"These men have families. They have children to feed. They think of you as the enemy because this is the only life they know. You may think you see only anger. You may hear only angry words. But they're afraid, and they deserve your compassion. Even if they hate you. Even if they do hateful things."

Then he led them back up the slope, onto the logging road, up to the gate. As they chained themselves by the wrist or by the neck, he pointed out the orange and yellow chanterelles pushing up through the spongy soil in the shadows of the old-growth Douglas firs. It was important, he said, to know the names of things.

For a long time there was only the sound of the wind in the treetops.

"Wouldn't it be funny," someone said, "if they just didn't come today?"

But half an hour later, one of Bull Wilson's logging crews arrived, with an escort of state police.

11. With a Gift

Jack watches the river a moment longer. He gets up. He sits closer to Bull. Closer, but still not too close. And he says, "You've got it wrong. You've got it backward."

Bull looks at him, seems to know for the first time who he is.

"The mud and dust you have collected there," Jack says, "it's not protection."

Bull unclenches his fist, draws the cartridge to his palm, considers.

"The ghosts are *in* there," Jack says. "You brought them with you."

Narrowing his eyes, Bull says, "How would *you* know." Now Jack is sure that Bull recognizes him, knows who he is, who he used to be.

"I know," Jack says. "I just do."

Bull loosens his tie. Jack takes that as a good sign, says softly, "Let 'em go."

So Bull Wilson unscrews the container, the hollowed-out shell and casing. A few flakes of dust fall.

"Let the river have them," Jack says. He isn't sure he's right. In any case, he doesn't expect any immediate sign. But when Bull throws it all into the Willamette, shell, dust, casing, and chain, Jack feels something change in the air, as if the river has drawn a breath.

The air gets unstable. Light moves. Jack smells a hint of cordite, of rotten fish, of green decay. Then he can see them, in black pajamas and uniforms of the NVA. In U.S. Army jungle fatigues. The outlines of dead men, the barest hints of memory, standing in the river.

Bull sees them, too. Old buddies and old enemies, unreconciled, made of thirty-year-old fear.

No other miracle happens. Jack doesn't expect one, although he feels he is waiting for something. The ghosts are waiting, too.

12. A Woman Is a Body of Water

Over the years, the women Jack loved, the women who stayed for longer or shorter times under his tin roof, were of a certain sort. They still wore tie-dyed or granny dresses, strung their own beads. None of them shaved their legs. They ate organic, or vegetarian, or vegan. Some of them said wildly delusional things about Republicans on one hand and witches on the other.

On some nights when such a woman slept beside him, or on other nights when Jack slept alone, Diane would come to him. The Diane of seventeen, of the spring of 1968. But she'd be mixed with the Diane he had sometimes seen with her husband at public hearings, a woman still trim, carefully packaged, running a business of her own. Or so he'd guessed. He never spoke to her. He invented the details he didn't know.

She would come, this Diane who was many Dianes, and offer her breasts to his mouth, the curve of her thighs to his hands. He would stroke himself, feeling the crisp sheets of her bed. Hot summer nights, he would feel the breeze of air-conditioning that made her shiver even as his penetrating fingers made her arch and moan.

He would glide into her, filling her, merging the river of his blood with hers.

Wiping the stickiness from his belly with the sheet, he would always feel empowered, relieved, ashamed. The fantasy rooted him in many things he wanted to be free of. Revenge. Old injuries. New enmities. Christ, even air-conditioning.

13. Mist

Rain drums so loud on Jack's tin roof that the first sign he has of Diane is the sound of her car door closing. He opens his door before she can knock.

She's wearing blue jeans and a sweater, yellow boots smeared with the mud of his driveway. She has left the car running, lights on, windshield wipers gliding silently from side to side. "Thank you," she says.

"I don't suppose he's altogether whole."

"Who ever is?" Diane laughs. "He's better. He's so much better."

The rain lets up a bit and the wipers begin to squeak. Diane watches his face, and he watches her watching. He wants something, and she seems to know that, but he doesn't have a name for what it is that he wants.

As she says, "If there's anything I can ...," Jack says, "It bothers me that..."

She waits. He says, "I know who Bull is. We'll never be friends, but I know who he is." He looks at her, droplets of rain in her hair. "I want to know who you are. Who you have become."

She could take this the wrong way. But she says, "Let's go for a drive."

They follow the rain-slick highway into town. Jack twice thinks he is about to say, *I never stopped wanting you.* He doesn't say it.

"I grow orchids," Diane tells him. "It started as a hobby when the girls were little, but it turned into a business by the time Rae was in high school."

Jack laughs.

"What?" Diane asks.

But he only shakes his head.

She says, "Remember how you tried to impress me with the names of trees?"

"I remember."

Now it's her turn to be silent, to leave him wondering.

There is no sign on the greenhouse. Jack has been by here before, seen the glass roofs, and never imagined that Diane owned them. Inside, the air is hot and moist. Jungle air, but sweeter. Some of the flowers are spotted or striped. One is patterned with gold and rust and white. The ornate petals remind Jack of lace.

"Fascination," she says. "New Moon. Flirtation. Peter Pan." She catches his eye. She is trying not to laugh. "Madonna. Dos Pueblos. Virginia Night. Nikki."

He laughs, and he follows her among the tables, beneath the lights and misting rods, accepting her gift.

From Forever Peace

JOE HALDEMAN

Joe Haldeman burst upon the science fiction scene in 1975 with a closely observed novel of hard times in an interstellar war of vast proportions, *The Forever War*. It made his reputation, won him the Hugo, Nebula, and Ditmar (Australia) awards, and framed his central concerns. In 1997 he repeated this success with *Forever Peace,* a thematic sequel set in 2043. The novel follows "soldierboys," indestructible war machines run by remote control by soldiers safely far away. This is a logical extension of current American casualty-minimizing strategy, which diminishes domestic opposition to foreign engagements while relying on ever-evolving technology.

The novel is larger in its concerns than *The Forever War,* ranging into theoretical physics and sketching in a thoroughly believable world less than a century hence. Written with Haldeman's laconic grace, it is thoroughly enjoyable.

I have probably known Joe longer than anyone in the field, as he and I were physics students at the University of Oklahoma together. We never spoke of science fiction as I remember, and Joe was soon off to Maryland and then Vietnam, where he was severely wounded. Only while slowly recovering did he begin writing for publication. His fiction reflects a wry insight into our darker faces, with a shrewdness uncommon in fiction; Haldeman has earned his views.

It was not quite completely dark, thin blue moonlight threading down through the canopy of leaves. And it was never completely quiet.

A thick twig popped, the noise muffled under a heavy weight. A male howler monkey came out of his drowse and looked down. Something moved down there, black on black. He filled his lungs to challenge it.

There was a sound like a piece of newspaper being torn. The monkey's midsection disappeared in a dark spray of blood and shredded organs. The body fell heavily through the branches in two halves.

Would you lay off the goddamn monkeys? Shut up! *This place is an ecological preserve.* My watch, shut up. Target practice.

Black on black it paused, then slipped through the jungle like a heavy silent reptile. A man could be standing two yards away and not see it. In infrared it wasn't there. Radar would slither off its skin.

It smelled human flesh and stopped. The prey maybe thirty meters upwind, a male, rank with old sweat, garlic on his breath. Smell of gun oil and smokeless powder residue. It tested the direction of the wind and backtracked, circled around. The man would be watching the path. So come in from the woods.

It grabbed the man's neck from behind and pulled his head off like an old blossom. The body shuddered and gurgled and crapped. It eased the body down to the ground and set the head between its legs.

Nice touch. Thanks.

It picked up the man's rifle and bent the barrel into a right angle. It lay the weapon down quietly and stood silent for several minutes.

Then three other shadows came from the woods, and they all converged on a small wooden hut. The walls were beaten-down aluminum cans nailed to planks; the roof was cheap glued plastic.

It pulled the door off and an irrelevant alarm sounded as it switched on a headlight brighter than the sun. Six people on cots, recoiling.

"—Do not resist," it boomed in Spanish. "—You are prisoners

of war and will be treated according to the terms of the Geneva Convention."

"*Mierda.*" A man scooped up a shaped charge and threw it at the light. The tearing-paper sound was softer than the sound of the man's body bursting. A split second later, it swatted the bomb like an insect and the explosion blew down the front wall of the building and flattened all the occupants with concussion.

The black figure considered its left hand. Only the thumb and first finger worked, and the wrist made a noise when it rotated.

Good reflexes. Oh, shut up.

The other three shapes turned on sunlights and pulled off the building's roof and knocked down the remaining walls.

The people inside looked dead, bloody and still. The machines began to check them, though, and a young woman suddenly rolled over and raised the laser rifle she'd been concealing. She aimed it at the one with the broken hand and did manage to raise a puff of smoke from its chest before she was shredded.

The one checking the bodies hadn't even looked up. "No good," it said. "All dead. No tunnels. No exotic weapons I can find."

"Well, we got some stuff for Unit Eight." They turned off their lights and sped off simultaneously, in four different directions.

The one with the bad hand moved about a quarter mile and stopped to inspect the damage with a dim infrared light. It beat the hand against its side a few times. Still, only the two digits worked.

Wonderful. We'll have to bring it in.

So what would you have done?

Who's complaining? I'll spend part of my ten in base camp.

The four of them took four different routes to the top of a treeless hill. They stood in a row for a few seconds, arms upraised, and a cargo helicopter came in at treetop level and snatched them away.

Who got the second kill there? thought the one with the broken hand.

A voice appeared in all four heads. "Berryman initiated the response. But Hogarth commenced firing before the victim was unambiguously dead. So by the rules, they share the kill."

The helicopter with the four soldierboys dangling slipped down the hill and screamed through the night at treetop level, in total darkness, east toward friendly Panama.

I didn't like Scoville having the soldierboy before me. You have to monitor the previous mechanic for twenty-four hours before you take it over, to warm up and become sensitive to how the soldierboy might have changed since your last shift. Like losing the use of three fingers.

When you're in the warm-up seat you're just watching; you're not jacked into the rest of the platoon, which would be hopelessly confusing. We go in strict rotation, so the other nine soldierboys in the platoon also have replacements breathing over their mechanics' shoulders.

You hear about emergencies, where the replacement has to suddenly take over from the mechanic. It's easy to believe. The last day would be the worst even without the added stress of being watched. If you're going to crack or have a heart attack or stroke, it's usually on the tenth day.

Mechanics aren't in any physical danger, deep inside the Operations bunker in Portobello. But our death and disability rate is higher than the regular infantry. It's not bullets that get us, though; it's our own brains and veins.

It would be rough for me or any of my mechanics to replace people in Scoville's platoon, though. They're a hunter/killer group, and we're "harassment and interdiction," H & I; sometimes loaned to Psychops. We don't often kill. We aren't selected for that aptitude.

All ten of our soldierboys came into the garage within a couple of minutes. The mechanics jacked out and the exoskeleton shells eased open. Scoville's people climbed out like little old men and women, even though their bodies had been exercised constantly and adjusted for fatigue poisons. You still couldn't help feeling as if you'd been sitting in the same place for nine days.

I jacked out. My connection with Scoville was a light one, not at all like the near-telepathy that links the ten mechanics in the platoon. Still, it was disorienting to have my own brain to myself.

We were in a large white room with ten of the mechanic shells and ten warm-up seats, like fancy barber chairs. Behind them, the wall was a huge backlit map of Costa Rica, showing with lights of various colors where soldierboy and flyboy units were working. The other walls were covered with monitors and digital readouts with jargon labels. People in white fatigues walked around checking the numbers.

Scoville stretched and yawned and walked over to me.

"Sorry you thought that last bit of violence was unnecessary. I felt the situation called for direct action." God, Scoville and his academic airs. Doctorate in Leisure Arts.

"You usually do. If you'd warned them from outside, they would've had time to assess the situation. Surrender."

"Yes indeed. As they did in Ascensión."

"That was one time." We'd lost ten soldierboys and a flyboy to a nuclear booby trap.

"Well, the second time won't be on my watch. Six fewer pedros in the world." He shrugged. "I'll go light a candle."

"Ten minutes to calibration," a loudspeaker said. Hardly enough time for the shell to cool down. I followed Scoville into the locker room. He went to one end to get into his civvies; I went to the other end to join my platoon.

Sara was already mostly undressed. "Julian. You want to do me?"

Yes, like most of our males and one female, I *did*, as she well knew, but that's not what she meant. She took off her wig and handed me the razor. She had three weeks' worth of fine blond stubble. I gently shaved off the area surrounding the input at the base of her skull.

"That last one was pretty brutal," she said. "Scoville needed the body count, I guess."

"It occurred to him. He's eleven short of making E-8. Good thing they didn't come across an orphanage."

"He'd be bucking for captain," she said.

I finished her and she checked mine, rubbing her thumb around the jack. "Smooth," she said. I keep my head shaved off duty, though it's unfashionable for black men on campus. I don't mind long bushy hair, but I don't like it well enough to run around all day wearing a hot wig.

Louis came over. "Hi, Julian. Give me a buzz, Sara." She reached up—he was six feet four and Sara was small—and he winced when she turned on the razor.

"Let me see that," I said. His skin was slightly inflamed on one side of the implant. "Lou, that's going to be trouble. You should've shaved before the warm-up."

"Maybe. You gotta choose." Once you were in the cage you were there for nine days. Mechanics with fast-growing hair and sensitive skin, like Sara and Lou, usually shaved once, between warm-up and the shift. "It's not the first time," he said. "I'll get some cream from the medics."

Bravo platoon got along pretty well. That was a partly a matter of chance, since we were selected out of the pool of appropriate draftees by body size and shape, to fit the platoon's cages and the aptitude profile for H & I. Five of us were survivors of the original draft pick: Candi and Mel as well as Lou, Sara, and me. We've been doing this for four years, working ten days on and twenty off. It seems like a lot longer.

Candi is a grief counselor in real life; the rest of us are academics of some stripe. Lou and I are science, Sara is American politics, and Mel is a cook. "Food science," so called, but a hell of a cook. We get together a few times a year for a banquet at his place in St. Louis.

We went together back to the cage area. "Okay, listen up," the loudspeaker said. "We have damage on units one and seven, so we won't calibrate the left hand and right leg at this time."

"So we need the cocksuckers?" Lou asked.

"No, the drains will not be installed. If you can hold it for forty-five minutes."

"I'll certainly try, sir."

"We'll do the partial calibration and then you're free for ninety minutes, maybe two hours, while we set up the new hand and leg modules for Julian and Candi's machines. Then we'll finish the calibration and hood up the orthotics, and you're off to the staging area."

"Be still my heart," Sara murmured.

We lay down in the cages, working arms and legs into stiff sleeves, and the techs jacked us in. For the calibration we were tuned down to about ten percent of a combat jack, so I didn't hear actual words from anybody but Lou — a "hello there" that was like a faint shout from a mile away. I focused my mind and shouted back.

The calibration was almost automatic for those of us who'd been doing it for years, but we did have to stop and back up twice for Ralph, a neo who'd joined us two cycles ago when Richard stroked out. It was just a matter of all ten of us squeezing one muscle group at a time, until the red thermometer matched the blue thermometer on the heads-up. But until you're used to it, you tend to squeeze too hard and overshoot.

After an hour they opened the cage and unjacked us. We could kill ninety minutes in the lounge. It was hardly worth wasting time getting dressed, but we did. It was a gesture. We were about to live in each other's bodies for nine days, and enough was enough.

Familiarity breeds, as they say. Some mechanics become lovers, and sometimes it works. I tried it with Carolyn, who died three years ago, but we could never bridge the gap between being combat-jacked and being civilians. We tried to work it out with a relator, but the relator had never been jacked, so we might as well have been talking Sanskrit.

I don't know that it would be "love" with Sara, but it's academic. She's not really attracted to me, and of course can't hide her feelings, or lack of same. In a physical way we're closer than any civilian pair could be, since in full combat jack we are this one creature with twenty arms and legs, with ten brains, with five vaginas and five penises.

Some people call the feeling godlike, and I think there have been gods who were constructed along similar lines. The one I grew up with was an old white-bearded Caucasian gent without even one vagina.

We'd already studied the order of battle, of course, and our specific orders for the nine days. We were going to continue in Scoville's area, but doing H & I, making things difficult in the cloud forest of Costa Rica. It was not a particularly dangerous assignment, but it was distasteful, like bullying, since the rebels didn't have anything remotely like soldierboys.

Ralph expressed his discomfort. We had sat down at the dining table with tea and coffee.

"This overkill gets to me," he said. "That pair in the tree last time."

"Ugly," Sara said.

"Ah, the bastards killed themselves," Mel said. He sipped the coffee and scowled at it. "We probably wouldn't have noticed them if they hadn't opened up on us."

"It bothers you that they were children?" I asked Ralph.

"Well, yeah. Doesn't it you?" He rubbed the stubble on his chin. "Little girls."

"Little girls with machine guns," Karen said, and Claude nodded emphatically. They'd come in together about a year ago, and were lovers.

"I've been thinking about that, too," I said. "What if we'd known they were little girls?" They'd been about ten years old, hiding in a tree house.

"Before or after they started shooting?" Mel said.

"Even after," Candi said. "How much damage can they do with a machine gun?"

"They damaged *me* pretty effectively!" Mel said. He'd lost one eye and the olfactory receptors. "They knew exactly what to aim for."

"It wasn't a big deal," Candi said. "You got field replacements."

"Felt like a big deal to me."

"I know. I was there." You don't exactly feel pain when a sensor goes out. It's something as strong as pain, but there's no word for it.

"I don't think we would've had to kill them if they were out in the open," Claude said. "If we could see they were just kids and lightly armed. But hell, for all we knew they were FOs who could call in a tac nuke."

"In Costa Rica?" Candi said.

"It happens," Karen said. It had happened once in three years. Nobody knew where the rebels had gotten the nuke. It had cost them two towns, the one the soldierboys were in when they were vaporized, and the one we took apart in retaliation.

"Yeah, yeah," Candi said, and I could hear in those two words all she wasn't saying: that a nuke on our position would just destroy ten machines. When Mel flamed the tree house he roasted two little girls, probably too young to know what they were doing.

There was always an undercurrent in Candi's mind, when we were jacked. She was a good mechanic, but you had to wonder why she hadn't been given some other assignment. She was too empathetic, sure to crack before her term was up.

But maybe she was in the platoon to act as our collective conscience. Nobody at our level knew why anybody was chosen to be a mechanic, and we only had a vague idea why we were assigned to the platoon we got. We seemed to cover a wide range of aggressiveness, from Candi to Mel. We didn't have anybody like Scoville, though. Nobody who got that dark pleasure out of killing. Scoville's platoon always saw more action than mine, too; no coincidence. Hunter/killers—they're definitely more congenial with mayhem. So when the Great Computer in the Sky decides who gets what mission, Scoville's platoon gets the kills and ours gets reconnaissance.

Mel and Claude, especially, grumbled about that. A confirmed kill was an automatic point toward promotion, in pay grade if not in rank, whereas you couldn't count on the PPR—Periodic Performance Review—for a dime. Scoville's people got the kills, so they averaged about twenty-five percent higher pay than my people. But what could you spend it on? Save it up and buy our way out of the army?

"So we're gonna do trucks," Mel said, "Cars and trucks."

"That's the word," I said. "Maybe a tank if you hold your mouth right." Satellites had picked up some IR traces that probably meant the rebels were being resupplied by small stealthed trucks, probably robotic or remote. One of those outbursts of technology that kept the war from being a totally one-sided massacre.

I suppose if the war went on long enough, the enemy might have soldierboys, too. Then we could have the ultimate in something: ten-million-dollar machines reducing each other to junk while their operators sat hundreds of miles away, concentrating in air-conditioned caves.

People had written about that, warfare based on attrition of wealth rather than loss of life. But it's always been easier to make new lives than new wealth. And economic battles have long-established venues, some political and some not, as often among allies as not.

Well, what does a physicist know about it? My science has rules and laws that seem to correspond to reality. Economics describes reality after the fact, but isn't too good at predicting. Nobody predicted the nanoforges.

The loudspeaker told us to saddle up. Nine days of truck-stalking.

All ten people in Julian Class's platoon had the same basic weapon—the soldierboy, or Remote Infantry Combat Unit: a huge suit of armor with a ghost in it. For all the weight of its armor, more than half of the RICU's mass was ammunition. It could fire accurate sniper rounds to the horizon, two ounces of depleted uranium, or at close range it could hose a stream of supersonic flechettes. It had high explosive and incendiary rockets with eyes, a fully automatic grenade launcher, and a high-powered laser. Special units could be fitted with chemical, biological, or nuclear weapons, but those were only used for reprisal in kind.

(Fewer than a dozen nuclear weapons, small ones, had been used in twelve years of war. A large one had destroyed Atlanta, and although the Ngumi denied responsibility, the Alliance responded by giving twenty-four hours' notice, and then leveling Mandellaville and São

Paulo. Ngumi contended that the Alliance had cynically sacrificed one non-strategic city so it could have an excuse to destroy two important ones. Julian suspected they might be right.)

There were air and naval units, too, inevitably called flyboys and sailorboys, even though most flyboys were piloted by females.

All of Julian's platoon had the same armor and weapons, but some had specialized functions. Julian, being platoon leader, communicated directly and (in theory) constantly with the company coordinator, and through her to the brigade command. In the field, he received constant input in the form of encrypted signals from flyover satellites as well as the command station in geosynchronous orbit. Every order came from two sources simultaneously, with different encryption and a different transmission lag, so it would be almost impossible for the enemy to slip in a bogus command.

Ralph had a "horizontal" link similar to Julian's "vertical" one. As platoon liaison, he was in touch with his opposite number in each of the other nine platoons that made up Bravo. They were "lightly jacked"— the communication wasn't as intimate as he had with other members of the platoon, but it was more than just a radio link. He could advise Julian as to the other platoons' actions and even feelings, morale, in a quick and direct way. It was rare for all the platoons to be engaged in a single action, but when they were, the situation was chaotic and confusing. The platoon liaisons then were as important as the vertical command links.

One soldierboy platoon could do as much damage as a brigade of regular infantry. They did it quicker and more dramatically, like huge invincible robots moving in silent concert.

They didn't use actual armed robots for several reasons. One was that they could be captured and used against you; if the enemy could capture a soldierboy they would just have an expensive piece of junk. None had ever been captured intact, though; they self-destruct impressively.

Another problem with robots was autonomy: the machine has to be able to function on its own if communications are cut off. The image, as well as the reality, of a heavily armed machine making spot combat decisions was not something any army wanted to deal with. (Soldierboys had limited autonomy, in case their mechanics died or passed out. They stopped firing and went for shelter while a new mechanic was warmed up and jacked.)

The soldierboys were arguably more effective psychological weapons than robots would be. They were like all-powerful knights, heroes. And they represented a technology that was out of the enemy's grasp.

The enemy did use armed robots, like, as it turned out, the two tanks that were guarding the convoy of trucks that Julian's platoon was sent to destroy. Neither of the tanks caused any trouble. In both cases they were destroyed as soon as they revealed their position by firing. Twenty-four robot trucks were destroyed, too, after their cargos had been examined: ammunition and medical supplies.

After the last truck had been reduced to shiny slag, the platoon still had four days left on its shift, so they were flown back to the Portobello base camp, to do picket duty. That could be pretty dangerous, since the base camp was hit by rockets a couple of times a year, but most of the time it was no challenge. Not boring, though — the mechanics were protecting their own lives, for a change.

Sometimes it took me a couple of days to wind down and be a civilian again. There were plenty of joints in Portobello willing to help ease the transition. I usually did my unwinding back in Houston, though. It was easy for rebels to slip across the border and pass as Panamanians, and if you got tagged as a mechanic you were a prime target. Of course there were plenty of other Americans and Europeans in Portobello, but it's possible that mechanics stood out: pale and twitchy, collars pulled up to hide the skull jacks, or wigs.

We lost one that way last month. Arly went into town for a meal and a movie. Some thugs pulled off her wig, and she was hauled into an alley and beaten to a pulp and raped. She didn't die but she didn't recover, either. They had pounded the back of her head against a wall until the skull fractured and the jack came out. They shoved the jack into her vagina and left her for dead.

So the platoon was one short this month. (The neo Personnel delivered couldn't fit Arly's cage, which was not surprising.) We may be short two next month: Samantha, who is Arly's best friend, and a little bit more, was hardly there this week. Brooding, distracted, slow. If we'd been in actual combat she might have snapped out of it; both of them were pretty good soldiers — better than me, in terms of actually liking the work — but picket duty gave her too much time to meditate, and the truck assignment before that was a silly exercise a flyboy could have done on her way back from something else.

We all tried to give Samantha support while we were jacked, but it was awkward. Of course she and Arly couldn't hide their physical attraction for one another, but they were both conventional enough to be embarrassed about it (they had boyfriends on the outside), and had encouraged kidding as a way of keeping the complex relationship manageable. There was no banter now, of course.

She had spent the past three weeks visiting Arly every day at the convalescent center, where the bones of her face were growing back, but that was a constant frustration, since the nature of her injuries meant they couldn't be jacked, couldn't be close. Never. And it was Samantha's nature to want revenge, but that was impossible now. The five rebels involved had been apprehended immediately, slid through the legal system, and were hanged a week later in the public square.

I'd seen it on the cube. They weren't hanged so much as slowly strangled. This in a country that hadn't used capital punishment in generations, before the war.

Maybe after the war we'll be civilized again. That's the way it has always happened in the past.

Julian usually went straight home to Houston, but not when his ten days were up on a Friday. That was the day of the week when he had to be the most social, and he needed at least a day of preparation for that. Every day you spent jacked, you felt closer to the other nine mechanics. There was a terrible sense of separation when you unjacked, and hanging around with the others didn't help. What you needed was a day or so of isolation, in the woods or in a crowd.

Julian was not the outdoor type, and he usually just buried himself in the university library for a day. But not if it was Friday.

He could fly anywhere for free, so on impulse he went up to Cambridge, Massachusetts, where he'd done his undergraduate work. It was a bad choice, dirty slush everywhere and thin sleet falling in a constant sting, but he grimly persisted in his quest to visit every bar he could remember. They were full of inexplicably young and callow people.

Harvard was still Harvard; the dome still leaked. People made a point of not staring at a black man in uniform.

He walked a mile through the sleet to his favorite pub, the ancient

Plough and Stars, but it was padlocked, with a card saying BAHAMA! taped inside the window. So he squished back to the Square on frozen feet, promising to simultaneously get drunk and not lose his temper.

There was a bar named after John Harvard, where they brewed nine kinds of beer on the premises. He had a pint of each one, methodically checking them off on the blotter, and flowed into a cab that decanted him at the airport. After six hours of off-and-on slumber, he flew his hangover back to Houston Sunday morning, following the sunrise across the country.

Back at his apartment he made a pot of coffee and attacked the accumulated mail and memos. Most of it was throwaway junk. Interesting letter from his father, vacationing in Montana with his new wife, not Julian's favorite person. His mother had called twice about a money problem, but then called again to say never mind. Both brothers called about the hanging; they followed Julian's "career" closely enough to realize that the woman who'd been attacked was in his platoon.

His actual career had generated the usual soft sifting pink snowfall of irrelevant interdepartmental memos, which he did have to at least scan. He studied the minutes of the monthly faculty meeting, just in case something real had been discussed. He always missed it, since he was on duty from the tenth to the nineteenth of every month. The only way that might have hurt his career would be jealousy from other faculty members.

And then there was a hand-delivered envelope, a small square under the memos, addressed "J." He saw a corner of it and pulled it out, pink slips fluttering, and ripped open the flap, over which a red flame had been rubber-stamped: it was from Blaze, who Julian was allowed to call by her real name, Amelia. She was his coworker, ex-advisor, confidante, and sexual companion. He didn't say "lover" in his mind, yet, because that was awkward, Amelia being fifteen years older than him. Younger than his father's new wife.

The note had some chat about the Jupiter Project, the particle-physics experiment they were engaged in, including a bit of scandalous gossip about their boss, which did not alone explain the sealed envelope. "Whatever time you get back," she wrote, "come straight over. Wake me up or pull me out of the lab. I need my little boy in the worst way. You want to come over and find out what the worst way is?"

Actually, what he'd had in mind was sleeping for a few hours. But he could do that afterward. He stacked the mail into three piles and dropped one pile into the recycler. He started to call her but then put the phone down unpunched. He dressed for the morning cool and went downstairs for his bicycle.

The campus was deserted and beautiful, redbuds and azaleas in bloom under the hard blue Texas sky. He pedaled slowly, relaxing back into real life, or comfortable illusion. The more time he spent jacked, the harder it was to accept this peaceful, monocular view of life as the real one. Rather than the beast with twenty arms; the god with ten hearts.

At least he wasn't menstruating anymore.

He let himself into her place with his thumbprint. Amelia was actually up at nine Sunday morning, in the shower. He decided against surprising her there. Showers were dangerous places—he had slipped in one once, experimenting with a fellow clumsy teenager, and he wound up with a cut chin and bruises and a decidedly unerotic attitude toward the location (and the girl, for that matter).

So he just sat up in her bed, quietly reading the newspaper, and waited for the water to stop. She sang bits of tunes, happy, and switched the shower from fine spray to coarse pulse and back. Julian could visualize her there and almost changed his mind. But he stayed on the bed, fully clothed, pretending to read.

She came out toweling and started slightly when she saw Julian; then recovered: "Help! There's a strange man in my bed!"

"I thought you liked strange men."

"Only one." She laughed and eased alongside him, hot and damp.

Genre and Genesis: A Discussion of Science Fiction's Literary Role

JONATHAN LETHEM

GORDON VAN GELDER

GEORGE ZEBROWSKI

DAVID HARTWELL

BILL WARREN

In 1998 Jonathan Lethem published in the *Village Voice* and the *New York Review of Science Fiction* a provocative essay on the literary reputation of the science fiction genre, and the roots of its present predicament.

Many disagreed with him. In my introduction to this book I take a somewhat different path, and following Lethem's cogent piece, I have asked several major critical figures to render their arguments. Gordon Van Gelder is both a book editor for St. Martin's Press and editor of *The Magazine of Fantasy and Science Fiction;* his piece appeared there in slightly different form as an editorial. George Zebrowski is a well-known writer and former editor of the *Nebula Awards* volumes. David Hartwell is senior editor at Tor Books and one of the most prominent anthologists in the field's history; his remarks are drawn from his speech at the banquet where this volume's awards were given.

Bill Warren is a noted critic of film and television science fiction. His remarks go to the heart of the mismatch between written SF and its visual forms. Because we are mostly known through films and TV produced by those who know little of the genre's literary forms (except to loot them for ideas, of course, a now universal practice), we should understand the genre's uniquely schizophrenic role in popular culture: neglected in books, triumphant in the visual.

The treatment of science fiction has been unique among genres in this century—reflecting, I think, a deep fear in the conventional literary culture both of science and of the future itself. I hope this selection will give a cross section of responses, and depict how the genre is understanding both its own past and its future prospects.

Why Can't We All Just Live Together?
A Vision of Genre Paradise Lost

JONATHAN LETHEM

In 1973 Thomas Pynchon's *Gravity's Rainbow* was awarded the Nebula, the highest honor available in the field once known as "Science Fiction"—a term now mostly forgotten. From our current perspective, the methods and approaches of the so-called "SF Writers" seem so central to the literature of our century that the distinction has no value, and the historical fact of a separate genre is a footnote, of scholarly interest at best.

Notoriously shy, Pynchon sent beloved comedian Lenny Bruce to accept the award in his place...

Sorry, just dreaming. In our world Bruce is dead, while Bob Hope lurches on. And, though *Gravity's Rainbow* really was nominated for the 1973 Nebula, it was passed over for *Rendezvous with Rama*, by Arthur C. Clarke, which commentator Carter Scholz rightly deemed "less a novel than a schematic diagram in prose." Pynchon's nomination now stands as a hidden tombstone marking the death of the hope that science fiction was about to merge with the mainstream.

That hope was born in the hearts of writers, who, without any particular encouragement from the larger literary world, for a little while dragged the genre to the brink of respectability. The "New Wave" of the sixties and seventies was often word-drunk, applying modernist techniques willy-nilly to the old genre motifs, adding compensatory dollops of alienation and sexuality to characters who'd barely shed their slide rules. But the New Wave also made possible books like Samuel Delany's *Dhalgren*, Philip K. Dick's *A Scanner Darkly*, Ursula Le Guin's *The Dispossessed*, and Tom Disch's *334*, work to stand with the best American fiction of the 1970s — labels, categories, and genres aside. In a seizure of ambition, SF even flirted with renaming itself "Speculative Fabulation," a lit-crit term both pretentiously silly and dead right.

For what makes SF wonderful and complicated is that mix of *speculation* and *the fabulous*: SF is both think-fiction and dream-fiction. For the first sixty-odd years of the century American fiction was deficient in exactly those qualities SF offered in abundance, however inelegantly. While fabulists like Borges, Abe, Cortazar, and Calvino flourished abroad, a strain of literary Puritanism quarantined imaginative and surreal writing from respectability here. Another typical reflex, that anti-intellectualism which dictates that novelists shouldn't pontificate, extrapolate, or theorize, only *show* and *feel*, meant the novel of ideas was for decades pretty much the exclusive domain of, um, Norman Mailer. What's more, a reluctance in the humanities to acknowledge the technocratic impulse that was transforming contemporary culture left certain themes untouched. For decades SF filled the gap, and during those decades it added characterization, ambiguity, and reflexivity, evolving toward something like a literary maturity — or at least the ability to throw up an occasional masterpiece.

But a funny thing happened on the way to the revolution. In the sixties, just as SF's best writers began to beg the question of whether SF might be literature, American literary fiction began to open to the modes it had excluded. Writers like Donald Barthelme, Richard Brautigan, and Robert Coover restored the place of the imaginative and surreal, while others like Don DeLillo and Joseph McElroy began to contend with the emergent technoculture. William Burroughs and Thomas Pynchon did a little of both. The result was that the need to recognize SF's accomplishments dwindled away. Why seek in those gaudy paperbacks what was readily available in reputable packages? Why tangle with claims of legitimacy for a legion of disenfranchised writers when they carried an awkward legacy of pulpy techno-advocacy? So what followed was mostly critical rejection, or indifference.

Meanwhile, on the other side of the genre ghetto walls, a retrenchment was under way. A backlash. Though the stakes aren't nearly as crucial, it's hard not to see SF's attempt at self-liberation as typical of other equality movements which peaked in political strength around the same time, then retreated into identity politics. Fearing the loss of a distinctive oppositional identity, and bitter over lack of access to the Ivory Tower, SF took a step backward, away from its broadest literary aspirations. Not that SF of brilliance wasn't written in the years following, but with a few key exceptions it was overwhelmed on the shelves (and award ballots) by a reactionary SF as artistically dire as it was comfortingly familiar.

In the '80s cyberpunk was taken as a sign of hope, for its verve, its polish, its sensory alertness to the way our conceptions of the future had changed. But even cyberpunk's best writers mostly peddled surprisingly macho and regressive fantasies of rebellion as transcendence — and verve and polish were thin meat for those who recalled the mature depths of the best of the New Wave. Anyway, cyberpunk's best were quickly swamped themselves, by gelled-and-pierced photocopies of adolescent power fantasies that were already very, very old.

Which brings us to today. Where, against all odds, SF deserving of greater attention from a literary readership is *still* written. Its relevance, though, since the collapse of the notion that SF should and would converge with literature, is unclear at best. SF's literary writers exist now in a twilight world, neither respectable nor commercially viable. Their work drowns in a sea of garbage in bookstores, while much of SF's promise is realized elsewhere by writers too savvy or oblivious to bother with the stigmatized identity. SF's failure to present its own best face, to win proper respect, was never so tragic as now, when its strengths are so routinely preempted. In a literary culture where Pynchon, DeLillo, Barthelme, Coover, Jeanette Winterson, Angela Carter, and Steve Erickson are ascendant powers, isn't the division meaningless?

But the *literary* traditions reinforcing that division are only part of the story.

Among the factors arrayed against acceptance of SF as serious writing, none is more plain to outsiders than this: the books are *so fucking ugly.* Worse, they're all ugly in the same way, so you can't distinguish those meant for grown-ups from those meant for twelve-year-olds. Sadly enough, that confusion is intentional, and the explanation brings us back again to the mid-seventies.

It's now a commonplace in film criticism that George Lucas and Steven Spielberg together brought to a crashing halt the most progressive and interesting decade in American film since the thirties. What's eerie is that the same duo are the villains in SF's tragedy as well, though you might want to add a third—J. R. R. Tolkien. The vast popular success of the imagery and archetypes purveyed by those three savants of children's literature expanded the market for "Sci-Fi"—a cartoonified, castrated, and deeply nostalgic version of the budding literature—a thousandfold. What had been a negligible, eccentric publishing niche, permitted to go its own harmless way, was now a potential cash cow. (Remember when *Star Trek* was resurrected overnight, a moribund TV cult suddenly at the center of popular culture?) As stakes rose, marketers encamped on the territory—for a handy comparison, recall the cloning of Grunge Rock after Nirvana. Books were produced to meet this vast, superficial new appetite, rotten books, millions of them—and fine books were repackaged to fit the paradigm. Out with the hippie-surrealist book jackets of the sixties, with their promise of grown-up abstractions and ambiguities. In with that leaden and literal style so perfectly abhorrent to the literary bookbuyer. The golden mean of an SF jacket since 1976 looks, well, exactly like the original poster for *Star Wars*. Men of the future were once again thinking with their swords—excuse me, *lightsabers*. This passive sellout would make more sense if the typical writer of literary SF had actually made any money out of it. Instead the act is still too often rewarded with wages resembling those of a poet—an untenured poet, that is.

Other obstacles to acceptance remain hidden in the culture of SF, ambushes on a road no one's taking. Along with being a literary genre or mode, SF is also an ideological site. Anyone who's visited is familiar with the "home truths"—that the colonization of space is desirable; that rationalism will prevail over superstition; that cyberspace has the potential to transform individual and collective consciousness. Tangling with this inheritance has resulted in work of genius—Barry Malzberg tarnishing the allure of astronautics, J. G. Ballard gleefully unraveling the presumption that technology extends from rationalism, James Tiptree Jr. (née Alice Sheldon) replacing the body and its instincts in an all-too-disembodied discourse. But the pressure against heresy can be surprisingly strong, reflecting the emotional hunger for solidarity in marginalized groups. For SF can also function as a clubhouse, where members share the resentments of the excluded, and a defensive fondness for stories which thrived in twelve-year-old imaginations but shrivel on first contact with an adult brain. In its unqualified love for its own junk stratum SF may be as postmodern as Frederic Jameson's dreams, but it's also as sentimental about itself as an Elks Lodge, or a family.

Marginality, it should be said, isn't always the worst thing for artists. Silence, exile, and cunning remain a writer's allies, and despised genres have been a plentiful source of exile for generations of iconoclastic American fictioneers. And sure, hipster audiences always resent seeing their favorite cult item grow too popular. But an outsider art courts precious self-referentiality if it too strongly resists incorporation. The remnants of the jazz which refused the bebop transformation are those guys in pinstripe suits playing Dixieland, and the separate-but-unequal postseventies SF field, preening over its lineage and fetishizing its rejection, sometimes sounds an awful lot like Dixieland—as refined, as calcified, as sweetly irrelevant.

If good writing is neglected because of genre boundaries, so it goes—good writing goes unread for lots of reasons. The shame is in what's left unwritten, in artists internalizing prejudice as crippling self-doubt. Great art mostly occurs when creators are encouraged to entertain the possibility of their relevance. Might a Phil Dick have learned to revise his first drafts instead of flinging them despairingly into the marketplace if *The Man in the High Castle* had been recognized by the literary critics of 1964? Might another five or ten fledgling Phil Dicks have appeared shortly thereafter? We'll never know. And there are artistic costs on the other side of the breach as well. Consider Kurt Vonnegut, who, in dodging the indignities of the SF label, apparently renounced the iconographic fuel that fed his best work.

What would a less-prejudiced model of SF's relation to the larger enterprise look like? Well, nobody likes to be labeled an experimental writer, yet experimental writing flourishes in quiet pockets of the literary landscape—and, however little read, is granted its place. When claims are made for the wider importance of this or that experimental writer— Dennis Cooper, say, or Mark Leyner—those claims aren't rebuffed on grounds that are, quite literally, *categorical*. SF could ask this much: that its more hermetic or hardcore writers be respected for pleasing their small audience of devotees, that its rising stars be given a fair chance on the main stage. What's missing, too, is a "Great Books" theory of post-1970 SF — one which asserts a shelf of Disch, Ballard, Dick, Le Guin, Delany and Russell Hoban, Joanna Russ, Geoff Ryman, Christopher Priest, David Foster Wallace, plus books like Pamela Zoline's *The Heat Death of the Universe*, Walter Tevis's *Mockingbird*, D. G. Compton's *The Continuous Katherine Mortenhoe*, Lawrence Shainberg's *Memories of Amnesia*, Ted Mooney's *Easy Travel to Other Planets*, Margaret Atwood's *Handmaid's Tale*, and Thomas Palmer's *Dream Science* as the standard. Such a theory would also have to push a lot of the genre's self-enshrined but archaic "classics" onto the junkheap.

Tomorrow's readers, born in dystopian cities, educated on computers, and steeped in media recursions of SF iconography, won't notice if the novels they read are set in the future or the present. Savvy themselves, they won't care if certain characters babble techno-jargon and others don't. Some of those readers, though, will graduate from a craving for fictions that flatter and indulge their fantasies to that precious appetite for fictions that provoke, disturb, and complicate by a manipulation of those same narrative cravings. They'll learn to appreciate the difference, say, between Terry McMillan and Toni Morrison, between Tom Robbins and Thomas Pynchon, between Roger Zelazny and Samuel Delany — distinctions forever too elusive to be made in publishers' categories, or on booksellers' shelves.

Of course, short of a utopian reconfiguration of the publishing, bookselling, and reviewing apparatus the barrier — though increasingly contested and absurd — will remain. Still, we can dream. The 1973 Nebula Award *should* have gone to *Gravity's Rainbow*, the 1976 award to *Ratner's Star*. Soon after, the notion of "science fiction" ought to have been gently and lovingly dismantled, and the writers dispersed: children's fantasists here, hardware-fetish thriller writers here, novelizers of films-both-real-and-imaginary here. Most important, a ragged handful of heroically enduring and ambitious speculative fabulators should have embarked for the rocky realms of midlist, out-of-category fiction. And there — don't wake me now, I'm fond of this one — they should have been welcomed.

Respectability

GORDON VAN GELDER

Unlike a lot of SF fans I know, I'm neither a first nor an only child. My older brother had been around for three and a half years when I came along, and he never let me forget that fact. As per the rules of *The Official Older Sibling Handbook* (I'm *sure* that such a book exists, I just know it, but rule number one is that younger siblings can never ever see it). Nothing I did ever impressed my brother. Whatever I said or did, my brother had already seen or done better.

As I grew up, I recognized that I couldn't win this game, so I stopped trying so hard to impress him. And that, of course, was when I discovered he'd been impressed all along.

Various critics credit the birth of science fiction to Mary Shelley, Edgar Allan Poe, Jules Verne, H. G. Wells, or Hugo Gernsback, but nobody yet has suggested that SF is older than realistic, "mainstream" fiction. As Robert Killheffer points out in his column this month, SF is like many other contemporary genres in that it matured in the pulps during the early part of this century.

When is it ever going to realize it can't win the game of trying to impress the mainstream?

My lament this month is brought on by an article in the June *Village Voice Literary Supplement* by Jonathan Lethem. In "Close Encounters: The Squandered Promise of Science Fiction," Jonathan argues that science fiction missed its opportunity in the 1970s to bring down the genre walls and merge with the mainstream. He uses the fact that Arthur C. Clarke's *Rendezvous with Rama* beat out Thomas Pynchon's *Gravity's Rainbow* for the 1973 Nebula Award as a tombstone to mark the point where science fiction blew its chance.

I consider Jonathan one of the most widely and well-read people I know—it's scarcely a coincidence that he contributes this month's "Curiosities" column, since he has been steering me toward good books for years. But I think he's off target here.

Jonathan's main argument is that SF's 1960s New Wave produced masterpieces in the early 1970s like *Dhalgren*, *A Scanner Darkly*, *The Dispossessed*, and *334*, and as a result of these books it stood poised on the brink of literary acceptability. Then:

just as SF's best writers began to beg the question of whether SF might be literature, American literary fiction began to open to the modes it had excluded. Writers like Donald Barthelme, Richard Brautigan, and Robert Coover restored the place of the imaginative and surreal, while others like Don DeLillo and Joseph McElroy began to contend with the emergent technoculture. William Burroughs and Thomas Pynchon did a little of both. The result was that the need to recognize SF's accomplishments dwindled away.

The result, says Jonathan, is that

SF's literary writers exist now in a twilight world, neither respectable nor commercially viable. Their work drowns in a sea of garbage in bookstores, while much of SF's promise is realized elsewhere by writers too savvy or oblivious to bother with its stigmatized identity.

Jonathan goes on to wish that:

the notion of "science fiction" ought to have been gently and lovingly dismantled, and the writers dispersed: children's fantasists here, hardware-fetish thriller writers here, novelizers of films-both-real-and-imaginary here. Most important, a ragged handful of heroically enduring and ambitious speculative fabulators should have embarked for the rocky realms of midlist, out-of-category fiction.

Okay, let me say now that aesthetically I'm very sympathetic with Jonathan—in fact, I proposed something similar on a convention panel in 1992, only to have Barry Malzberg lecture me for twenty minutes. "I turned my back on science fiction in 1976," declared Barry, "and I was wrong. The genre is bigger than us; we are here because of it."

Having spent four years in ivy-covered academic halls and ten years at a mainstream publisher editing books in this so-called twilight world, I agree mostly with Barry nowadays.

Today the term "science fiction" encompasses so much that I'm leery of generalizing about it, but indulge me. Of all the genres, SF is fundamentally the most radical—unlike mysteries or romances or westerns, it can rewrite all the rules, or make up the rules as it goes along. (Indeed, Jonathan Lethem's *Amnesia Moon* is a good example of a book that plays fair with the reader but changes the rules in midstream.) As John W. Campbell always argued, it has the widest scope and the most freedom of any literary form, and consequently it intimidates many readers. A science fiction novel can challenge a reader in ways no other novel can.

In a *New Yorker* review circa 1990, John Updike argued that SF relies on spectacle for its entertainment value, and as Aristotle taught us, spectacle is the most base of all artistic goals. Personally, I think it's foolish to deny the spectacular nature of SF. This genre is a form of *popular* literature; its inherent goal is to entertain (unlike much mainstream fiction). Some people will forever adopt the attitude espoused by John Updike and look down on SF because it remains a story-driven and primarily popular art form.

Those people seem to be the ones whose respect Jonathan seeks, if I understand him correctly when he refers to "literary respectability." When I hear those words, I think of green pastures on the other side of the fence. They mark the exact spot where I disagree with Jonathan. For one thing, as I've stated many times in many places, things are not better in the mainstream than they are in the genre. Indeed, they're generally worse: "the rocky realms of midlist, out-of-category fiction" are the one place where books get ignored most. I once sat on a panel with William Trotter, whose first novel *Winter Fire* was published handsomely in those rocky realms. "How many reviews did you get?" I asked. "Well, we got the trade reviews, and the *Times* review was okay." When I asked if he got any other reviews, he said, "Yes, there was one other — in *Deathrealm*."

The commercial prospects are even worse. It would be improper for me to cite sales figures and such, but I believe that the careers of such novelists as Jack Womack, Jonathan Carroll, and Jack Cady would have foundered on those rocky shores after two or three novels each were it not for the genre and genre editors. I could go on. I could cite the careers of mainstream novelists that *have* petered out because nobody would publish their third or fourth books, but to keep this short I'll limit myself to pointing out the ironic fact that some of the writers Jonathan names as "ascendant powers" in our "literary culture" don't sell nearly as well as do Jonathan's own books. Trust me. I've seen the figures.

Enough about the grass-is-greener syndrome; every writer is prone to some envy. It's an occupational hazard. What I really want to address is this notion of "literary respectability." I have grave problems with it. Perhaps in 1973 it meant something different, but here in 1998, it's more than forty years after such American masterpieces as A *Canticle for Leibowitz* and *Fahrenheit 451* were born in the SF genre, thirty-plus years since Daniel M. Keyes illuminated the human condition with help from a mouse named Algernon, more than a quarter of a century after J. G. Ballard *Crash*ed into the literary field and Harlequin let loose those jelly beans. The science fiction field has fostered and grown numerous such works whose literary merits are, to my mind, incontrovertible. In light of the evidence they provide, I think that any critic who summarily dismisses SF is guilty of literary bigotry, prejudging the fiction by the color of its cover. (Please note that I'm not questioning anyone's right to read whatever suits their tastes. But, I think that a critic who dismisses an entire category of fiction — any category — shouldn't keep a closed mind.)

And who really needs Archie Bunker's respect? At least my older brother kept an open mind, but people like some editors at the *New York Times Book Review* obviously don't, and I see no virtue in seeking their approval.

I do think Jonathan Lethem's right in pointing out that the SF genre no longer means what it used to mean. The SF publishing category hasn't entirely kept pace with the tastes of American readers. A lot of writers and readers are stuck in the twilight because publishing doesn't know the right way to put the two together (and the few efforts at doing so, such as Dell's "Cutting Edge" trade paperback line about four years ago, never really got a chance). But I think the answer lies in shifting the boundaries of the genre, not in knocking them down.

Let me end with one brief anecdote. In college, I studied with novelist Stephen Wright (*M31, Going Native*) and I still run into him occasionally. Last time I saw him, we got on the subject of how nice it was that Steven Millhauser won the Pulitzer Prize, and Stephen — who is wonderfully opinionated — started sounding off about the Pulitzers. "Did you know that those bastards at Columbia wouldn't give the prize to *Gravity's Rainbow*? The judges all wanted it to win, but the award administrators were afraid of it, so they gave it to something safe . . . some Civil War novel, I think."

In point of fact, Michael Shaara's lovely novel *The Killer Angels* won the Pulitzer in 1975 (Eudora Welty's *The Optimist's Daughter* won in 1973, and no award was given in 1974). But if there's any truth to Stephen's claim, and I believe there is, are we to conclude that the mainstream missed its opportunity to merge with SF? Or should we just decide that we're different from our big brother and get on with life?

Gatekeepers and Literary Bigots

GEORGE ZEBROWSKI

The community of science fiction writers and readers can take pride in two things.

One is the body of novels and short fiction, now going back more than a century, which is considered of permanent value (we'll call it the canon).

Another is the claim that SF is a literature of ideas, and that thinking, both scientific and philosophical, is the center of it.

Let's consider the "canon" idea first. In order to have such a body of work, in which a novel like *The Stars My Destination* by Alfred Bester, to take an example that is agreed upon by even the most oppositely minded individuals in the field, may be considered one of the permanent works, one must start with a set of measuring sticks, according to which the work succeeds or fails. These measures can clearly be discerned in the agreed-upon canon.

But one might start with a different set of values for great science fiction—ones of thoughtfulness and ideas, and above all the demand that "thinking" be present in a work—and come up with a perhaps unfamiliar canon. One might even go on to ask which values "should" one hold, and even whether this question can be usefully asked.

I have often attempted to make such a "canon of ideas and thought" and been quite surprised to realize that the accepted canon exists as part of a literary social system, which we are free, if we think for ourselves, to reject.

More on the above later.

Criticism and reviewing also exist as part of a social convention of comment, commercial struggle, and cultural struggle over turf—who will say what is what and who is who—and that these gatekeepers work to prevent free and independent judgment among both readers and writers (though they may deny it), by putting forward certain kinds of value-models to be admired and copied, just as an organism's DNA strives to project itself into the future.

At the end of these considerations one may come to the conclusion that one is free to follow not "what is" but "what should be," and that "what should be" is a diversity of things.

How much of a field of action is there in all fiction, in the SF novel; how much possibility, how many value-models yet undiscovered, how many one-of-a-kind models? All these kinds of searching questions should be necessary to the science fiction reader, and to the writer engaged in the enterprise that is perhaps more ambitious than anyone realizes, so important that its still wide-open way cannot be adequately discussed without serious theorizing. Certainly the purely literary approach must fail, because it will hold up aesthetics over the demands of originality and thought, and it almost always refuses to discuss the "experience" of reading an individual author, whose fleeting magic may escape one reader and not another, and whose "way" may outweigh all other considerations for a large group of readers.

Nabokov once said that he divided all novels into those he wished he'd written and those he had written. At first this seems silly, but why should any writer admit to the virtues of a book he knows is great, a part of the canon according to law, but which he cannot appreciate? There are those who seem to cast a wide net and appreciate great variety, but they do recall the "girl who liked all the boys," or the "boy who chased anything in skirts."

A good theoretician will carve up the map into the variety of good books, as they exist even in territories foreign to him. He can then say that these are the discovered ways of being good and give them a salute; but, if he is ambitious, he will head off for parts unknown. He will include, but he will also search the frontier.

Recent discussions about SF have lost the simplicity of truthful observation and statement, and appear to justify whatever a particular author or reader happens to be doing in the marketplace. But in fact the theoretical questions about SF's possibilities, especially its critical potential, were answered successfully a long time ago, but are simply being ignored by people unwilling to think rigorously. Discussions about SF have lost their sense of reality—both of SF's proper subject matter and its manner of publication.

You can learn the insights achieved by SF's best theoreticians by rote, and even find that the catechism is supremely flexible and open when you encounter the difficulties of practicing it. "Science fiction is about the human impact of future changes in science and technology," Asimov wrote with cogency, echoing the conclusive thought of Campbell, Blish, Tenn, and later taken up by Lem to great outcry by the damned. The "human impact" makes it fiction, the "changes," whether they be strictly of science or technology, make it SF. You can just go with the changes and the human impact, if you like, which broadens it all inclusively.

The question I often ask is: if one is going to write SF, why not go the distance? Why water it down? Why not learn all the needed science, technology, and thinking to do the work? Well, you don't have to do all that to write science fiction, a colleague once told me with a smile, and the assumptions behind the idea filled me with horror, because content and actual thought are the heart of SF. Think about the human impact of science, about our human experience of science and its philosophical consequences (and philosophical means nothing more than the effort to actually think about subject matter in a rigorous way—the birthright of every human being: you either think successfully or you don't is all that the word philosophical means).

Think of the massive body of science and its philosophy as a great attractor around which we wordsmiths circle, thinking of the dramatic, human possibilities. Suddenly there is an expansion, as with the early inflation of the universe, or the jump to blastocyst in an organism—and from there the work begins to grow and acquire character.

Freeman Dyson has written that great works of science—Einstein's equations, Goedel's Proof, the description of black holes—are also works of art, because they possess the qualities of uniqueness, beauty, and unexpectedness, and because they are constructions describing an imagination greater than our own—nature's. He is describing the wellspring of all great SF, the growing body of knowledge and theory in a hundred different arenas that is the proper central sun of SF, about which we should think critically and write of hopeful and fearful possibilities for our kind.

That's all there is to it; but try to do it. Discussions of SF, because they rarely start at genuine "first things," exhibit a poverty of assumptions, making the speakers travelers who plan their departure from the middle and then attempt the journey whose starting point is impossible and the chance of arriving nil.

The agony is that well thought and well written beats brilliantly written and badly thought. Is the content more important? Yes—but try not to ignore the literary graces; one would not wish to eat the efforts of a great chef off the floor. But significance does not lie in a mandarin cultivation of grace over content. We don't have to deliberately ignore the literary virtues; but there will be writers of great thought and minor literary skills. Right now we have more of the skilled over the thoughtful.

So how to get there? Avoid fashions and think for yourself, away from the homogenized fiction of workshops and credentials. To start one must try, then one must work at it. One must think, not only be a good writer. One must be ready to hold the love of SF's possibilities and accomplishment above popularity. A hard road—which is why all the other roads are taken so often. This is not advice that financial survivors wish to hear. It is a call to accomplishment that was made by James Blish and others in past times, and which they did not always heed themselves.

"Did you ever admire an empty-headed writer for his style?" Kurt Vonnegut once asked. We do it all the time, unfortunately; but the new wrinkle in SF's discussion groups is that we now have empty-headed theoreticians who fail to start at the beginning before they grope the elephant.

The theoretical answers to the confusions of critics like Jonathan Lethem or the exhaustion of Thomas Disch have been stated definitively by Gregory Benford: ". . . the quantity of fine written SF has never been higher . . ." To know this one must go out and examine the production of several years, something that many critics do not seem to do; instead, they rely on their unscholarly impressions, which may be years old. Benford continues, "The advance of hard SF after them (the New Wave of the '60s and '70s) used weaponry they had devised . . ." But—"At the core of SF lies the experience of science. This makes the genre finally hostile to ... fashions in criticism, for it values its empirical ground. ... SF novels give us worlds which are not to be taken as metaphors, but as real. We are asked to participate in wrenchingly strange events, not merely watch them for clues as to what they're really about. SF pursues a 'realism of the future' and so does not take its surrealism neat, unlike much avant-garde which is easily confused with it. The social-realist followers of James have yet to fathom this. The Mars and stars and digital deserts of our best novels are, finally, to be taken as real, as if to say: life isn't like this, it *is* this."

That *Gravity's Rainbow* lost to *Rendezvous with Rama* in the 1973 Nebula voting is significant today only if we understand that the subtleties of each novel lay in vastly different worlds, and that they each resonated with a very different database within their supportive readers. Yet the proponents of Pynchon reacted with literary bigotry, ignoring the fact that Pynchon's very nomination was a tribute (quite something to an outsider to SF circles), and spoke of Clarke with the derisiveness of French critics referring to British Cinema as an oxymoron. Clarke's novel possesses rich subtleties that belong to SF and to science, but which exist behind a screen to the insufficiently prepared (who simply do not know how to read Clarke). It is a graceful piece of writing, and bears rereading. It tries not to exist in its time, but looks beyond temporal provincialisms, as does all of Clarke's work. "Throughout this century, conventional literature persistently avoided thinking about conceptually altered tomorrows, and retreated into a realist posture of fiction of ever-smaller compass," writes Benford. It is to this degree that watered-down SF, often so well written, continues to emulate contemporary letters, and by which it fails, along with its theoretical defenders, to be a match for the writers and thinkers of hard SF, who unlike their detractors have willingly learned from all the examples around them, who do not repudiate the past but see into it (we are all time travelers, are we not?) questioningly, asking what it was that made sense to the readers of the time, rather than reducing it to nonsense with present-blinded eyes.

There is another canon of SF in this century, outside the territories of today's gatekeepers and literary bigots, whose first aim is to hold the power of saying who's who and what's what, with money or with insistent words. It is a canon that speaks only from its pages, to readers who read and think for themselves, free of critics and reviewers who presuppose everything and thus skew unfettered reactions. Unknown to each other, these readers, many of them writers, have made a list, to which they add yearly. It cannot be collated into one list, except by Borges, who cannot and would not show it to us. And I wish I had that list.

I showed this essay to a sci-fi writer who lives down the street from me, figuratively speaking.

"Well, what do you think?"

"Are you kidding? It's too hard to do, what you're asking."

"So what do you do instead? What do you use?"

He shrugged. "Other SF, where it's all predigested."

"Don't you feel any shame?"

"Nah, it's all rock and roll. I'm a star. I get the money and the girls."

"And you're happy with that?"

"Yeah, I am."

"Really?" I asked.

"It's all I learned to do."

"And it's too late now?"

"Yeah, it's too late. Look, you're a nice guy. But what do you want from me, anyway? To make me look bad?"

"Well, no, I'm sorry. You do that yourself in the eyes of people who think."

"Look, my readers read with their gut, not with their brains. I know it looks bad . . . so make me some new readers."

"Who made them that way?" I asked. When he failed to answer, I said, "Of course, you're free to write whatever you please, except that you may not be doing that. You may be writing what someone unknown to you, or the marketplace's demand for entertainment, has taught you, without you even thinking about it. And when you make a token effort to think about it, you start your argument so far along that your premise is virtually your conclusion. That's not thinking. It's repeating the premise, following a recipe, begging the question."

"Science fiction is not about thinking. It's about fiction — and style. Ideas are a dime a dozen, and thinking is a bore."

"Well, then all is given away, all is lost. The looters from the media are at the gates of SF City, but it has already destroyed itself from within, having fed itself too long on its own inheritance. New SF City can rise only by reflecting an ever-expanding knowledge base, not weaving ever more finely spun versions of hand-me-down ideas and themes."

"Are you fucking serious?" he asked.

"Look. Imaginings are like lines of credit. They can go on for some time by borrowing from each other. But somewhere in the activity there must be an inflow of real money. In science and science fiction that inflow comes in the form of new observations and experiments — or the imaginings grow and are shored up only within their own frames of reference, with diminishing hold on the world outside. The result is bankruptcy in the financial world, failed theories in science, and triviality in science fiction."

"But it sells!"

"Only because not enough readers have seen what's been done. That's accomplished by abolishing backlists."

"So? A book you haven't read is new to you."

"Fine, if money is all you want. How about the accomplishment? It's the same even if it's never published, just like the high jump record no one can ever take away from you."

"Yeah, yeah, yeah. Get real."

"Get real? Literature's great creative genre has to get real and give away everything to get published?"

"You force me to say yes. T. S. Eliot, I think, once said that man can't stand too much reality. I need a drink. Happy now?"

And I knew that it had cost him to write against the grain.

Good News about SF in Bad Publishing Times; or, Growth, Change, and the Preservation of Quality in the Literature of Genre

DAVID G. HARTWELL

This evening is a celebration of many successes, and we have cause to approach the future of science fiction and fantasy optimistically. I remind both the nominees and those who wish they'd been nominated that there are more awards for SF and fantasy than ever before in the late '90s, and in more places in the world too, even one recently held in the Eiffel Tower — and according to Norman Spinrad, we might have a

Nebula ceremony there one day. And even outside the genre, we have had some pleasant surprises in recent years—a PEN-West best novel award to Molly Gloss's *The Dazzle of Day*, surely the most prestigious literary award yet given in the United States to an SF novel. We have also in our community a MacArthur grant winner, Octavia Butler. So to reverse Jerry Pournelle's famous line, delivered when accepting an award for another writer, awards and award nominations will help get you through times of no money.

Books   After the 1995 consolidation of North American wholesale distributors, which was the biggest distribution disaster to hit United States magazines and paperback books since the demise of the American New Company in 1957, there are SF and fantasy genre lines at fewer companies, and even fewer sales forces. While a great deal of time and energy has so far been spent developing electronic text retrieval systems and bookselling, these are not yet significant economic forces in SF and fantasy, except in selling used and rare books—it seems there is a great demand for out-of-print material. Also, little or no editing occurs with original material published through the Internet, so that readers may experience online the delights and horrors of the slush pile, without the intervention of editors, copy editors, or even type designers. However, nearly every SF line now has a hardcover component that is essential to its publishing program. While fewer books in our genres will be published in mass market paperback this year than last, a trend accelerating since 1995, more fantasy and SF is appearing in hardcover than ever before, even more than in the boom years of the 1980s.

I have been working for the last decade or so to help Tor, my employer, build the largest SF and fantasy hardcover line in the history of SF publishing, and now Tor alone publishes more hardcover SF in a season than the whole industry did a little over a decade ago. This trend began in the early 1980s and has now changed the field so completely that SF is no longer principally driven by mass market sales. This is the biggest economic and publishing change since the late 1950s, when the dominance of the magazines gave way to the paperbacks. The lion's share of the best books in SF each year is now published first in hardcover.

This is good for the field. Hardcovers are "real books"—they get reviewed, preserved on library shelves, are not disposable the way magazines and paperbacks are, or at least the way they are outside of the genre. Hardcovers are sold in bookstores, mainly, and are kept on bookstore shelves for months, sometimes years, until they are sold or remaindered. Paperbacks have a short sales life in bookstores, and an even shorter one on racks in airports and drugstores and newsstands. They regularly get used up and discarded after only a few readings. And most magazines are sold for a week or a month and, if sold, are thrown away after a month or two. People outside the field perceive SF and fantasy as more adult, more serious, and higher class if it is in hardcover.

Meanwhile the Science Fiction Book Club is expanding, buying more titles per month, adding more money into the profit calculations in SF and fantasy publishing, and the club selects primarily from the pool of hardcover titles. The chief beneficiaries may be younger readers, who do not otherwise buy many, or any, hardcovers.

Of course a large number of new books and reprints of older books are now released in trade paperback. The contraction of the backlist in mass market paperbacks has been going on for more than twenty years, at the same time as the frontlist has been growing, but that combination of trends is slowing considerably as the superstores stock backlist in depth while the frontlist shrinks. Trade paperbacks have come to the forefront as the economical way to reprint after a hardcover edition and enlarge the readership, and to make a profit on a sale of a few thousand copies in cases where you cannot print a mass market edition — either because you have no mass market slot or because the projected distribution in mass market is not profitable. Of course you can also reprint a classic work. (At least two new classics lines in trade paperback are appearing this year, one in the United Kingdom and one in the United States.) Or you can launch a new writer in trade paperback, and that is happening with some regularity now. The trade paperback is perceived as the more literary form of paperback publishing, the medium in which the cutting-edge literary fiction of the mainstream is published.

The covers of the hardbacks and trade paperbacks are on the whole sophisticated and deliberately literary, not the traditional illustration we in the genre have been used to for decades. This strategy seems to be working well, in part because it is aimed at adults, and adults, not teenagers, buy the majority of hardcovers and trade paperbacks. In the face of Gallup polls and other published market research in the 1990s, no one can support the claim that SF is still a literature for kids. Most SF and fantasy today sells to an adult audience; the typical buyer is over thirty, and getting older. This is why so much effort in recent years has been put into Reading for the Future, and into publishing specifically young adult SF—we want to regain the young SF audience that the field outgrew in the 1970s and 1980s. It is ironic that the trade paperbacks of today in SF look more like the Ballantine books of the 1950s, when Richard Powers did all the covers, than they look like contemporary mass market SF.

And yet to the best of my knowledge every SF line is experiencing continuing success with their lead books in mass market. The huge companies that now do mass market distribution want to sell leads effectively, without the distractions of smaller books. So there is an upside to the mass distribution consolidation, namely that the top books by established writers can be distributed more efficiently and often in greater numbers than ever before. We may disagree with this principle, and nearly every editor I know does, because it so limits what else can be published in the mass market, but it certainly benefits the top writers in all fields and their publishers.

So if you are a first novelist and you manage to sell your first novel, you are much more likely to be published in hardcover, which means a more enduring book, more reviews, and so on. If you are an established writer whose books are published as lead titles, more copies of them will be sold. And if you are a writer in midcareer whose books were published in the midlist but who was shaken out in the recent shakeouts in the marketplace, there is an increasingly competent small-press movement that has increasingly sophisticated technological tools and is looking for good books to publish.

Many of you are readers of the *New York Review of Science Fiction*, which I publish, whose editorial policy is to discuss the strengths and weaknesses of good books. We at the *NYRSF* find six to ten books a month to discuss, and do not feel we succeed in covering all the good books available to review, so it is clear to me that the field is producing an abundance of good books.

Short Fiction   In recent years I have been doing an annual *Year's Best SF* volume for HarperPrism and so have had a chance to read widely in short fiction. I can say confidently that the news is good there. In the major magazines the quality control is excellent; competent professional editing is nearly universal, whatever the editorial taste. While the original anthologies are usually not as good as the average issue of one of the magazines, they still constitute a significant market and have supported an abundance of genre writing this year.

So a lot of short fiction is getting published professionally, making writers' reputations and growing name recognition for them. A significant though smaller proportion of the short fiction is getting published in reprint anthologies, a form that has always underpinned the field. Although generally avoided by the major houses these days, reprint anthologies crop up frequently in the late 1990s, thanks to book clubs, small presses that have benefited enormously from the new electronic technologies, and book chains (some of which are now instant remainder publishers). There are fewer copies of fewer professional genre magazines than ever, but more SF and fantasy anthologies and collections are being published in more places.

It is in short fiction that the small press is making a particularly significant contribution in recent years, both in the growth of semiprofessional magazines such as *Interzone, On Spec,* and *Eidolon* and in the continuing publication of single-author collections, a form that was taken over in the 1980s by small-press publishers from Arkham to Ziesing, some of whom are actually thriving. We will all feel the absence of Jim Turner, whose nearly thirty years of editorship at Arkham and then Golden Gryphon showed what a fine editor could accomplish in the small press. Jim's taste and professionalism put many to shame, and gave his peers a standard to live up to.

Postmodern Publishing and SF   Speculative fiction—at least that part of it attempting to escalate out of genre into the mainstream—has never been healthier, although much of it is published completely outside genre markets by publishers and editors who are under the impression that they are publishing contemporary nongenre fiction. And perhaps they are. Examples are Mary Doria Russell's novels, Jonathan Lethem's recent work, and the Four Walls Eight Windows publishing program. But speculative fiction is subject to the ups and downs of the cold world of the mainstream literary midlist, where a much higher percentage of books lose money than in genre.

The hallmark of such publishing programs (and I suppose I should include the trade paper reprints from Vintage) is that, somewhat like Hollywood, they make little effort to distinguish between fantasy and SF, in part because they see no difference. This means quality control is based entirely upon the prose style and literary marketing signals generated by the text. Postmodern is the cool thing to be just now. So a lot of writers of real talent who are more comfortable outside genre publishing—for example, Karen Joy Fowler, William Gibson, James Morrow, Jack Womack, Paul Di Filippo, and Octavia Butler—are finding homes in nongenre lists and yet still sticking with the social field of SF, appearing at conventions and so forth. Some of them are in the room today. Genre virtues such as consistent world building or scientific verisimilitude are somewhat irrelevant to the marketing of their works now, but genre subculture support still underpins much of their careers.

The important thing for us is that they do not reject genre support. From Tennessee Williams to Kurt Vonnegut to Donald E. Westlake, writers have started out associated with genre SF and fantasy and then left—that's not new. These 1990s writers are sticking around. We always knew that top-notch scientists in the mainstream (Eric Temple Bell, Norbert Wiener, Sheldon Glashow, Marvin Minsky, and many others) paid attention to SF, and still do—Freeman Dyson is going to be Science Guest of Honor at a convention (VikingCon) next year—but now some of our more ambitious writers are getting mainstream publication and attention without having to deny us (in the Biblical sense).

The mainstream, at least a little bit, is joining us. Sure, there are some self-consciously postmodern writers who appropriate SF as just another pop culture repository of collage-making material, but they are not terribly important on the literary scene or relevant to SF and fantasy. More significant, there are a lot of literary writers whose work, had it paid a little more attention to genre attitudes and virtues such as verisimilitude and plotting, would have fallen solidly in the genre. And sometimes does—Russell's first two novels, *The Sparrow* and *Children of God,* are more closely related to genre SF, without being labeled so by the publisher, than some works that appear wearing the genre trademark. Last year John Updike, Gore Vidal, and others published novels that were by every useful standard SF. And Vintage Contemporaries, the leading literary trade paperback line in the United States, having reprinted almost all of the works of Philip K. Dick is now doing Alfred Bester, Theodore Sturgeon, and Thomas M. Disch's SF—as literature. As a consequence less academic attention is paid to SF and fantasy as a discrete genre in the late 1990s than there was in the 1970s or 1980s, but the attention is of higher quality. The genre label is less stigmatizing than it used to be, and more works are talked about for their ideas and execution. There is now an academic establishment, several journals, many serious SF courses, and fewer shallow courses that merely use our genre to teach science or religion or whatever. Many academics do not share the goals and attitudes of SF writers or of the SF community, but they now recognize that those goals exist and often take them into account when discussing writers and works. And the SF community has spawned its own academics: Samuel R. Delany, Joanna Russ, Brian Stableford, John Kessel, Kim Stanley Robinson, Damien Broderick, F. Brett Cox, and Andy Duncan. In differing ways these critics are influencing the way our literature is taught and studied.

But that's a topic for another day. Tonight we have considered growth and change and the preservation of quality in the marketplace as a prelude to celebrating high excellence and achievement in the SF and fantasy literature of the recent past. Tonight is the eve of the greatest media event of the decade in SF, whether that invokes the new *Star Wars* film, the Y2K problem, or the turn of the millennium itself, and while we all anticipate riding the next big wave into the future, it is fitting that we stop for a moment and honor the literature that is the source of all the cultural spinoffs and the wellspring of images that feeds the media.

The Truth about Sci-Fi Movies, Revealed at Last

BILL WARREN

Growing up in a small town on the Oregon coast, I felt isolated from the people around me, and immersed myself in science fiction. I loved the books (though rarely read the magazines, since, or so I thought, all the good stuff would wind up in anthologies), I loved comic books — and I loved the movies, too. Later, I encountered science fiction fandom, and then "prodom" as well, assuming that I would meet others who loved all three of those sources of my great childhood and adolescent joy. I was puzzled that while I often met people who liked comic books and movies, or books and comics, or sometimes even books and movies, I virtually never encountered anyone who loved all three. The movies were often viewed with contempt and scorn, sometimes because they weren't like written science fiction.

That baffled me, because as far as I was concerned, it was akin to complaining that watermelon wasn't like pizza. Both food, to be sure, both fun to eat — but so different in their very nature that I was mystified people even bothered to compare them. I never did. They were both in one broad category: popular entertainment in the form of science fiction, and that was about it. Even when plots were similar, I never thought of the cliché "the book is better than the movie." The movie may not be *like* the book, but it wasn't to me a matter of the book being *better*, just that the book was intended for a particular, rather narrow audience, and the movie was intended for a different, more general audience. I still feel much the same way, which can sometimes drive friends to distraction. Sure, I knew that *The Day the Earth Stood Still* was better than *The Day the World Ended*, but I wanted to see both of them. I didn't expect either to be any more like each other than either were like written SF, even if *The Day the Earth Stood Still* was based on a published SF story. It was better than the Corman movie because it was better *cinematically*, not because it was more like written SF.

Some people consider that attacking SF movies for failing to be like SF books is a holy crusade; while victory may never be achieved, the battle has to be continued for the honor of science fiction. To me, this implies that they think science fiction fans/readers and writers somehow *own* science fiction. It's less a matter of being upset that Hollywood makes bad science fiction movies now and then, but more of a sense of indignation, moral outrage: how *dare* they use *our* stuff and not use it in ways that *we* approve.

While there are many people in the science fiction field, both fans and pros, who understand movies and who judge science fiction films on the same basis they judge other *movies*, rather than books, too many simply don't get this distinction at all. "The book was better than the movie," they claim — and they don't mean that as a book, the book was better than the movie was as a movie. They think the two can be directly compared.

But except in a very limited, essentially pointless sense, they can't be. It's not just a matter of the basic differences between the two media (a book doesn't have a music track, for example), but of how we respond to the two. For one thing, reading a book is generally a solitary experience; watching a movie, under ideal circumstances anyway, is a group experience, and this distinction not only affects how we respond to the work itself, but how the creators are able to evoke responses. Even the greatest comedies work better — are *funnier* — when viewed with a responsive audience than while alone. The same is true of thrillers, mysteries, musicals, etc. Suspense can be heightened when you're in a group that is responding in much the same manner as you.

In a book, we can read back over earlier material without any trouble; except on home video, movies are perceived linearly; we have to take them as they come, or not at all — and this is built into how movies are constructed. It makes not less narrative complexity, but complexity of a different order. Also, with movies, it's (usually) not a matter of reaching for the lowest common denominator, but broadening the experience, making it accessible to most of the audience. Sometimes, this is the same thing; it's hard to find subtlety in *Armageddon* — but *Dark City* is sophisticated and intelligent, while still satisfying most of the needs of the action crowd.

Movies are not the same as books, but they are not intrinsically inferior to books, unless you tautologically believe that writing is the ultimate art form. Movies are not intended to compete with or to supplant books, not even the ones they're based on. A friend once asked James M. Cain how he could let Hollywood ruin his books. Cain said that the books weren't ruined; there they were, right there on the shelf. . . .

There are some who want, almost desperately, to believe that Hollywood makes "sci-fi" but, say, Larry Niven writes science fiction. The trouble is that this "sci-fi is bad science fiction" definition exists exclusively within SF fandom, and not even every fan goes along with it. To the world at large, "sci-fi" means "science fiction," good and bad, plausible and im-, space opera and diamond-hard science fiction. But still, on the Internet, in letters, some fanzines, and elsewhere, you'll find the narrower definition of "sci-fi" offered as Revealed Truth, not just an opinion. (You can make the eyes of these people turn into little pinwheels by pointing out that the term was apparently coined twice, quite independently: once by Forrest J. Ackerman, and once by Robert A. Heinlein, who used it in correspondence. And just like Ackerman, when he used the term, Heinlein meant "science fiction.")

Sometimes, this shifts into a belief that it's the scientific implausibilities that make science fiction movies bad (even though, for example, "Cavorite" doesn't make Wells's *The First Men in the Moon* a bad novel). At least one company was started that, for a fee, would vet scripts for scientific blunders and offer alternatives of greater scientific verisimilitude. The founders of the company were genuinely surprised, even hurt, that Hollywood didn't give a damn. Even bad screenwriters and directors are aware that being scientifically accurate won't make a movie better — except for a tiny segment of the population, who, if they all stayed away from the movie, wouldn't make the tiniest dent in the box-office results. On the other hand, with some movies — in 1998, *Soldier* was a good example — the lack of scientific accuracy underscores the fact that the movie is bad in most other ways, too.

The bottom line in Hollywood is, of course, money. This isn't evil, it's a simple fact of economic life; those who rail against Hollywood are trying somehow to hold it to a higher standard than other big businesses. But that's what it is: a big business. A new version of *When Worlds Collide*, based on the novel rather than the George Pal movie, might well have resulted in a very good film — but would it have made as much money as the god-awful *Armageddon*? *Armageddon* was a much more surefire bet, with Bruce Willis playing his usual smart-ass, tough-as-nails role, a director whose last film (*The Rock*) had done very well, and a loud, noisy approach that included far more special effects than *When Worlds Collide* would have. *Deep Impact*, which was more like *When Worlds Collide* than it was like *Armageddon*, didn't do as well as *Armageddon*. And the idea is to make money.

To understand why Hollywood ends up making the choices it does, you have to think like a Hollywood executive. Not only does this mean deciding on the project most likely to make the most money — to hell with any considerations of quality — but there are aspects of pissing contests, too. As a "suit" you want your movie to make money, but also *more* money than your rival makes.

And there's more, too. I once asked a screenwriter (Terry Rossio) who's very savvy about written science fiction — read it all the time growing up — just why it is that movies are so rarely based on written science fiction. He said that it was a very good question, and there was a very long answer, but the short answer was that the kind of people who grow up reading science fiction don't become studio executives. They might well become movie writers, directors, special effects experts, even producers sometimes—but they don't run the studios.

And it's the people who *do* run the studios who decide what gets filmed. They don't *get* out-of-the-ordinary material, and assume the audiences don't, either, so they don't produce musicals or Westerns anymore. They don't understand the appeal of science fiction or horror (beyond "boo!"), so they finance spoofs of SF, horror, superhero adventures, etc., because they do understand comedy, and can't quite understand why anyone would take this kind of thing seriously. (Warners executives understood Joel Schumacher's approach to Batman, but never could figure out the more serious direction.) So budget considerations, lack of familiarity, and ignorance combine to cut back on the number of SF movies.

Don't think science fiction novels are being singled out to be ignored. The movie business has changed over the years. In the 1930s and '40s, people over twenty-one made up most of the moviegoing audience. Movies were often based on books and plays not so much because the ticket buyers were familiar with them, but because they appealed to the same demographics. As time passed, as television came in, and as people *under* twenty-one got more disposable income, those movies aimed at kids tended to make more money—sometimes a lot more money—than those aimed at adults. Movies based on novels and plays declined in number; when a novel is filmed today, often it's something along the lines of a Tom Clancy thriller, while the rest of even the best-seller list goes unfilmed (though some of them end up as TV miniseries).

In short, hardly *any* books are being filmed these days, because the target audience doesn't read books, and because the books that are written don't tell the stories that this audience wants to see. Like many generalizations, this is, of course, only generally true.

In the last twenty years, science fiction became redefined as a subset of the action thriller. The audience doesn't make a major distinction between, say, *Lethal Weapon 4* and *Armageddon*; they're both action thrillers, and that one happens to be science fiction simply means it will have more special effects in it. Which, of course, is another problem: special effects are goddamned expensive. Why, they can sometimes cost as much as half of Jim Carrey's salary—maybe even more—for a movie on the scale of the SF/action thrillers today.

So a filtering process is built in: even if you're one of the rare suits who reads and likes science fiction and who wants to film Heinlein or Asimov or Gibson or Niven or Bear or whoever won the last Nebula, you still have to answer to your bosses. Your movie is going to cost somewhere between eighty and a hundred million dollars; either you go the star route (like *Armageddon*) or the wow-look-at-these-effects route (like *Deep Impact*), but you have to be sure you're going to have a *return* on that money, or you'll be out of work a week after the movie flops at the box office. (And "flop" is a relative term; despite making about two hundred million dollars worldwide, *Armageddon* was considered a bit of a financial disappointment, in ratio of cost to profit.) And you reluctantly put aside your dream project of filming Vernor Vinge, and, sighing, try to figure a way to fit Leonardo DiCaprio into a big splashy space adventure—short on brains but long on action and thrills.

Of course, studios should take bigger chances on science fiction as well as in other areas, and like anyone who loves SF, I have my own list of books I think would make entertaining and profitable movies. This article isn't a defense of Hollywood; it's a regrettable explanation.

On the other hand, in the last few years, there has been an increasing number of attempts at filming science fiction "the right way" (i.e., like any other serious drama or adventure). Sometimes, the results aren't what SF fans and readers wanted—*Starship Troopers* is a case in point. I happen to like the film but many others didn't, and the film was a box-office failure—not because it didn't "live up to Heinlein," but because the intentions of director Paul Verhoeven didn't match the expectations of the general audience. *The Postman*, based on the novel by David Brin, has become the latest bad-movie whipping boy, although, like *Troopers*, it's a much better movie than its detractors claim. (In this case, it would *have* to be.)

And *Contact*, while more highly regarded than those two, also was felt to be lacking in some regard, although it was extremely faithful to Carl Sagan's novel. Bob Zemeckis clearly understands science fiction—his approach to time travel in the *Back to the Future* movies was as stringent as any hardcore SF fan could want—and he knew exactly what kind of movie he was making in *Contact*. It was made in a more direct style than *Starship Troopers* (which tried a European approach of playing it straight and satiric at the same time), and was less cluttered and ambitious than *The Postman*, and yet there was a lack here, too.

But despite the claims of some, in these cases, whatever's wrong with the movies has little or nothing to do with their being science fiction. Any mistakes that were made were the same kind you'd find in non–science fiction movies—and actually, these three films were more honestly conceived than an audience-manipulating melodrama like, say, *Stepmom*. Today, there are very few obstacles in Hollywood to filming science fiction, as long as a profit is visible. And as computer graphic effects improve, they'll become cheaper, which will allow slightly more marginal projects to be tackled.

But don't expect the members of SFWA to suddenly become squillionaires; most written SF is still too "esoteric" in the eyes of the people guarding the big stacks of money. The door has been cracked just a little; Asimov's *Bicentennial Man* is beginning production as I write. And Hollywood does recognize the name of Philip K. Dick. (He seems an unlikely choice, since so many of his stories consist of *internal* action— the thought processes of the hero—but he dealt a lot with paranoia, and that's an attitude Hollywood not only understands, but is proficient at translating into movie terms.)

I suspect that on the average, SFWA members are a bit more hip to the movie jive than an equivalent section of the general populace might be, but still they're mostly aware of the big-scale pictures—simply because those are the projects needing the biggest publicity pushes. Even so, how many recognized *The Truman Show* as science fiction? (Fans did, as it was nominated for a Hugo.) And how many had even heard of *Dark City*? These were the two best and most intelligent science fiction movies of 1998; what it lacked in originality, *The Truman Show* more than made up in style, wit, and compassion, and such a thorough development of its theme that it practically seethes with metaphorical interpretations. (Those who think the movie should have continued after Truman goes through the door simply don't understand what the movie was about.)

Dark City was a PKDick–like tale of paranoia, carefully worked out; initially, things are very weird, but the movie offers one revelation after another, until by the end, what has seemed to be a wildly stylized fantasy is revealed as a pretty straightforward science fiction tale. Yes, it's very pulpish, like a book Dick might have done as half of an Ace Double Novel, such as *Dr. Bloodmoney*. But it's honest, it sticks to its own premises very carefully, and is a very satisfying production all the way around.

The year had a few TV tie-ins, from a low of *Lost in Space* through an okay *Star Trek: Insurrection* to a modest high of *The X-Files*. And there was the usual junk — some really bad (*Disturbing Behavior*), some okay for what it was (*Deep Rising, The Faculty*), most of it, as with all creative endeavors, in the middle (*Phantoms*). The great huge hulking megaproductions in the SF arena were no better than those outside; *Armageddon* was the worst of the lot, while *Godzilla*, cursed with a moronic script, did manage to feature a few impressive monster-on-the-loose scenes. *Soldier* was just another hackneyed attempt to retell *Shane* in another venue, with a particularly foolish background.

Until the suits who never read science fiction, and have a hard time getting it now, are out of the way, or producers and directors knowledgeable about science fiction get a lot more clout than they currently have, there simply isn't going to be filmed science fiction with some of the sophistication and intelligence of the best written SF, at least not among the big-budgeted films. If you want to enjoy these movies, follow Queen Victoria's advice: lie there and think of England.

But things are gradually changing. *Gattaca*, in 1997, wasn't exactly hard SF, but its science fictional premise was tightly linked to the characters — the story was all of a piece. Stylistically, writer/director Andrew Niccol blundered, but he's an especially good writer, shown again in his well-structured, very thorough script for *The Truman Show*. David Twohy is another writer/director to pay attention to; he had nothing new out in 1998, but his *The Arrival* of the year before, while familiar and routine in its SF elements, treated them with respect and even wit.

Dark City plays with classic SF themes with respect, authority, and intelligence. Yes, this sort of thing has been done in written SF for years, but there's no reason to expect *filmed* SF not to head down some well-trodden paths. SF readers have no right to expect movies to leap ahead to the place written SF has reached at the turn of the millennium. Changes take place, but they take place slowly, and sometimes in unexpected venues. *The Matrix* of 1999 is an action-adventure movie that, when all trappings are stripped away, is about a band of superheroes out to save the world from itself. The science fiction elements are familiar to SF readers, but new to SF moviegoers, and again, writer-directors the Wachowski brothers know the literature as well as the movies and comic books.

Movies are a mass medium; written SF — for the most part — is not, and never will be. To hold mass entertainment up to the standards set by literature created for a smaller group is a mistake, whether it's science fiction, jazz, or commercial art. There are a lot of good movies that are science fiction; don't make the mistake of demanding that they also be good science fiction — or rather, don't assume that "good science fiction" is anything more than a perspective, a viewpoint, one that works for you, but doesn't necessarily work for those who buy movie tickets.

Winter Fire

GEOFFREY A. LANDIS

Dr. Geoffrey Landis works for NASA. He helped build the So-journer rover that explored Mars in 1997. I have worked with him, co-authoring a paper on how to find wormholes, and in recent research on the dynamics of sending sails driven by microwave beams out into the solar system. He is a wide-ranging intelligence and an adroit storyteller, with awards to his credit. The story to follow is a rather stern look at our species and what will all too probably occur in the next century—more conflict that increasingly looks, up close, worse than meaningless.

I am nothing and nobody; atoms that have learned to look at themselves; dirt that has learned to see the awe and the majesty of the universe.

The day the hover-transports arrived in the refugee camps, huge windowless shells of titanium floating on electrostatic cushions, the day faceless men took the ragged little girl that was me away from the narrow, blasted valley that had once been Salzburg to begin a new life on another continent: that is the true beginning of my life. What came before then is almost irrelevant, a sequence of memories etched as with acid into my brain, but with no meaning to real life.

Sometimes I almost think that I can remember my parents. I remember them not by what was, but by the shape of the absence they left behind. I remember yearning for my mother's voice, singing to me softly in Japanese. I cannot remember her voice, or what songs she might have sung, but I remember so vividly the missing of it, the hole that she left behind.

My father I remember as the loss of something large and warm and infinitely strong, prickly and smelling of—of what? I don't remember. Again, it is the loss that remains in my memory, not the man. I remember remembering him as more solid than mountains, something eternal; but in the end he was not eternal, he was not even as strong as a very small war.

I lived in the city of music, in Salzburg, but I remember little from before the siege. I do remember cafés (seen from below, with huge tables and the legs of waiters and faces looming down to ask me if I would like a sweet). I'm sure my parents must have been there, but that I do not remember.

And I remember music. I had my little violin (although it seemed so large to me then), and music was not my second language but my first. I thought in music before ever I learned words. Even now, decades later, when I forget myself in mathematics I cease to think in words, but think directly in concepts clear and perfectly harmonic, so that a mathematical proof is no more than the inevitable majesty of a crescendo leading to a final, resolving chord.

I have long since forgotten anything I knew about the violin. I have not played since the day, when I was nine, I took from the rubble of our apartment the shattered cherry-wood scroll. I kept that meaningless piece of polished wood for years, slept with it clutched in my hand every night until, much later, it was taken away by a soldier intent on rape. Probably I would have let him, had he not been so ignorant as to think my one meager possession might be a weapon. Coitus is nothing more than the natural act of the animal. From songbirds to porpoises, any male animal will rape an available female when given a chance. The action is of no significance except, perhaps, as a chance to contemplate the impersonal majesty of the chain of life and the meaninglessness of any individual's will within it.

When I was finally taken away from the city of music, three years later and a century older, I owned nothing and wanted nothing. There was nothing of the city left. As the hoverjet took me away, just one more in a seemingly endless line of ragged survivors, only the mountains remained, hardly scarred by the bomb craters and the detritus that marked where the castle had stood, mountains looking down on humanity with the gaze of eternity.

My real parents, I have been told, were rousted out of our apartment with a tossed stick of dynamite, and shot as infidels as they ran through the door, on the very first night of the war. It was probably fanatics of the New Orthodox Resurgence that did it, in their first round of ethnic cleansing, although nobody seemed to know for sure.

In the beginning, despite the dissolution of Austria and the fall of the federation of free European states, despite the hate-talk spread by the disciples of Dragan Vukadinović, the violent cleansing of the Orthodox church, and the rising of the Pan-Slavic unity movement, all the events that covered the news-nets all through 2108, few people believed there would be a war, and those that did thought that it might last a few months. The dissolution of Austria and eastern Europe into a federation of free states was viewed by intellectuals of the time as a good thing, a recognition of the impending irrelevance of governments in the post-technological society with its burgeoning sky-cities and prospering free-trade zones. Everyone talked of civil war, but as a distant thing; it was an awful mythical monster of ancient times, one that had been thought dead, a thing that ate people's hearts and turned them into inhuman gargoyles of stone. It would not come here.

Salzburg had had a large population of Asians, once themselves refugees from the economic and political turmoil of the twenty-first century, but now prosperous citizens who had lived in the city for over a century. Nobody thought about religion in the Salzburg of that lost age; nobody cared that a person whose family once came from the Orient might be a Buddhist or a Hindu or a Confucian. My own family, as far as I know, had no religious feelings at all, but that made little difference to the fanatics. My mother, suspecting possible trouble that night, had sent me over to sleep with an old German couple who lived in a building next door. I don't remember whether I said good-bye.

Johann Achtenberg became my foster-father, a stocky old man, bearded and forever smelling of cigar smoke. "We will stay," my foster-father would often say, over and over. "It is our city; the barbarians cannot drive us out." Later in the siege, in a grimmer mood, he might add, "They can kill us, but they will never drive us out."

The next few months were full of turmoil, as the Orthodox Resurgence tried, and failed, to take Salzburg. They were still disorganized, more a mob than an army, still evolving toward the killing machine that they would eventually become. Eventually they were driven out of the city, dynamiting buildings behind them, to join up with the Pan-Slavic Army rolling in from the devastation of Graz. The roads in and out of the city were barricaded, and the siege began.

For that summer of 2109, the first summer of the siege, the life of the city hardly changed. I was ten years old. There was still electricity, and water, and stocks of food. The cafés stayed open, although coffee became hard to obtain, and impossibly expensive when it was available, and at times they had nothing to serve but water. I would watch the pretty girls, dressed in colorful Italian suede and wearing ornately carved Ladakhi jewelry, strolling down the streets in the evenings, stopping to chat with T-shirted boys, and I would wonder if I would ever grow up to be as elegant and poised as they. The shelling was still mostly far away, and everybody believed that the tide of world opinion would soon stop the war. The occasional shell that was targeted toward the city caused great commotion, people screaming and diving under tables even for a bird that hit many blocks away. Later, when civilians had become targets, we all learned to tell the caliber and the trajectory of a shell by the sound of the song it made as it fell.

After an explosion there is silence for an instant, then a hubbub of crashing glass and debris as shattered walls collapse, and people gingerly touch each other, just to verify that they are alive. The dust would hang in the air for hours.

Toward September, when it became obvious that the world powers were stalemated, and would not intervene, the shelling of the city began in earnest. Tanks, even modern ones with electrostatic hover and thin coilguns instead of heavy cannons, could not maneuver into the narrow alleys of the old city and were stymied by the steep-sided mountain valleys. But the outer suburbs and the hilltops were invaded, crushed flat, and left abandoned.

I did not realize it at the time, for a child sees little, but with antiquated equipment and patched-together artillery, my besieged city clumsily and painfully fought back. For every fifty shells that came in, one was fired back at the attackers.

There was an international blockade against selling weapons to the Resurgence, but that seemed to make no difference. Their weapons may not have had the most modern of technology, but they were far better than ours. They had superconducting coilguns for artillery, weapons that fired aerodynamically shaped slugs—we called them birds—that maneuvered on twisted arcs as they moved. The birds were small, barely larger than my hand, but the metastable atomic hydrogen that filled them held an incredible amount of explosive power.

Our defenders had to rely on ancient weapons, guns that ignited chemical explosives to propel metal shells. These were quickly disassembled and removed from their position after each shot, because the enemy's computers could backtrail the trajectory of our shells, which had only crude aeromaneuvering, to direct a deadly rain of birds at the guessed position. Since we were cut off from regular supply lines, each shell was precious. We were supplied by ammunition carried on mules whose trails would weave through the enemy's wooded territory by night and by shells carried one by one across dangerous territory in backpacks.

But still, miraculously, the city held. Over our heads the continuous shower of steel eroded the skyline. Our beautiful castle Hohensalzburg was sandpapered to a hill of bare rock; the cathedral towers fell and the debris by slow degrees was pounded into gravel. Bells rang in sympathy with explosions until at last the bells were silenced. Slowly, erosion softened the profiles of buildings that once defined the city's horizon.

Even without looking for the craters, we learned to tell from looking at the trees which neighborhoods had had explosions in them. Near a blast, the city's trees had no leaves. They were all shaken off by the shock waves. But none of the trees lasted the winter anyway.

My stepfather made a stove by pounding with a hammer on the fenders and door panels of a wrecked automobile, with a pipe made of copper from rooftops and innumerable soft-drink cans. Floorboards and furniture were broken to bits to make fuel for us to keep warm. All through the city, stovepipes suddenly bristled through exterior walls and through windows. The fiberglass sides of modern housing blocks, never designed for such crude heating, became decorated with black smoke trails like unreadable graffiti, and the city parks became weirdly empty lots crossed by winding sidewalks that meandered past the craters where the trees had been.

Johann's wife, my foster-mother, a thin, quiet woman, died by being in the wrong building at the wrong time. She had been visiting a friend across the city to exchange chat and a pinch of hoarded tea. It might just as easily have been the building I was in where the bird decided to build its deadly nest. It took some of the solidity out of Johann. "Do not fall in love, little Leah," he told me, many months later, when our lives had returned to a fragile stability. "It hurts too much."

In addition to the nearly full-time job of bargaining for those necessities that could be bargained for, substituting or improvising those that could not, and hamstering away in basements and shelters any storable food that could be found, my stepfather Johann had another job, or perhaps an obsession. I only learned this slowly. He would disappear, sometimes for days. One time I followed him as far as an entrance to the ancient catacombs beneath the bird-pecked ruins of the beautiful castle Hohensalzburg. When he disappeared into the darkness, I dared not follow.

When he returned, I asked him about it. He was strangely reluctant to speak. When he did, he did not explain, but only said that he was working on the molecular still, and refused to say anything further, or to let me mention it to anyone else.

As a child I spoke a hodgepodge of languages; the English of the foreigners, the French of the European Union, the Japanese that my parents had spoken at home, the book-German of the schools, and the Austrian German that was the dominant tongue of the culture I lived in. At home we spoke mostly German, and in German, "Still" is a word that means quietude. Over the weeks and months that followed, the idea of a molecular still grew in my imagination into a wonderful thing, a place that is quiet even on the molecular level, far different from the booming sounds of war. In my imagination, knowing my stepfather was a gentle man who wanted nothing but peace, I thought of it as a reverse secret weapon, something that would bring this wonderful stillness to the world. When he disappeared to the wonderful molecular still, each time I would wonder whether this would be the time that the still would be ready, and peace would come.

And the city held. "Salzburg is an idea, little Leah," my stepfather Johann would tell me, "and all the birds in the world could never peck it away, for it lives in our minds and in our souls. Salzburg will stand for as long as any one of us lives. And, if we ever abandon the city, then Salzburg has fallen, even if the city itself still stands."

In the outside world, the world I knew nothing of, nations quarreled and were stalemated with indecision over what to do. Our city had been fragilely connected to the western half of Europe by precarious roads, with a series of tunnels through the Alps and long arcing bridges across narrow mountain valleys. In their terror that the chaos might spread westward, they dynamited the bridges, they collapsed the tunnels. Not nations, but individuals did it. They cut us off from civilization, and left us to survive, or die, on our own.

Governments had become increasingly unimportant in the era following the opening of the resources of space by the free-trade zones of the new prosperity, but the trading consortia that now ruled America and the far east in the place of governments had gained their influence only by assiduously signing away the capacity to make war, and although the covenants that had secured their formation had eroded, that one prohibition still held. Only governments could help us, and the governments tried negotiation and diplomacy as Dragan Vukadinović made promises for the New Orthodox Resurgence and broke them.

High above, the owners of the sky-cities did the only thing that they could, which was to deny access to space to either side. This kept the war to the ground, but hurt us more than it hurt the armies surrounding us. They, after all, had no need for satellites to find out where we were.

To the east, the Pan-Slavic Army and the New Orthodox Resurgence were pounding against the rock of the Tenth Crusade; farther south they were skirmishing over borders with the Islamic Federation. Occasionally the shelling would stop for a while, and it would be safe to bring hoarded solar panels out into the sunlight to charge our batteries — the electric grid had gone long ago, of course — and huddle around an antique solar-powered television set watching the distant negotiating teams talk about our fate. Everybody knew that the war would be over shortly; it was impossible that the world would not act.

The world did not act.

I remember taking batteries from wrecked cars to use a headlight, if one happened to survive unbroken, or a taillight, to allow us to stay up past sunset. There was a concoction of boiled leaves that we called "tea," although we had no milk or sugar to put in it. We would sit together, enjoying the miracle of light, sipping our "tea," perhaps reading, perhaps just sitting in silence.

With the destruction of the bridges, Salzburg had become two cities, connected only by narrow-beam microwave radio and the occasional foray by individuals walking across the dangerous series of beams stretched across the rubble of the Old Stone Bridge. The two Salzburgs were distinct in population, with mostly immigrant populations isolated in the modern buildings on the east side of the river, and the old Austrians on the west.

It is impossible to describe the Salzburg feeling, the aura of a sophisticated ancient city, wrapped in a glisteningly pure blanket of snow, under siege, faced with the daily onslaught of an unseen army that seemed to have an unlimited supply of coilguns and metastable hydrogen. We were never out of range. The Salzburg stride was relaxed only when protected by the cover of buildings or specially constructed barricades, breaking into a jagged sprint over a stretch of open ground, a cobbled forecourt of crossroads open to the rifles of snipers on distant hills firing hypersonic needles randomly into the city. From the deadly steel birds, there was no protection. They could fly in anywhere, with no warning. By the time you heard their high-pitched song, you were already dead, or, miraculously, still alive.

Not even the nights were still. It is an incredible sight to see a city cloaked in darkness suddenly illuminate with the blue dawn of a flare sent up from the hilltops, dimming the stars and suffusing coruscating light across the glittering snow. There is a curious, ominous interval of quiet: the buildings of the city dragged blinking out of their darkness and displayed in a fairy glow, naked before the invisible gunners on their distant hilltops. Within thirty seconds, the birds would begin to sing. They might land a good few blocks away, the echo of their demise ringing up and down the valley, or they might land in the street below, the explosion sending people diving under tables, windows caving in across the room.

They could, I believe, have destroyed the city at any time, but that did not serve their purposes. Salzburg was a prize. Whether the buildings were whole or in parts seemed irrelevant, but the city was not to be simply obliterated.

In April, as buds started to bloom from beneath the rubble, the city woke up, and we discovered that we had survived the winter. The diplomats proposed partitioning the city between the Slavs and the Germans — Asians and other ethnic groups, like me, being conveniently ignored — and the terms were set, but nothing came of it except a cease-fire that was violated before the day was over.

The second summer of the siege was a summer of hope. Every week we thought that this might be the last week of the siege; that peace might yet be declared on terms that we could accept, that would let us keep our city. The defense of the city had opened a corridor to the outside world, allowing in humanitarian aid, black-market goods, and refugees from other parts of the war. Some of the people who had fled before the siege returned, although many of the population who had survived the winter used the opportunity to flee to the west. My foster-father, though, swore that he would stay in Salzburg until death. It is civilization, and if it is destroyed, nothing is worthwhile.

Christians of the Tenth Crusade and Turks of the Islamic Federation fought side by side with the official troops of the Mayor's Brigade, sharing ammunition but not command, to defend the city. High above, cities in the sky looked down on us, but, like angels who see everything, they did nothing.

Cafés opened again, even those without black-market connections that could only serve water, and in the evenings there were nightclubs, the music booming even louder than the distant gunfire. My foster-father, of course, would never let me stay up late enough to find out what went on in these, but once, when he was away tending his molecular still, I waited for darkness and then crept through the streets to see.

One bar was entirely Islamic Federation Turks, wearing green turbans and uniforms of dark maroon denim, with spindly railgun-launchers slung across their backs and knives and swords strung on leather straps across their bodies. Each one had in front of him a tiny cup of dark coffee and a clear glass of whisky. I thought I was invisible in the doorway, but one of the Turks, a tall man with a pocked face and a dark mustache that drooped down the side of his mouth, looked up, and, without smiling, said, "Hoy, little girl, I think that you are in the wrong place."

In the next club, mercenaries wearing cowboy hats, with black uniforms and fingerless leather gloves, had parked their guns against the walls before settling in to pound down whisky in a bar where the music was so loud that the beat reverberated across half the city. The one closest to the door had a shaven head, with a spider web tattooed up his neck, and daggers and weird heraldic symbols tattooed across his arms. When he looked up at me, standing in the doorway, he smiled, and I realized that he had been watching me for some time, probably ever since I had appeared. His smile was far more frightening than the impassive face of the Turk. I ran all the way home.

In the daytime, the snap of a sniper's rifle might prompt an exchange of heavy machine-gun fire, a wild, rattling sound that echoed crazily from the hills. Small-arms fire would sound, tak, tak, tak, answered by the singing of small railguns, tee, tee. You can't tell the source of rifle fire in an urban environment; it seems to come from all around. All you can do is duck, and run. Later that summer the first of the omniblasters showed up, firing a beam of pure energy with a silence so loud that tiny hairs all over my body would stand up in fright.

Cosmetics, baby milk, and whisky were the most prized commodities on the black market.

I had no idea what the war was about. Nobody was able to explain it in terms that an eleven-year-old could understand; few even bothered to try. All I knew was that evil people on hilltops were trying to destroy everything I loved, and good men like my foster-father were trying to stop them.

I slowly learned that my foster-father was, apparently, quite important to the defense. He never talked about what he did, but I overheard other men refer to him with terms like "vital" and "indispensable," and these words made me proud. At first I simply thought that they merely meant that the existence of men like him, proud of the city and vowing never to leave, were the core of what made the defense worthwhile. But later I realized that it must be more than this. There were thousands of men who loved the city.

Toward the end of the summer the siege closed around the city again. The army of the Tenth Crusade arrived and took over the ridgetops just one valley to the west; the Pan-Slavic Army and the Orthodox Resurgence held the ridges next to the city and the territory to the east. All that autumn the shells of the Tenth Crusade arced over our heads toward the Pan-Slavs, and beams of purple fire from pop-up robots with omniblasters would fire back. It was a good autumn; mostly only stray fire hit the civilians. But we were locked in place, and there was no way out.

There was no place to go outside, no place that was safe. The sky had become our enemy. My friends were books. I had loved storybooks when I had been younger, in the part of my childhood before the siege that even then I barely remembered. But Johann had no storybooks; his vast collection of books were all forbidding things, full of thick blocks of dense text and incomprehensible diagrams that were no picture of anything I could recognize. I taught myself algebra, with some help from Johann, and started working on calculus. It was easier when I realized that the mathematics in the books was just an odd form of music, written in a strange language. Candles were precious, and so in order to keep on reading at night, Johann made an oil lamp for me, which would burn vegetable oil. This was nearly as precious as candles, but not so precious as my need to read.

A still, I had learned from my reading—and from the black market—was a device for making alcohol, or at least for separating alcohol from water. Did a molecular still make molecules?

"That's silly," Johann told me. "Everything is made of molecules. Your bed, the air you breathe, even you yourself, nothing but molecules."

In November, the zoo's last stubborn elephant died. The predators, the lions, the tigers, even the wolves, were already gone, felled by simple lack of meat. The zebras and antelopes had gone quickly, some from starvation-induced illness, some killed and butchered by poachers. The elephant, surprisingly, had been the last to go, a skeletal apparition stubbornly surviving on scraps of grass and bits of trash, protected against ravenous poachers by a continuous guard of armed watchmen. The watchmen proved unable, however, to guard against starvation. Some people claim that kangaroos and emus still survived, freed from their hutches by the shelling, and could be seen wandering free in the city late at night. Sometimes I wonder if they survive still, awkward birds and bounding marsupials, hiding in the foothills of the Austrian Alps, the last survivors of the siege of Salzburg.

It was a hard winter. We learned to conserve the slightest bit of heat, so as to stretch a few sticks of firewood out over a whole night. Typhus, dysentery, and pneumonia killed more than the shelling, which had resumed in force with the onset of winter. Just after New Year, a fever attacked me, and there was no medicine to be had at any price. Johann wrapped me in blankets and fed me hot water mixed with salt and a pinch of precious sugar. I shivered and burned, hallucinating strange things, now seeing kangaroos and emus outside my little room, now imagining myself on the surface of Mars, strangling in the thin air, and then instantly on Venus, choking in heat and darkness, and then floating in interstellar space, my body growing alternately larger than galaxies, then smaller than atoms, floating so far away from anything else that it would take eons for any signal from me to ever reach the world where I had been born.

Eventually the fever broke, and I was merely back in my room, shivering with cold, wrapped in sheets that were stinking with sweat, in a city slowly being pounded into rubble by distant soldiers whose faces I had never seen, fighting for an ideology that I could never understand.

It was after this, at my constant pleading, that Johann finally took me to see his molecular still. It was a dangerous walk across the city, illuminated by the glow of the Marionette Theater, set afire by incendiary bombs two days before. The still was hidden below the city, farther down even than the bomb shelters, in catacombs that had been carved out of rock over two thousand years ago. There were two men there, a man my stepfather's age with a white mustache, and an even older Vietnamese-German man with one leg, who said nothing the whole time.

The older man looked at me and said in French, which perhaps he thought I wouldn't understand, "This is no place to bring a little one."

Johann replied in German, "She asks many questions." He shrugged, and said, "I wanted to show her."

The other said, still in French, "She couldn't understand." Right then I resolved that I would make myself understand, whatever it was that they thought I could not. The man looked at me critically, taking in, no doubt, my straight black hair and almond eyes. "She's not yours, anyway. What is she to you?"

"She is my daughter," Johann said.

The molecular still was nothing to look at. It was a room filled with curtains of black velvet, doubled back and forth, thousands and thousands of meters of blackness. "Here it is," Johann said. "Look well, little Leah, for in all the world, you will never see such another."

Somewhere there was a fan that pushed air past the curtains; I could feel it on my face, cool, damp air moving sluggishly past. The floor of the room was covered with white dust, glistening in the darkness. I reached down to touch it, and Johann reached out to still my hand. "Not to touch," he said.

"What is it?" I asked in wonder.

"Can't you smell it?"

And I could smell it, in fact, I had been nearly holding my breath to avoid smelling it. The smell was thick, pungent, almost choking. It made my eyes water. "Ammonia," I said.

Johann nodded, smiling. His eyes were bright. "Ammonium nitrate," he said.

I was silent most of the way back to the fortified basement we shared with two other families. There must have been bombs, for there were always the birds, but I do not recall them. At last, just before we came to the river, I asked, "Why?"

"Oh, my little Leah, think. We are cut off here. Do we have electrical generators to run coilguns like the barbarians that surround us? We do not. What can we do, how can we defend ourselves? The molecular still sorts molecules out of the air. Nitrogen, oxygen, water; this is all that is needed to make explosive, if only we can combine them correctly. My molecular still takes the nitrogen out of the air, makes out of it ammonium nitrate, which we use to fire our cannons, to hold the barbarians away from our city."

I thought about this. I knew about molecules by then, knew about nitrogen and oxygen, although not about explosives. Finally something occurred to me, and I asked, "But what about the energy? Where does the energy come from?"

Johann smiled, his face almost glowing with delight. "Ah, my little Leah, you know the right questions already. Yes, the energy. We have designed our still to work by using a series of reactions, each one using no more than a gnat's whisker of energy. Nevertheless, you are right, we must needs steal energy from somewhere. We draw the thermal energy of the air. But old man entropy, he cannot be cheated so easily. To do this we need a heat sink."

I didn't know then enough to follow his words, so I merely repeated his words dumbly: "A heat sink?"

He waved his arm, encompassing the river, flowing dark beneath a thin sheet of ice. "And what a heat sink! The barbarians know we are manufacturing arms; we fire the proof of that back at them every day, but they do not know where! And here it is, right before them, the motive power for the greatest arms factory of all of Austria, and they cannot see it."

Molecular still or not, the siege went on. The Pan-Slavics drove back the Tenth Crusade, and resumed their attack on the city. In February the armies entered the city twice, and twice the ragged defenders drove them back. In April, once more, the flowers bloomed, and once more, we had survived another winter.

It had been months since I had had a bath; there was no heat to waste on mere water, and in any case, there was no soap. Now, at last, we could wash, in water drawn directly from the Salzach, scrubbing and digging to get rid of the lice of winter.

We stood in line for hours waiting for a day's ration of macaroni, the humanitarian aid that had been air-dropped into the city, and hauled enormous drums across the city to replenish our stockpile of drinking water.

Summer rain fell, and we hoarded the water from rain gutters for later use. All that summer the smell of charred stone hung in the air. Bullet-riddled cars, glittering shards of glass, and fragments of concrete and cobblestone covered the streets. Stone heads and gargoyles from blasted buildings would look up at you from odd corners of the city.

Basements and tunnels under the city were filled out with mattresses and camp beds as makeshift living quarters for refugees, which became sweaty and smelly during summer, for all that they had been icy cold in winter. Above us, the ground would shake as the birds flew in, and plaster dust fell from the ceiling.

I was growing up. I had read about sex, and knew it was a natural part of the pattern of life, the urging of chromosomes to divide and conquer the world. I tried to imagine it with everybody I saw, from Johann to passing soldiers, but couldn't ever make my imagination actually believe in it. There was enough sex going on around me—we were packed together tightly, and humans under stress copulate out of desperation, out of boredom, and out of pure instinct to survive. There was enough to see, but I couldn't apply anything of what I saw to myself.

I think, when I was very young, I had some belief that human beings were special, something more than just meat that thought. The siege, a unrelenting tutor, taught me otherwise. A woman I had been with on one day, cuddled in her lap and talking nonsense, the next day was out in the street, bisected by shrapnel, reduced to a lesson in anatomy. If there was a soul it was something intangible, something so fragile that it could not stand up to the gentlest kiss of steel.

People stayed alive by eating leaves, acorns, and, when the humanitarian aid from the sky failed, by grinding down the hard centers of corncobs to make cakes with the powder.

There were developments in the war, although I did not know them. The Pan-Slavic Army, flying their standard of a two-headed dragon, turned against the triple cross of the New Orthodox Resurgence, and to the east thousands of square kilometers of pacified countryside turned in a day into flaming ruin, as the former allies savaged each other. We could see the smoke in the distance, a huge pillar of black rising kilometers into the sky.

It made no difference to the siege. On the hilltops the Pan-Slavic Army drove off the New Orthodox Resurgence, and when they were done, the guns turned back on the city. By the autumn the siege had not lifted, and we knew we would have to face another winter.

Far over our heads, through the ever-present smoke we could see the lights of freedom, the glimmering of distant cities in the sky, remote from all of the trouble of Earth. "They have no culture," Johann said. "They have power, yes, but they have no souls, or they would be helping us. Aluminum and rock, what do they have? Life, and nothing else. When they have another thousand years, they will still not have a third of the reality of our city. Freedom, hah. Why don't they help us, eh?"

The winter was slow frozen starvation. One by one, the artillery pieces that defended our city failed, for we no longer had the machine shops to keep them in repair, nor the tools to make shells. One by one the vicious birds fired from distant hilltops found the homes of our guns and ripped them apart. By the middle of February we were undefended.

And the birds continued to fall.

Sometimes I accompanied Johann to the molecular still. Over the long months of siege they had modified it so that it now distilled from air and water not merely nitrate, but finished explosive ready for the guns, tons per hour. But what good was it now, when there were no guns left for it to feed? Of the eight men who had given it birth, only two still survived to tend it, old one-legged Nguyen and Johann.

One day Nguyen stopped coming. The place he lived had been hit, or he had been struck in transit. There was no way I would ever find out.

There was nothing left of the city to defend, and almost nobody able to defend it. Even those who were willing were starved too weak to hold a weapon.

All through February, all through March, the shelling continued, despite the lack of return fire from the city. They must have known that the resistance was over. Perhaps, Johann said, they had forgotten that there was a city here at all, they were shelling the city now for no other reason than that it had become a habit. Perhaps they were shelling us as a punishment for having dared to defy them.

Through April, the shelling continued. There was no food, no heat, no clean water, no medicine to treat the wounded.

When Johann died it took me four hours to remove the rubble from his body, pulling stones away as birds falling around me demolished a building standing a block to the east and two blocks north. I was surprised at how light he was, little more than a feather pillow. There was no place to bury him; the graveyards were all full. I placed him back where he had lain, crossed his hands, and left him buried in the rubble of the basement where we had spent our lives entwined.

I moved to a new shelter, a tunnel cut out of the solid rock below the Mönchsberg, an artificial cavern where a hundred families huddled in the dark, waiting for an end to existence. It had once been a parking garage. The moisture from three hundred lungs condensed on the stone ceiling and dripped down on us.

At last, at the end of April, the shelling stopped. For a day there was quiet, and then the victorious army came in. There were no alleys to baffle their tanks now. They came dressed in plastic armor, faceless soldiers with railguns and omniblasters thrown casually across their backs; they came flying the awful standard of the Pan-Slavic Army, the two-headed dragon on a field of blue crosses. One of them must have been Dragan Vukadinović, Dragan the Cleanser, the Scorpion of Bratislava, but in their armor I could not know which one. With them were the diplomats, explaining to all who would listen that peace had been negotiated, the war was over, and our part of it was that we would agree to leave our city and move into camps to be resettled elsewhere.

Would the victors write the history? I wondered. What would they say, to justify their deeds? Or would they, too, be left behind by history, a minor faction in a minor event forgotten against the drama of a destiny working itself out far away?

It was a living tide of ragged humans that met them, dragging the crippled and wounded on improvised sledges. I found it hard to believe that there could be so many left. Nobody noticed a dirty twelve-year-old girl, small for her age, slip away. Or if they did notice, where could she go?

The molecular still was still running. The darkness, the smell of it, hidden beneath a ruined, deserted Salzburg, was a comfort to me. It alone had been steadfast. In the end the humans who tended it had turned out to be too fragile, but it had run on, alone in the dark, producing explosives that nobody would ever use, filling the caverns and the dungeons beneath a castle that had once been the proud symbol of a proud city. Filling it by the ton, by the thousands of tons, perhaps even tens of thousands of tons.

I brought with me an alarm clock, and a battery, and I sat for a long time in the dark, remembering the city.

And in the darkness, I could not bring myself to become the angel of destruction, to call down the cleansing fire I had so dreamed of seeing brought upon my enemies. In order to survive you must become tough, Johann had once told me; you must become hard. But I could not become hard enough. I could not become like them.

And so I destroyed the molecular still, and fed the pieces into the Salzach. For all its beauty and power it was fragile, and when I had done there was nothing left by which someone could reconstruct it, or even understand what it had been. I left the alarm clock and the battery, and ten thousand tons of explosive, behind in the catacombs.

Perhaps they are there still.

It was, I am told, the most beautiful, the most civilized city in the world. The many people who told me that are all dead now, and I remember it only through the eyes of a child, looking up from below and understanding little.

Nothing of that little girl remains. Like my civilization, I have remade myself anew. I live in a world of peace, a world of mathematics and sky-cities, the opening of the new renaissance. But, like the first re-naissance, this one was birthed in fire and war.

I will never tell this to anybody. To people who were not there, the story is only words, and they could never understand. And to those who were there, we who lived through the long siege of Salzburg and some-how came out alive, there is no need to speak.

In a very long lifetime, we could never forget.

Lethe

WALTER JON WILLIAMS

Walter Jon Williams has been a professional writer most of his life, and had written historical novels earlier in his career. His talents in setting and character have served him well in both science fiction and fantasy, and his imagination in such novels as *Hardwired* showed a prodigious range of sheer invention in thinking about the near future.

He looks like the hero of a historical novel himself—tall, muscular, bearded in a handsome way. He lives south of Albuquerque and has an unfailingly sunny disposition. Williams is widely liked in the SF community, and one wonders sometimes why he did not become a politician—except, of course, that he has good taste.

His story here caught my attention because its discussion of cloning particularly goes far beyond the clichéd discourse of mainstream thinking, and indeed, rings changes upon even the advanced ideas that have been depicted in the SF literature for decades. As an identical twin, I have watched the fervent moralizing about cloning with a skeptical eye; many do not seem to realize that twins are a common biological strategy among mammals, and could be an instructive case for the earnest "ethicists" of the present. In any case, Williams's drama is gripping in its own right.

Davout had himself disassembled for the return journey. He had already been torn in half, he felt: the remainder, the dumb beast still alive, did not matter. The Captain had ruled, and Katrin would not be brought back. Davout did not want to spend the years between the stars in pain, confronting the gaping absence in his quarters, surrounded by the quiet sympathy of the crew.

Besides, he was no longer needed. The terraforming team had done its work, and then, but for Davout, had died.

Davout lay down on a bed of nano and let the little machines take him apart piece by piece, turn his body, his mind, and his unquenchable longing into long strings of numbers. The nanomachines crawled into his brain first, mapping, recording, and then shut down his mind piece by piece, so that he would feel no discomfort during what followed, or suffer a memory of his own body being taken apart.

Davout hoped that the nanos would shut down the pain before his consciousness failed, so that he could remember what it was like to live without the anguish that was now a part of his life, but it didn't work out that way. When his consciousness ebbed, he was aware, even to the last fading of the light, of the knife-blade of loss still buried in his heart.

The pain was there when Davout awoke, a wailing voice that cried, a pure contralto keen of agony, in his first dawning awareness. He found himself in an early-Victorian bedroom, blue-striped wallpaper, silhouettes in oval frames, silk flowers in vases. Crisp sheets, light streaming in the window. A stranger—shoulder-length hair, black frock coat, cravat carelessly tied—looked at him from a Gothic-revival armchair. The man held a pipe in the right hand and tamped down tobacco with the prehensile big toe of his left foot.

"I'm not on the *Beagle*," Davout said.

The man gave a grave nod. His left hand formed the mudra for <correct>. "Yes."

"And this isn't a virtual?"

<Correct> again. "No."

"Then something has gone wrong."

<Correct> "Yes. A moment, sir, if you please." The man finished tamping, slipped his foot into a waiting boot, then lit the pipe with the anachronistic lighter in his left hand. He puffed, drew in smoke,

exhaled, put the lighter in his pocket, and settled back in the walnut embrace of his chair.

"I am Dr. Li," he said. <Stand by> said the left hand, the old finger position for a now-obsolete palmtop computer, a finger position that had once meant *pause*, as <correct> had once meant *enter*, enter because it was correct. "Please remain in bed for a few more minutes while the nanos double-check their work. Redundancy is frustrating," puffing smoke, "but good for peace of mind."

"What happens if they find they've made a mistake?"

<Don't be concerned> "It can't be a very large mistake," said Li, "or we wouldn't be communicating so rationally. At worst, you will sleep for a bit while things are corrected."

"May I take my hands out from under the covers?" he asked.

"Yes."

Davout did so. His hands, he observed, were brown and leathery, hands suitable for the hot, dry world of Sarpedon. They had not, then, changed his body for one more suited to Earth, but given him something familiar.

If, he realized, they were on Earth.

His right fingers made the mudra <thank you>.

<Don't mention it> signed Li.

Davout passed a hand over his forehead, discovered that the forehead, hand, and the gesture itself were perfectly familiar.

Strange, but the gesture convinced him that he was, in a vital way, still himself. Still Davout.

Still alive, he thought. Alas.

"Tell me what happened," he said. "Tell me why I'm here."

Li signed <stand by>, made a visible effort to collect himself. "We believe," he said, "that the *Beagle* was destroyed. If so, you are the only survivor."

Davout found his shock curiously veiled. The loss of the other lives — friends, most of them — stood muted by the precedent of his own earlier, overriding grief. It is as if the two losses were weighed in a balance, and the *Beagle* found wanting.

Li, Davout observed, was waiting for Davout to absorb this information before continuing.

<Go on> Davout signed.

"The accident happened seven light-years out," Li said. "*Beagle* began to yaw wildly, and both automatic systems and the crew failed to correct the maneuver. *Beagle's* automatic systems concluded that the ship was unlikely to survive the increasing oscillations, and began to use its communications lasers to download personality data to collectors in Earth orbit. As the only crew member to elect disassembly during the return journey, you were first in the queue. The others, we presume, ran to nano disassembly stations, but communication was lost with the *Beagle* before we retrieved any of their data."

"Did Katrin's come through?"

Li stirred uneasily in his chair. <Regrettably> "I'm afraid not."

Davout closed his eyes. He had lost her again. Over the bubble of hopelessness in his throat he asked, "How long has it been since my data arrived?"

"A little over eight days."

They had waited eight days, then, for *Beagle*—for the *Beagle* of seven years ago—to correct its problem and reestablish communication. If *Beagle* had resumed contact, the mass of data that was Davout might have been erased as redundant.

"The government has announced the loss," Li said. "Though there is a remote chance that the *Beagle* may come flying in or through the system in eleven years as scheduled, we have detected no more transmissions, and we've been unable to observe any blueshifted deceleration torch aimed at our system. The government decided that it would be unfair to keep sibs and survivors in the dark any longer."

<Concur> Davout signed.

He envisioned the last moments of the *Beagle*, the crew being flung back and forth as the ship slammed through increasing pendulum swings, the desperate attempts, fighting wildly fluctuating gravity and inertia, to reach the emergency nanobeds . . . no panic, Davout thought, Captain Moshweshwe had trained his people too well for that. Just desperation, and determination, and, as the oscillations grew worse, an increasing sense of futility, and impending death.

No one expected to die anymore. It was always a shock when it happened near you. Or *to* you.

"The cause of the *Beagle's* problem remains unknown," Li said, the voice far away. "The Bureau is working with simulators to try to discover what happened."

Davout leaned back against his pillow. Pain throbbed in his veins, pain and loss, knowledge that his past, his joy, was irrecoverable. "The whole voyage," he said, "was a catastrophe."

<I respectfully contradict> Li signed. "You terraformed and explored two worlds," he said. "Downloads are already living on these worlds, hundreds of thousands now, millions later. There would have been a third world added to our commonwealth if your mission had not been cut short due to the, ah, first accident..."

<Concur> Davout signed, but only because his words would have come out with too much bitterness.

<Sorry>, a curt jerk of Li's fingers. "There are messages from your sibs," Li said, "and downloads from them also. The sibs and friends of *Beagle's* crew will try to contact you, no doubt. You need not answer any of these messages until you're ready."

<Understood>

Davout hesitated, but the words were insistent; he gave them tongue. "Have Katrin's sibs sent messages?" he asked.

Li's grave expression scarcely changed. "I believe so." He tilted his head. "Is there anything I can do for you? Anything I can arrange?"

"Not now, no," said Davout. <Thank you> he signed. "Can I move from the bed now?"

Li's look turned abstract as he scanned indicators projected somewhere in his mind. <Yes> "You may," he said. He rose from his chair, took the pipe from his mouth. "You are in a hospital, I should add," he said, "but you do not have the formal status of patient, and may leave at any time. Likewise, you may stay here for the foreseeable future, as long as you feel it necessary."

<Thank you> "Where is this hospital, by the way?"

"West Java. The city of Bandung."

Earth, then. Which Davout had not seen in seventy-seven years. Memory's gentle fingers touched his mind with the scent of durian, of ocean, of mace, cloves, and turmeric.

He knew he was never in Java before, though, and wondered whence the memory came. From one of his sibs, perhaps?

<Thank you> Davout signed again, putting a touch of finality, a kind of dismissal, into the twist of his fingers.

Dr. Li left Davout alone, in his new/old body, in the room that whispered of memory and pain.

In a dark-wood armoire Davout found identification and clothing, and a record confirming that his account had received seventy-eight years' back pay. His electronic in-box contained downloads from his sibs and more personal messages than he could cope with—he would have to construct an electronic personality to answer most of them.

He dressed and left the hospital. Whoever supervised his reassembly—Dr. Li perhaps—had thoughtfully included a complete Earth atlas in his internal ROM, and he accessed it as he walked, making random turnings but never getting lost. The furious sun burned down with tropical intensity, but his current body was constructed to bear heat, and a breeze off the mountains made pleasant even the blazing noontide.

The joyful metal music of the gamelans clattered from almost every doorway. People in bright clothing, agile as the siamang of near Sumatra, sped overhead along treeways and ropeways, arms and hands modified for brachiation. Robots, immune to the heat, shimmered past on silent tires. Davout found it all strangely familiar, as if he had been here in a dream.

And then he found himself by the sea, and a pang of familiarity knifed through his heart. *Home!* cried his thoughts. Other worlds he had built, other beauties he had seen, but he had never beheld *this* blue, *this* perfection, anywhere else but on his native sphere. Subtle differences in atmospherics had rendered this color unnatural on any other world.

And with the cry of familiarity came a memory: it had been Davout the Silent who had come here, a century or more ago, and Katrin had been by his side.

But Davout's Katrin was dead. And as he looked on Earth's beauty, he felt his world of joy turn to bitter ashes.

<Alas!> His fingers formed the word unbidden. <Alas!>

He lived in a world where no one died, and nothing was ever lost. One understood that such things occasionally occurred, but never—hardly ever—to anyone that one knew. Physical immortality was cheap and easy, and was supported by so many alternate systems: backing up the mind by downloading, or downloading into a virtual reality system or into a durable machine. Nanosystems duplicated the body or improved it, adapted it for different environments. Data slumbered in secure storage, awaiting the electron kiss that returned it to life. Bringing a child to term in the womb was now the rarest form of reproduction, and bringing a child to life in a machine womb the next rarest.

It was so much easier to have the nanos duplicate you as an adult. Then, at least, you had someone to talk to.

No one died, and nothing is ever lost. But Katrin died, Davout thought, and now I am lost, and it was not supposed to be this way.

<Alas!> Fingers wailed the grief that was stopped up in Davout's throat. <Alas!>

Davout and Katrin had met in school, members of the last generation in which womb-breeding outnumbered the alternatives. Immortality whispered its covenant into their receptive ears. On their first meeting, attending a lecture (Dolphus on "Reinventing the Humbolt Sea") at the College of Mystery, they looked at each other and *knew*, as if angels had whispered into their ears, that there was now one less mystery in the world, that each served as an answer to another, that each fitted neatly into a hollow that the other had perceived in his or her soul, dropping into place as neatly as a butter-smooth piece in a finely made teak puzzle — or, considering their interests, as easily as a carbolic functional group nested into place on an indole ring.

Their rapport was, they freely admitted, miraculous. Still young, they exploded into the world, into a universe that welcomed them.

He could not bear to be away from her. Twenty-four hours was the absolute limit before Davout's nerves began to beat a frustrated little tattoo, and he found himself conjuring a phantom Katrin in his imagination, just to have someone to share the world with — he *needed* her there, needed this human lens through which he viewed the universe.

Without her, Davout found the cosmos veiled in a kind of uncertainty. While it was possible to apprehend certain things (the usefulness of a coenocytic arrangement of cells in the transmission of information-bearing proteins and nuclei, the historical significance of the Yucatán astrobleme, the limitations of the Benard cell model in predicting thermic instabilities in the atmosphere), these things lacked *nóesis*, existed only as a series of singular, purposeless accidents. Reflected through Katrin, however, the world took on brilliance, purpose, and genius. With Katrin he could feast upon the universe; without her the world lacked savor.

Their interests were similar enough for each to generate enthusiasm in the other, diverse enough that each was able to add perspective to the other's work. They worked in cozy harmony, back-to-back, two desks set in the same room. Sometimes Davout would return from a meeting, or a coffee break, and find that Katrin had added new paragraphs, sometimes an entire new direction, to his latest effort. On occasion he would return the favor. Their early work—eccentric, proliferating in too many directions, toward too many specialties—showed life and promise and more than a hint of brilliance.

Too much, they decided, for just the two of them. They wanted to do too much, and all at once, and an immortal lifetime was not time enough.

And so, as soon as they could afford it, Red Katrin, the original, was duplicated—with a few cosmetic alterations—in Dark Katrin and later Katrin the Fair; and nanomachines read Old Davout, blood and bone and the long strands of numbers that were his soul, and created perfect copies in Dangerous Davout, later called the Conqueror, and Davout the Silent.

Two had become six, and a half a dozen, they now agreed, was about all the universe could handle for the present. The wild tangle of overlapping interests was parceled out between the three couples, each taking one of the three most noble paths to understanding. The eldest couple chose History as their domain, a part of which involved chronicling the adventures of their sibs; the second couple took Science; the third Psyche, the exploration of the human mind. Any developments, any insights, on the part of one of the sibs could be shared with the others through downloads. In the beginning they downloaded themselves almost continually, sharing their thoughts and experiences and plans in a creative frenzy. Later, as separate lives and more specialized careers developed, the downloads grew less frequent, though there were no interruptions until Dangerous Davout and Dark Katrin took their first voyage to another star. They spent over fifty years away, though to them it was less than thirty; and the downloads from Earth, pulsed over immense distances by communications lasers, were less frequent, and less frequently resorted to. The lives of the other couples, lived at what seemed speeded-up rates, were of decreasing relevance to their own existence, as if they were lives that dwelled in a half-remembered dream.

<Alas!> the fingers signed. <Alas!> for the dream turned to savage nightmare.

The sea, a perfect terrestrial blue, gazed back into Davout's eyes, indifferent to the sadness frozen into his fingers.

"Your doctors knew that to wake here, after such an absence, would result in a feeling of anachronism," said Davout's sib, "so they put you in this Victorian room, where you would at least feel at ease with the kind of anachronism by which you are surrounded." He smiled at Davout from the neo-Gothic armchair. "If you were in a modern room, you might experience a sensation of obsolescence. But everyone can feel superior to the Victorians, and besides one is always more comfortable in one's past."

"Is one?" Davout asked, fingers signing <irony>. The past and the present, he found, were alike a place of torment.

"I discover," he continued, "that my thoughts stray for comfort not to the past, but to the future."

"Ah." A smile. "That is why we call you Davout the Conqueror."

"I do not seem to inhabit that name," Davout said, "if I ever did."

Concern shadowed the face of Davout's sib. <Sorry> he signed, and then made another sign for <profoundly>, the old *multiply* sign, multiples of sorrow in his gesture.

"I understand," he said. "I experienced your last download. It was . . . intensely disturbing. I have never felt such terror, such loss."

"Nor had I," said Davout.

It was Old Davout whose image was projected into the Gothic-revival armchair, the original, womb-born Davout of whom the two sibs were copies. When Davout looked at him it was like looking into a mirror in which his reflection had been retarded for several centuries, then unexpectedly released—Davout remembered, several bodies back, once possessing that tall forehead, the fair hair, the small ears flattened close to the skull. The gray eyes he had still, but he could never picture himself wearing the professorial little goatee.

"How is our other sib?" Davout asked.

The concern on Old Davout's face deepened. "You will find Silent Davout much changed. You haven't uploaded him, then?"

<No> "Due to the delays, I'm thirty years behind on my uploading."

"Ah." <Regret> "Perhaps you should speak to him, then, before you upload all those years."

"I will." He looked at his sib and hoped the longing did not burn in his eyes. "Please give my best to Katrin, will you?"

"I will give her your *love*," said Old Davout, wisest of the sibs.

The pain was there when Davout awoke next day, fresh as the moment it first knifed through him, on the day their fifth child, the planet Sarpedon, was christened. Sarpedon had been discovered by astronomers a couple of centuries before, and named, with due regard for tradition, after yet another minor character in Homer; it had been mapped and analyzed by robot probes; but it had been the *Beagle's* terraforming team that had made the windswept place, with its barren mountain ranges and endless deserts, its angry radiation and furious dust storms, into a place suitable for life.

Katrin was the head of the terraforming team. Davout led its research division. Between them, raining nano from Sarpedon's black skies, they nursed the planet to life, enriched its atmosphere, filled its seas, crafted tough, versatile vegetation capable of withstanding the angry environment. Seeded life by the tens of millions, insects, reptiles, birds, mammals, fish, and amphibians. Re-created themselves, with dark, leathery skin and slit pupils, as human forms suitable for Sarpedon's environment, so that they could examine the place they had built.

And—unknown to the others—Davout and Katrin had slipped bits of their own genetics into almost every Sarpedan life-form. Bits of redundant coding, mostly, but enough so that they could claim Sarpedon's entire world of creatures as their children. Even when they were junior terraformers on the *Cheng Ho's* mission to Rhea, they had, partly as a joke, partly as something more calculated, populated their creations with their genes.

Katrin and Davout spent the last two years of their project on Sarpedon among their children, examining the different ecosystems, different interactions, tinkering with new adaptations. In the end Sarpedon was certified as suitable for human habitation. Preprogrammed nanos constructed small towns, laid out fields, parks, and roads. The first human Sarpedans would be constructed in nanobeds, and their minds filled with the downloaded personalities of volunteers from Earth. There was no need to go to the expense and trouble of shipping out millions of warm bodies from Earth, running the risks of traveling for decades in remote space. Not when nanos could construct them all new on site.

The first Sarpedans — bald, leather-skinned, slit-eyed — emerged blinking into their new red dawn. Any further terraforming, any attempts to fine-tune the planet and make it more Earthlike, would be a long-term project and up to them. In a splendid ceremony, Captain Moshweshwe formally turned the future of Sarpedon over to its new inhabitants. Davout had a few last formalities to perform, handing certain computer codes and protocols over to the Sarpedans, but the rest of the terraforming team, most fairly drunk on champagne, filed into the shuttle for the return journey to the *Beagle*. As Davout bent over a terminal with his Sarpedan colleagues and the *Beagle*'s first officer, he could hear the roar of the shuttle on its pad, the sustained thunder as it climbed for orbit, the thud as it crashed through the sound barrier, and then he saw out of the corner of his eye the sudden red-gold flare . . .

When he raced outside it was to see the blazing poppy unfolding in the sky, a blossom of fire and metal falling slowly to the surface of the newly christened planet.

There she was — her image anyway — in the neo-Gothic armchair; Red Katrin, the green-eyed lady with whom he in memory, and Old Davout in reality, had first exchanged glances two centuries ago while Dolphus expanded on what he called his "lunaforming."

Davout had hesitated about returning her call of condolence. He did not know whether his heart could sustain *two* knife-thrusts, both Katrin's death and the sight of her sib, alive, sympathetic, and forever beyond his reach.

But he couldn't *not* call her. Even when he was trying not to think about her, he still found Katrin on the edge of his perceptions, drifting through his thoughts like the persistent trace of some familiar perfume.

Time to get it over with, he thought. If it was more than he could stand, he could apologize and end the call. But he had to *know*...

"And there are no backups?" she said. A pensive frown touched her lips.

"No *recent* backups," Davout said. "We always thought that, if we were to die, we would die together. Space travel is hazardous, after all, and when catastrophe strikes it is not a *small* catastrophe. We didn't anticipate one of us surviving a catastrophe on Earth, and the other dying light-years away." He scowled.

"Damn Moshweshwe anyway! There were recent backups on the *Beagle*, but with so many dead from an undetermined cause he decided not to resurrect anyone, to cancel our trip to Astoreth, return to Earth, and sort out all the complications once he got home."

"He made the right decision," Katrin said. "If my sib had been resurrected, you both would have died together."

<Better so> Davout's fingers began to form the mudra, but he thought better of it, made a gesture of negation.

The green eyes narrowed. "There are older backups on Earth, yes?"

"Katrin's latest surviving backup dates from the return of the *Cheng Ho*."

"Almost ninety years ago." Thoughtfully. "But she could upload the memories she has been sending me ... the problem does not seem insurmountable."

Red Katrin clasped her hands around one knee. At the familiar gesture, memories rang through Davout's mind like change-bells. Vertigo overwhelmed him, and he closed his eyes.

"The problem is the instructions Katrin—we both—left," he said. "Again, we anticipated that if we died, we'd die together. And so we left instructions that our backups on Earth were not to be employed. We reasoned that we had two sibs apiece on Earth, and if they—you—missed us, you could simply duplicate yourselves."

"I see." A pause, then concern. "Are you all right?"

<No> "Of course not," he said. He opened his eyes. The world eddied for a moment, then stilled, the growing calmness centered on Red Katrin's green eyes.

"I've got seventy-odd years' back pay," he said. "I suppose that I could hire some lawyers, try to get Katrin's backup released to my custody."

Red Katrin bit her nether lip. "Recent court decisions are not in your favor."

"I'm very persistent. And I'm cash-rich."

She cocked her head, looked at him. "Are you all right talking to me? Should I blank my image?"

<No> He shook his head. "It helps, actually, to see you."

He had feared agony in seeing her, but instead he found a growing joy, a happiness that mounted in his heart. As always, his Katrin was helping him to understand, helping him to make sense of the bitter confusion of the world.

An idea began to creep into his mind on stealthy feet.

"I worry that you're alone there," Red Katrin said. "Would you like to come stay with us? Would you like us to come to Java?"

<No, thanks> "I'll come see you soon," Davout said. "But while I'm in the hospital, I think I'll have a few cosmetic procedures." He looked down at himself, spread his leathery hands. "Perhaps I should look a little more Earthlike."

After his talk with Katrin ended, Davout called Dr. Li and told him that he wanted a new body constructed.

Something familiar, he said, already in the files. His own, original form.

Age twenty or so.

"It is a surprise to see you . . . as you are," said Silent Davout.

Deep-voiced, black-skinned, and somber, Davout's sib stood by his bed.

"It was a useful body when I wore it," Davout answered. "I take comfort in . . . familiar things . . . now that my life is so uncertain." He looked up. "It was good of you to come in person."

"A holographic body," taking Davout's hand, "however welcome, however familiar, is not the same as a real person."

Davout squeezed the hand. "Welcome, then," he said. Dr. Li, who had supervised in person through the new/old body's assembly, had left after saying the nanos were done, so it seemed appropriate for Davout to stand and embrace his sib.

The youngest of the sibs was not tall, but he was built solidly, as if for permanence, and his head seemed slightly oversized for his body.

With his older sibs he had always maintained a kind of formal reserve that had resulted in his being nicknamed "the Silent." Accepting the name, he remarked that the reason he spoke little when the others were around is that his older sibs had already said everything that needed saying before he got to it.

Davout stepped back and smiled. "Your patients must think you a tower of strength."

"I have no patients these days. Mostly I work in the realm of theory."

"I will have to look up your work. I'm so far behind on uploads—I don't have any idea what you and Katrin have been doing these last decades."

Silent Davout stepped to the armoire and opened its ponderous mahogany doors. "Perhaps you should put on some clothing," he said. "I am feeling chill in this conditioned air, and so must you."

Amused, Davout clothed himself, then sat across the little rosewood side table from his sib. Davout the Silent looked at him for a long moment—eyes placid and thoughtful—and then spoke.

"You are experiencing something that is very rare in our time," he said. "Loss, anger, frustration, terror. All the emotions that in their totality equal *grief*."

"You forgot sadness and regret," Davout said. "You forgot memory, and how the memories keep replaying. You forgot *imagination*, and how imagination only makes those memories worse, because imagination allows you to write a different ending, but the world will not."

Silent Davout nodded. "People in my profession," fingers forming <irony>, "anyway those born too late to remember how common these things once were, must view you with a certain clinical interest. I must commend Dr. Li on his restraint."

"Dr. Li is a shrink?" Davout asks.

<Yes> A casual press of fingers. "Among other things. I'm sure he's watching you very carefully and making little notes every time he leaves the room."

"I'm happy to be useful." <Irony> in his hand, bitterness on his tongue. "I would give those people my memories, if they want them so much."

<Of course> "You can do that." Davout looked up in something like surprise.

"You know it is possible," his sib said. "You can download your memories, preserve them like amber, or simply hand them to someone else to experience. And you can erase them from your mind completely, walk on into a new life, *tabula rasa* and free of pain."

His deep voice was soft. It was a voice without affect, one he no doubt used on his patients, quietly insistent without being officious. A voice that made suggestions, or presented alternatives, but which never, ever, gave orders.

"I don't want that," Davout said.

Silent Davout's fingers were still set in <of course>. "You are not of the generation that accepts such things as a matter of course," he said. "But this, this *modular* approach to memory, to being, constitutes much of my work these days."

Davout looked at him. "It must be like losing a piece of yourself, to give up a memory. Memories are what make you."

Silent Davout's face remained impassive as his deep voice sounded through the void between them. "What forms a human psyche is not a memory, we have come to believe, but a pattern of thought. When our sib duplicated himself, he duplicated his pattern in us; and when we assembled new bodies to live in, the pattern did not change. Have you felt yourself a different person when you took a new body?"

Davout passed a hand over his head, felt the fine blond hair covering his scalp. This time yesterday, his head had been bald and leathery. Now he felt subtle differences in his perceptions—his vision was more acute, his hearing less so—and his muscle memory was somewhat askew. He remembered having a shorter reach, a slightly different center of gravity.

But as for *himself*, his essence—no, he felt himself unchanged. He was still Davout.

<No> he signed.

"People have more choices than ever before," said Silent Davout. "They choose their bodies, they choose their memories. They can upload new knowledge, new skills. If they feel a lack of confidence, or feel that their behavior is too impulsive, they can tweak their body chemistry to produce a different effect. If they find themselves the victim of an unfortunate or destructive compulsion, the compulsion can be edited from their being. If they lack the power to change their circumstances, they can at least elect to feel happier about them. If a memory cannot be overcome, it can be eliminated."

"And you now spend your time dealing with these problems?" Davout asked.

"They are not *problems,*" his sib said gently. "They are not *syndromes* or *neuroses.* They are *circumstances.* They are part of the condition of life as it exists today. They are environmental." The large, impassive eyes gazed steadily at Davout. "People choose happiness over sorrow, fulfillment over frustration. Can you blame them?"

<Yes> Davout signed. "If they deny the evidence of their own lives," he said. "We define our existence by the challenges we overcome, or those we don't. Even our tragedies define us."

His sib nodded. "That is an admirable philosophy—for Davout the Conqueror. But not all people are conquerors."

Davout strove to keep the impatience from his voice. "Lessons are learned from failures as well as successes. Experience is gained, life's knowledge is applied to subsequent occurrence. If we deny the uses of experience, what is there to make us human?"

His sib was patient. "Sometimes the experiences are negative, and so are the lessons. Would you have a person live forever under the shadow of great guilt, say for a foolish mistake that resulted in injury or death to someone else; or would you have them live with the consequences of damage inflicted by a sociopath, or an abusive family member? Traumas like these can cripple the whole being. Why should the damage not be repaired?"

Davout smiled thinly. "You can't tell me that these techniques are used only in cases of deep trauma," he said. "You can't tell me that people aren't using these techniques for reasons that might be deemed trivial. Editing out a foolish remark made at a party, or eliminating a bad vacation or an argument with the spouse."

Silent Davout returned his smile. "I would not insult your intelligence by suggesting these things do not happen."

<Q.E.D.> Davout signed. "So how do such people mature? Change? Grow in wisdom?"

"They cannot edit out *everything.* There is sufficient friction and conflict in the course of ordinary life to provide everyone with their allotted portion of wisdom. Nowadays our lives are very, very long, and we have a long time to learn, however slowly. And after all," smiling, "the average person's capacity for wisdom has never been so large as all that. I think you will find that as a species we are far less prone to folly than we once were."

Davout looked at his sib grimly. "You are suggesting that I undergo this technique?"

"It is called Lethe."

"That I undergo Lethe? Forget Katrin? Or forget what I feel for her?"

Silent Davout slowly shook his grave head. "I make no such suggestion."

"Good."

The youngest Davout gazed steadily into the eyes of his older twin. "Only you know what you can bear. I merely point out that this remedy exists, should you find your anguish beyond what you can endure."

"Katrin deserves mourning," Davout said.

Another grave nod. "Yes."

"She deserves to be remembered. Who will remember her if I do not?"

"I understand," said Silent Davout. "I understand your desire to feel, and the necessity. I only mention Lethe because I comprehend all too well what you endure now. Because," he licked his lips, "I, too, have lost Katrin."

Davout gaped at him. "You—" he stammered. "She is—she was killed?"

<No> His sib's face retained its remarkable placidity. "She left me, sixteen years ago."

Davout could only stare. The fact, stated so plainly, was incomprehensible.

"I—" he began, and then his fingers found another thought. <What happened?>

"We were together for a century and a half. We grew apart. It happens."

Not to us it doesn't! Davout's mind protested. *Not to Davout and Katrin!*

Not to the two people who make up a whole greater than its parts. Not to us. Not ever.

But looking into his sib's accepting, melancholy face, Davout knew that it had to be true.

And then, in a way he knew to be utterly disloyal, he began to hope.

"Shocking?" said Old Davout. "Not to us, I suppose."

"It was their downloads," said Red Katrin. "Fair Katrin in particular was careful to edit out some of her feelings and judgments before she let me upload them, but still I could see her attitudes changing. And knowing her, I could make guesses by what she left out.... I remember telling Davout three years before the split that the relationship was in jeopardy."

"The Silent One was still surprised, though, when it happened," Old Davout said. "Sophisticated though he may be about human nature, he had a blind spot where Katrin was concerned." He put an arm around Red Katrin and kissed her cheek. "As I suppose we all do," he added.

Katrin accepted the kiss with a gracious inclination of her head, then asked Davout, "Would you like the blue room here, or the green room upstairs? The green room has a window seat and a fine view of the bay, but it's small."

"I'll take the green room," Davout said. I do not need so much room, he thought, now that I am alone.

Katrin took him up the creaking wooden stair and showed him the room, the narrow bed of the old house. Through the window he could look south to a storm on Chesapeake Bay, blue-gray cloud, bright eruptions of lightning, slanting beams of sunlight that dropped through rents in the storm to tease bright winking light from the foam. He watched it for a long moment, then was startled out of reverie by Katrin's hand on his shoulder, and a soft voice in his ear.

"Are there sights like this on other worlds?"

"The storms on Rhea were vast," Davout said, "like nothing on this world. The ocean area is greater than that on Earth, and lies mostly in the tropics — the planet was almost called Oceanus on that account. The hurricanes built up around the equatorial belts with nothing to stop them, sometimes more than a thousand kilometers across, and they came roaring into the temperate zones like multi-armed demons, sometimes one after another for months. They spawned waterspots and cyclones in their vanguard, inundated whole areas with a storm surge the size of a small ocean, dumped enough rain to flood an entire province away.... We thought seriously that the storms might make life on land untenable."

He went on to explain the solution he and Katrin had devised for the enormous problem: huge strings of tall, rocky barrier islands built at a furious rate by nanomachines, a wall for wind and storm surge to break against; a species of silvery, tropical floating weed, a flowery girdle about Rhea's thick waist, that radically increased surface albedo, reflecting more heat back into space. Many species of deep-rooted, vinelike plants to anchor slopes and prevent erosion, other species of thirsty trees, adaptations of cottonwoods and willows, to line streambeds and break the power of flash floods.

Planetary engineering on such an enormous scale, in such a short time, had never been attempted, not even on Mars, and it had been difficult for Katrin and Davout to sell the project to the project managers on the *Cheng Ho*. Their superiors had initially preferred a different approach, huge equatorial solar curtains deployed in orbit to reflect heat, squadrons of orbital beam weapons to blast and disperse storms as they formed, secure underground dwellings for the inhabitants, complex lock and canal systems to control flooding.... Katrin and Davout had argued for a more elegant approach to Rhea's problems, a reliance on organic systems to modify the planet's extreme weather instead of assaulting Rhea with macro-tech and engineering. Theirs was the approach that finally won the support of the majority of the terraforming team, and resulted in their subsequent appointment as heads of *Beagle*'s terraforming team.

"Dark Katrin's memories were very exciting to upload during that time," said Katrin the Red. "That delirious explosion of creativity! Watching a whole globe take shape beneath her feet!" Her green eyes look up into Davout's. "We were jealous of you then. All that abundance being created, all that talent going to shaping an entire world. And we were confined to scholarship, which seemed so lifeless by comparison."

He looked at her. <Query> "Are you sorry for the choice you made? You two were senior: you could have chosen our path if you'd wished. You still could, come to that."

A smile drifts across her face. "You tempt me, truly. But Old

Davout and I are happy in our work—and besides, you and Katrin needed someone to provide a proper record of your adventures." She tilted her head, and mischief glittered in her eyes. "Perhaps you should ask Blonde Katrin. Maybe she could use a change."

Davout gave a guilty start: she was, he thought, seeing too near, too soon. "Do you think so?" he asked. "I didn't even know if I should see her."

"Her grudge is with the Silent One, not with you."

"Well." He managed a smile. "Perhaps I will at least call."

Davout called Katrin the Fair, received an offer of dinner on the following day, accepted. From his room he followed the smell of coffee into his hosts' office, and felt a bubble of grief lodge in his heart: two desks, back-to-back, two computer terminals, layers of papers and books and printout and dust... he could imagine himself and Katrin here, sipping coffee, working in pleasant compatibility.

<How goes it?> he signed.

His sib looked up. "I just sent a chapter to Sheol," he said. "I was making Maxwell far too wise." He fingered his little goatee. "The temptation is always to view the past solely as a vehicle that leads to our present grandeur. These people's sole function was to produce *us*, who are of course perfectly wise and noble and far superior to our ancestors. So one assumes that these people had *us* in mind all along, that we were what they were working toward. I have to keep reminding myself that these people lived amid unimaginable tragedy, disease and ignorance and superstition, vile little wars, terrible poverty, and *death*..."

He stopped, suddenly aware that he'd said something awkward—Davout felt the word vibrate in his bone, as if he were stranded inside a bell that was still singing after it had been struck—but he said, "Go on."

"I remind myself," his sib continued, "that the fact that we live in a modern culture doesn't make us better, it doesn't make us superior to these people—in fact it enlarges *them*, because they had to overcome so much more than we in order to realize themselves, in order to accomplish as much as they did." A shy smile drifted across his face. "And so a rather smug chapter is wiped out of digital existence."

"*Lavoisier* is looming," commented Red Katrin from her machine.

"Yes, that too," Old Davout agreed. His *Lavoisier and His Age* had won the McEldowney Prize and been shortlisted for other awards.

Davout could well imagine that bringing *Maxwell* up to *Lavoisier's* magisterial standards would be intimidating.

Red Katrin leaned back in her chair, combed her hair back with her fingers. "I made a few notes about the *Beagle* project," she said. "I have other commitments to deal with first, of course."

She and Old Davout had avoided any conflicts of interest and interpretation by conveniently dividing history between them: she would write of the "modern" world and her near-contemporaries, while he wrote of those securely in the past. Davout thought his sib had the advantage in this arrangement, because her subjects, as time progressed, gradually entered his domain, and became liable to his reinterpretation.

Davout cleared away some printout, sat on the edge of Red Katrin's desk. "A thought keeps bothering me," he said. "In our civilization we record everything. But the last moments of the crew of the *Beagle* went unrecorded. Does that mean they do not exist? Never existed at all? That death was *always* their state, and they returned to it, like virtual matter dying into the vacuum from which it came?"

Concern darkened Red Katrin's eyes. "They will be remembered," she said. "I will see to it."

"Katrin didn't download the last months, did she?"

<No> "The last eight months were never sent. She was very busy, and—"

"Virtual months, then. Gone back to the phantom zone."

"There are records. Other crew sent downloads home, and I will see if I can gain access either to the downloads, or to their friends and relations who have experienced them. There is *your* memory, your downloads."

He looked at her. "Will you upload my memory, then? My sib has everything in his files, I'm sure." Glancing at Old Davout.

She pressed her lips together. "That would be difficult for me. *Me* viewing *you* viewing *her* . . ." She shook her head. "I don't dare. Not now. Not when we're all still in shock."

Disappointment gnawed at his insides with sharp rodent teeth. He did not want to be so alone in his grief; he didn't want to nourish all the sadness by himself.

He wanted to share it with *Katrin*, he knew, the person with whom he shared everything. Katrin could help him make sense of it, the way she clarified all the world for him. Katrin would comprehend the way he felt.

<I understand> he signed. His frustration must have been plain to Red Katrin, because she took his hand, lifted her green eyes to his.

"I *will*," she said. "But not now. I'm not ready."

"I don't want *two* wrecks in the house," called Old Davout over his shoulder.

Interfering old bastard, Davout thought. But with his free hand he signed, again, <I understand>.

Katrin the Fair kissed Davout's cheek, then stood back, holding his hands, and narrowed her gray eyes. "I'm not sure I approve of this youthful body of yours," she said. "You haven't looked like this in — what — over a century?"

"Perhaps I seek to evoke happier times," Davout said.

A little frown touched the corners of her mouth. "*That* is always dangerous," she judged. "But I wish you every success." She stepped back from the door, flung out an arm. "Please come in."

She lived in a small apartment in Toulouse, with a view of the Allée Saint-Michel and the rose-red brick of the Vieux Quartier. On the whitewashed walls hung terra-cotta icons of Usil and Tiv, the Etruscan gods of the sun and moon, and a well cover with a figure of the demon Charun emerging from the underworld. The Etruscan deities were confronted, on another wall, by a bronze figure of the Gaulish Rosmerta, consort of the absent Mercurius.

Her little balcony was bedecked with wrought iron and a gay striped awning. In front of the balcony a table shimmered under a red and white checked tablecloth: crystal, porcelain, a wicker basket of bread, a bottle of wine. Cooking scents floated in from the kitchen.

"It smells wonderful," Davout said.

<Drink?> Lifting the bottle.

<Why not?>

Wine was poured. They settled onto the sofa, chatted of weather, crowds, Java. Davout's memories of the trip that Silent Davout and his Katrin had taken to the island were more recent than hers.

Fair Katrin took his hand. "I have uploaded Dark Katrin's memories, so far as I have them," she said. "She loved you, you know — absolutely, deeply." <Truth> She bit her nether lip. "It was a remarkable thing."

<Truth> Davout answered. He touched cool crystal to his lips, took a careful sip of his cabernet. Pain throbbed in the hollows of his heart.

"Yes," he said, "I know."

"I felt I should tell you about her feelings. Particularly in view of what happened with me and the Silent One."

He looked at her. "I confess I do not understand that business."

She made a little frown of distaste. "We and our work and our situation grew irksome. Oppressive. You may upload his memories if you like—I daresay you will be able to observe the signs that he was determined to ignore."

<I am sorry>

Clouds gathered in her gray eyes. "I, too, have regrets."

"There is no chance of reconciliation?"

<Absolutely not>, accompanied by a brief shake of the head. "It was over." <Finished> "And, in any case, Davout the Silent is not the man he was."

<Yes?>

"He took Lethe. It was the only way he had of getting over my leaving him."

Pure amazement throbbed in Davout's soul. Fair Katrin looked at him in surprise.

"You didn't know?"

He blinked at her. "I *should* have. But I thought he was talking about *me*, about a way of getting over..." Aching sadness brimmed in his throat. "Over the way my Dark Katrin left me."

Scorn whitened the flesh about Fair Katrin's nostrils. "That's the Silent One for you. He didn't have the nerve to tell you outright."

"I'm not sure that's true. He may have thought he was speaking plainly enough—"

Her fingers formed a mudra that gave vent to a brand of disdain that did not translate into words. "He knows his effects perfectly well," she said. "He was trying to suggest the idea without making it clear that this was his *choice* for you, that he wanted you to fall in line with his theories."

Anger was clear in her voice. She rose, stalked angrily to the bronze of Rosmerta, adjusted its place on the wall by a millimeter or so. Turned, waved an arm.

<Apologies>, flung to the air. "Let's eat. Silent Davout is the last person I want to talk about right now."

"I'm sorry I upset you." Davout was not sorry at all: he found this display fascinating. The gestures, the tone of voice, were utterly familiar, ringing like chimes in his heart; but the *style*, the way Fair Katrin avoided the issue, was different. Dark Katrin never would have fled a subject this way: she would have knit her brows and confronted the problem directly, engaged with it until she'd either reached understanding or catastrophe. Either way, she'd have laughed, and tossed her dark hair, and announced that now she understood.

"It's peasant cooking," Katrin the Fair said as she bustled to the kitchen, "which of course is the best kind."

The main course was a ragoût of veal in a velouté sauce, beans cooked simply in butter and garlic, tossed salad, bread. Davout waited until it was half consumed, and the bottle of wine mostly gone, before he dared to speak again of his sib.

"You mentioned the Silent One and his theories," he said. "I'm thirty years behind on his downloads, and I haven't read his latest work—what is he up to? What's all this theorizing about?"

She sighed, fingers ringing a frustrated rhythm on her glass. Looked out the window for a moment, then conceded. "Has he mentioned the modular theory of the psyche?"

Davout tried to remember. "He said something about modular *memory*, I seem to recall."

<Yes> "That's a part of it. It's a fairly radical theory that states that people should edit their personality and abilities at will, as circumstances dictate. That one morning, say, if you're going to work, you upload appropriate memories, and work skills, along with a dose of ambition, of resolution, and some appropriate emotions like satisfaction and eagerness to solve problems, or endure drudgery, as the case may be."

Davout looked at his plate. "Like cookery, then," he said. "Like this dish—veal, carrots, onions, celery, mushrooms, parsley."

Fair Katrin made a mudra that Davout didn't recognize. <Sorry?> he signed.

"Oh. Apologies. That one means, roughly, 'har-de-har-har.'" Finger formed <laughter>, then <sarcasm>, then slurred them together. "See?"

<Understood> He poured more wine into her glass.

She leaned forward across her plate. "Recipes are fine if one wants to be *consumed*," she said. "Survival is another matter. The human mind is more than just ingredients to be tossed together. The atomistic view of the psyche is simplistic, dangerous, and *wrong*. You cannot *will* a psyche to be whole, no matter how many *wholeness* modules are uploaded. A psyche is more than the sum of its parts."

Wine and agitation burnished her cheeks. Conviction blazed from her eyes. "It takes *time* to integrate new experience, new abilities. The modular theorists claim this will be done by a 'conductor,' an artificial intelligence that will be able to judge between alternate personalities and abilities and upload whatever's needed. But that's such *rubbish*, I — " She looked at the knife she was waving, then permitted it to return to the table.

"How far are the Silent One and his cohorts toward realizing this ambition?" Davout said.

<Beg pardon?> She looked at him. "I didn't make that clear?" she said. "The technology is already here. It's happening. People are fragmenting their psyches deliberately and trusting to their conductors to make sense of it all. And they're *happy* with their choices, because that's the only emotion they permit themselves to upload from their supply." She clenched her teeth, glanced angrily out the window at the Vieux Quartier's sunset-burnished walls. "All traditional psychology is aimed at integration, at wholeness. And now it's all to be *thrown away* . . ." She flung her hand out the window. Davout's eyes automatically followed an invisible object on its arc from her fingers toward the street.

"And how does this theory work in practice?" Davout asked. "Are the streets filled with psychological wrecks?"

Bitterness twisted her lips. "Psychological imbeciles, more like. Executing their conductors' orders, docile as well-fed children, happy as clams. They upload passions — anger, grief, loss — as artificial experiences, secondhand from someone else, usually so they can tell their conductor to avoid such emotions in the future. They are not *people* anymore, they're . . ." Her eyes turned to Davout.

"You saw the Silent One," she said. "Would you call him a *person*?"

"I was with him for only a day," Davout said. "I noticed something of a . . ." <Stand by> he signed, searching for the word.

"Lack of affect?" she interposed. "A demeanor marked by an extreme placidity?"

<Truth> he signed.

"When it was clear I wouldn't come back to him, he wrote me out of his memory," Fair Katrin said. "He replaced the memories with *facts*—he knows he was married to me, he knows we went to such-and-such a place or wrote such-and-such a paper—but there's nothing else there. No feelings, no real memories good or bad, no understanding, nothing left from almost two centuries together." Tears glittered in her eyes. "I'd rather he felt anything at all—I'd rather he hated me than feel this apathy!"

Davout reached across the little table and took her hand. "It is his decision," he said, "and his loss."

"It is *all* our loss," she said. Reflected sunset flavored her tears with the color of roses. "The man we loved is gone. And millions are gone with him—millions of little half-alive souls, programmed for happiness and unconcern." She tipped the bottle into her glass, received only a sluicing of dregs.

"Let's have another," she said.

When he left, some hours later, he embraced her, kissed her, let his lips linger on hers for perhaps an extra half-second. She blinked up at him in wine-muddled surprise, and then he took his leave.

"How did you find my sib?" Red Katrin asked.

"Unhappy," Davout said. "Confused. Lonely, I think. Living in a little apartment like a cell, with icons and memories."

<I know> she signed, and turned on him a knowing green-eyed look.

"Are you planning on taking her away from all that? To the stars, perhaps?"

Davout's surprise was brief. He looked away and murmured, "I didn't know I was so transparent."

A smile touched her lips. <Apologies> she signed. "I've lived with Old Davout for nearly two hundred years. You and he haven't grown so very far apart in that time. My fair sib deserves happiness, and so do you . . . if you can provide it, so much the better. But I wonder if you are not moving too fast, if you have thought it all out."

Moving fast, Davout wondered. His life seemed so very slow now, a creeping dance with agony, each move a lifetime.

He glanced out at Chesapeake Bay, saw his second perfect sunset in only a few hours — the same sunset he'd watched from Fair Katrin's apartment, now radiating its red glories on the other side of the Atlantic. A few water-skaters sped toward home on their silver blades. He sat with Red Katrin on a porch swing, looking down the long green sward to the bayfront, the old wooden pier, and the sparkling water, that profound, deep blue that sang of home to Davout's soul. Red Katrin wrapped herself against the breeze in a fringed, autumn-colored shawl. Davout sipped coffee from gold-rimmed porcelain, set the cup into its saucer.

"I wondered if I was being untrue to *my* Katrin," he said. "But they are really the same person, aren't they? If I were to pursue some other woman now, I would know I was committing a betrayal. But how can I betray Katrin with herself?"

An uncertain look crossed Red Katrin's face. "I've downloaded them both," hesitantly, "and I'm not certain that the Dark and Fair Katrins are quite the same person. Or ever were."

Not the same — of course he knew that. Fair Katrin was not a perfect copy of her older sib — she had flaws, clear enough. She had been damaged, somehow. But the flaws could be worked on, the damage repaired. Conquered. There was infinite time. He would see it done.

<Question> "And how do your sibs differ, then?" he asked. "Other than obvious differences in condition and profession?"

She drew her legs up and rested her chin on her knees. Her green eyes were pensive. "Matters of love," she said, "and happiness."

And further she would not say.

Davout took Fair Katrin to Tangier for the afternoon and walked with her up on the old palace walls. Below them, white in the sun, the curved mole built by Charles II cleaved the Middle Sea, a thin crescent moon laid upon the perfect shimmering azure. (Home! home!, the waters cried.) The sea breeze lashed her blond hair across her face, snapped little sonic booms from the sleeves of his shirt.

"I have sampled some of the Silent One's downloads," Davout said. "I wished to discover the nature of this artificial tranquillity with which he has endowed himself."

Fair Katrin's lips twisted in distaste, and her fingers formed a scatologue.

"It was . . . interesting," Davout said. "There was a strange, uncomplicated quality of bliss to it. I remember experiencing the download of a master sitting zazen once, and it was an experience of a similar cast."

"It may have been the exact same sensation." Sourly. "He may have just copied the zen master's experience and slotted it into his brain. That's how *most* of the vampires do it—award themselves the joy they haven't earned."

"That's a calvinistic point of view," Davout offered. "That happiness can't just happen, that it has to be earned."

She frowned out at the sea. "There is a difference between real experience and artificial or recapitulative experience. If that's calvinist, so be it."

<Yes> Davout signed. "Call me a calvinist sympathizer, then. I have been enough places, done enough things, so that it matters to me that I was actually there and not living out some programmed dream of life on other worlds. I've experienced my sibs' downloads—lived significant parts of their lives, moment by moment—but it is not the same as *my life*, as *being me*. I am," he said, leaning elbows on the palace wall, "I am myself, I am the sum of everything that happened to me, I stand on this wall, I am watching this sea, I am watching it with you, and no one else has had this experience, nor ever shall, it is *ours*, it belongs to us . . ."

She looked up at him, straw-hair flying over an unreadable expression. "Davout the Conqueror," she said.

<No> he signed. "I did not conquer alone."

She nodded, holding his eyes for a long moment. "Yes," she said. "I know."

He took Katrin the Fair in his arms and kissed her. There was a moment's stiff surprise, and then she began to laugh, helpless peals bursting against his lips. He held her for a moment, too surprised to react, and then she broke free. She reeled along the wall, leaning for support against the old stones. Davout followed, babbling, "I'm sorry, I didn't mean to—"

She leaned back against the wall. Words burst half-hysterical from her lips, in between bursts of desperate, unamused laughter. "So that's what you were after! My God! As if I hadn't had enough of you all after all these years!"

"I apologize," Davout said. "Let's forget this happened. I'll take you home."

She looked up at him, the laughter gone, blazing anger in its place. "The Silent One and I would have been all right if it hadn't been for you—*for our sibs!*" She flung her words like daggers, her voice breaking with passion. "You lot were the eldest, you'd already parceled out the world between you. You were only interested in psychology because my damned Red sib and your Old one wanted insight into the characters in their histories, and because you and your dark bitch wanted a theory of the psyche to aid you in building communities on other worlds. We only got created because *you were too damned lazy to do your own research!*"

Davout stood, stunned. <No> he signed, "That's not—"

"We were *third*," she cried. "We were *born in third place.* We got the jobs you wanted least, and while you older sibs were winning fame and glory, we were stuck in work that didn't suit, that you'd *cast off,* awarded to us as if we were charity cases—" She stepped closer, and Davout was amazed to find a white-knuckled fist being shaken in his face. "My husband was called The Silent because his sibs had already used up all the words! He was third-rate and knew it. It *destroyed* him! Now he's plugging artificial satisfaction into his head because it's the only way he'll ever feel it."

"If you didn't like your life," Davout said, "you could have changed it. People start over all the time—we'd have helped." He reached toward her. "I can help you to the stars, if that's what you want."

She backed away. "The only help we ever needed was to *get rid of you!*" A mudra, <har-de-har-har>, echoed the sarcastic laughter on Fair Katrin's lips. "And now there's another gap in your life, and you want me to fill it—*not this time.*"

<Never> her fingers echoed. <Never> The laughter bubbled from her throat again.

She fled, leaving him alone and dazed on the palace wall, the booming wind mocking his feeble protests.

"I am truly sorry," Red Katrin said. She leaned close to him on the porch swing, touched soft lips to his cheek. "Even though she edited her downloads, I could tell she resented us—but I truly did not know how she would react."

Davout was frantic. He could feel Katrin slipping farther and farther away, as if she were on the edge of a precipice and her handholds were crumbling away beneath her clawed fingers.

"Is what she said true?" he asked. "Have we been slighting them all these years? Using them, as she claims?"

"Perhaps she had some justification once," Red Katrin said. "I do not remember anything of the sort when we were young, when I was uploading Fair Katrin almost every day. But now," her expression growing severe, "these are mature people, not without resources or intelligence — I can't help but think that surely after a person is a century old, any problems that remain are *her* fault."

As he rocked on the porch swing he could feel a wildness rising in him. *My God,* he thought, *I am going to be* alone.

His brief days of hope were gone. He stared out at the bay — the choppy water was too rough for any but the most dedicated waterskaters — and felt the pain pressing on his brain, like the two thumbs of a practiced sadist digging into the back of his skull.

"I wonder," he said. "Have you given any further thought to uploading my memories?"

She looked at him curiously. "It's scarcely time yet."

"I feel a need to share . . . some things."

"Old Davout has uploaded them. You could speak to him."

This perfectly sensible suggestion only made him clench his teeth. He needed *sense* made of things, he needed things put in *order*, and that was not the job of his sib. Old Davout would only confirm what he already knew.

"I'll talk to him, then," he said.

And then never did.

The pain was worst at night. It wasn't the sleeping alone, or merely Katrin's absence: it was the knowledge that she would *always* be absent, that the empty space next to him would lie there forever. It was then the horror fully struck him, and he would lie awake for hours, eyes staring into the terrible void that wrapped him in its dark cloak. Fits of trembling sped through his limbs.

I will go mad, he sometimes thought. It seemed something he could choose, as if he were a character in an Elizabethan drama who turns to the audience to announce that he will be mad now, and then in the next scene is found gnawing bones dug out of the family sepulchre. Davout could see himself being found outside, running on all fours and barking at the stars.

And then, as dawn crept across the windowsill, he would look out the window and realize, to his sorrow, that he was not yet mad, that he was condemned to another day of sanity, of pain, and of grief.

Then, one night, he *did* go mad. He found himself squatting on the floor in his nightshirt, the room a ruin around him: mirrors smashed, furniture broken. Blood was running down his forearms.

The door leapt off its hinges with a heave of Old Davout's shoulder. Davout realized, in a vague way, that his sib had been trying to get in for some time. He saw Red Katrin's silhouette in the door, an aureate halo around her auburn hair in the instant before Old Davout snapped on the light.

Afterward Katrin pulled the bits of broken mirror out of Davout's hands, washed and disinfected them, while his sib tried to reconstruct the green room and its antique furniture.

Davout watched his spatters of blood stain the water, threads of scarlet whirling in Coriolis spirals. "I'm sorry," he said. "I think I may be losing my mind."

"I doubt that." Frowning at a bit of glass in her tweezers.

"I want to *know.*"

Something in his voice made her look up. "Yes?"

He could see his staring reflection in her green eyes. "Read my downloads. Please. I want to know if . . . I'm reacting normally in all this. If I'm lucid or just . . ." He fell silent. *Do it,* he thought. *Just do this one thing.*

"I don't upload other people. Davout can do that. *Old* Davout, I mean."

No, Davout thought. His sib would understand all too well what he was up to.

"But he's me!" he said. "He'd think I'm normal!"

"Silent Davout, then. Crazy people are his specialty."

Davout wanted to make a mudra of scorn, but Red Katrin held his hands captive. Instead he gave a laugh. "He'd want me to take Lethe. Any advice he gave would be . . . in that direction." He made a fist of one hand, saw drops of blood well up through the cuts. "I need to know if I can stand this," he said. "If—something drastic is required."

She nodded, looked again at the sharp little spear of glass, put it deliberately on the edge of the porcelain. Her eyes narrowed in thought—Davout felt his heart vault at that look, at the familiar lines forming at the corner of Red Katrin's right eye, each one known and adored.

Please do it, he thought desperately.

"If it's that important to you," she said, "I will."

"Thank you," he said.

He bent his head over her the basin, raised her hand, and pressed his lips to the flesh beaded with water and streaked with blood.

It was almost like conducting an affair, all clandestine meetings and whispered arrangements. Red Katrin did not want Old Davout to know she was uploading his sib's memories—"I would just as soon not deal with his disapproval"—and so she and Davout had to wait until he was gone for a few hours, a trip to record a lecture for Cavor's series on *Ideas and Manners.*

She settled onto the settee in the front room and covered herself with her fringed shawl. Closed her eyes. Let Davout's memories roll through her.

He sat in a chair nearby, his mouth dry. Though nearly thirty years had passed since Dark Katrin's death, he had experienced only a few weeks of that time; and Red Katrin was floating through these memories at speed, tasting here and there, skipping redundancies or moments that seemed inconsequential. . . .

He tried to guess from her face where in his life she dwelt. The expression of shock and horror near the start was clear enough, the shuttle bursting into flames. After the shock faded, he recognized the discomfort that came with experiencing a strange mind, and flickering across her face came expressions of grief, anger, and here and there amusement; but gradually there was only a growing sadness, and lashes wet with tears. He crossed the room to kneel by her chair and take her hand. Her fingers pressed his in response . . . she took a breath, rolled her head away . . . he wanted to weep not for his grief, but for hers.

The eyes fluttered open. She shook her head. "I had to stop," she said. "I couldn't take it—" She looked at him, a kind of awe in her wide green eyes. "My God, the sadness! And the *need*. I had no idea. I've never felt such need. I wonder what it is to be needed that way."

He kissed her hand, her damp cheek. Her arms went around him. He felt a leap of joy, of clarity. The need was hers, now.

Davout carried her to the bed she shared with his sib, and together they worshiped memories of his Katrin.

"I will take you there," Davout said. His finger reached into the night sky, counted stars, *one, two, three . . .* "The planet's called Atugan. It's boiling hot, nothing but rock and desert, sulfur and slag. But we can make it home for ourselves and our children — all the species of children we desire, fish and fowl." A bubble of happiness filled his heart. "Dinosaurs, if you like," he said. "Would you like to be parent to a dinosaur?"

He felt Katrin leave the shelter of his arm, step toward the moonlit bay. Waves rumbled under the old wooden pier. "I'm not trained for terraforming," she said. "I'd be useless on such a trip."

"I'm decades behind in my own field," Davout said. "You could learn while I caught up. You'll have Dark Katrin's downloads to help. It's all possible."

She turned toward him. The lights of the house glowed yellow off her pale face, off her swift fingers as she signed.

<Regret> "I have lived with Old Davout for nearly two centuries," she said.

His life, for a moment, seemed to skip off its internal track; he felt himself suspended, poised at the top of an arc just before the fall.

Her eyes brooded up at the house, where Old Davout paced and sipped coffee and pondered his life of Maxwell. The mudras at her fingertips were unreadable in the dark.

"I will do as I did before," she said. "I cannot go with you, but my other self will."

Davout felt his life resume. "Yes," he said, because he was in shadow and could not sign. "By all means." He stepped nearer to her. "I would rather it be you," he whispered.

He saw wry amusement touch the corners of her mouth. "It *will* be me," she said. She stood on tiptoe, kissed his cheek. "But now I am your sister again, yes?" Her eyes looked level into his. "Be patient. I will arrange it."

"I will in all things obey you, madam," he said, and felt wild hope singing in his heart.

Davout was present at her awakening, and her hand was in his as she opened her violet eyes, the eyes of his Dark Katrin. She looked at him in perfect comprehension, lifted a hand to her black hair; and then the eyes turned to the pair standing behind him, to Old Davout and Red Katrin.

"Young man," Davout said, putting his hand on Davout's shoulder, "allow me to present you to my wife." And then (wisest of the sibs) he bent over and whispered, a bit pointedly, into Davout's ear, "I trust you will do the same for me, one day."

Davout concluded, through his surprise, that the secret of a marriage that lasts two hundred years is knowing when to turn a blind eye.

"I confess I am somewhat envious," Red Katrin said as she and Old Davout took their leave. "I envy my twin her new life."

"It's your life as well," he said. "She is you." But she looked at him soberly, and her fingers formed a mudra he could not read.

He took her on honeymoon to the Rockies, used some of his seventy-eight years' back pay to rent a sprawling cabin in a high valley above the headwaters of the Rio Grande, where the wind rolled grandly through the pines, hawks spun lazy high circles on the afternoon thermals, and the brilliant clear light blazed on white starflowers and Indian paintbrush. They went on long walks in the high hills, cooked simply in the cramped kitchen, slept beneath scratchy trade blankets, made love on crisp cotton sheets.

He arranged an office there, two desks and two chairs, back-to-back. Katrin applied herself to learning biology, ecology, nanotech, and quantum physics — she already had a good grounding, but a specialist's knowledge was lacking. Davout tutored her, and worked hard at catching up with the latest developments in the field. She — they did not have a name for her yet, though Davout thought of her as "New Katrin" — would review Dark Katrin's old downloads, concentrating on her work, the way she visualized a problem.

Once, opening her eyes after an upload, she looked at Davout and shook her head. "It's strange," she said. "It's *me*, I know it's me, but the way she thinks —" <I don't understand> she signed. "It's not memories that make us, we're told, but patterns of thought. We are who we are because we think using certain patterns . . . but I do not seem to think like her at all."

"It's habit," Davout said. "Your habit is to think a different way."

<Possibly> she conceded, brows knit.

<Truth> "You — Red Katrin — uploaded Dark Katrin before. You had no difficulty in understanding her then."

"I did not concentrate on the technical aspects of her work, on the way she visualized and solved problems. They were beyond my skill to interpret — I paid more attention to other moments in her life." She lifted her eyes to Davout. "Her moments with you, for instance. Which were very rich, and very intense, and which sometimes made me jealous."

"No need for jealousy now."

<Perhaps> she signed, but her dark eyes were thoughtful, and she turned away.

He felt Katrin's silence after that, an absence that seemed to fill the cabin with the invisible, weighty cloud of her somber thought. Katrin spent her time studying by herself or restlessly paging through Dark Katrin's downloads. At meals and in bed she was quiet, meditative — perfectly friendly, and, he thought, not unhappy — but keeping her thoughts to herself.

She is adjusting, he thought. *It is not an easy thing for someone two centuries old to change.*

"I have realized," she said ten days later at breakfast, "that my sib — that Red Katrin — is a coward. That I am created — and the other sibs, too — to do what she would not, or dared not." Her violet eyes gazed levelly at Davout. "She wanted to go with you to Atugan — she wanted to feel the power of your desire — but something held her back. So I am created to do the job for her. It is my purpose . . . to fulfill *her* purpose."

"It's her loss, then," Davout said, though his fingers signed <surprise>.

<Alas!> she signed, and Davout felt a shiver caress his spine. "But I am a coward, too!" Katrin cried. "I am not your brave Dark Katrin, and I cannot become her!"

"Katrin," he said. "You are the same person — you *all* are!"

She shook her head. "I do not think like your Katrin. I do not have her courage. I do not know what liberated her from her fear, but it is something I do not have. And—" She reached across the table to clasp his hand. "I do not have the feelings for you that she possessed. I simply do not—I have tried, I have had that world-eating passion read into my mind, and I compare it with what I feel, and—what I have is as nothing. I *wish* I felt as she did, I truly do. But if I love anyone, it is Old Davout. And..." She let go his hand, and rose from the table. "I am a coward, and I will take the coward's way out. I must leave."

<No> his fingers formed, then <please>. "You can change that," he said. He followed her into the bedroom. "It's just a switch in your mind, Silent Davout can throw it for you, we can love each other forever..." She made no answer. As she began to pack, grief seized him by the throat and the words dried up. He retreated to the little kitchen, sat at the table, held his head in his hands. He looked up when she paused in the door, and froze like a deer in the violet light of her eyes.

"Fair Katrin was right," she said. "Our elder sibs are bastards—they use us, and not kindly."

A few moments later he heard a car drive up, then leave. <Alas!> his fingers signed. <Alas!>

He spent the day unable to leave the cabin, unable to work, terror shivering through him. After dark he was driven outside by the realization that he would have to sleep on sheets that were touched with Katrin's scent. He wandered by starlight across the high mountain meadow, dry soil crunching beneath his boots, and when his legs began to ache he sat down heavily in the dust.

"*I am weary of my groaning...*," he thought.

It was summer, but the high mountains were chill at night, and the deep cold soaked his thoughts. The word *Lethe* floated through his mind. Who would not choose to be happy? he asked himself. It is a switch in your mind, and someone can throw it for you.

He felt the slow, aching droplets of mourning being squeezed from his heart, one after the other, and wondered how long he could endure them, the relentless moments, each striking with the impact of a hammer, each a stunning, percussive blow...

Throw a switch, he thought, and the hammerblows would end.

"Katrin deserves mourning," he had told Davout the Silent, and now he had so many more Katrins to mourn, Dark Katrin and Katrin the Fair, Katrin the New and Katrin the Old. All the Katrins webbed by fate, alive or dead or merely enduring. And so he would, from necessity, endure. . . . *So long lives this, and this gives life to thee.*

He lay on his back, on the cold ground, gazed up at the world of stars, and tried to find the worlds, among the glittering teardrops of the heavens, where he and Katrin had rained from the sky their millions of children.

The Mercy Gate

MARK J. McGARRY

Mark J. McGarry published his first story in 1978, at the age of twenty, followed by two novels and many shorter works. He has published infrequently in the last decade, a time when he built a journalism career at three of the nation's top ten newspapers, *Newsday,* the *New York Times,* and the *Washington Post,* where he currently is an assistant news editor on the business desk. He also served as editor of the *Bulletin* of the Science Fiction and Fantasy Writers of America from 1995 through 1998. He lives in Georgetown.

Of his novelette, he writes:

The Mercy Gate *started with two questions: "What's the worst thing that ever happened to you?" and "What's in Pharaoh's tomb?" Despite the story's tortured development, I stayed close to the original concept, answering both questions: to the first, the death of a loved one; to the second, treasures and terrors both.*

Although my protagonists and I usually start out with lofty goals and high ideals, before long all we want is to get to the end in one piece. Evan Bergstrom had his problems, and I had mine.

For me, writing is always a wrestling match, and I get thrown nine falls out of ten. I did my first work on The Mercy Gate *in early 1989 and finished it six years later. It wasn't a continuous effort—I'm not that slow—but before it was over I had more than 100,000 words of drafts and notes. I don't recommend this method, but I seem to be stuck with it.*

This work reminds me of high-tech Zelazny—sharp and quick and stylishly brutal.

Anyone can stop a man's life,
but no one his death;
a thousand doors open on to it.
                              —Seneca

1

They came to the world that had died in a single night, the kurtikutt pentad, the Proteus, and the human pair, to the city that had lain undisturbed for a dozen centuries.

A handful of days was all the kurtikutt tomb robbers would allow Bergstrom for his work. At the end of that time the last of his remotes coursed lonely through pale yellow skies, a cold methane wind whistling across its wings. Through the robot's faceted eyes, he looked down on a canvas painted in X-rays and infrared, sonar and radar, gravimetric gradients and the visible spectrum, to render a cityscape of graceful towers, vast amphitheaters, and parklands run riot. This was a preindustrial world, less promising than most Bergstrom had visited in the past eight years; still, he could have spent a lifetime in the city the Hand of God had touched.

"Time to go home now, Evan."

The voice was small and distant, a bit of noise in the data stream, but it drew him down. He tipped one graphite wing and spiraled in, toward the plaza at the city's heart, and the black pearl set there—the place where lines of electromagnetic force were drawn tight and the gravitational well became infinitely deep, a gate to other worlds.

He swept along streets filled with evidence of the final hours' torment, past smashed merchants' stalls; rune-etched ruby steles, toppled and broken; draft animals' skeletons yoked to overturned carts; crude barricades; a pyramidal gallows, its victim's mummified remains curled beneath the open trap. Across a hundred worlds, the progression had been the same: the sudden onslaught, virulent panic, scattered episodes of compassion or heroism, the swift descent into chaos, the unending silence.

"*Evan?*" Cara's voice again, this time a bit more insistent. Bergstrom triggered the remote's rudimentary intelligence, instructing it to complete the descent, and slid regretfully from the interface. The virtual reality folded in on itself, bright colors smearing to gray, the world spinning about him, but strong hands bore him up before he could fall.

"Steady now, comrade," the kurtikutts' Second Born rumbled from behind him.

"All right, lover?" Cara Austen said, her voice made hollow by her helmet and his. "You were deep into it." Her mitt brushed the thick hide of his sleeve. Like his, her environmental suit was much patched, a centuries-old salvage job. Through her helmet's scarred visor, Bergstrom saw the fine-boned face and long, buttery hair, those electric blue eyes, and he smiled a bit.

"All right now," he said hoarsely. And, over his shoulder: "Thanks."

The kurtikutt let him go, his vibrissae twitching with some inscrutable sentiment. "Sure thing, comrade," he said, righting Bergstrom's camp chair. The brute was roughly anthropoid, two meters of dense bone and muscle wrapped in a thick hide. His glittery metallic robes stirred in the methane breeze; the small, enameled shield strapped to the small of his back indicated birth rank in the Ruhk'thmar Clutch. The Second Born needed no environmental suit, only a transparent mask tailored for its broad muzzle and a flask of oxygen-argon mix hanging from a knitted sash. Like the Vandals and Visigoths, the kurtikutts were rugged.

"Chief says we're almost ready to go," Cara said. "He wants to pull out in fifteen minutes." Bergstrom nodded, and began peeling the VR system's induction patches from his wrist seals and helmet.

The wind picked up, whistling through the broken doors and empty-eyed windows of the towers fronting the plaza. It set dust devils to capering among the ruby obelisks placed at intervals along the perimeter of the square and brushed clean the grooves cut into its alabaster paving stones. The pattern grew more complex toward the center of the square, where bands of untarnished metal bound the Portal to the face of the dead world. Tall as a three-story building, sharp-edged and seemingly solid, the black hemisphere hummed faintly.

Though the plaza was largely unscarred, soot blackened the stone walls of a low, circular building not far from the stargate. Its door was smashed and burned, the pavement outside buckled from the fire's heat. The Portals themselves, existing largely outside conventional space, were virtually indestructible, but the mechanisms that aligned one gate with another were more delicate. Neither they nor their operators had long survived on worlds the Hand had touched.

One of the kurtikutts' sledges sat nearby, runners bowed under the weight of a battered antimatter generator. The youngest kurtikutt perched atop the vintage power plant, thick fingers stroking the control surfaces of his hand-built tuning rig. Cables sprouted from the device, snaking across the pavement and passing seamlessly into the Portal. Reconstructing the Outstepper technology was an arcane craft, synchronizing two gates an art. Once the Fifth Born was done, a single step would return them to Chimerine.

"Evan?" Concern edged her voice. "How about it, love?"

Bergstrom took a deep breath, the air thick in his throat. It was as if he could taste some lingering poison through all the layers of his environmental suit, could feel its chill, its holocaust taint. Foolish, perhaps . . . but then, these places always got to him.

"My last bird is on its way in," he said, stooping to collect his battered recording gear. Twenty kilos of telefactoring systems, josephson arrays, and bubble storage — a modest container for a decade's work.

"Allow me," said Junior, taking the pack and Bergstrom's chair under one arm. He grinned, displaying a great many sharp teeth, and set off toward the tower where they had made camp.

"His big brother is grumbling about our shares again," Cara said after he had gone. "He's disappointed with the take and wants to make up for it on our end. I think I can hold the line, though."

"That damned pirate."

"It was worse with the last bunch," Cara reminded him. "At least we can be reasonably sure these pirates won't try to kill us in our sleep."

"Yes," he said flatly, "they're grave robbers, cheats, and barbarians, but they're not murderers."

He knelt to collect his remotes, a half-dozen robots he hung from his hip belt like game birds. "There's never enough time, Cara. Reisner had a decade just for Nubia."

"But you have a lot of good data, Evan."

"Not enough, and I haven't found any written records at all — just carvings that seem purely ornamental. This city is as sophisticated as Classical Athens, but you don't reach that level without some system of writing — you need it for trade, taxation, if nothing else."

"Evan," she said quietly, "we've been through this before. You get a glimpse of a new civilization and you want to study it down to the bones. Every one of them has a history as rich as ours. They each had a Parthenon, a Great Wall, a Jesus Christ, and a Genghis Khan. Most of them had their Neil Armstrongs and Harold Mawsons. Space platforms. Starships. Technology we could only guess at. It's all out there, waiting for you to dig it up. And you're a *good* archaeologist, lover... but we can't do that kind of work on our own. We can look at one problem — the most important one, as it happens — and just do the best we can."

"Sometimes I wonder if it's worth doing." He looked around. "We don't have a place to stand, Cara. Our own records are in pieces, and half the pieces are gone, either destroyed or locked up on worlds still hiding behind quarantine. The Portals themselves... We can use the technology but we don't understand it, and the Outsteppers have been dust for ten thousand years or more. All we have are theories, Cara — not even that. Guesses. Hunches."

"You've done good work," she insisted.

"We need to do more. There should be some sort of commission, an agency, to send expeditions to every world the Hand smashed... and some kind of police corps, to keep the vandals out of places like this." He exhaled loudly. "Maybe in another thousand years, when we've built everything up again and people aren't so afraid of the dark."

"We'll go out again in a few months," she said.

"Maybe." Then, his voice flatter: "You did all right, then?"

"Yes..." She paused, thinking. "A few hundred kilograms of the usual bangles and art objects, including some intricate stone carvings I'm sure I have a buyer for. Four sets of mummified remains —"

"I need those for my work," Bergstrom said sharply.

"And we'll have them recorded before we let them go. I know Findlay Broz will make a bid for those. We'll let *him* pay for the recording—full spectrum. Then there's the heavy earthenware and one of those ruby pylons. . . . After the Chief's cut, we'll have enough left over to buy our way onto another expedition and, say, six months' living expenses."

Bergstrom only nodded. The silence between them lengthened.

"Do you want me to put it all back?" Cara said finally.

"Of course not."

"Do you want to go back to living on your papers and my teaching?"

"You know we can't. Not and do fieldwork."

"I do know," she said. "I wanted to be sure you did." Then: "We'd better get moving. The Chief isn't in a mood to wait. And I, for one, want to get home again."

Home was Flanders. Cara's world had been spared the plague, but not the chaos following the collapse of interstellar trade, the refugee hordes and quarantine wars, famine and revolution. It was the work of generations to rebuild, and Flanders's one university was not very old when Bergstrom came to it.

Cara turned away, her back stiff; Bergstrom opened his mouth to speak, then winced as his suit radio awakened with a crash of static. "Home again, home again," the Proteus said across the link, the emission modulated to a crude counterfeit of Bergstrom's own voice. He scowled.

It swooped down from the saffron sky, took a turn around the square and plunged toward Bergstrom, buffeting him with the wind from its feathered wings. The pinions flowed like wax, two becoming four, an eagle's wings transforming to a honeybee's. The metamorph hovered, for now about a meter across, an amalgam of practical attributes sewed up in a scaly skin. From its limitless catalog it had selected a sleek, sinuous body, taloned feet, and a narrow head ringed with slitted eyes and less readily identifiable sensors.

"Carry?" it asked from a vaguely human mouth.

"You, no." But Bergstrom took a bulging sack from its claws. "This, yes."

"Gratitude," the Proteus said, fattening its lips to a sweetly smiling cupid's bow. "Kindly refrain from pilferage." It flew off in a flurry of transmogrification.

"Another pirate," Bergstrom said under his breath.

"More of a magpie, I think," Cara said. "But who knows? Maybe the little monster is a top archaeologist, too, back where he comes from."

Smiling sourly, Bergstrom hefted the pouch and loosened the drawstring. Nestled inside was a clutch of ruby eggs, finely polished, intricately etched, and glowing with some soft internal light. The same material as the obelisks ringing the plaza, the same runes. They would, he knew, fetch a fair price on the black markets of a dozen worlds.

Throat tight, he looked away and saw the square as it had been, the towers gleaming in the sun, the ruby steles glittering, standing tall above the throngs milling about the plaza. The people were small and fragile, with smooth, translucent skin, long arms and long, many-fingered hands, huge, dark eyes widely set in elongated skulls, slitted nostrils, small, lipless mouths. He heard their voices on the wind, a gentle keening, like the sound of cicadas across a distance.

"The creature does have a weakness for shiny things," he said, handing the bag to Cara. "I haven't seen these before."

She looked inside. "I have," she said. "In some of the towers. The uppermost rooms."

They had gone into the towers to die, most of them—floor after floor of withered, childlike corpses, flesh so soured by the Hand that it was toxic even to corrupting microorganisms. A thousand towers, a million rooms, legions of carcasses in this one city, and the same all across the planet—across a hundred planets.

"I left them," she said dully. "I just didn't want them."

Bergstrom took the pouch from her. "It's all right," he said.

He followed her across the plaza, frowning.

Trash lay scattered around the tower where they'd lived the past week, a tapered cylinder two hundred meters tall, its weathered facade the color of old bone. A portable airlock was cemented roughly across the entrance; rubbery fabric sealed the windows on the ground floor. The other two sledges were drawn up outside, one piled high with loot, the other with their equipment and the remaining stores.

Junior looked up as they approached, then went back to lashing down their gear. Without a word, Cara walked over to supervise. Bergstrom watched her a moment, his mouth set, before he cycled through the airlock.

The room on the other side took up most of the first floor. Beneath the rubbish scattered underfoot, inscribed tiles created complex patterns; thin, graceful columns poured upward into a vaulted ceiling. A dozen lamps floated about the chamber, projecting wan heat and a dull red luminescence. The bloody glow fell across two of the kurtikutts as they broke down the atmosphere plant. They worked side by side and in silence, perfectly coordinated, stoically efficient. Cara called them The Twins, though the Third Born outweighed his younger brother by at least twenty kilograms.

The pressurized shelter Bergstrom had shared with Cara sat in the far corner, collapsed and rolled into a neat bundle. He settled onto it, cracked open his helmet faceplate, and took a shallow breath: heavy, shockingly cold, stinking of methane and the kurtikutts' vinegar reek.

A shadow fell across him. "Your mate her treasure found, and we ours as well," said a voice so deep he felt it in his bones. "And you, Beergstromm?"

"I found what I was looking for," he said flatly. "Clues to how the Hand came, and why. Whether it will come again."

The First Born towered over him, a wall of scarred leather draped in elaborate robes. A jeweled scabbard hung from the silver sash knotted at his waist; one big, seven-fingered hand rested idly on the blade's hilt. His thick arms were bare, corded with muscle and old scars. More scar tissue ran like a river down one side of his head, across the hollow right eye socket and along his throat. His remaining eye was like an opal, unblinking, unreadable.

"Dusty words, and dust," the First Born growled. "Your mate's treasure is more of my liking."

"When the Hand reaches for you," Bergstrom said, "see if it will take a bag of gold instead."

The kurtikutt glared, then threw back his head and laughed, a coyote howl that sent shivers down Bergstrom's spine. "If the Hand comes," the First Born said, "I will send it to you, your sharp tongue to cut it, Beergstromm."

He grimaced. Cara had wanted to buy their way onto one of the kurtikutts' expeditions for years. The Ruhk'thmar pack had been working the fringes of the shadow trade for decades, buying coordinates and Portal access from corrupt operators, moving their loot through the black markets of a dozen worlds, and staying clear of both the syndicates and local authorities. They had no backers, no brokers, no permanent base of operations. Cara had finally caught up with the Chief a month ago, in a dive called The Cadaver Dog, not far from the stargate on Chimerine. Sooner or later, all the pirates came to Chimerine.

Behind him, the airlock cycled with a wheeze and a gasp of cold methane. Cara came through, then Junior.

"Your mate knows of value," the First Born said. "The Hand may come again—but she and I will be of wealth in the meantime, hey?"

Cara pulled off her helmet, gave the brute a sour glance, and barked a handful of words in the kurtikutts' language. The First Born glowered.

"Private joke," Cara explained to Bergstrom. She smiled up at the kurtikutt. "You're in a big hurry-up, Chief, but your littlest brother is taking all day to align the Portal. How about a remedy?"

The First Born considered. "His ass I will kick," he decided. He lumbered toward the airlock.

Cara touched Bergstrom's arm. "This won't take long," she said. "Shorty just doesn't know when to stop fussing."

"Better that than we end up scattered across the Arm. Teams do go out and never come back."

"That's not us, lover."

He took her hand. "I am an idiot, sometimes."

"Oh, you are not. Sometimes."

The Fourth Born brushed past, pushing a cart stacked with components of the atmosphere plant. His brother followed, carrying their shelter. After they had cycled through the airlock, Cara looked around the empty room and squeezed Bergstrom's hand. "Be a gentleman, sir, and walk me home?"

Shorty was still working at the tabs and levers of his homebrew device as Junior stood watch over the generator. The First Born paced alongside the Portal, then stalked up to the youngest kurtikutt. His bellow echoed from the towers. Eyes wide, Shorty ducked his head and stepped away from the apparatus. The First Born gestured sharply and The Twins dragged up the sledges, one brother yoked to each.

Junior moved forward, but the eldest kurtikutt put a hand to his brother's chest. Their conversation was like the rumbling of a waterfall. When it was over, Junior started back toward the tower they had occupied.

"Now what?" Cara demanded.

The First Born cocked his one eye in their direction. "Your treasure we carry," he growled. "You we do not." He pointed to the gate.

Cara shrugged. "Last one home, lover."

Bergstrom hesitated. "I still have a remote on its way in. I could—"

"We can't afford to write it off." She gave him a quick grin. "It's all right—you wait here until it finds its way back."

He watched her walk toward the Portal. Even bundled up in that clumsy suit, he could see the way she moved, the way she held herself. He remembered the nights on Flanders, and the warmth of her in the mornings, and he, too, wanted to be home again.

Static surged from his suit radio. "Just me, love," Cara said across the link. She looked over her shoulder, smiling. "Wanted to tell you not to wait *too* long . . . and remember I'll be waiting for you on the other side." He grinned. "And I wanted to tell you what I'd like to do when—"

The transmission cut off as she crossed the Portal's interface, the darkness closing around her.

"Tease," Bergstrom said under his breath, but he was still smiling. He looked up into the pale yellow skies. Horizon to horizon, they stretched empty. "Come on, damn it."

"Beergstromm!" the First Born thundered. "Time marches!" He raised one scarred arm and The Twins started forward, sledges groaning, their runners gouging the alabaster tiles. The Proteus fluttered overhead, squawking in the pirates' language.

The Portal loomed before him, a cut of night framed against the jasmine sky, a black so deep and formless it hurt to look at it for very long.

A glove reached from it, fingers clutching. An arm. And Cara staggered from the Portal.

Bergstrom caught her and went down with her to the cold stone. Her eyes were wide, her face ashen and sheened with sweat; blood trickled from her nose, smearing her visor. Her mouth worked. "Evan," she said, the word faint beneath rasp of labored breath.

"It'll be all right, sweetheart. Everything's all right." He checked her suit's seals, the telltales on the environmental pack: temperature, integrity, radiation count, pressure, power. "There's nothing *wrong*, damn it."

She coughed, bright red blood splashing the inside of her helmet. "Oh, lover," she got out. "Oh, Evan, it was worse than you thought."

"*Cara?*"

He looked over his shoulder. The Second Born stood over him, hands working at his sides, but the other kurtikutts had drawn back. "We have to get the shelter rigged again," Bergstrom said. "And the med kit—" The words tumbled from him. "First—get that first, before the shelter, while we can still—"

None of them moved. Then Junior knelt ponderously. "She is dead, comrade." He touched her helmet with one finger.

Bergstrom slapped his hand away. "Get away from us, you fucking monster," he said, his face wet. "Get the hell away or I'll kill you all."

2

"The answer must be ours," the Second Born said in a low rumble. "What happened, we must know it."

In the ruddy glow of a single floating lamp, dried blood painted black Cara's parted lips. Her eyes were closed, their lashes delicate traces against ivory skin. Golden hair spilled unruly across the blanket folded beneath her head.

It was the moment between one breath and another. Bergstrom had lived it before, with the sun coming up over the hills of Flanders, the light of dawn pouring through the bedroom window, as he waited for Cara to open her eyes and smile. It was the moment between sleeping and waking. He sat close by, and waited for her next breath.

"The Portal has murdered your mate," said the First Born, "and may yet us all." He sat on a crate away from the lamplight. "One exit there is, Beergstromm, and in time we must take it or wait for air and food to be exhausted." The other kurtikutts stirred, muttering.

"We are none of us chirurgeons, and we know little of your people," said Junior, his voice almost gentle. "Can you discover the means of her death?"

Bergstrom's eyes squeezed shut. "Just leave her alone."

The box creaked as the First Born stood. "The answer within her lies," he said, coming out of the darkness. Red light poured along the blade of his knife. "Perhaps I will search for it."

Junior reached for Bergstrom as he leaped, but his brother was quicker. The First Born's free hand clamped on Bergstrom's head, temples, and crown. Bergstrom grunted as the vise squeezed; his boots kicked at empty air.

"Time marches," the kurtikutt hissed, his vinegary breath washing across Bergstrom's face.

"*Murdering . . . bastard*," he forced out.

"The murderer I am not," said the First Born. "But hunted I have, and you are frail prey, Beergstromm."

The Second Born spoke a single harsh syllable. Blackness flooded Bergstrom's sight as the eldest tightened his grip and let loose a stream of words heavy as a hammer blow. Junior spoke again, vibrissae fanned stiffly from his wrinkled muzzle, and bared needle teeth.

The First Born snarled—this time something less than words—and spread his fingers wide. The floor came up at Bergstrom and smashed the breath from him. He lay there, his chest caught in bands of steel, his face to the icy flagstones. He winced at a hot, sweet stink, but it was Junior who came close and said, "You are not the sixth brother of our clutch, but you are our comrade of the hunt." He helped Bergstrom from the floor, set him on his feet as if he weighed nothing, and steadied him with one hand. "No harm will come to you, or further harm to your mate."

"She is dead," the First Born snarled. "We must find the reason."

"In your own way, comrade, will you try?"

"He will," said the First Born, "or—"

"Or he will not," said Junior. "Comrade?"

Bergstrom looked down the long, wavy blade of the First Born's kris. *Remember I'll be waiting for you on the other side*, she had said. He took a shallow breath—all he could manage—and measured the distance. Then the First Born shoved the dagger into its scabbard and folded his arms across his chest: the moment had passed.

"Weak prey," the kurtikutt grunted. "Too weak even to save himself."

"If we find the way, it will be a scholar who leads, not a hunter." Junior turned to Bergstrom. "Later, comrade?" he said quietly. "But not much later."

From the darkness at the back of the room, the atmosphere plant wheezed and grumbled. Near it, the remaining stores formed a small, untidy pile. And in the shadows a few meters away, a still form lay beneath a weathered tarpaulin. Bergstrom sank back.

The kurtikutts sat in a circle on the other side of the room, speaking in low voices. Junior glanced up as Bergstrom stirred, murmured a few words to the First Born, then stood and came over. "We discuss the paths we may take," he said. "My brother invites you to join us."

Bergstrom looked up, his face blank. Junior studied him for a few moments before settling onto his haunches alongside him. "This time you have spent with her, comrade — for you this hour was fleeting, but for us it stretched. Do you see my meaning?"

"I hear you."

"Come, then." He put a heavy hand on Bergstrom's arm. "On Chimerine, no one waits for us. In this trap we are alone. No one will save us unless it is we ourselves."

Bergstrom shrugged him off. "It should have been you, you know. You were going in first, the Chief stopped you, and it was her instead."

Junior's nostrils flared. "There were, here, lengths of gold cloth my brother remembered, a part of our treasure. I was sent to retrieve it. There was nothing more than that."

"Then show me the cloth."

"You are hunting, comrade, but there is no prey here."

"Show me the cloth," Bergstrom repeated. "We may be your comrades of the hunt, but we're not part of the clutch. Your little brother does a fair job on the Portal, but there's always a risk. The Chief let her take it."

"You know I mourn her," Junior said heavily. "In all the journeyings of the Ruhk'thmar, nothing of this like has happened. Always, all among us, kin and stranger both, returned safely home."

"Not this time," Bergstrom said.

She waited for him in the shadows. He went to her.

Bergstrom knelt by her side and slowly pulled back the tarp. He did not move again for a long while; then, when he did, it was to brush a few strands of hair from her face. Her skin was cold and hard as stone, but he did not pull away.

After a time he drew his fingers along her cheek, then across the ceramic helmet seal, to the suit's heavy, quilted fabric, the environmental pack. The status lights glowed wanly under his outstretched hand. The suit still lived, storage cells near capacity, air canisters charged, pressure regulators and recycling systems in readiness. He brought up the diagnostic displays in sequence: all green.

He paused, then lifted her nearer arm from the floor, wincing at its weight and stiffness, then flinched again as the mitt flopped loosely at the wrist. He fumbled at the wrist seal . . . and it slipped from his nerveless fingers, her arm hitting the floor with a dull thud. A small sound came from the back of his throat.

"Comrade." Junior came over. "The glove?"

Bergstrom only nodded.

Junior worked silently at the seal. Soon the mitt came free, rough cloth rasping on smooth skin. Her hand was pale, almost luminescent; thin fingers clutched at nothing. Bergstrom motioned, and the kurtikutt passed him the mitt. "Now the other one," Bergstrom said. "Wait . . . the helmet first, over there."

The Second Born reached across Cara's legs, lifted the helmet easily with one hand, and put it in Bergstrom's arms. "Are there tools I will need?" the kurtikutt asked, not looking at him.

Bergstrom stared at the helmet, the smear of blood inside the visor, the dozen or so long, blond hairs caught in the convolutions of the foam padding. "I won't let you cut her," he said. "You'll have to kill me first." His fingers trembled against the chill metal, the faceplate's crystal, the roughness of scrapes and scratches left by generations of explorers, and uncounted explorations. He knew them all . . . but for one, fresher than the rest.

Junior reached for her other hand. "If there were a thing to find within her, we would not see it," the kurtikutt said. "I will tell my brother this." He unfastened the cuff seal, then grasped her tightly clenched fist and, gently, opened it.

A sullen fire burned in her palm. The kurtikutt inhaled sharply, the breath whistling through his teeth. "Comrade . . ."

The jewel fell free, watery red light pouring along its smooth curves, glittering on the etched patterns, gathering within its heart. Bergstrom caught it as it fell, hissing as the cold stone burned him. He closed his fist around it, holding the hurt.

The kurtikutt shrank back. "My brother took a few of these," he said. "But for me, there is a stink to them."

"She thought so, too." The ruby egg warmed slowly in his hand. "But it is, I know, nothing but dead stone."

"Yes."

"Do you think there are spectres, comrade?" the kurtikutt said suddenly.

Bergstrom looked up, the blood pounding in his head.

"A spirit that wears the body," the Second Born said, his eyes on Bergstrom's. "A thing that lives on after the body dies."

Looking away, Bergstrom shook his head. "No. But I wish I did."

The First Born stalked over to them. "You did not dig deeply," he growled.

Junior glided to his feet. "There was no need," he said. "The scent, I think we have it now."

"This?" The First Born took the jewel from Bergstrom and held it up to the light. "A bit of treasure it is, and nothing more. I have many like it." Black lips skinned back from yellowed fangs. "You would sell this, Beergstromm? Soon, perhaps, for air to breathe."

"She didn't have it when she went through the Portal," Bergstrom said. "She had it when she came back."

The First Born glared. "Fools, both of you, and I trapped with you."

"Her suit is intact," Bergstrom said. "Operational. No sign of radiation, pressure, acceleration, electrical shock, tidal forces. Nothing."

"This we already suspected. These would have left their mark. But inside her? In the mouth there is blood."

"She bit her tongue," Bergstrom said. "Her nose is bloody. She hurt herself. Her face hit the inside of the helmet."

"What reason for this?" the First Born snapped. "If she stumbled, where did she fall? If she was put to ground, what hunted her?" He snarled. "What remains is meat. *She* is gone, Beergstromm. Too much time have we wasted, respectful of meat." He swung toward Junior. "You said it should be so. She is his, yes, but if there is answer in her, it is ours."

"She had time enough to realize what was happening," Bergstrom said. "It might have been a heart attack. Or stroke."

"And of this there would be no sign?" the First Born demanded.

"To a medician, yes," Bergstrom said. "To us, no. The damage would be too subtle. For a stroke, a burst blood vessel somewhere in the brain. For a heart attack . . . I don't know if that produces any visible sign at all. Maybe a change in the blood chemistry."

"You may deceive us in this," the First Born said.

"Yes," Bergstrom said. "Does it matter? *You* wouldn't find anything, and I won't look."

"There is a strength in you, Beergstromm," the kurtikutt growled, "though it is buried deep." Junior opened his mouth, but the eldest cut him off with a snarl. "We are as hatchlings, eyes still closed! We do not know the means of her death—whether from within her, or of the Portal, or by some hunter on the other side. We must learn the truth of it, and set right the Portal if we can."

"It may be operating as intended," Bergstrom said flatly. "On my world, an ancient civilization constructed magnificent tombs for their royalty. Their treasure was buried with them, so they would have it in the afterlife. And thick walls, hidden passages, traps, and sorcerers' curses protected their treasure from thieves in this life."

"You believe we are accursed, Beergstromm?"

"These people knew their world was being murdered. Maybe they set a trap for the murderer and it caught us, instead."

"*Fanciful.*" The whisper drifted from the back of the room. Behind it came wet, meaty sounds, growing louder. Something moved there in the darkness, half-seen, unfolding itself until it stood close to three meters tall. "*Their technology was vastly inadequate,*" said the graveyard voice.

"Holy Father," Bergstrom whispered.

It came out of the shadows, muscles squirming beneath a scaly hide, red lamplight glinting from the spikes that flared across its massive shoulders. One large eye, black and moist, gleamed from beneath a thick ridge of bone. The wide mouth parted slightly, revealing rows of thorns painted with faintly luminescent drool. The thorns rustled, producing words: "*We must explore the Portal.*"

Distantly, Bergstrom heard Junior make a sound not far from a whine, barely audible and quickly stilled. Behind him, the younger kurtikutts backed away.

"You wear a hunter's skin now," the First Born said, "but I remember when you were but a small bird." His nostrils flared. "A brainless bird, and ill-spoken. Your form is not all that changes."

Towering over the kurtikutt, the Proteus smiled with its mouth full of thorns. Beneath his battered hide, the First Born's muscles were rigid with tension. But he kept his hand well away from the hilt of his knife.

"*If we are to live, we need more information,*" said the Proteus. It indicated one of The Twins, who cowered. "*This one is not vital. It will enter the Portal.*"

Junior took a step forward. "No one of my brothers will be sacrificed." He glanced at Bergstrom, then quickly away. "No one else will be sacrificed."

The Proteus hissed. "*Do not challenge me in this,*" it said. "*I move to save us all.*" It spread its hands, steely serrated claws gleaming in the lamplight. Junior crouched and moved slowly to one side, flanking the monster. The First Born fell back, the kris suddenly appearing in his hand.

"Be careful with him," Bergstrom said, his mouth dry, "but he's not all he seems to be."

The Proteus swung its ridged skull toward him. A faint reek of ozone wafted from the creature.

Bergstrom looked up into its faceted eye. "That's a frightening package," he said, "but you can't mass more than fifteen or twenty kilograms. Stick him with your knife, Chief, and he'll pop like a balloon."

"Beergstromm, what is your tongue after now?" He did not look away from the shapeshifter.

"How much would you say he weighs?" Bergstrom asked. "Twice what you do?"

"Perhaps," said the kurtikutt, "but I have taken larger prey."

"And when he wore wings and feathers, how much did he weigh then?" Bergstrom said steadily. "He can't create mass, just redistribute it. Keep watching him, though. He may not be in your weight class, but he's got the reach."

Junior's muzzle wrinkled. His tongue lolled from his mouth and he raised one hand to cover it. Laughter, Bergstrom realized.

The First Born glared at the Proteus for a moment more, then shoved the kris into its scabbard. "Trickery," he growled. "And as time runs from us."

The Proteus shrugged, a quite human gesture. "*We require stronger leadership,*" it said. It was already shrinking, softening, the spikes and ridges withdrawing into its oily hide. *"Our status remains unchanged. One must enter the Portal."*

Junior looked at Bergstrom. "Comrade, what of your robots? Send one machine into the Portal, and look through its eyes."

He shook his head. "Not once it crosses the interface. Nothing can —"

"Transmission of information across the Portal would violate relativity," the Proteus said in a voice now blurred and vaguely feminine.

The creature's hide had smoothed. Its trunk narrowed; arms and legs thinned. The head became an ovoid, featureless except for a narrow, lipless slit for a mouth.

"That includes nerve impulses," Bergstrom said, his heart racing as the Proteus transformed itself. "Otherwise I'd suggest you stick your head in and look around, Chief."

The Proteus smiled at Bergstrom with white, even teeth. The skin stretched across its skull fell in, leaving two round holes. Eyes surfaced from within them, black pupils ringed by electric blue irises. The head tilted back; graceful fingers caressed golden hair. Delicate laughter echoed.

"Is this form more to your liking, Bergstrom?" it said with her voice. Her eyes stared at him; her hands roamed over her throat, her breasts, her stomach. "Or do you still find me frightening?"

Bergstrom looked away. "Not now, comrade," Junior said quietly from behind him. "But later. Yes, later."

The First Born sighed. "These games go on too long," he said. "I am thinking now of your ancient kings, Beergstromm."

"A pretty theory," the Proteus said in her voice, "but these people did not have the means."

"They may have traded for the technology," Junior said, "in the time before the Hand. Or a visitor may have laid the trap, if trap there is."

"Trap or accident," the First Born said, "the answer we must find, and quickly." He knuckled the scar tissue around his empty eye socket. "We put aside air, water, and food to last the span of the hunt and little more. Even the power goes, too quickly. The motes at its heart, the light and shadow ..." His teeth clashed. "Beergstromm, your tongue be damned!"

"The antimatter within the generator decays at a constant rate," Junior explained. "We can tap its power, but not conserve it. And when it is gone, we cannot tame the Portal."

"How long do we have?" Bergstrom asked.

Junior looked across the chamber and spoke a few words of kurtikutt; Shorty's reply was barely audible. "Twelve hours remain to us before the power has grown too weak," Junior said. "Even before that, my brother tells me, grasping the Portal at Chimerine grows difficult."

"Then perhaps you'll finally accept the wisdom of my advice," the Proteus said to Bergstrom, running her hands over her hips. "You know I'm right, lover. Tell them."

The First Born sprang, silent, and put his kris to the side of the Proteus's neck. Blue eyes widened, but otherwise the creature remained motionless.

"This game tires me," the kurtikutt said low in his throat. "End it, or your head I will take."

The Proteus smiled thinly. "You must know that wouldn't kill me."

"It would be of an inconvenience," the First Born said. It pressed knife to skin, drawing a thin rivulet of blood. Despite everything, Bergstrom's eyes stung to see it.

"Why do you take his part?" the Proteus asked mildly. "He is useless to us."

The kurtikutt's knife arm trembled. "He is our comrade of the hunt," he said. "End it, now."

The Proteus shrugged. "If it will please you." Without moving its head, the monster shifted its eyes to Bergstrom's. Its smile broadened, becoming sad and sweet as the familiar curves flattened, the pink skin bleached white, and the long, buttery hair withdrew into the scalp. The lips went last, leaving the mouth a narrow slit with ends upturned.

When it was over, the metamorph stood a meter and a half tall, fragile and childlike, its translucent skin taut over thin bones. The lipless mouth smiled, the slitted nostrils flared slightly, and the fiend looked at him with eyes that had through the metamorphosis remained warm and wide and blue.

Bergstrom looked into Cara's eyes and said: "There may be another way."

3

The wind blew along the streets of the dead city, rushing in through all its gaping windows and running out through all its empty doors. It stole across the merchants' stalls and whispered through the gallows' open trap. In the plaza, it lifted a shroud of dust and set the motes to glittering against the stargate's starless night. Bergstrom sat close by, and felt in him the Portal's vast emptiness.

A dozen meters off, Shorty's fingers moved slowly across the control surfaces of his handmade tuning rig. The First Born towered over him, one hand on his jeweled scabbard. Shorty had been at work for the better part of an hour, but the First Born stayed silent.

Twisting a coiled rope, Junior settled alongside Bergstrom's camp chair. "Is there a thing I can do?" the kurtikutt asked, his voice muffled only slightly by the transparent breathing mask he wore.

Sunlight glinted from Bergstrom's visor as he looked into the empty saffron sky. "There's one still out there," he said half to himself. "I was waiting for it, and she went through first. It never came back."

"Later, comrade. Later."

"She'd be angry. Half our profits to replace it." He closed a panel in the robot's breast. The device was inert for a few seconds, then shook its graphite wings. Its head began to turn on its thin neck, back and forth, scanning.

"It will remember for us now?" the kurtikutt said.

"It was built to relay data to my recording rig in real time," Bergstrom said tonelessly, "but it has some onboard storage. I've reconfigured most of the memory, disabled half the sensors, stepped down the resolution of the others. It won't see much, but it'll remember what it sees — an hour's worth, at least, which is more than we need." Standing, he looked toward the First Born.

The eldest squatted beside Shorty and spoke with him for a few moments, then got to his feet again and came over. "My brother says the Portal is seemingly as it was before," he said, "as if it would lead to Chimerine." He glanced down. "I tire of small birds."

"This one may save your miserable hide." Bergstrom handed the remote to Junior, who shook free a few meters of rope. Working quickly, he fashioned a harness that slipped over the robot's wings and was drawn tight across its breast. He finished it with a square knot and passed the remote back to Bergstrom. "It will not escape us," the kurtikutt said.

The First Born snatched the bird from Bergstrom before he could react. "You have a strength, Beergstromm, but it is not in your arm." He looped the free end of the rope around his waist, knotted it, then began whirling the robot over his head, paying out more line with each revolution.

Bergstrom stepped back. "Be careful with it, you bastard." The First Born wrinkled his muzzle and let the remote fly free. It arced toward the Portal, rope trailing, and met the ebony dome two-thirds of the way up. The robot seemed to hang there for an instant, then was gone. The rope fell after it, the first dozen meters or so disappearing into the interface, the rest hitting the paving stones with a muffled slap.

"Give it fifteen minutes," Bergstrom said, settling into his chair. His heart pounded.

The First Born took some of the slack out of the rope and began looping it around his scarred forearm. "If there is a hunter on the other side," he said, "I am ready should your little bird it take for bait." He slid his kris from its scabbard, set it on the ground before him, and settled onto his haunches, waiting.

Bergstrom pressed a switch. And remembered: a carousel of images. The Portal, an arc of night. Bone-white towers, yellow sky. The plaza, three figures standing on the dusty stones, falling away (the kurtikutts, lambent in infrared, the First Born's hand still open, arm outstretched, and alongside them the environmental suit's cooler signature). The Portal again, a wall that grew to close out everything else. A shock, a surge, a deeper night, a time unending.

Then: the rush of air again across graphite wings, a sensation of falling, impact, and darkness.

But this was merely the absence of light. Obeying a deeply ingrained subroutine, the remote righted itself and looked around.

Painted in shades of sonar, the gallery stretched beyond his sensors' range. Ranks of willowy columns flowed from the etched floor and into the barrel ceiling high overhead. Elaborate patterns flowered along the stonework to frame row on row of shallow niches, making them part of the design. And within each niche a ruby egg, finely polished, intricately inscribed. A thousand rows, millions upon millions of stones.

The scene slid left, then right as the remote's head panned, the image repainting itself in radar, in infrared, then again in the visible spectrum before cycling back to sonar. Nothing moved. Nothing changed.

Long minutes passed. Then the view juddered, swaying crazily, the walls of the gallery slowly sliding past as the remote was drawn backward. Again the shock of translation across the infinite, the surge, and utter darkness. Now light again, the black wall stretching upward and the pale yellow sky above it, a mitted hand reaching down, and beyond it a crystal visor framing a drawn face: Bergstrom's own.

The playback ended, the virtual reality shattering, the sense of the dead world pouring in on him, the weight of his own meat and bone, stink of sweat, the sour taste in his mouth, and everything spinning, spinning.

"Comrade . . . ?" Junior squatted before him, his hands on Bergstrom's shoulders, his face too near. Weakly, Bergstrom pushed him away.

"No hunter," he said thickly. "No threat. A room, vast, somewhere near." He shook his head to clear it, then forced himself to his feet. "Like a church, dark, empty. Somewhere on this world, maybe in this city." He swayed and put a hand on the back of the chair, steadying himself. His environmental suit was awash in sweat. "Underground," he said. "I'm sure of it. It may be right under us."

The First Born stared at him, his teeth set in a carnivore rictus. "Nothing to have murdered your mate?"

"It's an empty room, damn it. No one there. No enemy for you to fight."

The kurtikutt looked at him a moment longer, then stalked off . . . not toward their camp, but across the square, and away. Junior watched him go. "Now we know no more than before," he said. "Your mate may have crossed into a place where the hunter lives, but you saw another land. Or the hunter may have gone from it. What you saw may have been a trick, a dream put into the machine. Or perhaps this is my dream, comrade." He looked up at the sound of wingbeats. "Or nightmare."

The Proteus swept down from the yellow sky, circling the Portal once before alighting a few meters away. Its head was human, or nearly so — stylized, glossy, a mannequin's head with high cheekbones, blue eyes, and long blond hair. The body was monstrous, an amalgam of raptor and reptile, with a thick, snakelike torso and clawed feet.

"You didn't listen to me," the Proteus said, its voice Cara's once again. "Now you've lost valuable time. And for you, time has nearly run out."

"But not for you," Bergstrom said.

The Proteus twisted its lips into a parody of a smile. "You know I am very adaptable," it said. "And very patient. If you do not find a way out, in time others will come. One of them will find the way." The creature flexed its harpy's wings. "I wish you could stay and keep me company, Evan, but I'm afraid you won't last long. You may have enough water, heat, and air for a while, but the food will go more quickly — if not yours, then the kurtikutts'. And when they grow hungry, lover, they will forget you are their comrade of the hunt."

"My brother should have taken your head," Junior snarled. His eyes slid to Bergstrom. "Comrade, you know we would never —"

"Of course you would," Bergstrom said. "The monster is right about that . . . about a lot of things."

He walked slowly across the paving stones, each step raising a little cloud of dust. The black wall of the Portal loomed over him, closing out the city and the sky. He felt again its depth, its vast emptiness, and then a subtle vibration as he passed between the bands of smooth, gray metal that held fast the stargate.

"*Comrade!*"

The kurtikutt's voice echoed, the echoes lost as Bergstrom stepped into the Portal. Darkness enfolded him.

Utter lightlessness. Unspeakable cold. Silence, unmarked even by surge of blood or sough of breath. Time stretched, time enough to believe he would never draw breath again. A pressure, a straining, as if he were being pulled in a hundred different directions. Shapes formed within the darkness, patterns of night and shadow, taking on form, becoming the walls of the vault streaming past him, the unending cavern lit by the foxfire glow of a million jewels. Then a sudden surge, a burst of light, and Bergstrom was through to the other side . . .

And he was a merchant selling sweetbeetles, fruit vines, and northlands succulents from his stall along the radian of the philosophers...

And she was a chancellor drinking up the vernal sun and the loving touch of her husbands in a parkland on the eastern verge...

And he was a sculptor shaping melancholy in his studio not far from the assembly of souls...

And she was a wright turning the shape of the Outsteppers' gate, and from her station watching another party of visitors stream into the world...

And he was a missioner falling to his knees on the bright alabaster stones.

"Comrade?"

Strong hands put him on his feet. He looked up, into the hard stones of a kurtikutt's eyes, and read in them not concern but mere curiosity—an almost predatory interest, abstract yet marbled with a primal taste for blood. More intriguing, though, was the undercurrent of profound loneliness.

"Your kind does not often hunt alone," the missioner said in the kurtikutt's own language, barks and grunts that came awkwardly to him.

Beneath its transparent breathing mask, the animal's muzzle twitched. "I hunt here for trade, while my brothers await word."

"Passage is dear," the missioner said. The kurtikutt's lip curled, but he said nothing.

"Our world is poor," the missioner continued, "but I wish you good hunting." He felt in the kurtikutt's gaze a vague but growing suspicion. "Good hunting," he repeated, and turned away.

The tide of new arrivals surged around him, molegs and Yaenites, a small mob of kappans, a Simonswood in its articulated rambler, towering above all the others—a dozen or more breeds, and everywhere the humans, who roamed across all the worlds of the Outsteppers' net. His was a backwater planet to all their races, but still they came in search of trade, knowledge, adventure... or to try to satisfy the vague but powerful need that gnawed at so many of them. Their unruly personae spread across the plaza and along the city's radians, carrying with them subtle disorder.

The missioner closed his eyes and pushed himself outward, embracing the city, and it welcomed him with its gleaming towers and windswept streets, the places of assembly and sun-warmed commons, all suffused by the presence of his brothers and sisters, each soul a thread in the tapestry that wrapped the world: the Bonding. He sent himself out along the design, casting after the thread that bound him here most tightly and, finding it, he felt that soul tremble beneath the touch of his. She bore him up in warmth and love, and he knew he was home again.

And felt, only distantly, the vibration of heavy footsteps, his wife's quickening alarm as the rambler bore down on him. He stepped back, meeting up against rough, unyielding fabric. A hand clamped on his shoulder, holding him fast though he struggled. Venting steam and stink, the machine's metal foreleg swept past, close enough to stir his tunic, then the rear leg in turn. The Simonswood looked back from its throne, leafy ocher sensors rustling with agitation.

The hand fell from his shoulder. "You could have been killed." The tone was one of indifference.

The missioner turned, and shivered. It was a human, sealed up in the rude second skin that carried her environment. Lips pressed to a thin line, she stared at him through the bubble enclosing her head. Looking into her cold blue eyes, he saw . . . nothing. He had fallen against her, he had not known she was there, close by, because there was in her no life or thought, only a cold emptiness. *Nothing*.

The thing tilted its head, as if listening to something in the distance. "You are frightened," it said, and its voice was a hundred voices. "What are you frightened of?"

"*You.*" His gathering fear set a strain on the fabric; in answer he felt vague concern, and one bright chord of alarm from his wife. "Stay away," the missioner said, as much to her as to the monster.

It gripped his hand in its heavy mitt, and smiled. The crowd streamed past, heedless, the wide-eyed kappans pointing at the fine, gleaming towers, the Yaenite mob grumbling and muttering, a pair of humans looking all around them and everywhere at once. From them he felt anxiety and anticipation and determination and wariness: life.

The creature's grip tightened. Muscle bruised, bone creaked; the missioner nearly cried out, but did not. "You feel it coming," it said in its terrible chorus. "I see it in you."

"What *are* you?" he gasped.

"You know who I am," it said. "I was here long before these others, long before even your kind. I have always walked among them, these vermin, and since last we met, I have watched their numbers grow, their contagion spread. The Bonding put a name to me long ago, speaking it only in the darker places."

"No." He recoiled as the monster reached with its other mitt, but it merely caressed the side of his face, the rough cloth oddly gentle on his skin. "We destroyed you."

"You tried, you and the Outsteppers. But you only wounded me. You drove me from the light of all your suns, into the shadows." It paused, seeming to listen again, and its smile became a snarling rictus. "I rested there, gathering strength, watching. Learning how to exterminate you, as I did the Outsteppers."

It began to change, the curves and folds of the environmental suit softening. The lines of its face melted, the eyes fell in. The helmet puffed out and then collapsed, flowing into the streaming flesh. Cloth and meat fell away from the hand that still brushed his face, baring a claw of gleaming bone. He bit back a scream as the talons sank into his flesh.

Around him, the crowd twitched as if stung. A cry went up; a shriek; confusion and fright rushed outward, diminishing as it rippled through the mob, those dim intelligences even a few meters away remaining oblivious.

The missioner cast across the Bonding and it strained, it *tore*, as bright points of fear blossomed in the fabric. It was everywhere; whatever it was, it was everywhere in his world at once.

A big hand lashed out, slapping the claw away in a spray of black muck and flecks of the monster's brittle bone, and the missioner fell. The kurtikutt stood over him, nostrils flared, shaking. He snarled, the sound cutting through the rush and rumble of the mob.

In the sudden silence the demon laughed, a wet, bubbling sound that welled from its depths. It raised its arms, stretching itself against the sky. Its skin grew taut and smooth, paled, turning smoky, then transparent as the monster spread itself on the wind. Taller than the Outsteppers' gate, then higher than any of the towers, barely visible now, a stain, ghostly, billowing, still growing, still laughing—a thin, vaporous laugh, a memory, a nightmare.

The shouting began. The screams. The mob buffeted him, visitors running from the square. A human female brushed by him, and he saw in her bright, metallic fear. An omblegenna came after, its four snakelike arms flailing. The Simonswood's rambler stampeded back toward the gate; one of the kappans fell under the churning metal legs, its high-pitched screams quickly silenced. The missioner felt its pain only distantly before that, too, was extinguished.

The missioner put one hand to his face and it came away wet with blood. The kurtikutt pulled him roughly to his feet. "You will live," he said, "but not if we stay here."

The sky had turned gray, the sun dim behind it. It was, he knew, the same all across his world.

"Comrade . . ." the kurtikutt rasped, the fear boiling off him. "This hunter — we must find a place away from it."

"If you can," said the missioner, and laid his hand on the beast's head. The kurtikutt flinched at the contact, but some of the fear slipped from him.

"My brothers —"

"I think you will be with them soon."

The demon's shape filled half the sky, the vaguest of shadows, a breath of night, nearly imperceptible. It continued to stretch, shafts of saffron sunlight pushing through . . . then it burst, becoming a cloud of gray dust that drifted down, dreamlike.

On the winds he heard its laughter.

He closed his eyes. The clamor of the mob receded, and the kurtikutt's next words, the sounds of his own heart and breath. He found his wife waiting, filled with fear and love and longing. He wrapped himself in her, then cast himself further out, across the fabric of the Bonding.

It was the same all over: a hundred soulless, lightless monsters; their transformation; twilight everywhere; now a rain of dust.

The missioner opened his eyes again as a stillness settled over the square. The kurtikutt stood close by, breathing hard, watching the dust drift down. It stained the alabaster paving stones and drew a film across the towers. It settled on the missioner's outstretched hands, black against his white skin, fading to gray, vanishing. Burrowing. Leaving trails of white heat through his flesh.

The kurtikutt howled, slapping at himself. "Comrade . . ." Eyes fierce, it turned on him. The missioner braced himself . . . but the kurtikutt shook himself once all over and sprinted into the crowd, leaving a trail of dazed and fallen visitors.

The Outsteppers' gate stood impassive above the mob, dark and empty, a hole cut through the universe, humming faintly.

Twitching, the missioner hugged himself. Screams echoed from the towers. The wind carried to him the stinks of smoke and gore. A kappan blundered into him, bleeding from a dozen cuts. An omblegenna clutched at him with its tentacles, then was carried away. The missioner turned, and stared into the face of one of his brothers. One eye, nearly closed, wept blood; the other was wide and wild. The missioner held him for a moment, the pain washing over him, drowning him, then pushed him away. So much pain, a world of it. He sent himself into it, covered himself with it, to find the one he loved.

I am coming.

He went out into the city.

Smoke and chaos filled its radians. A team of helpbeasts dragged an overturned cart. A gray-muzzled kurtikutt crouched in a doorway, pawing at anything that came near. Merchants' stalls were upended. A pack of kappans stoned a human; helmet broken, she choked on bitter air before her skull was crushed. Guideposts were toppled; lost and frightened, newly released souls circled the ruins of their blood-red lattices. The missioner hurried past a gallows, where brothers murdered brothers.

Through smoke and over barricades, sometimes seeking the shadows while violence passed, down streets where blood ran free. Then he was home, stumbling over the corpse in the doorway, up the stairs, higher and higher, to where she waited. He took her in his arms and held her, taking up her love and warmth, and put his hands to her throat. Her soul was freed, flying above the city, the smoke, the death and madness, hurrying away, to the other side.

He could not follow. Instead he climbed higher, into the tower's uppermost reaches, and then outward, across the torn and burning fabric of the world . . .

And he was a merchant, the life seeping from him in a smashed stall along the radian of the philosophers . . .

And she was a chancellor, giving her husbands release in a parkland on the eastern verge before turning the blade on herself . . .

And he was a sculptor, shaping rage and torment in his studio not far from the assembly of souls, as his blood ran from half a hundred wounds . . .

And she was a wright, turning the shape of the Outsteppers' gate so death could not escape, as the mob screamed outside her station's door and fire blackened her skin . . .

And he was a man, standing in the gallery, a chamber big enough to hold a world, column upon graceful column, line upon finely etched line, row upon row of recesses carved into living stone, in each a ruby egg, millions upon millions, polished, glittering, glowing, warm. *Souls.*

. . . and he fell to his knees on the dusty stones. He lay there, face pressed to the inside of his helmet, chest heaving, stale, recycled air sawing his throat, until big hands turned him gently onto his back. Junior looked down at him. "You live," he said. "Comrade, *you live.*"

Bergstrom swallowed bile and coughed, spattering his faceplate with filmy blood. His tongue was thick in his mouth; sounds came out, but no words. His left hand clutched at Junior's robes; his right arm was dead weight. The kurtikutt helped him sit up, cradling Bergstrom against his chest. The First Born looked on, and behind him the Proteus, still wearing its harpy's wings.

"Beergstromm," said the eldest, "that strength you have, I think it is not in your head, either." He bared yellow teeth.

"Mon . . . ster," Bergstrom slurred. "Bass . . . tard."

Junior tensed. "Comrade, there is no need—"

The Proteus folded its wings and stared at him with hard eyes. A smile split its mannequin's face.

"*Kill . . . it,*" Bergstrom got out. "*Kill it!*"

Sunlight flashed on the First Born's kris, but the Proteus was suddenly elsewhere, its form blurring as it moved. Leathery wings stretched and thinned in an instant, becoming a nest of lashing tentacles. Its skull lengthened, becoming lean and predatory, its mouth agape. The kurtikutt backed away, knife extended. A tentacle briefly wrapped his forearm, coming away with a sucking sound. Blood sprayed from flesh made ragged; bone shone bright white deep within the wound. Silent, the First Born passed the kris to his other hand.

He circled, the blade moving slowly back and forth. Blood streamed down his arm and onto the paving stones. "Beergstromm . . ." he hissed.

"His kind . . ." Bergstrom fought to make the words. "They . . . brought the plague. They *are* . . . the Hand."

The First Born grinned. "When you were a small bird," he told the Proteus, "I should have taken your head then." He lunged, and missed.

232 Nebula Awards Showcase 2000

A tentacle shot out, slapping his leg. Flesh ripped, blood gouted, and the First Born went down, rolling in the dust. The Proteus's neck telescoped, the head lunging forward, jaws wide, fangs gleaming wetly—snapping shut on nothing as the First Born rolled underneath, the kris slashing upward, cutting through the scaly neck.

Black sap fountained from the stump. The head rolled for meters.

The First Born struggled to his feet, the blood running from him. Tentacles whipped blindly. He gripped them one after the other, severing each. The trunk lay at his feet, inky slime pulsing from its wounds.

"Not dead," the First Born said raggedly. "But inconvenienced." He swayed, the kris slipping from his fingers to clatter on the pavement. Blood drenched his tunic. Junior went to his side, then looked across the plaza and called his brothers with a howl that made Bergstrom shiver.

Bergstrom got his legs under him and stood.

"Comrade," Junior said, "you are hurt."

"Nerve damage," Bergstrom said, the words still indistinct. "Stroke, maybe. Like her." He started toward the kurtikutts, his right foot dragging.

"We both are battle-scarred, Beergstromm." The First Born's muzzle twitched. "I could die now, I think."

The other kurtikutts ran up, their gnarls and growls filling the square. Junior cut them off with a roar, then lowered the First Born to the ground. He ripped his own tunic into strips and began binding his brother's wounds. The First Born grunted, his eye closing.

"You will not die," Bergstrom said, the barks and grunts strange in his mouth. "Not unless you are too much a miser to pay a chirurgeon on Chimerine."

Junior gaped at him. The First Born's good eye fluttered open. "You did not know our tongue before," he said.

"I know it now." Bergstrom's face twisted. "I *remember* it."

"If a trick this is . . ." The First Born tried to rise. "No, it is madness upon you. A wound in the brain, you said, it may have murdered your mate, and now in you . . ." He fell back, breathing hard. "And mad was I to listen to you."

Junior put his hand on his brother's head. "Comrade. *Comrade!*" Bergstrom looked at him, trying to focus. "What is this thing in you?"

He shook his head. A thousand voices filled his ears, a million remembrances crowded in on him, filling him. But already they were fading, slipping from him one by one.

"Memories," he said. "Answers." He staggered, but the Fifth Born steadied him before he could fall. "These people . . . the Bonding. What it was like to be here when the Hand came down. To die . . . to feel a million deaths, all at once. How they twisted the Portal, so it led just one way. How to get home. *How we can get home.*"

"Madness," the First born muttered.

"Or not," Junior said. "We can follow him, or wait here for death. For you it will come sooner, without a chirurgeon, but it will come for all of us soon enough." To Bergstrom: "You can find the way to Chimerine?"

"With Shorty's help. But first, there's something else that needs doing." He turned to The Twins. "Bring the shapeshifter to the Outsteppers' gate," he said in their language. "*Now.*"

They looked to Junior, who barked his assent. They hurried off. Shorty trailed Bergstrom as he followed unsteadily.

When he reached The Twins, they were standing well back from the Proteus's head. One kurtikutt held its trunk, which writhed sluggishly in its grasp; the other held the tentacles far from its body.

The Proteus's teeth clashed as Bergstrom knelt in front of the sleek skull. It was metamorphosing, but haltingly. Buds formed on its underside — the start of legs, perhaps. Bony ridges thickened, the Proteus's eyes burning from beneath them. The teeth snapped again, then shortened, withdrawing into the jaw. Lips formed, wrinkled, spat out: "Death to you. Death to you."

He grasped the skull behind its ferocious mouth, its oily hide writhing under his hands. "And you're going to live forever," Bergstrom said, "in the room where all your victims are waiting."

Grunting, he threw the Proteus toward the wall of night.

Its scream was cut short, leaving only silence.

4

The sun came up over the western hills and set the morning mist aglow. The fog wrapped wooded slopes and green valleys, a turquoise lake burning with dawn's light. High clouds streaked a delicate blue sky.

Not Flanders's sun or sky, but Chimerine's; still, it made his throat ache to see it. Bergstrom had the bed raise him up, and held the jewel to the light. The sunlight poured like molten fire along the lines and channels etched into it, forming patterns he could no longer read.

The door opened tentatively. "Comrade?" Junior looked in. "It was a long hunt to find you, the hospital is so large."

"It needs to be," Bergstrom said. "A lot of people get hurt out there." He slipped the ruby egg under the covers. "Come in."

"Sure thing." He held the door open and the First Born hobbled in, one arm and one leg wrapped in sleek green bandages. Junior pulled a chair away from the wall and his brother settled into it.

"I wondered if you could bear to pay a medician," Bergstrom said.

"Thieves, all of them," the First Born growled. "But, good fortune, they don't know how to bargain. And you, Beergstromm? A damage to the nerves, they tell me."

"They're repairing it, but it takes time."

"And treasure," the First Born said, "but that hunts for you now. The knowledge of that place gathered a high price."

"We shouldn't have sold it."

"Make of it a charity?" the First Born rumbled. "And for charity they would heal both of us, and give you means to live until you are well enough to go out again? This is the way of it, Beergstromm: To everything there is a price. Better than most, you know that."

Silence fell across the room. Into it Junior said, "Across all the worlds we hunt them."

"And how many of us have they killed?"

The eldest's look turned sour. "Able hunters they are. The fight will be long."

"It'll never end," Bergstrom said. "They're all pieces of the same organism, like a cancer—leave one piece alive and it will all grow back. Next time it will be stronger, smarter. Its hate will be stronger, too. It wants the universe to itself again."

"My hate also is strong," the First Born said.

Bergstrom sat up with a muffled groan. "We're like animals to them—vermin. The war probably started when my ancestors were still in the trees. The Outsteppers fell first, but the Proteus were beaten back. When the shapeshifters returned, it was as the Hand, making themselves into new strains for each species. Then the Bonding fell . . . along with a hundred other races. Now we're the only ones left to stand against them — the survivors."

"The Bonding were a gentle people," Junior said.

"Yes." Bergstrom's look was distant. Their memories were gone from him, but he recalled their flavor. Each of his brothers and sisters, their experiences stored in crystal matrices — not dead histories, but undying souls. The gallery — not a dusty library, or a monument, but a temple. "You have to be gentle, when you can read another's thoughts and feel another's pain."

"We are not a gentle people," Junior said. "And we do not have to learn how to be hunters."

The First Born shifted in his chair, wincing. "For the hurt both we took," he said, "for the death of Cara Ausstenn, we will kill them each. There is a bounty, and I will be of wealth from it. You will visit me in the house they build for the Ruhk'thmar."

Bergstrom frowned. "Not if you get any slower, Chief."

The First Born barked a laugh. Junior tried to help him to his feet, but the eldest shrugged him off. "I am not so feeble as believes our scholar." Suddenly he took Bergstrom's hand in his; the kurtikutt's skin was warm and coarse. "Comrades of the hunt, Beergstromm — and sixth brother of the Ruhk'thmar, if you will honor me."

Bergstrom looked into the obsidian eye, flat and dead. "Brothers," he said.

The First Born gripped his hand more tightly, then released him. He glanced over his shoulder. "My stomach is hollow! The food here is of a garbage heap, and there's little of it."

"We will search out something fit," Junior said. He watched as his brother limped from the room, then turned back to Bergstrom. "He will not hunt again, but he will keep his promise. From his bed he began gathering teams of hunters. They will be his claws and teeth." He came up to the bed. "And where does the hunt bring you?"

"I'm going to take Cara home," Bergstrom said. "After that . . . I don't know. I've spent my whole life sifting the ruins for bits of the past. For a few moments, I knew it all. I *lived* it. I could spend the rest of my life trying to get that back again."

"It would be a good life, I think," Junior said. "After you take her home, comrade, come and find us."

When he had gone, Bergstrom looked out over the green hills and blue skies, so much like home's. He put his hand around the jewel again and felt in it a familiar warmth, and a longing. *I'm waiting for you on the other side.*

"I'm sorry, sweetheart," he said as the dawn's light poured through the window. "You'll have to wait a while longer."

The 1998 Author Emeritus
WILLIAM TENN

GEORGE ZEBROWSKI

A Swift and Klassic Man

To know Phil Klass is to be powerless to prevent humorous con-
ceits from falling out of one's head into one's mouth—or slipping
through one's fingers if you're trying to write about him. Thinking about
him makes this happen to a writer trained in his ways (make that influenced by his ways). It's inevitable, so bear with me in this brief personal
appreciation and first-time-ever revelations about this Swift[1] and Klassic
man (proofreaders be warned that it's a big S and a big K), who as Author
Emeritus is now the Klass of 1998—all by himself.

William Tenn, the well-known pseudonym of the equally well-
known Phil Klass (the ignorant are divided from the faithful when they
mistake him for the UFO writer Philip J. Klass), is the SF satirist who
came to prominence in the 1950s, '60s, and '70s (and who is still promi-
nencing), and the one great source from which all such SF flows. He
was the most trenchant of all who chose this path, and preceded nearly
all American writers who can be spoken of with respect in this century,
and is likely to outlast all who have thrown themselves into this scolding
flame (and having been burned, they continue to draw soothing firewater[2] from his well).

[1]Jonathan Swift, who wrote *Gulliver's Travels*.
[2]"Firewater!" *Astounding Science Fiction*, February 1952.

He has been writing satirical science fiction since his first story was published in the March 1946 issue of John W. Campbell's *Astounding*. Most of Tenn's stories have been reprinted in many anthologies and best-of-the-year collections, in more than a dozen languages; they have been gathered into six often-reprinted collections. His two well-regarded novels, one science fiction and one fantasy, are *Of Men and Monsters* (1968) and *A Lamp for Medusa* (1968). The first has been at least twice imitated.[3] Two new novels are soon to be published, and one of them will win a Nebula and all the other awards (Phil knows which novel will win) he so clearly deserves.

Tenn also edited the influential early theme anthology *Children of Wonder* (1953), which was a first offering of the Science Fiction Book Club. Tenn the essayist has published both scholarly and popular nonfiction, and holds the title of Professor Emeritus of English and comparative literature at Pennsylvania State University, where he taught courses in writing, science fiction, and the literature of humor, as well as an honors course in scientific prediction and prophecy. In 1976 he received the Lindback All-University Award for distinguished teaching. He now lives in Pittsburgh, Pennsylvania.

Although he is described by many as a satirist, his best science fiction, "Firewater!" and "Brooklyn Project," to name two early stories, features a level of verisimilitude not usually associated with the "just kidding" school of satire. These are plausibly worked out, seriously presented stories. "Firewater!" has the distinction of having made John Campbell relax his ban on stories in which human beings are bested by aliens.

Tenn is SF's ultimate "straight man," and so hypothetical verismo may be just one of his masks; truth telling is another, but he only wears it when he's lying. I suspect that William Tenn's unmasked gaze, which I have glimpsed and since carefully avoided, would either make the subject explode into divine laughter or implode into a personal black hole.[4]

I have one anecdote (entirely fictionalized for his own protection) to tell about Phil. He has told me, in complete confidence, which I now betray in a good cause, that he has correctly guessed that Alpha Centauri

[3]By two unnamed writers of novels.
[4]Read Stephen Hawking.

B has six planets, and that the one Earthlike world has two small moons that orbit around the planet in the wrong way.[5]

Pass it on.

With this entirely fortuitous discovery, our own Author Emeritus has achieved the virtue of being doubly, if not triply, unmistakable. So many of us, in so many moments, flow from his wit and intelligence, that we can only hope that he continues in his Klassic way.

A classic writer.[6]

My typing fingers are too short to have pun with "Tenn." Believe me, I tried to have Tenn footnotes, but perfection is not mine.

[5]Following Swift's example in his blind discovery of the moons of Mars.
[6]I was going to say Vlassic, but that would get me in a pickle.

My Life and Hard Times in SF

WILLIAM TENN

Thank you. Thank you.

This business of giving the Author Emeritus Award to people who are no longer quite so active: I am finishing a novel for St. Martin's Press. I have written five short stories in the past few years. I get into my pants every morning (with the aid of a cane). Who the hell's "not active"?

All right, perhaps I'm not as violently active as I used to be.

Now, when I got up to make this speech my wife pulled at my sleeve and said, "Don't mention Harlan Ellison." I honor my wife, and I usually give in to her requests — but what the hell kind of speech would that be? A speech without even one anecdote about Harlan Ellison — Migod!

Well, truth to tell, I did originally try to be a bit different about this talk.

I called the president of SFWA, Paul Levinson, a couple of days ago, and I said that in my speech — my acceptance speech, I guess you might call it, for the Emeritus award — I would like to make a large statement. I wanted to sum up what I think science fiction is, what it has been, where it is going. He said, "No. We have J. Michael Straczynski. We have David Hartwell. They are going to make the statements. Keep it short. Keep it light." Well, some of you know me: you know I don't keep things short. Tonight, however, I'll try.

But—how can you give a short, light speech at a moment like this? First of all, I have not ever been a member of SFWA. I won't say that it's been my loss; I will say that it has been SFWA's loss. (Notice, please, I'm keeping it short and keeping it light.)

I bought the issue of *Locus* that the announcement of my new status would be in. I was curious, of course, about what the announcement itself would be like. I was also curious about what the picture of me that illustrated the announcement would be like. I know what Charlie Brown has done to pictures of me in the past.

I didn't think that this time he would absolutely surpass himself. There is a picture of me in this issue of *Locus*, announcing the award, that makes me look like I am a refugee from flood-ravaged Atlantis. Absolutely libelous! I got away two full weeks before the flood.

But I picked up this issue and I said, I must find out what's doing with SFWA—this organization to which I don't belong, but into which, they tell me, I am being forced . . . permanently!

So I open the issue to read about SFWA and there is a headline: "SFWA President Sawyer Resigns." I read the article and SFWA President Sawyer says, in his resignation speech, "Enough is enough! No *more!*" And Paul Levinson becomes president, and it turns out that Norman Spinrad immediately announces that he is going to attack him publicly.

So this is the organization I've stayed out of. And they are now making me a permanent member! And they want me to make a short and light speech — and not mention Harlan Ellison, even!

Well, let me tell you something: This is not the fault of Old President Sawyer, nor the fault of Present President Levinson, nor the fault even of Charlie Brown (though there are many things that *are* Charlie Brown's fault). All that I have just mentioned—all I've read from *Locus*—has to do with The Essence of Science Fiction.

Now, what *is* The Essence of Science Fiction? (Remember, I'm not giving you the long speech—this is the short, light one.) Is The Essence of Science Fiction prediction? Is it, as I've often tried to believe, preparation for a brave new world a-coming? Is it, as I used to tell my classes at Penn State (lying in my very dentures), the new form of literature for modern industrial man? No. That is not The Essence of Science Fiction. As I sat and thought about it and went through as much literature as I could in preparation for this talk, I concluded that The Essence of Science Fiction is—quarrelsomeness. Science fiction is the most quarrelsome genre that ever has been seen, on land or sea or in intergalactic space.

You know, mystery writers don't argue with each other. Western writers don't argue. Romance writers—well, I won't tell you what they do, but at least they don't argue when they do it. But SF writers? Most of them were once science fiction fans, and they are the ugliest bunch of irritating, argumentative bastards you ever want to see. They *always* fight—because as fans they have always fought.

I am going to give you a very brief run-through of the quarrels of science fiction. Very brief. Very short. Very *light*. And after that, I am going to come to my place in it, and then I am going to look at the essence of it: Why does this occur? And what might we at least hope for in the future?

Look. Way back in the forties there was something called the Eastern Science Fiction Association, and the Queens Science Fiction League, as well as something else called the Futurians. And they engaged in battle: titanic, never-ending battle, from borough to shell-shocked borough in New York City. Sam Moskowitz was with, I believe, the Eastern Science Fiction Association, with its headquarters in Newark, New Jersey. From time to time, he crossed the Hudson into New York and, when he did, he carried howitzers and mortars with him.

Sam Moskowitz? He had the loudest, strongest, yellingest voice ever heard on a mortal man. When he called for a cab in Newark, New Jersey, there was a traffic jam on Market Street in San Francisco, California. When he stood up at a rival science fiction club meeting and shouted, "Mr. Chairman, point of order!"—the very windows cracked and the very housebeams splintered.

At the first science fiction convention I attended (the PhilCon, in either 1948 or '49), I met a very bright young man and we talked about many things—history, science, logic.... I was very impressed with him and I told him so. I said, "What's your name?" And he said that his name was not important. He said, "I am merely a satrap of Sam Moskowitz's." And that was all he wanted to be known as.

Sam Moskowitz fought Will Secora of the Queens Science Fiction League. He would show up—with his Eastern Science Fiction

Association cohorts — at a Queens Science Fiction League meeting and he and his followers would start a riot. They would point out that the story under discussion had not been published in September 1929; it was published in *November* 1929, as any dumb son-of-a-bitch slob would know. And the hall would erupt in beer-stein throwing and screams and so forth. According to Harry Warner Jr., in his history of fandom, *All Our Yesterdays*, at one of these to-dos Will Secora's wife lost a very good purse when she repeatedly banged it on Sam Moskowitz's head. The purse was ruined. It was a very expensive purse, and she said that his head had ruined it forever.

The Futurians, who were organized by Donald Wollheim, were a Marxist group, unlike the Queens bunch and Moskowitz's bunch who were extremely devout capitalists. The Futurians followed the theoretical Marxian lead of John Michel and called themselves Michelists. They and Moskowitz and Secora fought *very* complicated battles. They fought them in beer halls and subway cars and Coney Island beaches. They fought them in mimeographed broadsides and the letter columns of science fiction magazines.

And they also fought battles in smeary, ink-stained publications called fanzines. These fanzines, devoted to convention announcements, analyses of stories in science fiction periodicals, and profiles of science fiction authors, later came under the astonished scrutiny of Richard B. Gehman in the *New Republic*. After digesting them for several pages, he attempted to capture their special quality for his readers by saying they were absolutely "the damndest mixture of *Screen Romances* and *Partisan Review*."

Besides that, they were the damndest mixture of shrill polemic, hurled anathema, and justification of violence yet to come.

Sam Moskowitz wrote all of this up. He wrote all of the history of these fights in a book called *The Immortal Storm*. It was a sort of follow-up to another history of science fiction written by a fellow named Spear and entitled *Up to Now*. It has been said of *Up to Now* that it set an unfortunate precedent: overemphasis on the fans and organizations who engaged in the most quarrels and had the least effect on science fiction.

Sam Moskowitz then wrote *The Immortal Storm*, and of that it has been said that it covered a year or two more time and quarrels than *Up to Now*, at more than ten times the length. In 1951, I think, the book was published in mimeograph form—I have it somewhere at home, dissolving in a cellulose mist in my bookcase, and it is an enormous work. In about '51 or '52, Sam Merwin, the editor of *Thrilling Wonder Stories*, reviewed it. He said of it that "if read immediately after the history of World War II, it does not seem like an anticlimax."

It was at about this time that many fans became professional writers. The Futurians were the most notable group. Donald Wollheim organized a group of young fans, much younger than he (he was nineteen, they were seventeen). He called a meeting, I have been told, and he raised his hand and said, "We will now have a science fiction group called the Futurians, of which I will be president." And it was morning, and it was evening of the first day.

The Futurians lasted I don't know quite how many years—through battles with Moskowitz, battles with Secora, and extremely bloody battles with dirty pacifists. Many of the Futurians became professionals chiefly because Wollheim was publishing a real professional magazine with a wonderful idea: having his membership write stories for the magazine for no money whatsoever.

And then Fred Pohl, one of the Futurians—he had finally reached the magisterial age of nineteen—sold a publisher on the creation of a magazine called *Astonishing Stories* and another magazine called *Super Science Stories* (of which Damon Knight many years later was editor, and after him my brother, Morton Klass, was editor). But the idea behind *Super Science* and *Astonishing* was originally a version of Wollheim's, an idea basic to the pulp magazines of the day: You get writers and you don't pay them much—if possible, you don't pay them anything. The youngest writer of all was Cyril Kornbluth, and, according to one wild legend, because of his extreme youthfulness, Cyril was expected to *pay* small sums just for the honor of getting published at his age. He wrote some of his best stuff in that period, as did the rest of them, including, I believe, Ike Asimov. Cyril and Ike both told me they kept card files on different ways to murder Fred Pohl, even though they both agreed, later in life, that he was the best editor they had ever encountered.

In any event, the Futurians eventually broke up because the rank and file got into a violent quarrel with their president, Donald Wollheim, and, much to his astonishment, expelled him from the organization—something he claimed was constitutionally impossible. He thereupon sued them for something like $35,000. This event is known in science fiction as The Seven Against Wollheim. He claimed that his expulsion from the Futurians had damaged his professional reputation and income permanently. The rank-and-file Futurians managed to win the battle in open court, but it cost them money to pay their attorney — $500 apiece, which was more money than any of them had at the time. I spoke to my agent Virginia Kidd today (she and Judy Merril and Damon Knight and Jim Blish were four of the seven), and she told me that Fred Pohl, who was the only one making a living then, paid the lawyer's fees for most of them out of his own savings account.

All right, you say, these were fans, science fiction fans. You might expect anything of fans. Fans are nasty and noisy troublemakers and are completely outside the law. What has this to do with science fiction pros?

Look: I was once a member of a science fiction group myself, a club full of professionals, every one a well-published writer or illustrator or editor. It was called the Hydra Club. It was organized in the late forties and it flourished for several years. We had a permanent membership committee of nine. *Permanent membership committee?* Well, you see these were all science fiction ex-fans, except for me. They'd had a lot of unpleasant experience with science fiction organizations. And they wanted to make sure that no one would ever be able to take over this organization, so the nine of us who met that first night were established as the Permanent Membership Committee.

The constitution specifically read: "No member of the Permanent Membership Committee can ever be expelled or suspended for *any reason whatsoever, no matter what they do.*" The Permanent Membership Committee, or PMC as it was known in the club, was to be the nucleus of the organization, and we were to vote on all new members — one black ball meant you were rejected. My brother, Morton Klass, was the first to join. He had arrived at the first meeting a half hour late — just thirty minutes too late to become a member of the Permanent Membership Committee. He was therefore always referred to as The First Genuine Member.

Two of the members of the Permanent Membership Committee were Fred Pohl and Judy Merril, and they helped organize it in their apartment. They were married at the time. When the marriage broke up, Fred and Judy chose opposite sides and became the leaders of the antagonistic factions. The organization then met in a very unusual session—a rump membership meeting to which half of the PMC was not invited. And the constitution was destroyed—it disappeared completely. A new constitution was written on the spot, despite vigorous protests, and various people were expelled from the organization.

I want to tell you who was expelled, and why. As I said, Fred and Judy were on opposing sides, most *bitterly* opposing sides: It was a marriage made, after all, not in heaven, but in the lowest level of hell. Judy's side lost. Judy was expelled because she "did not show sufficient respect." That was it—that was the reason given. I was expelled because I was a notorious friend of Judy's. My brother, Morton Klass, was expelled because he was my brother. Harry Harrison was expelled because he was a friend of my brother's. Larry Shaw was expelled because he was a friend of Harry Harrison's. And a writer by the name of Larry Harris was expelled (Larry later changed his name to Lawrence Janifer and wrote many stories with Randall Garrett)—Larry Harris was expelled because his first name was Larry, the same as Larry Shaw's, and his last name was Harris. . . .

So much for quarrelsome fans and even quarrelsome writers. But *editors*? Are they like that? Were they like that? The really great, towering editors of our field—editors like John W. Campbell and Horace Gold and Tony Boucher?

Only one anecdote about editors—because I've just received a note telling me I have five minutes left, and I'd better close up shop and go away.

I was in Horace Gold's apartment in 1952 or 1953, going over a rewrite of a story I'd written for *Galaxy*—I think it was "Betelgeuse Bridge." The telephone rang, and Evelyn, Horace's wife, answered it. The voice that boomed out of the receiver and filled the entire apartment was immediately recognizable to me. I didn't need to hear Evelyn call out to Horace, "John Campbell. For you."

Horace picked up the phone across the room from me, and said, "Hi, John. What's up?"

"Horace!" came the voice of the editor of the competing magazine, *Astounding*, now many angry decibels louder. "What is this vicious slander I hear you have been circulating about me?"

"Which particular vicious slander?" Horace asked.

"You have been telling people that you consider me a dogmatic person."

"And, if I have?"

Campbell's voice now made the walls quiver. There was a loud clang as his fist apparently came down on the table from which he was calling. "That's a lie, a rotten, ugly, filthy lie. I AM NOT DOGMATIC!"

So. Where do we come from? How did we get this way? Is quarrelsomeness endemic to science fiction? Well, this is my favorite story about our field.

Consider George Orwell. George Orwell and H. G. Wells.

George Orwell had a tremendous admiration for H. G. Wells. He had always wanted very, very much to meet Wells—this was all back in the early 1940s, during World War II. Wells refused to meet him. Wells called him a Trotskyist with big feet. (Which is still, perhaps, a way of indicating some mild affection.) Orwell refused to give up. And finally Orwell, pulling all kinds of strings, managed to get invited to a dinner at which Wells was present. And he sat next to Wells. And he charmed him. He told him how great he, Wells, was. He told him how he had really created an entire new generation of thinkers. How he was the first real twentieth-century man. And Wells was impressed, and left feeling quite warm and friendly toward Orwell.

And Wells got home and turned on the radio, and there was a speech that Orwell had forgotten about—he had made it two weeks before for the BBC about H. G. Wells—in which he said that Wells was "an uncritical apostle of scientific progress" and the "Wellsian utopias were merely paradises of technology." He said that Wells believed—and that this was fundamental to the entire corpus of Wells's writings—that science can solve all the ills that man is heir to.

H. G. Wells sat himself down and wrote a single postcard back to Orwell—a one-line postcard which still is in existence. Here is the line: "I don't say that at all. Read my early works, you shit!"

With this as our background and with these as our forebears, what the hell hope do we have?

The Grand Master Award
HAL CLEMENT

POUL ANDERSON

Fifty-seven years since Hal Clement first shone like a nova on the science fiction universe? Can't be! I don't mean that's a ridiculously long time for us to wait before openly honoring one of our greatest, though it is. We have done so all along in our hearts. But "Proof" stands before me as fresh and vivid as if I read it yesterday.

And why not? If it's unfamiliar to you—and chances are you weren't born when the June 1942 *Astounding* came out—seek it among the anthologies. You'll be delighted. Time does not tarnish fine work. The idea of intelligent beings who live in the stars is admittedly fanciful, but what we have since learned about the physics of plasmoids may make it a little more plausible, and in any case it is brilliant.

From there Hal Clement went on to the possibilities in known laws of nature and well-grounded hypotheses, creating world after world, life-form after life-form, utterly strange and yet believable. Today, as our spacecraft and instruments reveal more and more about the universe, humankind in general has begun to appreciate how various it is, how magnificently full of surprises. Hal Clement's mind ranged far ahead, far earlier, to show his readers this.

In consequence, his influence on science fiction has been much larger and more profound than most people realize. He set the standard for the "hard" kind, which is of course not the only legitimate sort but is certainly basic to the field. I hope he, a modest man, won't think it pretentious if I call him a maker in the old and true sense of that word — a seer of marvels and mightinesses, who brings them home to us.

And he's always moonlighted at it! When "Proof" appeared, Harry Clement Stubbs was an undergraduate at Harvard, majoring in astronomy. He adopted a semipseudonym because he was afraid that publishing a science fiction story would be disreputable. Later he found out that a distinguished professor of his had tried unsuccessfully to do the very same thing.

Wartime military service interrupted. Afterward he continued in the Air Force Reserve until he retired with the rank of colonel. On the civilian side, he took master's degrees in education and chemistry, became a science teacher at a prestigious academy, and has remained a devoted husband, father, and now grandfather. He has been active in teachers' organizations and civic affairs, including regular blood donation; last I heard, he was up to eighteen gallons, and that was two decades ago. This has not in the least affected his robust health. He was, I believe, the first science fiction writer to address a convention of the American Association for the Advancement of Science in that avowed capacity, in 1961. The growth in respectability and recognition of our literature owes much to the intelligence and integrity evident in his contributions to it.

As for those, you'll probably agree that they are essentially in the tradition of Jules Verne, the extraordinary voyage and the exploration of ideas. Not that he neglects the human element. His characters of whatever planet and species are interesting and usually likable, people you'd enjoy meeting. He was among the first of our writers to consistently put strong, capable females into stories. Many of his colleagues share these virtues. However, where it comes to depicting the wonderfulness of the cosmos and efforts to understand and deal with it, Hal Clement is unrivaled. I submit that this is as noble and challenging a theme as any.

His tales are fewer than we'd eagerly read, but each is outstanding and some are — well, "classics" is an overworked word, but "foundation stones" seems about right. Let me offer just two rather early examples. *Needle* disproved editor John Campbell's assertion that a science fiction detective story is impossible because the author can pull anything out of a hat. Hal came up with a marvelously conceived alien police officer and criminal, and all the clues to the solution are honestly set forth. Campbell was pleased no end. Subsequently we have seen a number of science fiction mysteries. Hal opened the way. For *Mission of Gravity* and its gigantic, furiously rotating world Mesklin, he worked out the details so richly that his readers were *there*. If discoveries and theories in recent years have made such bodies appear unlikely, that could not be known at the time; and maybe in the future the astronomers will change their minds again. No matter. *Mission of Gravity* abides as a towering achievement.

I'd love to go on about the rest of his oeuvre, but space here is limited, unlike the space of his knowledge and imagination. Let me simply add that he also paints astronomical scenes, which he exhibits under yet another pseudonym so that they will be judged strictly on their own merits. This is typical of the man. You'll find him to be personally soft-spoken, congenial, the best of company.

At last we are making some small return for all that he has given us.

Uncommon Sense

HAL CLEMENT

"So you've left us, Mr. Cunningham!" Malmeson's voice sounded rougher than usual, even allowing for headphone distortion and the ever-present Denebian static. "Now, that's too bad. If you'd chosen to stick around, we would have put you off on some world where you could live, at least. Now you can stay here and fry. And I hope you live long enough to watch us take off—without you!"

Laird Cunningham did not bother to reply. The ship's radio compass should still be in working order, and it was just possible that his erstwhile assistants might start hunting for him, if they were given some idea of the proper direction to begin a search. Cunningham was too satisfied with his present shelter to be very anxious for a change. He was scarcely half a mile from the grounded ship, in a cavern deep enough to afford shelter from Deneb's rays when it rose, and located in the side of a small hill, so that he could watch the activities of Malmeson and his companion without exposing himself to their view.

In a way, of course, the villain was right. If Cunningham permitted the ship to take off without him, he might as well open his face plate; for, while he had food and oxygen for several days' normal consumption, a planet scarcely larger than Luna, baked in the rays of one of the fiercest radiating bodies in the galaxy, was most unlikely to provide further supplies when these ran out. He wondered how long it would take the men to discover the damage he had done to the drive units in the few minutes that had elapsed between the crash landing and their breaking through the control room door, which Cunningham had welded shut when he had discovered their intentions. They might not notice at all; he had severed a number of inconspicuous connections at odd points. Perhaps they would not even test the drivers until they had completed repairs to the cracked hull. If they didn't, so much the better.

Cunningham crawled to the mouth of his cave and looked out across the shallow valley in which the ship lay. It was barely visible in the starlight, and there was no sign of artificial luminosity to suggest that Malmeson might have started repairs at night. Cunningham had not expected that they would, but it was well to be sure. Nothing more had come over his suit radio since the initial outburst, when the men had discovered his departure; he decided that they must be waiting for sunrise, to enable them to take more accurate stock of the damage suffered by the hull.

He spent the next few minutes looking at the stars, trying to arrange them into patterns he could remember. He had no watch, and it would help to have some warning of approaching sunrise on succeeding nights. It would not do to be caught away from his cave, with the flimsy protection his suit could afford from Deneb's radiation. He wished he could have filched one of the heavier work suits; but they were kept in a compartment forward of the control room, from which he had barred himself when he had sealed the door of the latter chamber.

He remained at the cave mouth, lying motionless and watching alternately the sky and the ship. Once or twice he may have dozed; but he was awake and alert when the low hills beyond the ship's hull caught the first rays of the rising sun. For a minute or two they seemed to hang detached in a black void, while the flood of blue-white light crept down their slopes; then one by one, their bases merged with each other and the ground below to form a connected landscape. The silvery hull gleamed brilliantly, the reflection from it lighting the cave behind Cunningham and making his eyes water when he tried to watch for the opening of the air lock.

He was forced to keep his eyes elsewhere most of the time, and look only in brief glimpses at the dazzling metal; and in consequence, he paid more attention to the details of his environment than he might otherwise have done. At the time, this circumstance annoyed him; he has since been heard to bless it fervently and frequently.

Although the planet had much in common with Luna as regarded size, mass, and airlessness, its landscape was extremely different. The daily terrific heatings which it underwent, followed by abrupt and equally intense temperature drops each night, had formed an excellent substitute for weather; and elevations that might at one time have rivaled the Lunar ranges were now mere rounded hillocks, like that containing Cunningham's cave. As on the Earth's moon, the products of the age-long spalling had taken the form of fine dust, which lay in drifts everywhere. What could have drifted it, on an airless and consequently windless planet, struck Cunningham as a puzzle of the first magnitude; and it bothered him for some time until his attention was taken by certain other objects upon and between the drifts. These he had thought at first to be outcroppings of rock; but he was at last convinced that they were specimens of vegetable life — miserable, lichenous specimens, but nevertheless vegetation. He wondered what liquid they contained, in an environment at a temperature well above the melting point of lead.

The discovery of animal life — medium-sized, crablike things, covered with jet-black integument, that began to dig their way out of the drifts as the sun warmed them — completed the job of dragging Cunningham's attention from his immediate problems. He was not a zoologist by training, but the subject had fascinated him for years; and he had always had money enough to indulge his hobby. He had spent years wandering the Galaxy in search of bizarre life forms — proof, if any were needed, of a lack of scientific training — and terrestrial museums had always been more than glad to accept the collections that resulted from each trip and usually to send scientists of their own in his footsteps. He had been in physical danger often enough, but it had always been from the life he studied or from the forces which make up the interstellar traveler's regular diet, until he had overheard the conversation which informed him that his two assistants were planning to do away with him and appropriate the ship for unspecified purposes of their own. He liked to think that the promptness of his action following the discovery at least indicated that he was not growing old.

But he did let his attention wander to the Denebian life forms.

Several of the creatures were emerging from the dust mounds within twenty or thirty yards of Cunningham's hiding place, giving rise to the hope that they would come near enough for a close examination. At that distance, they were more crablike than ever, with round, flat bodies twelve to eighteen inches across, and several pairs of legs. They scuttled rapidly about, stopping at first one of the lichenous plants and then another, apparently taking a few tentative nibbles from each, as though they had delicate tastes which needed pampering. Once or twice there were fights when the same tidbit attracted the attention of more than one claimant; but little apparent damage was done on either side, and the victor spent no more time on the meal he won than on that which came uncontested.

Cunningham became deeply absorbed in watching the antics of the little creatures, and completely forgot for a time his own rather precarious situation. He was recalled to it by the sound of Malmeson's voice in his headphones.

"Don't look up, you fool; the shields will save your skin, but not your eyes. Get under the shadow of the hull, and we'll look over the damage."

Cunningham instantly transferred his attention to the ship. The air lock on the side toward him — the port — was open, and the bulky figures of his two ex-assistants were visible standing on the ground beneath it. They were clad in the heavy utility suits which Cunningham had regretted leaving, and appeared to be suffering little or no inconvenience from the heat, though they were still standing full in Deneb's light when he looked. He knew that hard radiation burns would not appear for some time, but he held little hope of Deneb's more deadly output coming to his assistance; for the suits were supposed to afford protection against this danger as well. Between heat insulation, cooling equipment, radiation shielding, and plain mechanical armor, the garments were so heavy and bulky as to be an almost insufferable burden on any major planet. They were more often used in performing exterior repairs in space.

Cunningham watched and listened carefully as the men stooped under the lower curve of the hull to make an inspection of the damage. It seemed, from their conversation, to consist of a dent about three yards long and half as wide, about which nothing could be done, and a series of radially arranged cracks in the metal around it. These represented a definite threat to the solidity of the ship, and would have to be welded along their full lengths before it would be safe to apply the stresses incident to second-order flight. Malmeson was too good an engineer not to realize this fact, and Cunningham heard him lay plans for bringing power lines outside for the welder and jacking up the hull to permit access to the lower portions of the cracks. The latter operation was carried out immediately, with an efficiency which did not in the least surprise the hidden watcher. After all, he had hired the men.

Every few minutes, to Cunningham's annoyance, one of the men would carefully examine the landscape; first on the side on which he was working, and then walking around the ship to repeat the performance. Even in the low gravity, Cunningham knew he could not cross the half mile that lay between him and that inviting air lock, between two of those examinations; and even if he could, his leaping figure, clad in the gleaming metal suit, would be sure to catch even an eye not directed at it. It would not do to make the attempt unless success were certain; for his unshielded suit would heat in a minute or two to an unbearable temperature, and the only place in which it was possible either to remove or cool it was on board the ship. He finally decided, to his annoyance, that the watch would not slacken so long as the air lock of the ship remained open. It would be necessary to find some means to distract or — an unpleasant alternative for a civilized man — disable the opposition while Cunningham got aboard, locked the others out, and located a weapon or other factor which would put him in a position to give them orders. At that, he reflected, a weapon would scarcely be necessary; there was a perfectly good medium transmitter on board, if the men had not destroyed or discharged it, and he need merely call for help and keep the men outside until it arrived.

This, of course, presupposed some solution to the problem of getting aboard unaccompanied. He would, he decided, have to examine the ship more closely after sunset. He knew the vessel as well as his own home — he had spent more time on her than in any other home — and knew that there was no means of entry except through the two main locks forward of the control room, and the two smaller, emergency locks near the stern, one of which he had employed on his departure. All these could be dogged shut from within; and offhand he was unable to conceive a plan for forcing any of the normal entrances. The view ports were too small to admit a man in a spacesuit, even if the panes could be broken; and there was literally no other way into the ship so long as the hull remained intact. Malmeson would not have talked so glibly of welding them sufficiently well to stand flight, if any of the cracks incurred on the landing had been big enough to admit a human body — or even that of a respectably healthy garter snake.

Cunningham gave a mental shrug of the shoulders as these thoughts crossed his mind, and reiterated his decision to take a scouting sortie after dark. For the rest of the day he divided his attention between the working men and the equally busy life forms that scuttled here and there in front of his cave; and he would have been the first to admit that he found the latter more interesting.

He still hoped that one would approach the cave closely enough to permit a really good examination, but for a long time he remained unsatisfied. Once, one of the creatures came within a dozen yards and stood "on tiptoe" — rising more than a foot from the ground on its slender legs, while a pair of antennae terminating in knobs the size of human eyeballs extended themselves several inches from the black carapace and waved slowly in all directions. Cunningham thought that the knobs probably did serve as eyes, though from his distance he could see only a featureless black sphere. The antennae eventually waved in his direction, and after a few seconds spent, apparently in assimilating the presence of the cave mouth, the creature settled back to its former low-swung carriage and scuttled away. Cunningham wondered if it had been frightened at his presence; but he felt reasonably sure that no eye adapted to Denebian daylight could see past the darkness of the threshold, and he had remained motionless while the creature was conducting its inspection. More probably it had some reason to fear caves, or merely darkness.

That it had reason to fear something was shown when another creature, also of crustacean aspect but considerably larger than those Cunningham had seen to date, appeared from among the dunes and attacked one of the latter. The fight took place too far from the cave for Cunningham to make out many details, but the larger animal quickly overcame its victim. It then apparently dismembered the vanquished, and either devoured the softer flesh inside the black integument or sucked the body fluids from it. Then the carnivore disappeared again, presumably in search of new victims. It had scarcely gone when another being, designed along the lines of a centipede and fully forty feet in length, appeared on the scene with the graceful flowing motion of its terrestrial counterpart.

For a few moments the newcomer nosed around the remains of the carnivore's feast, and devoured the larger fragments. Then it appeared to look around as though for more, evidently saw the cave, and came rippling toward it, to Cunningham's pardonable alarm. He was totally unarmed, and while the centipede had just showed itself not to be above eating carrion, it looked quite able to kill its own food if necessary. It stopped, as the other investigator had, a dozen yards from the cave mouth; and like the other, elevated itself as though to get a better look. The baseball-sized black "eyes" seemed for several seconds to stare into Cunningham's more orthodox optics; then, like its predecessor, and to the man's intense relief, it doubled back along its own length and glided swiftly out of sight. Cunningham again wondered whether it had detected his presence, or whether caves or darkness in general spelled danger to these odd life forms.

It suddenly occurred to him that, if the latter were not the case, there might be some traces of previous occupants of the cave; and he set about examining the place more closely, after a last glance which showed him the two men still at work jacking up the hull.

There was drifted dust even here, he discovered, particularly close to the walls and in the corners. The place was bright enough, owing to the light reflected from outside objects, to permit a good examination — shadows on airless worlds are not so black as many people believe — and almost at once Cunningham found marks in the dust that could easily have been made by some of the creatures he had seen. There were enough of them to suggest that the cave was a well-frequented neighborhood; and it began to look as though the animals were staying away now because of the man's presence.

Near the rear wall he found the empty integument that had once covered a four-jointed leg. It was light, and he saw that the flesh had either been eaten or decayed out, though it seemed odd to think of decay in an airless environment suffering such extremes of temperature — though the cave was less subject to this effect than the outer world.

Cunningham wondered whether the leg had been carried in by its rightful owner, or as a separate item on the menu of something else. If the former, there might be more relics about.

There were. A few minutes' excavation in the deeper layers of dust produced the complete exoskeleton of one of the smaller crablike creatures; and Cunningham carried the remains over to the cave mouth, so as to examine them and watch the ship at the same time.

The knobs he had taken for eyes were his first concern. A close examination of their surfaces revealed nothing, so he carefully tried to detach one from its stem. It finally cracked raggedly away, and proved, as he had expected, to be hollow. There was no trace of a retina inside, but there was no flesh in any of the other pieces of shell, so that proved nothing. As a sudden thought struck him, Cunningham held the front part of the delicate black bit of shell in front of his eyes; and sure enough, when he looked in the direction of the brightly gleaming hull of the spaceship, a spark of light showed through an almost microscopic hole. The sphere *was* an eye, constructed on the pinhole principle — quite an adequate design on a world furnished with such an overwhelming luminary. It would be useless at night, of course, but so would most other visual organs here; and Cunningham was once again faced with the problem of how any of the creatures had detected his presence in the cave — his original belief, that no eye adjusted to meet Deneb's glare could look into its relatively total darkness, seemed to be sound.

He pondered the question, as he examined the rest of the skeleton in a half-hearted fashion. Sight seemed to be out, as a result of his examination; smell and hearing were ruled out by the lack of atmosphere; taste and touch could not even be considered under the circumstances. He hated to fall back on such a time-honored refuge for ignorance as "extrasensory perception," but he was unable to see any way around it.

It may seem unbelievable that a man in the position Laird Cunningham occupied could let his mind become so utterly absorbed in a problem unconnected with his personal survival. Such individuals do exist, however; most people know someone who has shown some trace of such a trait; and Cunningham was a well-developed example. He had a single-track mind, and had intentionally shelved his personal problem for the moment.

His musings were interrupted, before he finished dissecting his specimen, by the appearance of one of the carnivorous creatures at what appeared to constitute a marked distance — a dozen yards from his cave mouth, where it rose up on the ends of its thin legs and goggled around at the landscape. Cunningham, half in humor and half in honest curiosity, tossed one of the dismembered legs from the skeleton in his hands at the creature. It obviously saw the flying limb; but it made no effort to pursue or devour it. Instead, it turned its eyes in Cunningham's direction, and proceeded with great haste to put one of the drifts between it and what it evidently considered a dangerous neighborhood.

It seemed to have no memory to speak of, however; for a minute or two later Cunningham saw it creep into view again, stalking one of the smaller creatures which still swarmed everywhere, nibbling at the plants. He was able to get a better view of the fight and the feast that followed than on the previous occasion, for they took place much nearer to his position; but this time there was a rather different ending. The giant centipede, or another of its kind, appeared on the scene while the carnivore was still at its meal, and came flowing at a truly surprising rate over the dunes to fall on victor and vanquished alike. The former had no inkling of its approach until much too late; and both black bodies disappeared into the maw of the creature Cunningham had hoped was merely a scavenger.

What made the whole episode of interest to the man was the fact that in its charge, the centipede loped unheeding almost directly through a group of the plant-eaters; and these, by common consent, broke and ran at top speed directly toward the cave. At first he thought they would swerve aside when they saw what lay ahead; but evidently he was the lesser of two evils, for they scuttled past and even over him as he lay in the cave mouth, and began to bury themselves in the deepest dust they could find. Cunningham watched with pleasure, as an excellent group of specimens thus collected themselves for his convenience.

As the last of them disappeared under the dust, he turned back to the scene outside. The centipede was just finishing its meal. This time, instead of immediately wandering out of sight, it oozed quickly to the top of one of the larger dunes, in full sight of the cave, and deposited its length in the form of a watch spring, with the head resting above the coils. Cunningham realized that it was able, in this position, to look in nearly all directions and, owing to the height of its position, to a considerable distance.

With the centipede apparently settled for a time, and the men still working in full view, Cunningham determined to inspect one of his specimens. Going to the nearest wall, he bent down and groped cautiously in the dust. He encountered a subject almost at once, and dragged a squirming black crab into the light. He found that if he held it upside down on one hand, none of its legs could get a purchase on anything; and he was able to examine the underparts in detail in spite of the wildly thrashing limbs. The jaws, now opening and closing futilely on a vacuum, were equipped with a set of crushers that suggested curious things about the plants on which it fed; they looked capable of flattening the metal finger of Cunningham's spacesuit, and he kept his hand well out of their reach.

He became curious as to the internal mechanism that permitted it to exist without air, and was faced with the problem of killing the thing without doing it too much mechanical damage. It was obviously able to survive a good many hours without the direct radiation of Deneb, which was the most obvious source of energy, although its body temperature was high enough to be causing the man some discomfort through the glove of his suit; so "drowning" in darkness was impractical. There might, however, be some part of its body on which a blow would either stun or kill it; and he looked around for a suitable weapon.

There were several deep cracks in the stone at the cave mouth, caused presumably by thermal expansion and contraction; and with a little effort he was able to break loose a pointed, fairly heavy fragment. With this in his right hand, he laid the creature on its back on the ground, and hoped it had something corresponding to a solar plexus.

It was too quick for him. The legs, which had been unable to reach his hand when it was in the center of the creature's carapace, proved supple enough to get a purchase on the ground; and before he could strike, it was right side up and departing with a haste that put to shame its previous efforts to escape from the centipede.

Cunningham shrugged, and dug out another specimen. This time he held it in his hand while he drove the point of his rock against its plastron. There was no apparent effect; he had not dared to strike too hard, for fear of crushing the shell. He struck several more times, with identical results and increasing impatience; and at last there occurred the result he had feared. The black armor gave way, and the point penetrated deeply enough to insure the damage of most of the interior organs. The legs gave a final twitch or two, and ceased moving, and Cunningham gave an exclamation of annoyance.

On hope, he removed the broken bits of shell, and for a moment looked in surprise at the liquid which seemed to have filled the body cavities. It was silvery, even metallic in color; it might have been mercury, except that it wet the organs bathed in it and was probably at a temperature above the boiling point of that metal. Cunningham had just grasped this fact when he was violently bowled over, and the dead creature snatched from his grasp. He made a complete somersault, bringing up against the rear wall of the cave; and as he came upright he saw to his horror that the assailant was none other than the giant centipede.

It was disposing with great thoroughness of his specimen, leaving at last only a few fragments of shell that had formed the extreme tips of the legs; and as the last of these fell to the ground, it raised the fore part of its body from the ground, as the man had seen it do before, and turned the invisible pinpoints of its pupils on the spacesuited human figure.

Cunningham drew a deep breath, and took a firm hold of his pointed rock, though he had little hope of overcoming the creature. The jaws he had just seen at work had seemed even more efficient than those of the plant-eater, and they were large enough to take in a human leg.

For perhaps five seconds both beings faced each other without motion; then to the man's inexpressible relief, the centipede reached the same conclusion to which its previous examination of humanity had led it, and departed in evident haste. This time it did not remain in sight, but was still moving rapidly when it reached the limit of Cunningham's vision.

The naturalist returned somewhat shakily to the cave mouth, seated himself where he could watch his ship, and began to ponder deeply. A number of points seemed interesting on first thought, and on further cerebration became positively fascinating. The centipede had not seen, or at least had not pursued, the plant-eater that had escaped from Cunningham and run from the cave. Looking back, he realized that the only times he had seen the creature attack were after "blood" had been already shed — twice by one of the carnivorous animals, the third time by Cunningham himself. It had apparently made no difference where the victims had been — two in full sunlight, one in the darkness of the cave. More proof, if any were needed, that the creatures could see in both grades of illumination. It was not strictly a carrion eater, however; Cunningham remembered that carnivore that had accompanied its victim into the centipede's jaws. It was obviously capable of overcoming the man, but had twice retreated precipitately when it had excellent opportunities to attack him. What was it, then, that drew the creature to scenes of combat and bloodshed, but frightened it away from a man; that frightened, indeed, all of these creatures?

On any planet that had a respectable atmosphere, Cunningham would have taken one answer for granted — scent. In his mind, however, organs of smell were associated with breathing apparatus, which these creatures obviously lacked.

Don't ask why he took so long. You may think that the terrific adaptability evidenced by those strange eyes would be clue enough; or perhaps you may be in a mood to excuse him. Columbus probably excused those of his friends who failed to solve the egg problem.

Of course, he got it at last, and was properly annoyed with himself for taking so long about it. An eye, to us, is an organ for forming images of the source of such radiation as may fall on it; and a nose is a gadget that tells its owner of the presence of molecules. He needs his imagination to picture the source of the latter. But what would you call an organ that forms a picture of the source of smell?

For that was just what those "eyes" did. In the nearly perfect vacuum of this little world's surface, gases diffused at high speed — and their molecules traveled in practically straight lines. There was nothing wrong with the idea of a pinhole camera eye, whose retina was composed of olfactory nerve endings rather than the rods and cones of photosensitive organs.

That seemed to account for everything. Of course the creatures were indifferent to the amount of light reflected from the object they examined. The glare of the open spaces under Deneb's rays, and the relative blackness of a cave, were all one to them — provided something was diffusing molecules in the neighborhood. And what doesn't? Every substance, solid or liquid, has its vapor pressure; under Deneb's rays even some rather unlikely materials probably evaporated enough to affect the organs of these life forms — metals, particularly. The life fluid of the creatures was obviously metal — probably lead, tin, bismuth, or some similar metals, or still more probably, several of them in a mixture that carried the substances vital to the life of their body cells. Probably much of the makeup of those cells was in the form of colloidal metals.

But that was the business of the biochemists. Cunningham amused himself for a time by imagining the analogy between smell and color which must exist here; light gases, such as oxygen and nitrogen, must be rare, and the tiny quantities that leaked from his suit would be absolutely new to the creatures that intercepted them. He must have affected their nervous systems the way fire did those of terrestrial wild animals. No wonder even the centipede had thought discretion the better part of valor!

With his less essential problem solved for the nonce, Cunningham turned his attention to that of his own survival; and he had not pondered many moments when he realized that this, as well, might be solved. He began slowly to smile, as the discrete fragments of an idea began to sort themselves out and fit properly together in his mind — an idea that involved the vapor pressure of metallic blood, the leaking qualities of the utility suits worn by his erstwhile assistants, and the bloodthirstiness of his many-legged acquaintances of the day; and he had few doubts about any of those qualities. The plan became complete, to his satisfaction; and with a smile on his face, he settled himself to watch until sunset.

Deneb had already crossed a considerable arc of the sky. Cunningham did not know just how long he had, as he lacked a watch; and it was soon borne in on him that time passes much more slowly when there is nothing to occupy it. As the afternoon drew on, he was forced away from the cave mouth; for the descending star was beginning to shine in. Just before sunset, he was crowded against one side; for Deneb's fierce rays shone straight through the entrance and onto the opposite wall, leaving very little space not directly illuminated. Cunningham drew a sigh of relief for more reasons than one when the upper limb of the deadly luminary finally disappeared.

His specimens had long since recovered from their fright, and left the cavern; he had not tried to stop them. Now, however, he emerged from the low entryway and went directly to the nearest dust dune, which was barely visible in the starlight. A few moments' search was rewarded with one of the squirming plant-eaters, which he carried back into the shelter; then, illuminating the scene carefully with the small torch that was clipped to the waist of his suit, he made a fair-sized pile of dust, gouged a long groove in the top with his toe; with the aid of the same stone he had used before, he killed the plant-eater and poured its "blood" into the dust mold.

The fluid was metallic, all right; it cooled quickly, and in two or three minutes Cunningham had a silvery rod about as thick as a pencil and five or six inches long. He had been a little worried about the centipede at first; but the creature was either not in line to "see" into the cave, or had dug in for the night like its victims.

Cunningham took the rod, which was about as pliable as a strip of solder of the same dimensions, and, extinguishing the torch, made his way in a series of short, careful leaps to the stranded spaceship. There was no sign of the men, and they had taken their welding equipment inside with them — that is, if they had ever had it out; Cunningham had not been able to watch them for the last hour of daylight. The hull was still jacked up, however; and the naturalist eased himself under it and began to examine the damage, once more using the torch. It was about as he had deduced from the conversation of the men; and with a smile, he took the little metal stick and went to work. He was busy for some time under the hull, and once he emerged, found another plant-eater, and went back underneath. After he had finished, he walked once around the ship, checking each of the air locks and finding them sealed, as he had expected.

He showed neither surprise nor disappointment at this; and without further ceremony he made his way back to the cave, which he had a little trouble finding in the starlight. He made a large pile of the dust, for insulation rather than bedding, lay down on it, and tried to sleep. He had very little success, as he might have expected.

Night, in consequence, seemed unbearably long; and he almost regretted his star study of the previous darkness, for now he was able to see that sunrise was still distant, rather than bolster his morale with the hope that Deneb would be in the sky the next time he opened his eyes.

The time finally came, however, when the hilltops across the valley leaped one by one into brilliance as the sunlight caught them; and Cunningham rose and stretched himself. He was stiff and cramped, for a spacesuit makes a poor sleeping costume even on a better bed than a stone floor.

As the light reached the spaceship and turned it into a blazing silvery spindle, the air lock opened. Cunningham had been sure that the men were in a hurry to finish their task, and were probably awaiting the sun almost as eagerly as he in order to work efficiently; he had planned on this basis.

Malmeson was the first to leap to the ground, judging by their conversation, which came clearly through Cunningham's phones. He turned back, and his companion handed down to him the bulky diode welder and a stack of filler rods. Then both men made their way forward to the dent where they were to work. Apparently they failed to notice the bits of loose metal lying on the scene — perhaps they had done some filing themselves the day before. At any rate, there was no mention of it as Malmeson lay down and slid under the hull, and the other began handing equipment in to him.

Plant-eaters were beginning to struggle out of their dust beds as the connections were completed, and the torch started to flame. Cunningham nodded in pleasure as he noted this; things could scarcely have been timed better had the men been consciously co-operating. He actually emerged from the cave, keeping in the shadow of the hillock, to increase his field of view; but for several minutes nothing but plant-eaters could be seen moving.

He was beginning to fear that his invited guests were too distant to receive their call, when his eye caught a glimpse of a long, black body slipping silently over the dunes toward the ship. He smiled in satisfaction; and then his eyebrows suddenly rose as he saw a second snaky form following the tracks of the first.

He looked quickly across his full field of view, and was rewarded by the sight of four more of the monsters — all heading at breakneck speed straight for the spaceship. The beacon he had lighted had reached more eyes than he had expected. He was sure that the men were armed, and had never intended that they actually be overcome by the creatures; he had counted on a temporary distraction that would let him reach the air lock unopposed.

He stood up, and braced himself for the dash, as Malmeson's helper saw the first of the charging centipedes and called the welder from his work. Malmeson barely had time to gain his feet when the first pair of attackers reached them; and at the same instant Cunningham emerged into the sunlight, putting every ounce of his strength into the leaps that were carrying him toward the only shelter that now existed for him.

He could feel the ardor of Deneb's rays the instant they struck him; and before he had covered a third of the distance the back of his suit was painfully hot. Things were hot for his ex-crew as well; fully ten of the black monsters had reacted to the burst of—to them—overpoweringly attractive odor—or gorgeous color?—that had resulted when Malmeson had turned his welder on the metal where Cunningham had applied the frozen blood of their natural prey; and more of the same substance was now vaporizing under Deneb's influence as Malmeson, who had been lying in fragments of it, stood fighting off the attackers. He had a flame pistol, but it was slow to take effect on creatures whose very blood was molten metal; and his companion, wielding the diode unit on those who got too close, was no better off. They were practically swamped under wriggling bodies as they worked their way toward the air lock; and neither man saw Cunningham as, staggering even under the feeble gravity that was present, and fumbling with eye shield misted with sweat, he reached the same goal and disappeared within.

Being a humane person, he left the outer door open; but he closed and dogged the inner one before proceeding with a more even step to the control room. Here he unhurriedly removed his spacesuit, stopping only to open the switch of the power socket that was feeding the diode unit as he heard the outer lock door close. The flame pistol would make no impression on the alloy of the hull, and he felt no qualms about the security of the inner door. The men were safe, from every point of view.

With the welder removed from the list of active menaces, he finished removing his suit, turned to the medium transmitter, and coolly broadcast a call for help and his position in space. Then he turned on a radio transmitter, so that the rescuers could find him on the planet; and only then did he contact the prisoners on the small set that was tuned to the suit radios, and tell them what he had done.

"I didn't mean to do you any harm," Malmeson's voice came back. "I just wanted the ship. I know you paid us pretty good, but when I thought of the money that could be made on some of those worlds if we looked for something besides crazy animals and plants, I couldn't help myself. You can let us out now; I swear we won't try anything more — the ship won't fly, and you say a Guard flyer is on the way. How about that?"

"I'm sorry you don't like my hobby," said Cunningham. "I find it entertaining; and there have been times when it was even useful, though I won't hurt your feelings by telling you about the last one. I think I shall feel happier if the two of you stay right there in the air lock; the rescue ship should be here before many hours, and you're fools if you haven't food and water in your suits."

"I guess you win, in that case," said Malmeson.

"I think so, too," replied Cunningham, and switched off.

Rhysling Award Winners
JOHN GREY
LAUREL WINTER

The Science Fiction Poetry Association gives the awards annually for best short poem (under fifty lines) and best long poem (more than fifty) of the year. The award is named for the wandering Blind Singer of the Spaceways in Robert A. Heinlein's classic story, "The Green Hills of Earth."

This year's winners are John Grey, who has published several works before, and Laurel Winter, who said of herself:

Laurel Winter lives in a passive-solar, earth-bermed smart house with her husband and thirteen-year-old twin sons. She grew up in the mountains of Montana and attended a one-room country grade school with one teacher for eight years. She turned forty on Earthday 1999 and is enjoying it a great deal.

Her short story of several years ago, "Infinity Syrup," was an evocative tale of Zen shopping.

Explaining Frankenstein to His Mother

JOHN GREY

His blinkered passion
has robbed him of much of
what you remember.
The Baron makes mockery
of your good and dutiful training
in the winding corridors,
the hundred and one frigid rooms
of that joyless castle.
He completely ignores
the rules and regulations
you drummed into him from birth
to when he slipped your net,
fell prey to the radical ideas that enmeshed
that accursed Swiss college tighter than ivy.
No, he has not followed the plot you wrote for him.
He seldom changes out of that
ragged coat, those faded gray pantaloons.
He does not pick up after himself,
not even the blood.
He is disrespectful of his elders,
especially the ultimate elder, God.
And he writes you no letters,
saves his quill for crazed diary scribblings.
He has become more a bleak personification
of his own crazed concept
than the well respected man of science you envisioned.
And worse, though he has not married
and settled down like the rest of your brood,
he has given you a grandchild,
a hideous thing made from
the flotsam and jetsam of corpses.
Unloved, it roams the landscape,
clumsily plunging misunderstanding
into terror.

"Life! I have created life!" was the
last thing he said to me.
An old saying of yours, as I understand it.

why goldfish shouldn't use power tools

LAUREL WINTER

first, they would probably be
electrocuted, as it is dangerous
to mix water and electricity.
>*but what about battery power,*
>you ask, *for example a cordless drill*
>*with modified trigger,*
>*sensitive enough to respond*
>*to a filmy pectoral fin,*
>*so that even an angel fish*
>*could activate the bit?*
>*I mean—you say—what about Navy S.E.A.L.s?*
>*don't they use power tools underwater?*
>*couldn't those be modified?*
well, yes, technically it could be done,
but think about it: your goldfish
swimming round in their bowl
atop your Louis whatever pedestal table
and an antique doily handed down from
great-aunt beatrice—who could have given you
a million dollars but no it was the doily instead—
those gold fish with a dazed expression
and vacant eyes and no cerebral cortex to speak of?
do you really want to give them
that kind of power? those kinds of tools?
think about it.
think about water damage
and how foolish you'd feel
filling out the insurance claim,
admitting that the bowl broke

because you empowered your goldfish,
gave them power tools and power over their destiny.
and how would you know
if one of your goldfish had a death wish?
it could be murder/suicide
and you would be an accessory.

> *but what about goldfish rights?* you say
> *what about the artistic possibilities,*
> *the fine engraving they might do*
> *on the inside of the bowl,*
> *which i could then sell for a million dollars*
> *— take that aunt beatrice — and what if*
> *they're yearning for expression?*

okay, fine, expression is good,
but steer them in other directions.
how about performance art?
turn a video camera on the bowl
and give them the opportunity
to reveal their souls that way.
you can always tape over
the boring parts;
goldfish don't seem to understand
dramatic structure.
or power tools —
or the projected angst you are misdirecting.
you want a power tool? get one
for yourself.
buy the goldfish a plastic castle
and a bag of colored marbles,
or maybe one of those bubbly skeleton things
that goes up and down.
you want to give them
more than they need.
your own curved reflection
stares back at you
from inside the bowl.

APPENDIXES

About the Nebula Awards

The Nebula Awards are chosen by the members of the Science Fiction and Fantasy Writers of America. In 1998 they were given in four categories: short story—under 7,500 words; novelette—7,500 to 17,499 words; novella—17,500 to 39,999 words; and novel—more than 40,000 words. SFWA members read and nominate the best SF stories and novels throughout the year, and the editor of the "Nebula Awards Report" collects these nominations and publishes them in a newsletter. At the end of the year, there is a preliminary ballot and then a final one to determine the winners.

The Nebula Awards are presented at a banquet at the annual Nebula Awards Weekend, held originally in New York and, over the years, in places as diverse as New Orleans; Eugene, Oregon; and aboard the *Queen Mary*, in Long Beach, California.

The Nebula Awards originated in 1965, from an idea by Lloyd Biggle Jr., the secretary-treasurer of SFWA at that time, who proposed that the organization select and publish the year's best stories, and have been given ever since.

The award itself was originally designed by Judith Ann Blish from a sketch by Kate Wilhelm. The official description: "a block of Lucite four to five inches square by eight to nine inches high into which a spiral nebula of metallic glitter and a geological specimen are embedded."

SFWA also gives the Grand Master Award, its highest honor. It is presented for a lifetime of achievement in science fiction. Instituted in 1975, it is awarded only to living authors and is not necessarily given every year. The Grand Master is chosen by SFWA's officers, past presidents, and board of directors.

The first Grand Master was Robert A. Heinlein in 1974. The others are Jack Williamson (1975), Clifford Simak (1976), L. Sprague de Camp (1978), Fritz Leiber (1981), Andre Norton (1983), Arthur C. Clarke (1985), Isaac Asimov (1986), Alfred Bester (1987), Ray Bradbury (1988), Lester del Rey (1990), Frederik Pohl (1992), Damon Knight (1994), A. E. van Vogt (1995), Jack Vance (1996), Poul Anderson (1997), and Hal Clement (1998).

The thirty-fourth annual Nebula Awards banquet was held at the Marriott City Center in Pittsburgh, Pennsylvania, on May 1, 1999.

Selected Titles from the 1998 Preliminary Nebula Ballot

NOVELS

Alpha Centauri, William Barton and Michael Capobianco (Avon)
Cosm, Gregory Benford (Avon Eos)
Komarr, Lois McMaster Bujold (Baen Books)
Days of Cain, J. R. Dunn (Avon)
The Pleistocene Redemption, Dan Gallagher (Cypress House)
Commitment Hour, James Alan Gardner (Avon Eos)
The Dazzle of Day, Molly Gloss (Tor Books)
Brown Girl in the Ring, Nalo Hopkinson (Warner Aspect)
Maximum Light, Nancy Kress (Tor Books)
Cold Iron, Melisa Michaels (Roc)
Saint Leibowitz and the Wild Horse Woman, Walter M. Miller Jr. (with Terry Bisson) (Bantam Spectra)
Once a Hero, Elizabeth Moon (Baen Books)
Vast, Linda Nagata (Bantam Spectra)
Hand of Prophecy, Severna Park (Avon Eos)
Kirinyaga, Mike Resnick (Del Rey)
Children of God, Mary Doria Russell (Villard Books)

Frameshift, Robert J. Sawyer (Tor Books)
Jovah's Angel, Sharon Shinn (Ace)
The Night Watch, Sean Stewart (Ace)
Island in the Sea of Time, S. M. Stirling (Roc)
Reckoning Infinity, John Stith (Tor Books)
Jack Faust, Michael Swanwick (Avon)
The Merro Tree, Katie Waitman (Del Rey)
Darwinia, Robert Charles Wilson (Tor Books)

NOVELLAS

"Cold at Heart," Brian A. Hopkins (*StarLance Publications*)
"In the Furnace of the Night," James Sarafin (*Asimov's Science Fiction*)

NOVELETTES

"The Moon Girl," M. Shayne Bell (*Asimov's Science Fiction*)
"Tal's Tale," Nancy Varian Berberick (*Adventures in Sword and Sorcery*)
"Content with the Mysterious," Maya Kaathryn Bohnhoff (*Analog*)
"Approaching Perimelasma," Geoffrey A. Landis (*Asimov's Science Fiction*)
"Little Differences," Paul Levinson (*Analog Science Fiction and Fact*)
"The Orchard," Paul Levinson (*Analog Science Fiction and Fact*)
"Crossing Chao Meng Fu," G. David Nordley (*Analog Science Fiction and Fact*)
"Noodle You, Noodle Me," B. J. Thrower (*Asimov's Science Fiction*)
"Lustman," Pat York (*Realms of Fantasy*)

SHORT STORIES

"Cosmic Corkscrew," Michael A. Burstein (*Analog Science Fiction and Fact*)
"Kaleidoscope," Kate Daniel (*Realms of Fantasy*)
"Children of Tears," Adrienne Gormley (*Alternate Tyrants*, ed. Resnick and Greenberg, Tor Books)
"Walter's Christmas-Night Musik," Susan J. Kroupa (*Realms of Fantasy*)
"Monstrosity," Mary Soon Lee (*The Magazine of Fantasy & Science Fiction*)
"Advantage, Bellarmine," Paul Levinson (*Analog Science Fiction and Fact*)
"Tiger, Tiger," Severna Park (*Realms of Fantasy*)

"The Hand You're Dealt," Robert J. Sawyer (*Free Space*, ed.
   Linaweaver and Kramer, Tor Books)
"Waiting for Victor," Del Stone Jr. (*Alfred Hitchcock's Mystery Magazine*)
"Silver Apples," Beverly Suarez-Beard (*Realms of Fantasy*)
"The Big One," Jim Van Pelt (*Analog Science Fiction and Fact*)
"The Ballad of Kansas McGriff," Bud Webster (*Hobo Times*)

Past Nebula Award Winners

1965

Best Novel: *Dune* by Frank Herbert
Best Novella: "The Saliva Tree" by Brian W. Aldiss and "He Who
   Shapes" by Roger Zelazny (tie)
Best Novelette: "The Doors of His Face, the Lamps of His Mouth" by
   Roger Zelazny
Best Short Story: "'Repent, Harlequin!' Said the Ticktockman" by
   Harlan Ellison

1966

Best Novel: *Flowers for Algernon* by Daniel Keyes and *Babel-17* by
   Samuel R. Delany (tie)
Best Novella: "The Last Castle" by Jack Vance
Best Novelette: "Call Him Lord" by Gordon R. Dickson
Best Short Story: "The Secret Place" by Richard McKenna

1967

Best Novel: *The Einstein Intersection* by Samuel R. Delany
Best Novella: "Behold the Man" by Michael Moorcock
Best Novelette: "Gonna Roll the Bones" by Fritz Leiber
Best Short Story: "Aye, and Gomorrah" by Samuel R. Delany

1968

Best Novel: *Rite of Passage* by Alexei Panshin
Best Novella: "Dragonrider" by Anne McCaffrey

Best Novelette: "Mother to the World" by Richard Wilson
Best Short Story: "The Planners" by Kate Wilhelm

1969

Best Novel: *The Left Hand of Darkness* by Ursula K. Le Guin
Best Novella: "A Boy and His Dog" by Harlan Ellison
Best Novelette: "Time Considered as a Helix of Semi-Precious Stones"
    by Samuel R. Delany
Best Short Story: "Passengers" by Robert Silverberg

1970

Best Novel: *Ringworld* by Larry Niven
Best Novella: "Ill Met in Lankhmar" by Fritz Leiber
Best Novelette: "Slow Sculpture" by Theodore Sturgeon
Best Short Story: no award

1971

Best Novel: *A Time of Changes* by Robert Silverberg
Best Novella: "The Missing Man" by Katherine MacLean
Best Novelette: "The Queen of Air and Darkness" by Poul Anderson
Best Short Story: "Good News from the Vatican" by Robert Silverberg

1972

Best Novel: *The Gods Themselves* by Isaac Asimov
Best Novella: "A Meeting with Medusa" by Arthur C. Clarke
Best Novelette: "Goat Song" by Poul Anderson
Best Short Story: "When It Changed" by Joanna Russ

1973

Best Novel: *Rendezvous with Rama* by Arthur C. Clarke
Best Novella: "The Death of Doctor Island" by Gene Wolfe
Best Novelette: "Of Mist, and Grass, and Sand" by Vonda N. McIntyre
Best Short Story: "Love Is the Plan, the Plan Is Death" by James
    Tiptree Jr.

Best Dramatic Presentation: *Soylent Green*
    Stanley R. Greenberg for screenplay (based on the novel *Make Room! Make Room!*)
    Harry Harrison for *Make Room! Make Room!*

1974

Best Novel: *The Dispossessed* by Ursula K. Le Guin
Best Novella: "Born with the Dead" by Robert Silverberg
Best Novelette: "If the Stars Are Gods" by Gordon Eklund and
    Gregory Benford
Best Short Story: "The Day Before the Revolution" by Ursula K. Le Guin
Best Dramatic Presentation: *Sleeper* by Woody Allen
Grand Master: Robert A. Heinlein

1975

Best Novel: *The Forever War* by Joe Haldeman
Best Novella: "Home Is the Hangman" by Roger Zelazny
Best Novelette: "San Diego Lightfoot Sue" by Tom Reamy
Best Short Story: "Catch That Zeppelin!" by Fritz Leiber
Best Dramatic Writing: Mel Brooks and Gene Wilder for *Young Frankenstein*
Grand Master: Jack Williamson

1976

Best Novel: *Man Plus* by Frederik Pohl
Best Novella: "Houston, Houston, Do You Read?" by James Tiptree Jr.
Best Novelette: "The Bicentennial Man" by Isaac Asimov
Best Short Story: "A Crowd of Shadows" by Charles L. Grant
Grand Master: Clifford D. Simak

1977

Best Novel: *Gateway* by Frederik Pohl
Best Novella: "Stardance" by Spider and Jeanne Robinson
Best Novelette: "The Screwfly Solution" by Raccoona Sheldon

Best Short Story: "Jeffty Is Five" by Harlan Ellison
Special Award: *Star Wars*

1978

Best Novel: *Dreamsnake* by Vonda N. McIntyre
Best Novella: "The Persistence of Vision" by John Varley
Best Novelette: "A Glow of Candles, a Unicorn's Eye" by Charles L. Grant
Best Short Story: "Stone" by Edward Bryant
Grand Master: L. Sprague de Camp

1979

Best Novel: *The Fountains of Paradise* by Arthur C. Clarke
Best Novella: "Enemy Mine" by Barry Longyear
Best Novelette: "Sandkings" by George R. R. Martin
Best Short Story: "giANTS" by Edward Bryant

1980

Best Novel: *Timescape* by Gregory Benford
Best Novella: "The Unicorn Tapestry" by Suzy McKee Charnas
Best Novelette: "The Ugly Chickens" by Howard Waldrop
Best Short Story: "Grotto of the Dancing Deer" by Clifford D. Simak
Grand Master: Fritz Leiber

1981

Best Novel: *The Claw of the Conciliator* by Gene Wolfe
Best Novella: "The Saturn Game" by Poul Anderson
Best Novelette: "The Quickening" by Michael Bishop
Best Short Story: "The Bone Flute" by Lisa Tuttle*

1982

Best Novel: *No Enemy But Time* by Michael Bishop

---

*This Nebula Award was declined by the author.

Best Novella: "Another Orphan" by John Kessel
Best Novelette: "Fire Watch" by Connie Willis
Best Short Story: "A Letter from the Clearys" by Connie Willis

1983

Best Novel: *Startide Rising* by David Brin
Best Novella: "Hardfought" by Greg Bear
Best Novelette: "Blood Music" by Greg Bear
Best Short Story: "The Peacemaker" by Gardner Dozois
Grand Master: Andre Norton

1984

Best Novel: *Neuromancer* by William Gibson
Best Novella: "Press Enter ■" by John Varley
Best Novelette: "Bloodchild" by Octavia E. Butler
Best Short Story: "Morning Child" by Gardner Dozois

1985

Best Novel: *Ender's Game* by Orson Scott Card
Best Novella: "Sailing to Byzantium" by Robert Silverberg
Best Novelette: "Portraits of His Children" by George R. R. Martin
Best Short Story: "Out of All Them Bright Stars" by Nancy Kress
Grand Master: Arthur C. Clarke

1986

Best Novel: *Speaker for the Dead* by Orson Scott Card
Best Novella: "R & R" by Lucius Shepard
Best Novelette: "The Girl Who Fell into the Sky" by Kate Wilhelm
Best Short Story: "Tangents" by Greg Bear
Grand Master: Isaac Asimov

1987

Best Novel: *The Falling Woman* by Pat Murphy

Best Novella: "The Blind Geometer" by Kim Stanley Robinson
Best Novelette: "Rachel in Love" by Pat Murphy
Best Short Story: "Forever Yours, Anna" by Kate Wilhelm
Grand Master: Alfred Bester

1988

Best Novel: *Falling Free* by Lois McMaster Bujold
Best Novella: "The Last of the Winnebagos" by Connie Willis
Best Novelette: "Schrödinger's Kitten" by George Alec Effinger
Best Short Story: "Bible Stories for Adults, No. 17: The Deluge" by
    James Morrow
Grand Master: Ray Bradbury

1989

Best Novel: *The Healer's War* by Elizabeth Ann Scarborough
Best Novella: "The Mountains of Mourning" by Lois McMaster
    Bujold
Best Novelette: "At the Rialto" by Connie Willis
Best Short Story: "Ripples in the Dirac Sea" by Geoffrey Landis

1990

Best Novel: *Tehanu: The Last Book of Earthsea* by Ursula K. Le Guin
Best Novella: "The Hemingway Hoax" by Joe Haldeman
Best Novelette: "Tower of Babylon" by Ted Chiang
Best Short Story: "Bears Discover Fire" by Terry Bisson
Grand Master: Lester del Rey

1991

Best Novel: *Stations of the Tide* by Michael Swanwick
Best Novella: "Beggars in Spain" by Nancy Kress
Best Novelette: "Guide Dog" by Mike Conner
Best Short Story: "Ma Qui" by Alan Brennert

1992

Best Novel: *Doomsday Book* by Connie Willis
Best Novella: "City of Truth" by James Morrow
Best Novelette: "Danny Goes to Mars" by Pamela Sargent
Best Short Story: "Even the Queen" by Connie Willis
Grand Master: Frederik Pohl

1993

Best Novel: *Red Mars* by Kim Stanley Robinson
Best Novella: "The Night We Buried Road Dog" by Jack Cady
Best Novelette: "Georgia on My Mind" by Charles Sheffield
Best Short Story: "Graves" by Joe Haldeman

1994

Best Novel: *Moving Mars* by Greg Bear
Best Novella: "Seven Views of Olduvai Gorge" by Mike Resnick
Best Novelette: "The Martian Child" by David Gerrold
Best Short Story: "A Defense of the Social Contracts" by Martha
    Soukup
Grand Master: Damon Knight

1995

Best Novel: *The Terminal Experiment* by Robert J. Sawyer
Best Novella: "Last Summer at Mars Hill" by Elizabeth Hand
Best Novelette: "Solitude" by Ursula K. Le Guin
Best Short Story: "Death and the Librarian" by Esther M. Friesner
Grand Master: A. E. van Vogt

1996

Best Novel: *Slow River* by Nicola Griffith
Best Novella: "Da Vinci Rising" by Jack Dann
Best Novelette: "Lifeboat on a Burning Sea" by Bruce Holland Rogers

Best Short Story: "A Birthday" by Esther M. Friesner
Grand Master: Jack Vance

1997

Best Novel: *The Moon and the Sun* by Vonda N. McIntyre
Best Novella: "Abandon in Place" by Jerry Oltion
Best Novelette: "The Flowers of Aulit Prison" by Nancy Kress
Best Short Story: "Sister Emily's Lightship" by Jane Yolen
Grand Master: Poul Anderson

About the Science Fiction and Fantasy Writers of America

The Science Fiction and Fantasy Writers of America, Incorporated, includes among its members most of the active writers of science fiction and fantasy. According to the bylaws of the organization, its purpose "shall be to promote the furtherance of the writing of science fiction, fantasy, and related genres as a profession." SFWA informs writers on professional matters, protects their interests, and helps them in dealings with agents, editors, anthologists, and producers of nonprint media. It also strives to encourage public interest in and appreciation of science fiction and fantasy.

Anyone may become an active member of SFWA after the acceptance of and payment for one professionally published novel, one professionally produced dramatic script, or three professionally published pieces of short fiction. Only science fiction, fantasy, and other prose fiction of a related genre, in English, shall be considered as qualifying for active membership. Beginning writers who do not yet qualify for active membership may join as associate members; other classes of membership include illustrator members (artists), affiliate members (editors, agents, reviewers, and anthologists), estate members (representatives of the estates of active members who have died), and institutional members (high schools, colleges, universities, libraries, broadcasters, film producers, futurist groups, and individuals associated with such an institution).

Anyone who is not a member of SFWA may subscribe to *The*

SFWA Bulletin. The magazine is published quarterly, and contains articles by well-known writers on all aspects of their profession. Subscriptions are $15 a year or $27 for two years. For information on how to subscribe to the *Bulletin,* write to:

SFWA Bulletin
1436 Altamont Ave.
PMB 292
Schenectady, NY 12303-2977

Readers are also invited to visit the SFWA site on the World Wide Web at the following address: http://www.sfwa.org

PERMISSIONS
ACKNOWLEDGMENTS